A
Fairytale
Bride

BESTSELLING AUSTRALIAN AUTHORS
ALLY BLAKE & JUSTINE LEWIS

MILLS & BOON

A FAIRYTALE BRIDE © 2024 by Harlequin Books S.A.

CINDERELLA ASSISTANT TO THE BOSS'S BRIDE
© 2023 by Ally Blake
Australian Copyright 2023
New Zealand Copyright 2023

First Published 2023
First Australian Paperback Edition 2024
ISBN 978 1 038 90012 8

BEAUTY AND THE PLAYBOY PRINCE
© 2024 by Justine Lewis
Australian Copyright 2024
New Zealand Copyright 2024

First Published 2024
First Australian Paperback Edition 2024
ISBN 978 1 038 90012 8

MIX
Paper | Supporting
responsible forestry
FSC® C001695
www.fsc.org

Published by
Mills & Boon
An imprint of Harlequin Enterprises (Australia) Pty Limited (ABN 47 001 180 918), a subsidiary of HarperCollins Publishers Australia Pty Limited (ABN 36 009 913 517)
Level 19, 201 Elizabeth Street
SYDNEY NSW 2000
AUSTRALIA

® and ™ (apart from those relating to FSC®) are trademarks of Harlequin Enterprises (Australia) Pty Limited or its corporate affiliates. Trademarks indicated with ® are registered in Australia, New Zealand and in other countries. Contact admin_legal@Harlequin.ca for details.

Printed and bound in Australia by McPherson's Printing Group

CONTENTS

Cinderella Assistant

Ally Blake

Australian author **Ally Blake** loves reading and strong coffee, porch swings and dappled sunshine, beautiful notebooks and soft, dark pencils. Her inquisitive, rambunctious, spectacular children are her exquisite delights. And she adores writing love stories so much she'd write them even if nobody else read them. No wonder, then, having sold over four million copies of her romance novels worldwide, Ally is living her bliss. Find out more about Ally's books at allyblake.com.

Books by Ally Blake

Billion-Dollar Bachelors

Whirlwind Fling to Baby Bombshell
Fake Engagement with the Billionaire

A Fairytale Summer!

Dream Vacation, Surprise Baby

Hired by the Mysterious Millionaire
A Week with the Best Man
Crazy About Her Impossible Boss
Brooding Rebel to Baby Daddy
The Millionaire's Melbourne Proposal
The Wedding Favor

Visit the Author Profile page at millsandboon.com.au for more titles.

Dear Reader,

I come to you filled with bittersweet feelings, as *Cinderella Assistant to Boss's Bride* is the final story in the Billion-Dollar Bachelors series.

It's been wonderful spending the past year with sweet Ted Fincher, charming Sawyer Mahoney and gorgeous, grumpy Ronan Gerard; the brains, brawn and brass behind what I think is the best company that ever existed (even if only in my head), Big Think Corp.

The Big Think boys have big reputations and big personalities to match. So, finding the right heroines to match with them has been great fun.

As the fourth musketeer, Hadley Moreau gave them all a run for their money. Ronan especially. Having watched them snipe and sass one another in the previous two books, I could not wait to see how they might find their way to a happy-ever-after.

If you haven't yet, I'd love for you to read *Whirlwind Fling to Baby Bombshell* and *Fake Engagement with the Billionaire*, the first two books in the series. Not only because I love them, but so you can see how Ronan and Hadley's fiery relationship changed and grew over time.

And now, I leave the Billion-Dollar Bachelors forever in your good hands.

Happy reading!

Ally

To the gorgeously wonderous Amy Andrews, Clare Connelly and Jennifer St. George, my fellow founders of www.HowtoWriteLove.com; the online course that we created with the heartfelt intent to share all we have learned in our years spent writing romance novels. I am ever grateful to be basking in their collective glow.

Praise for
Ally Blake

"I found *Hired by the Mysterious Millionaire* by Ally Blake to be a fascinating read... The story of how they get to their HEA is a page-turner. 'Love conquers all' and does so in a very entertaining way in this book."

—*Harlequin Junkie*

CHAPTER ONE

THE DAY HADLEY MOREAU resigned as executive assistant to her billionaire boss, she wore black. And not just any black—the kind of black that made a woman feel as if she were made of pure steel: fitted black tuxedo pants, black toenails peeking out of black peep-toe pumps and a high-necked black silk shirt with an oversized bow at the neck. The press of it against her throat, against the hard pulse of her jugular, was a reminder not to say anything that might give him even the slightest indication that he could change her mind.

"What the hell is this?" The infamous, the inimitable, the *impossible* Ronan Gerard looked up at Hadley from his seat at the head of the table in the Big Think Founders' Room, the back of the chair curling behind his shoulders like a not-so-subtle imitation of a throne.

"I think you'll find it's a letter of resignation," said Hadley, her voice crisp as she glanced pointedly at the piece of paper clenched in Ronan's claw, while every cell in her body remained braced for his response.

Ronan's gaze hardened; his nostrils flared. She could feel the sweep of his displeasure as it blew about the room like a tornado. And yet his lips remained tightly closed.

Say something, she thought. For, the moment he said something, she could say something back. And snap, crackle, pop: their sharply honed repartee would siphon the electricity from the air.

And yet...crickets.

No *Don't be ridiculous.*

No *You're not going anywhere.*

No *Stay, please, I can't do this without you and, more than that, I don't want to.*

Fine. There was as much chance of Ronan Gerard saying those words as there was of Big Think Tower growing wings and flying away.

But what about the standard *"why?"*

That had to be eating at him. How a person could choose not to work for Big Think Corp would make no sense to Ronan Gerard. His company was his everything. It was his life, his passion, his obsession. Nothing mattered to him more. Nothing.

Hadley gave him a smidge longer to respond, in case he was building up to something. Despite the current statue-like comportment, she knew he was gathering steam from the muscle ticking in his jaw, the shadows in his crisp blue eyes. She'd made a career of understanding the man's most minute tells, after all, so that she might give him what he needed before he even knew he needed it.

Then again, Ronan's refusal to give, to soften even a little, was but one of the reasons why this day had finally come.

When it became clear she'd have to be the next to speak, Hadley notched back her shoulders and looked to her tablet—a super-fast prototype developed by Big Think, and one of many things she'd have to leave behind. "I'm sending you a link to Pitch Perfect employment agency to source my replacement. High-end corporate is their niche."

She glanced up to see if *that* got a reaction, but the man was the human version of a storm cloud in a snow globe: dark, brooding, threatening thunder but safely encased in an impenetrable barrier.

So, she went on. "As noted in my letter, I'm offering a generous eight weeks' notice—the first four to finish any outstanding work and to train your new assistant. The next four, you will pay me as a contractor to project manage the Big Think Ball to completion. I've provided an amount I believe to be fair compensation for that role."

At *that* Ronan stood, slowly. He was pure restrained power in a bespoke suit as he pressed back his chair with a level of calm that had Hadley's heart thudding against the tight bow at her throat.

If he tried to negotiate, to push for more time or lower compensation for her work, she was ready to fight him. In fact, a good fiery debate would make this so much easier. Their disagreements always did: benign release valves that kept things from spilling over into some comment, or action, they couldn't take back.

Only, he remained silent, merely making his way round the table. Slowly, his eyes on her—those unfairly perceptive, deceptively warm, midnight-blue eyes—the paper still clenched in his fist.

If he thought this "prowling panther" move might make her waver, cower, he had another think coming. She held her ground. Held his gaze. Held tight to the myriad reasons why she could no longer work for the man—the ones she'd happily admit to, and those she never would.

Until she noticed the uneven knot of his tie.

The man, for all his skills, had never mastered that one. As always, the impulse to go to him, to fix it, to make sure he looked as perfectly put together on the outside as he was on the inside, flooded through her. Instead, Hadley's thumb began tracing the tattoo that ran around the base of her right ring-finger: a bow of thin black string, a talisman. A reminder to remember always to trust her instinct.

The same instinct that told her it was time to move on.

Only, Ronan noticed the move; his gait paused, his dark

gaze dropped to her hand. Just as she'd come to know him over the past several years, and despite her best efforts to preserve a safe level of opacity, he'd found ways and means to come to know her too.

His blue gaze lifted to hers, locking on, seeing a knowing glint. A single eyebrow rose in question, making it clear he knew she did not feel nearly as cool as she was making out.

Oh, buddy, she thought, heat rushing through her, a thready pulse now beating at her temples, *you have no idea.*

In fact, maybe she ought to tell him every last reason why she had to leave. That would wipe that assured smile from his face—the thought of which was nearly enough for her to let it out.

But that was never going to happen.

For, while Ronan Gerard was stubborn—a stubbornness born of extreme privilege—Hadley was more so. Only, she was street-smart stubborn: gritty, wily and survival-level stubborn. Yes, working for a successful company had given her the taste and means for the finer things, but deep down she was still the scrappy kid who'd grown up sleeping in her mother's car, or on a couch belonging to her mum's latest boyfriend.

Remembering *that,* Hadley left her tattoo alone, gripped her tablet in both hands, pressed her toes into the points of her shoes and stared the man down, even as he continued his prowl down the length of the room.

Neither of them said another word until he stopped. The delicious notes of his aftershave, the questions in his hard blue eyes that he was mulishly refusing to voice and the uneven knot of that damn tie vied for attention in her head.

"You're really doing this?" he finally asked.

His deep voice and velvety tones washed over her like a winter fog. She only just managed to keep a shiver at bay.

"You're really leaving me."

A note of sorrow, of disbelief, light but there, had Hadley's gaze whipping from the knot of his tie to his eyes and their gazes tangled. For a breath, moments, memories and history curled between them like a whisper, like a wish.

But, no. She was done wishing. Done putting herself in a position that would only end in pain as, in her experience, such things always would. It took every fragment of those street smarts to keep her voice even, her expression composed, as she said, deadpan, "I'm not leaving *you*, Ronan. I'm resigning. From a *job*."

A muscle jerked in Ronan's cheek and she thought perhaps she had him. That she'd cracked the smooth, polished, marble armour he wore like a second skin. But then he breathed out slowly, the tautness in his jaw easing as he slid his hands into his pockets and leant back against the desk, before flicking at some speck of nothing on his jacket.

As if that was that. As if he'd said all he would say on the matter. As if the last seven years stood for nothing.

And the tension swirling between them—the tension that was always there, watching, waiting—only grew, till it felt as if rope was winding about her ankles, her thighs and her chest, threatening to crush her.

"Okay, then," said Hadley, when the tension became too much. Cynicism dripped from the words, giving her away. "If that's all, I'll head to HR to lodge my resignation, to make it official and set in motion next steps."

Then, because it would stay with her all day if she didn't, Hadley hooked her tablet under her arm, stepped in, grabbed the knot of his tie and yanked it into place.

The insides of his knees bumped against the outsides of hers. The warmth of his skin pulsed towards her fingers. His aura—dark and delectable—clouded around her. She told herself that she was fixing his tie because it was best to ease back on such tasks, rather than go cold turkey. Not that she was *addicted* to straightening the man's tie. Not at all.

She tightened the thing a smidge more than entirely necessary.

"Better?" Ronan asked, lifting a hand to run his fingers over the knot, as if tracing the place her fingers had been.

"Infinitely," said Hadley.

Then, with one final acute glance at those knowing blue eyes, she stepped back, spun on a high heel, walked out of the room and shut the door behind her with a very slight bang.

To think his day had started with such promise, Ronan thought.

First, an email from Paris, informing him of his nomination for the International Humanitarian Award for his company's inroads regarding renewable energy and disease control. A hell of a thing for the son of a man who'd earned his fortune greasing political palms by the way of oil and coal.

While also providing him with possible leverage with the one man he'd been trying—and failing—to bring into the Big Think fold for years? Cattle baron, beloved by all sides of politics and one of Australia's most influential figures, Holt Waverly was famously tight-fisted when it came to spending his money or political cache on anything beyond the scope of his tightknit family. Waverly was proving to be the ultimate ungettable get, but Ronan wanted him on board as a benefactor, or even as a supporter, with a ferocity he couldn't quite explain. Yet every phone call, every request for a meeting, every pitch, had thus far failed in courting Waverly's favour.

Ronan had been imagining how a prestigious award focussed on Big Think's future-proofing success might tug on the sun-weathered heartstrings of a man with three grown daughters—with grandkids surely on the way soon—when Hadley had sauntered in.

Her dark hair had been flicked and falling over one eye, lips slicked in red, channelling Bette Davis or Greta Garbo—knock-out Hollywood glamour with an underlying thread of *don't mess with me or I will cut you.*

To say the woman had sapped his breath from his lungs as

thoroughly as if he'd been sucker-punched would be an understatement. To say she'd done so every day for several years was on him. At least he'd learned how to manage it: with constant vigilance and by bracing himself for impact.

Managing had been a necessity, for Hadley was a weapon—*his* weapon. At least that was what he'd always thought till that morning, barely a moment after he'd collected his wits, when she'd dropped her bombshell.

"I think you'll find it's a letter of resignation."

And every feeling of promise, every damn thought, had been crushed by the fallout.

Now that the aftershocks had settled, the ripples faded to a swirling red mist and a mid-grade tightness in his neck, he had moved onto trying to figure out what the hell had set her off, so that he could fix it.

Fixing things was what he did. Putting things to rights. For that, he needed Hadley. And he always got his way in the end.

"Earth to Ronan? Hey! *Gerard!*"

Ronan, back in his seat at the head of the table, found his way through the red mist, and looked up to find his business partners—Ted Fincher and Sawyer Mahoney—taking up their usual spots in the Big Think Founders' Room. Ted was in his father's ancient, beaten-up lounger, with Sawyer sitting backwards on whatever chair he'd found.

The Big Think Founders' Room was not the elegant haven of thought and creativity—the kind of place Aristotle or Da Vinci would have found inspiring—he'd imagined when Big Think Tower had been no more than a collective twinkle in their eyes. This room, in which bright minds made game-changing decisions and where billions were earned and spent, veered more towards the eclectic simplicity of the university dorm lounge in which they'd first met.

Proof, perhaps, that Ronan did not always get his way. Which was not the reminder he needed right now.

"Did he hear a word we said?" Sawyer said out of the side of his mouth, glancing at Ted as he grabbed a hand ball from the bowl he kept on the table and began juggling it with his left hand.

Ignoring Hadley's offensive sheet of paper for now, Ronan said, "I'm assuming you were nattering about window treatments. Or your next book club pick."

Sawyer—quicker off the mark than Ted, whose phenomenal scientific brain was likely computing what window treatments might be—said, "The latest Brené Brown, naturally."

A smile flitted at the edge of Ronan's subconscious but did not penetrate, for his head was full—of Hadley. And not in the way it usually was. Instead, he wondered what the hell had happened to bring her to the point of leaving.

She was a fighter. She never pulled back from saying her piece. If she had a gripe, she let it be known. It was a big part of why she fitted so well. For the inner circle didn't have time for politeness, or vacillation. Humour, yes; the work they did was serious enough to require respite. But never hesitation.

And Hadley had been a part of Big Think for as long as it had existed. Her supernatural ability to take their wild ideas and plan, delegate and make them happen was stitched into the company's very fabric.

Yes, the two of them spent more time sniping at one another than not, but that was part of the magic, the kinetic energy, the push-and-pull that fuelled him. Her resistance to half-heartedness reminded him, daily, of his mission to do better. To *be* better.

So, what the hell had gone wrong?

When he realised Sawyer was actually filling Ted in about the latest book he'd read, Ronan growled, "It's been a hell of a day already, so let's just get on with it."

"But we wait for Hadley," Ted noted, glancing towards the door to the spot where she usually stood.

Ronan had always imagined she saw herself as their bodyguard, ready to bite anyone who dared attempt to enter the inner sanctum. Now he wondered if she'd had one eye on the exit the whole time.

Growling again, this time at himself, Ronan snapped, "No waiting. Let's get on with it."

"But Hadley has the agenda," said Ted.

Ronan looked at his laptop, realising Ted was right. At which point he coughed out a laugh, not even an inkling of humour in or around it.

"You okay over there?" Sawyer asked, head cocked, as if he realised this wasn't a Ronan-juggling-a-hundred-things-at-once level distraction but a whole other thing.

"Peachy," Ronan shot back. Then closed his eyes, a headache pressing behind his left eye.

"You sure?" Sawyer asked. "Because you look like you just heard Wall Street fell down a sink hole. Or Tom Ford stopped making suits."

Hell. He had to tell them. For, while Hadley was his, the others leant on her constantly and had long since adopted her into the fold.

Strike that—Hadley was not *his*. Though Ted and Sawyer leaned on her constantly, she officially worked for him alone, as *his* executive assistant. His right hand. The voice to his thoughts. The strong arm to his determinations. The veil people had to get through to get to him. And if she left…

Something shifted in his chest. No, not his *chest*—his base instincts. He felt rumblings of impending disaster, like the earth quaking before a volcano blew its top.

That settled him back into his body like nothing else. Big Think was not about to go bang. It was too big, too important, too necessary. Which was why Hadley had to stay.

Ronan curled his hands into fists, his nails pressing into his palms, and ground out, "Hadley is not here, as this morning she gave me a letter of resignation. No concern of yours. I'll sort it out—"

"I'm sorry," Sawyer interjected, both hands out in front, as if pushing back Ronan's words. "Did you just say Hadley *quit*?"

Ronan nodded.

"She quit?" Ted asked, now fully engaged, rather than having half a mind on whatever scientific breakthrough he was currently working on. "Why?"

Sawyer asked, "Has she been headhunted? If so, we match it."

Ronan shook his head. "It's not that. People have tried, for years. I've shut every one of them down, matching any offer and then some."

"Of course you have. You're Ronan Freaking Gerard."

"Then why?" Ted tried again.

To that, Ronan gave no response. For he'd not actually asked. Had he instinctively known he wouldn't like he answer?

Ted, well-used to asking questions and getting answers, asked, "How much notice has she given? Does it give us time to change her mind?"

"What does her contract stipulate?" Sawyer added, before Ted's and his gazes both swung back to Ronan.

This Ronan did know, and it wasn't pretty. He'd readily have prevaricated if he'd believed the situation required it, but in the end went with knowledge being power.

"There is no contract," Ronan stated. "There never has been."

Sawyer sat forward, and carefully placed his hand ball on the table. "I know I'm stating the obvious here, but what the hell, Ronan? *No contract?* We don't do handshake deals. We don't move an inch on any project without having the legals in place. Your rule."

A nerve fluttered under Ronan's right eye.

Sawyer was right, of course. But the way he and Hadley had come to work together had been born in such fraught and complicated circumstances, choosing delicacy over conformity had seemed the right thing to do. And he'd never regretted that choice. Not for a moment.

Now, not having circled back to that felt like the most colossal error of judgement in his life.

"As to Ted's question, Hadley has given eight weeks' notice and she has agreed to train her replacement."

Sawyer shook his head. "The Sawyers of this world are replaceable. The Ronans are dime a dozen. The Hadley Moreaus are *not*."

"Don't you think I know that?" Ronan seethed, only to hear the strain in the words that echoed back at him. And it had nothing to do with how hard he'd worked not to be some cookie-cutter suit a man from his background and social position might have chosen to be. But the point was taken.

Hadley was wholly unique. Her background had not naturally eased her into the work she now did, but she was tenacious, whip-smart and highly motivated. Like a T-1000 Terminator, knock her down and she'd come at you more determined than before.

He tried picturing some other person running these highly sensitive meetings and coordinating his precariously balanced calendar. They'd require a key to his home, his passwords and his medical history. He ran a hand up the back of his neck, which felt as if it had come out in a sudden stress rash.

Then he tried picturing some other person leaning in, fixing the knot of his tie, and he recoiled…physically.

A day at Big Think without Hadley—without her work ethic, her ability to get stuff done—felt inconceivable. How to fix it? More money, time off, a contract, an island in the Bahamas? The truth was, Ronan would give her whatever it took to change her mind.

With that, the final vestiges of red mist curling about his mind dissolved. Ronan leaned forward and looked his partners down. "Rest assured, this is not over. Now, we need to move on. If you remember, we have a company to run. A company that is bigger than any one of us."

Ted looked concerned, Sawyer compassionate. Ronan refused to acknowledge either.

"Forget the agenda. Sawyer—updates on the Centres for Physical Therapy. Go."

Sawyer narrowed his eyes Ronan's way a moment longer, before his enthusiasm for his pet project took over—an ode to the treatment he'd received after breaking his leg in a career-ending football game years before.

Then Ted waxed lyrical about an elegant new vaccine created to combat the cancer-causing Epstein-Barr virus and now ready for trial.

All the while, Ronan found his gaze shifting constantly to the empty doorway. While trying to imagine some other person taking her place was impossible, imagining Hadley was as easy as breathing.

He imagined her standing in her usual spot, tablet in hand, expression absorbed, the whole of her impossibly chic.

He imagined her looking up, her gaze finding his and lingering, a beat longer than it should. Those dark eyes of hers searing right into his soul, making him start to believe he might actually have one.

Ronan looked down to find his hand was resting on the paper she'd handed him, smoothing out the creases. Breathing in deeply, he could all but sense a waft of her perfume lifting from the page, rich, warm and sophisticated. Circling him. Mocking him. Dragging him under.

"So, I can let Adelaid know it's a go?"

Ronan came to as Sawyer said, "Fingers crossed. Petra just agreed to curate a collection in New York, so we might be home by Christmas, or just after."

Christmas, Ronan thought. A week before the Big Think Ball, which took place on New Year's Eve. After which Hadley would be gone…for ever. Unless he found a way to make her stay. Which he would do. For he *was* Ronan Freaking Gerard.

"Ronan?" Sawyer nudged. "Dinner at Ted and Adelaid's? Or are you busy Christmas Eve?"

Busy with *family*, Sawyer meant, though he didn't say the words, knowing they could be akin to a match to a tinderbox where Ronan was concerned.

He would try to carve out time to see his mother before the holidays. His father could go to hell and stay there.

This was his true family. Not the one he'd been born into— where recrimination and cocktails took pride of place on the on the family crest—but these good, smart, enterprising, fiercely loyal men and the women who'd recently swept into their lives, bringing with them balance, expansion and the space to let go of old wounds.

"Add it to the calendar," Ronan said, then remembered there was no one in the room to do that for him.

Ronan's jaw set so hard, he nearly cracked a bone. *Impossible*, he thought yet again. Hadley could lodge all the damned forms with HR she damned well liked. Ronan was not letting her go.

Hadley stood outside the Gilded Cage, waiting on the team they'd hired to help turn it from a nightclub to day-and-night event space, opening the way for high teas and the luxurious lunch crowd.

It was a job she could easily have outsourced, only the Gilded Cage was one of Big Think's most special properties, Sawyer and Petra having become engaged to one another there—twice.

And she'd needed to get out of the office.

The more time that went by before Ronan finally said something, or looked at her in some way that tugged at all those dark, hidden, yearning places inside that she was so desperate to leave behind, the greater the chance she'd change her mind.

She'd made a bargain with herself when she'd come to him all those years ago, cap in hand, asking for a job: one year. One year to learn all she could learn, then take those tools and create her own opportunities, never again beholden to anyone.

Only, she'd not expected to relish the work, to love the pace and the pressure, or to luck out with such monumental financial security. And she'd not expected *him*: his brilliance, his work ethic, his intractability that called to her own.

So, she'd stayed. And it was the only time she'd ever broken a promise to herself. The only time she ever would.

When her phone rang, Hadley jumped.

It was Sawyer's wife, Petra.

Checking the street to find still no contractor, Hadley answered, "Hey, what's up?"

"Ah, so I was just talking to Sawyer and he seems to think you're leaving Big Think."

Hadley rustled her fingers through her hair. She hadn't considered this—the speed of the Big Think information web. She would have liked to have told Petra and Ted's wife, Adelaid, herself, for over the past couple of years they'd become friends. She could only blame the rareness of lasting female friendships in her life for the slip.

"Say it isn't so," said Petra.

"It is so," Hadley avowed. "I handed Ronan my letter of resignation this morning."

"You gave an actual letter. Of resignation. To Ronan. In person. And lived to tell the tale?"

"I did."

"Wow. I mean…wow. I've always known you were a marvel of a woman, but that's impressive. The freaking cojones on you."

Hadley found herself laughing at Petra's response. A most unexpected thing, considering how tightly wound her insides still felt.

Then again, her friendship with Petra and Adelaid had been *the* most unexpected part of working at Big Think. Was that something else she'd have to let go upon leaving the company? Her insides twisted all the more.

"Did he melt down?" Petra asked. "Or did he go all stoic and manly. Or did he finally crack and drop to his knees and tell you he could not do what he does without you and insist you had to stay?"

"Stoic." Pure Ronan—unreadable, impenetrable, impossible. "With no insisting I had to stay."

"Excuse me? He's *letting* you *go*?" Petra asked on a gasp. "Just like *that*?"

Hadley fixed the hook of her structured bag over her elbow and moved up onto the stairs outside the club so she wasn't blocking the footpath. "There was no *letting*. I am not his to let. I resigned. I gave ample notice. That's that."

"Wow. You are stone-cold, my friend. Brilliant and brave, and bolshie as hell, but stone-cold. I am in awe.

"Hang on," said Petra, then after a few beeping sounds continued, "We have Adelaid. Adelaid, have you spoken to Ted?"

"Not since he left for work," said Adelaid breathily. Hadley pictured her fair flyaway hair fluttering and falling about her face, vintage maternity dress fluttering about her knees as she dropped awkwardly into a seat somewhere. "Why? What did I miss?"

"You won't believe what Hadley just did to Ronan," Petra teased.

There came a beat, then Adelaid squealed, "Really? Oh, that's brilliant! And about time!"

Hadley breathed a little easier, knowing her friends weren't pulling back or taking sides. The fact that they were romantically attached to the other Big Think founders would have given them every right.

Though, it turned out, Adelaid wasn't done. "Thank the gods we can all now stop tiptoeing around the two of you. The longing looks, the accidental touches, the sexual tension…. Big Think Tower could have run on the electricity you and Ronan produce. So, how was it? Incendiary?"

Belatedly, Hadley realised Adelaid's misunderstanding; the absolute assuredness that she and Ronan had…

Hadley's heart thumped against her ribs hard enough to

bruise as she blurted, "Wait, no! You've got that all wrong. We're not—I haven't—he would never—"

"Adelaid," Petra kindly took over when Hadley found herself in a glitch loop. "Hadley *resigned*."

Adelaid's pause was weighty. "From *Big Think*?"

Hadley was still too shaken by Adelaid's attestation that they'd all been "tiptoeing around" to speak in recognisable sentences. Though Adelaid was wildly fond of classic romance movies, so chances were she was projecting.

"But you *are* Big Think!" said Adelaid, doubling down. "The first day I walked into the place, there you were, coming at me across that big, scary foyer, so terrifyingly glamorous. Then you looked me in the eye, and as good as told me I belonged there as much as anyone. I could have hugged you forever."

Hadley swallowed, for Adelaid had unwittingly pressed on a bruise. It had taken Hadley years to feel as if *she* belonged there. The men had gravitated towards one another, naturally, like calling to like. While she'd slipped in through a crack, then hung on with all her might.

The irony was it had taken for her to finally understand her value, trust her instincts were on point and know her innate abilities were without peer, to then realise that for all those reasons she had to leave.

Because life wasn't fair. It was built that way. And she'd been born into the faction that got the short straw, eventually; always.

"How did Ronan take it?" Adelaid asked. "Did he beg? Plead? Offer an eye-watering raise? The jet? A small country?"

"He didn't even try to talk her out of it," Petra stage-whispered.

"Seriously?" Adelaid asked. "That man! I often think about how much he could do with a really good shake."

Hadley knew the feeling. Over the years she'd wanted to shake him, rage at him, poke him, pinch him…and other things. Things she imagined in the dark, in the quiet, in the space between sensible thoughts. All the ways she might get through to the man, to show him what was right in front of him.

Had resigning partly been a version of that—a kind of wake-up slap? If so, it had failed. For he'd stood there, looked her in the eye and given her nothing.

"You know what?" said Petra. "Ten bucks says he's sitting back in his lair right now, hatching plans and schemes to get you to stay. Possibly stroking a fluffy white cat in a slightly menacing manner while he's at it."

At that, Adelaid burst into laughter. "I can so see that. He has all the hallmarks of a Bond villain who took a wrong turn somewhere and ended up doing oodles of good instead."

As the other two went back and forth, coming up with more and more versions of Ronan as great villains of history but with a good streak, Hadley mused at how right they were.

That was the great paradox regards Ronan Gerard. He might be stubborn, gruff and entitled but, beneath the polished exterior, his motives were pure.

Ronan knew full well how easy it would have been to follow in his father's footsteps. Constantine Gerard had grown obscenely rich and well-protected, despite decades of nefarious dealings and unspeakable behaviour, by choosing to see the rules of business as meant for other people. Yet Ronan had made a deliberate decision to use his money and influence to enact real change in the world.

Big Think Corp was the *pièce de résistance*. A veritable funnel of grand ideas and lightning-quick action that had poured more investment into medical breakthroughs, renewable energy, disease control and community-led services for those in greatest need than any other private group could.

Yet his father's shadow remained, pushing Ronan to do better, be better. To the point Hadley wondered if there would ever be a time when Ronan could look himself in the mirror and say, *I am enough*. Whether he'd ever be able to outrun the demons that chased him.

Unluckily for her, it was that sliver of darkness, the knowledge of where he'd come from that could never be denied, that called to the darker conflicts that lived deep inside in her. Add the fact that he was utterly gorgeous, and knew it—all big and broad and bear-like with that strong, striking face, those entrancing dark-blue eyes and a voice like warm molasses—and how could she not have fallen deeply, painfully, regrettably in love with the man?

Or maybe it wasn't love. Maybe it was some inherited self-destructive streak—this constant, living ache she felt behind her ribs; the vivid dreams that left her shaking, sweating, spent; the way her body surged, her blood sparking, her belly tightening to the point of pain any time they were in the same room.

It was a miracle she'd not thrown away her career, her self-respect, all of it, for the chance to be with him just once. It was her mother's MO when it came to the men in her life, after all. She could see her mother's face, full of hope, despite all evidence to the contrary, thinking *What if he's the one?*

Only now things felt as if they were coming to a head.

Since Adelaid had swooped in and stolen big, brilliant Ted's heart—and Petra had finally realised she'd had Sawyer's heart in the palm of her hands for years—the dynamics at Big Think had changed practically overnight.

Leaving Ronan as the sole man at the helm for whom the company was his *raison d'être*. And—not that he would never admit it—Ronan was struggling. Working longer hours, meaning she did too. Pushing back more and more against her ideas, which she knew was his way of getting the best from her.

All of which meant the gravitational pull that had existed between them from day dot had grown stronger still. As if, without Sawyer and Ted there to act as foils, Hadley was hurtling towards a black hole.

No wonder she'd hit breaking point. And Hadley Moreau had zero intention of breaking. Not for him. Not for anyone. Giving her no choice but to do what her ever-hopeful mother had never been able to and be the one to walk away.

Her phone buzzed and, at the thought it might be Ronan, her skin tightened all over. Lifting the phone from her ear, she checked the screen and saw it was the contractor, saying he was close.

And, while to all the world she might still present as Hadley Moreau—cool, sharp, and focussed, like a machine—inside it stung that Ronan was yet to message, yet to call. Yet to say a damn thing! The ache that his continued ambivalence brought on, and the disappointment in herself for still wanting more, was so strong she could taste it on the back of her tongue.

Hadley blinked to find the contractor coming up the street, waving. She waved back and cleared her throat. "I have to go. Work beckons."

"Even now she's Little Miss On Top of Things," Adelaid said on a sigh. "You are my idol."

"Whatever happens from here, you've got this," Petra added. "Elephant in the room, our partners are invested in Big Think too, but we support you and we love you. No matter what."

"Thank you," Hadley managed, holding in the feelings swarming through her—emotions she was not equipped to handle.

They both rang off, leaving Hadley feeling unusually wobbly in her high heels.

She pulled herself together as the contractor arrived and was at about ninety percent capacity as she showed him round the space.

Her mind kept whirling back to Adelaid's words: *thank the gods we can all now stop tiptoeing around the two of you.*

All of us.

All this time.

Both Petra and Adelaid had asked about Ronan's reaction—both expecting it to have been spectacular. But neither had asked her *why* she was leaving. Was it possible they *all* somehow knew? That they'd seen the writing on the wall long before she had—Ronan included?

"Hadley?"

Hadley shook her way out of the fog and moved to the contractor, concentrating as he talked through ways he imagined they could switch things up with as little disruption to business as possible. Knowing she had to be at one hundred percent from here on in to get done everything she needed *done*.

Before she left Big Think—and Ronan—once and for all.

CHAPTER TWO

HADLEY ARRIVED A smidge late to the next Big Think founders' meeting in the hope she might slip in, run the agenda then slip out again and get on with the mountain of work she had to get through in the next three and a half weeks.

There was also the fact that somehow she'd managed not to find herself alone with Ronan since her announcement which, until that week, would have been unheard of. It made her wonder if he'd been avoiding her too. Which was ridiculous, considering nothing mattered more to the man than his company, and he'd work alongside an ogre if it meant the company's success.

Mind spinning into knots, Hadley didn't notice the room was empty until she was inside. She checked her watch. Had she got the time wrong? Or had they had the meeting without her? For all that that would be the case in the not-too-distant future, the very thought that Ronan might have...

"Hadley."

Hadley whipped round, the bell sleeves of her floaty white top spinning out, her leather skirt squeaking she spun so fast.

"Ronan," she said on an outshot of breath that sounded far huskier than she'd have liked.

For there he was, standing in the doorway. Her doorway. Well, not her doorway, but the one that felt like her doorway as that was where she stood for all their meetings—never quite in, never quite out.

And now, with Ronan's large, dark presence filling the doorway, she wasn't sure where she stood at all.

Not moving out of his way instantly was her first mistake. And once she hadn't, she couldn't, lest it seem that she was backing down. Where Ronan was concerned, she'd learned to stand her ground.

Looking up was her second mistake. For he was close—dangerously close. Close enough for her to see how deeply furrowed his brow was, and allow herself to wonder if that was her doing. Close enough to note every hair that shadowed his hard jaw, and a new tightness there, the planes of his already gloriously carved face looking like pure granite. Close enough to scent the subtle notes of his aftershave and to feel the warmth of his skin and the subtle shift of his breath against her hair.

Nearness wasn't uncommon, considering how closely they worked together: heads bowed over one another's desks; in and out of cramped cars; sitting together in planes and airport lounges; sharing hotel suites; their feet knocking against each other's at restaurant tables. She'd found ways to move past him, to protect her space, to glide through his world while still making as much impact as she could on the business she loved.

Only now it *felt* different. As if, since her resignation, the dynamic had shifted. There was an extra crackle in the air, the sense that things were not quite stable. And this time, instead of gliding out of his way, she held her space, owning it as if she had some final thing to prove.

"Hadley," he said again, only this time his voice was softer, rougher, as if he'd had to push the word free.

Even in her high-heeled ankle boots she had to look up, as if assenting to the way his gaze roved over her face, in much the same way hers had roved over his. As if both were checking to see what might have changed in the rare hours they'd spent apart.

"Yes?" she said.

"Can we just—?"

"Move!" a voice said from behind Ronan.

Ronan took a step her way till there was no space between them at all. His hands reached out, taking her by the upper arms, pressing her back against the wall as he shifted to cover her, to protect her as Sawyer, with his big, jock energy, hustled into the room behind him. Ronan's chest brushed against hers, his thumbs swept down up and down her arms and his stubble caught on her hair.

And then he was gone, following Sawyer, patting him on the back and asking after Petra and their New York plans, leaving Hadley standing against the middle of the back wall, her cheeks flushed, her chest heaving, her hair floating over her face.

It took her a good three seconds to come back into her skin, only to find that she was trembling, not with surprise, but with flutters of desire. Because, despite the speed of the interaction, she'd have bet good money Ronan Gerard had just taken the chance to sniff her hair.

When, even to her squirrely mind, that sounded ridiculous, she quickly ruffled her hair back into place, moved away from the wall, back to her spot by the door, and gave herself a good, strong talking to.

Enough with the projecting, she told herself. Painting her feelings and the reactions pulsing through her body onto Ronan was wholly unfair. All it had done was put her in the position whereby she had to give up the best job she would ever have so that these feelings didn't eat her alive.

Hadley looked up as Ted lumbered into the room, pushing his glasses higher onto his nose. His expression turned sweet and his ruddy eyebrows raised, as if asking if perhaps she'd changed her mind. While both Sawyer and Ted had bothered to track her down separately—asking if they could do anything, *anything at all*, to change her mind, then hugging her and wish-

ing her all the best when she'd made it clear they could not—
Ronan had not. Not once.

Hadley shook her head. And, when Ted reached out to touch
her arm in consolation, she felt like weeping. As Ted made his
way to his usual chair, Hadley made every effort to feign cool,
sharp unaffectedness, even while her insides still roiled, fumed,
and fluttered.

Things were bound to feel strange as she dealt with mentally and emotionally disentangling herself from the fabric of
this place. From Ronan, and the space he took up in her day-
to-day life. Until the day came when the ties could be cut with
a single, final, painless snip, sending her floating off into the
ether, untethered and alone.

While it had been quite some time since she'd been alone, it
was a place she knew well. A place less likely to break her heart.

"Hadley," Ronan called, his voice a gruff bark from his seat
at the head of the table. Then, "Agenda." It was as if nothing
had happened in the doorway. As if the air hadn't crackled like
mad. As if he hadn't looked at her face as if he'd missed it.

Pressing all that down into the deep, dark, hidden place in
which she kept all such moments, Hadley pulled up the agenda
on her tablet. Then, after only a moment's hesitation, she moved
past all the other bits and pieces, going straight for...

"The Big Think Ball."

Of all the projects she'd had a hand in at Big Think, the ball
was Hadley's baby. It had been the first big idea she'd floated
after joining the company. Having worked in hospitality since
she'd been sixteen—catering, waitressing and hustling for tips
behind numerous bars—it was one area she knew more about
than the phenomenally well-read men she worked for.

It was also Big Think's biggest PR event of the year, one
that brought more press than vaccinating a village for free, or
the patenting of a new electric motor ever had. It also raised a
great chunk of the funds that allowed them do both, much to
Sawyer's delight, Ted's discombobulation and Ronan's perpet-

ual disillusionment that people didn't simply see Big Think's brilliance and leap on board.

When she'd first broached it with Ronan a year or so after she'd started working with him, she'd been fully prepared for a "no." For he was quick with those, if something didn't fit within the parameters of his vision. When it had taken him about half a second to say, "Go for it," as if he'd been awaiting the day she'd stand up and ask for what she wanted, she might well have fallen for him then and there.

Now, Ronan waved a hand, as if giving her permission to start there if she must, and her feelings ran more to umbrage.

Ignoring Ronan completely, she made eye contact with the others before referring back to her tablet. "We have several weeks till the night of the ball. The theme is locked in—this year it's the 'Yellow Brick Road'. We scored a huge coup, landing Australia's favourite musical-theatre export as the MC. The tables sold out within minutes of going on sale. We are still accepting auction items, as my intention is not only to break our record for funds raised on the night, but to obliterate it."

She looked up to find Sawyer juggling hand balls, and Ted looking out of the window. And she could happily have throttled the lot of them then and there.

They were brilliant, all three of them, in their own specific fields. But—as often happened with brilliant men—they had long got away with lacking basic life skills, such as listening to anything that didn't directly concern them. And she wondered if they had a single clue as to the hustle *she* put in behind the scenes in order for their company to run as efficiently and effectively as it did.

Gritting her teeth, her gaze swept to Ronan, fully expecting him also to be otherwise engaged, only to find him watching her intently, a finger running back and forth across the seam of his lips. And she fast found herself caught in the tangle of that dark-blue gaze.

This was where she would usually narrow her eyes then look

away, or he would blink slowly then shift focus to talk to Ted or Sawyer. And both of them would act as if the moment had never happened. Only this time neither one of them moved. It was as if they were playing some new game of chicken.

Heat prickled at Hadley's skin as a bubble seemed to descend over them both, him trapping her with the pinpoint focus of his thoughts till she felt awash with warmth, with want. With so many feelings, she lost track of what she'd been saying.

No, a voice popped up in the back of her head. *Your words are important. Make them listen.*

Hadley frowned then dragged her gaze to her tablet. She scrambled for just the right thing to force them to pay attention, till she remembered a nascent idea she'd been playing with.

Big Think might own some of the world's coolest hotels and most successful scientific and tech labs—heck, they had their own jet—but the people in this room were its greatest assets. Big, burly Ted with his phenomenal brain, ginger beard and Clark Kent glasses. Sawyer, with that killer smile and the kind of charisma that could convince a nun to cartwheel.

And then there was Ronan. Never had there been a man with a greater sense of purpose and the means to make things happen. And, if that wasn't seductive enough, he looked like a Greek statue—all thick, curling hair, broad shoulders and devilish hooded eyes that could make a woman's knees melt at twenty paces.

Each on their own was a force to be reckoned with—together in the same room, on the *same stage*, they would be magic. Add the fact that, with this idea of hers, she'd be pushing all three out of their cosy little comfort zones, the more she thought about it, the more she loved it.

"As our grand finale at this year's ball," she said, lifting her voice to a neat shout that had Sawyer flinching, Ted blinking her way and Ronan settling deeper into his throne as if this was a side of her he particularly enjoyed, "We will be auctioning the three of you lugs off to the highest bidder."

Ted's eyes grew comically wide behind his smudged glasses. Sawyer lost track of a ball, the thing bouncing off to the other side of the room.

While Ronan... Ronan looked at her as if she'd just thrown a glove at his feet. But, rather than shoot the idea down, or smoulder with intense disapproval, the corner of his mouth lifted, creating a crease in his right cheek, as if he knew exactly what she was doing. She could all but hear the rough edge of his voice as he thought: *game on*. And the thrill that shot through her proved something was very wrong with her.

"What exactly do you mean by 'auction'?" asked Sawyer, eyes comically wide. "Like a *bachelor* auction?"

Ted held up both hands in surrender. "Ah, not a bachelor. So, I'm out."

"Ditto," said Sawyer. "Already found my special someone. Which leaves Ronan. He is the prettiest of the three of us. You've been so uptight of late, mate, sending you on a date could only do us all some good."

Hadley suddenly imagined some sophisticated, well-bred, well-off woman dropping gob-smacking coin to take Ronan on a date. Needless to say, the spitting green angst roiling in her belly was not something she was proud of.

"You'll take one for the team, won't ya?" Sawyer asked.

Ronan blinked once, that smile still hooking at the corner of his mouth, though his eyes had turned feral. They were gleaming, predatory and still on Hadley as he said, "What if I did have an excuse?"

"Right." Hadley snorted. Then, before she could stop herself, she said, "Like you have a 'special someone' out there that *I* don't know about."

At that, he lifted an eyebrow.

And Hadley felt the impact like an arrow to the heart.

What she'd *meant* was that she looked after his calendar, his dry cleaning and his grocery shopping. She'd even been tasked with sending break-up bouquets in the early days, something she'd refused to do after the third. Not only because it played with her already messed up heart, but because—as she told him point-blank—a good man must face up to the consequences of his actions.

She'd *know* if he was dating someone because it was her job to know.

Only Ronan was looking at her as if she had skin in the game. And the game of chicken continued. She could hear the crackle of electricity in the backs of her ears. Could feel the buzz of it in her veins. This strange new standoff played out between them, right out in the open.

When it felt as if every ounce of air had been sapped from the room Ronan cleared his throat and shifted in his chair, and Hadley had to stop herself from punching the air in victory.

"I was not, in fact, suggesting a *bachelor* auction," she said, gaze shifting easily over Ted and Sawyer, leaving Ronan well alone. "I'm not about to pimp you out. I am friends with your partners, for Pete's sake, so you can all settle down."

But the idea, or a version thereof, did have real, money-spinning merit.

She went on. "How about this? Whomever wins the auction gets a one-on-one with the founder of their choice. A pitch meeting, or a tour of the facility at your side. The chance to see behind the curtain. Something clean-cut, wholesome and brand-happy. For some strange reason, people are constantly at me for access to you lot, so let's make them pay for the privilege. Magnanimous and highly competitive… It would be the perfect big finish."

Her big finish. Ronan would be on stage, looking larger than life in his custom-made tuxedo, all broad shoulders and generational polish, squinting grumpily and gorgeously into a spotlight as she turned her back and walked away for the very last time.

Ted and Sawyer murmured preliminary approval, mostly out of relief, she reckoned. But that was enough for her.

"It's decided, then," she said. "The Big Think Founders' Auction it is. Now, I have photographers coming in Wednesday for new marketing imagery to advertise the ball."

"I'll get out my fancy suit," said Sawyer, tugging at the collar of his snug polo shirt.

"No suits," she said, for she'd had a few left-field ideas there too. This being her last ball, it was not the time to hold back. "And Sawyer, Ted—don't shave till after."

Ted gave her a thumbs-up, while Sawyer grinned as he rubbed at his scruffy cheeks. "I'm down with that. But what about Ronan? Please say he needs to wax—full body."

Ronan, now tapping something into his laptop, held up a single finger in response. Sawyer burst into laughter and finally the room felt normal again.

Until Ronan's gaze once again found Hadley's and the tension came back with a vengeance. "What do you need from me?"

While some part of her so wanted to take his words another way, she knew he meant for the photo shoot. "Light grey suit. Snow-white shirt. Silver tie. And don't let them take a single photo till I've checked the knot."

At that, she remembered fixing his tie the other morning— the feel of his knees pressing against hers, the scent of him in her nostrils—and felt all kinds of off kilter.

"So that's it from me," she said, fussing as she tucked her tablet under her arm. "I've emailed you the rest of the agenda, all items you are big enough to look after yourselves. Okay?"

Fully aware none of them would dare contradict her, she shot each a beatific smile then walked out of the room, wobbling only slightly as she passed through the doorway, remembering Ronan filling it as his gaze had roved hungrily over her face not many minutes before.

At the lift, she shook out her arms, her legs and her hair, shaking off any lingering sensations that were not of imminent use to her work—meaning any lingering sensations linked to Ronan. The touch of his hands on her arms, the tilt of his mouth as he read her like a book, and the look in his eyes that made her wonder if perhaps this wasn't as one-sided as she'd convinced herself it always had been.

Muttering to herself to get a grip, Hadley swiped her security fob over the sensor and headed up to Ronan's private floor where he kept an apartment, a gym and the kitchen for his personal chef. His gargantuan private office was there too, as was hers. They faced one another with a large open space in between, but were close enough so she was within shouting distance.

Not that she had anything to complain about there, for her office was gorgeous. Large and airy, it had plush rugs, a lounge suite, private dressing room, top-notch tech with the most beautiful pale-gold tiled ceiling and dark teal wallpaper that made the space feel like something out of a gothic novel. She'd designed every inch of the space herself, and loved it more than chocolate.

Though, secretly, she'd loved her first office too, back when Big Think had been little more than a dream and her "office" had been a tiny desk pushed up against Ronan's in a small ground-floor corner of a converted warehouse in Richmond. Ted had worked in a lab across town; Sawyer had had a couch, but had been mostly on the road, drumming up contacts even then, meaning headquarters had mostly been just the two of them.

It was where she and Ronan had built their close working habits, cooped up together in that intimate space, making plans and building something amazing. With limited funds and gigantic ideas, there had been little room for civility, hurt feelings or privacy. But it had suited them both—in the mud together, clawing their way towards something great.

But now, having exceeded every possible dream, Ronan was still restless, still hyper-focussed, still reaching for something. While Hadley felt as if she'd given all she was willing to give before she lost herself entirely.

The lift door opened and Hadley breathed out, reminding herself that melancholy would do her no good. She had to focus on the ball: the photo shoot, how it might lean into the theme, and now the auction. Plenty to keep her mind busy.

As Hadley neared her office, her assistant, Kyle, got up from behind his desk in a flutter of paper and puppy-dog enthusiasm.

"Any news?" he asked as he jogged behind her towards her office door.

By that, he meant had she changed her mind. Though born with St Bernard Syndrome—aka resting sad-face—Kyle had looked even more down-hearted since she'd given him the news of her imminent departure.

Hadley waited for him to catch up and shot him a half-smile. "Plenty. I've figured out how we are going to close out the ball."

She touched her thumb to the security pad and her smoky-glass office door swished open. Even though it had been a couple of years since they'd moved in, she felt a frisson of disbelief and pride that this space was actually hers—she an ex-waitress, high-school drop-out, daughter of a hot mess of a single mum who'd struggled her whole life to make ends meet.

Kyle dropped his tablet on the coffee table by the bookshelves before heading off to make them both coffees from Hadley's espresso machine, while Hadley popped her tablet on its charging pad and sank into her peacock-blue leather wonder of an office chair, sighing as it settled beneath her.

She sprayed a little water on Cactiss Everdeen: the mini-cactus Adelaid had given Ronan when he'd hosted a dinner party a while back, which Hadley had taken, knowing Ronan would forget it existed the second it was out of his sight.

Then she looked across to the open door of her office and beyond, to where the doors to Ronan's empty sat open across the way. For all the security—the thumbprints and personal fobs—he left his doors open more often than not. They'd both positioned their desks so that they could see one another, all that way away.

She startled when Kyle placed her coffee in its porcelain cup onto a leather coaster on her desk.

"You okay?" he asked.

When Hadley realised her hand was rubbing at the spot over her ribs right over her heart, she dropped a fist on the desk.

"Two things," she said.

Kyle held up a finger before hustling over to where he'd left his own fancy Big Think tablet. He sat, stylus aloft, and nodded.

"The grand finale of the Big Think Ball will now be a non-bachelor bachelor auction."

"Brilliant," said Kyle. "And whom are we auctioning?"

Hadley paused, looking at him pointedly.

Kyle shook his head. "Sawyer, Ronan and Ted. Of course! The Billion-Dollar Bachelor Auction. Love it."

"Only, we're not calling it a *bachelor* auction, as it's not a bachelor auction, because two out of the three are no longer bachelors."

"True that," said Kyle with a sigh. "Only, it's totally a bachelor auction, right?"

Hadley smiled, then felt a need to rub her ribs again when it hit her how much she'd miss working with Kyle. Easy, breezy and light, their relationship was the exact opposite of that with her boss.

Kyle grinned. "So, we sell them off in a completely G-rated, sophisticated, professional manner, while totally playing up their bangable-ness, because, hello, elephant in the room."

Hadley didn't dignify *that* with a response, but agreed wholeheartedly. For, while the ends absolutely justified the means, thinking about Ronan and that term had the wires in her brain short-circuiting.

"The second thing?" Kyle asked.

"It's time we start looking for my replacement."

Ronan swung his keys in his hand as he took the lift to the private garage below Big Think Tower, as if the smack of metal against his palm might unlock some insight into how the hell he could change Hadley's mind.

There'd been a moment—before the meeting that morning—when he'd sensed his chance to say something, before Sawyer had barrelled into the room and broken the spell.

No, he thought, scowling, there had been no *spell*. That made it sound transcendental, or magical, when it had merely been a moment alone. One on one, for the first time in days. Which was entirely his fault, as he'd absolutely been avoiding her—but only because he wanted to say *exactly the right thing* that would get her to rescind her resignation.

Problem was, he'd yet to come up with a reason that didn't sound as if he was commanding, or demanding, or rolling over and begging. Which was utterly infuriating. He was never this unsure—ever. But he needed to get this right so that they could get back to the way things had been.

Because it had *worked. They* had worked. Yes, they pushed one another's buttons, and their working relationship was far more hot-tempered than was in any way normal. The blame for that lay squarely in both corners. As a boss, he was no peach: his standards were high and his patience thin. While Hadley was tenacious and had a famously short fuse.

Their motivations, though, were perfectly in sync. She was a true Big Think believer, and had never let him rest on his laurels, even for a second. Since he'd known her, she'd made him do better, be better, every single day.

So, why the hell did she want to give all that up? Whatever the reason, there had to be some way to lure her back. Something she wanted. Something only he could give her.

Several rather specific ideas slithered, unbidden, into his head built on memories of a million moments when their eye contact had held far longer than usual. Times in near-empty lifts when they'd stood close enough their arms had brushed, and brushed again.

As always when he had such thoughts, he acknowledged them, then pushed them aside. For he would never act on them. He had infinite wells of self-control and would empty every single one if that was what it took not to be that man. Not to be anything like his father.

The lift doors opened and, as he stepped into the garage, his phone rang. He answered without checking, growling, "Ronan Gerard."

"What the hell is this I hear about you making a play for Holt Waverly?"

Ronan pulled the phone from his ear as if burnt, and saw *Don't Answer!* in lieu of his father's name on the screen. *Damn it.* If anyone had some nefarious radar that alerted him to the extremely rare moments when Ronan might think about him, it was Constantine Gerard.

While the urge to drop his phone and crush it underfoot was strong, Ronan tapped into the self-control he was so proud of, moved his phone to his other ear and said, "I'm well, thanks. And you?"

"Don't sass me, boy," Constantine Gerard barked back, his gravelly voice sending shards of aggravation through Ronan's nerves.

It had been some years since Ronan had done a single thing his father had told him to do, and he said not another word as he slid into his car, the soft, cream leather sinking under his bulk. The phone connected to the Bluetooth as Ronan gunned the engine and arced out of the private garage.

"How's Mum?" Ronan asked.

"She's fine," his father ground out.

She'd better be, Ronan thought.

As if the man had a clue. His parents' relationship—Constantine's simmering anger, his mother stoically taking it as payment for her comfortable life—had messed him up for a long time, until being out in the world had shown him how damaging it all was. But the scars remained.

When Ronan said nothing for long enough—sassy or otherwise—Constantine lost patience, as Constantine tended to do. "Holt Waverly is a no-go area."

That was the second reason why cultivating a relationship with cattle baron Holt Waverly appealed to Ronan: his father had famously fallen out with the man a decade before, over some land grab gone wrong, and had felt the cut of it ever since.

Ronan kept his attention on the traffic, which was heavy, and the sky above—a deep cerulean blue. "In case you hadn't realised, Big Think is not your company, and therefore its dealings are not your concern."

Ronan could all but hear his father's sneer. "Its mast bears my family name." There came a pause to let that sink in. "Waverly is a hard bastard. He'll eat you alive and you won't even know it's happening."

In direct contrast to the rising tension, Ronan gently tapped the indicator, checked his mirrors and changed lanes. "Appreciate the input, but we already have a list of people deemed unsuitable for investing in our projects, and Holt Waverly is not one of them."

His father's silence evidence the irony had not been lost on him.

For a second Ronan considered following up by telling his father about the award. But he couldn't be sure if he'd tell him to chafe the older man, or in the disturbing hope his father might actually be impressed. Old habits died hard.

Then his father scoffed, "Who put this supposed list of yours together? That girl—?"

"Don't," Ronan snapped as ice slid through his veins. "Don't even think about it." Don't even think about *her*.

Tolerance all used up, Ronan's voice was lifeless, cold, as he said, "I have an appointment. Say hi to my mother."

His father cleared his throat. "Son, that's not why I called. I—"

Ronan hung up, but not before the word "son" rattled against the sharp edges of his brain. Spying a gap in the lane over, he pressed his foot down, the acceleration shoving him back in his seat, his grip on the leather steering wheel painfully tight.

That girl.

The nerve of the man. The audacity, to dare to refer to Hadley at all. And force Ronan, in penance, to relive all that had gone down, as if it had happened days, not years, before.

It had been at a party—the first, in fact, back when his company had been little more than an idea. They hadn't even had a corporate name as yet, but word had been out that brilliant young scientist Ted Fincher, football star and Australian of the Year Sawyer Mahoney and Constantine Gerard's son were about to hit the world of philanthropy in a big way.

Ronan had used that momentum to pull together a soft launch. His father had been there, of course, along with his cronies. Which meant Ronan had spent much of the evening making sure the drinks trays discreetly avoided his father's corner of the room so that things didn't take a dark turn.

Then Ronan had seen his father make a beeline for the kitchen, just before the launch speeches were about to begin, and something, some instinct, had made him follow.

He'd imagined catching his father and reversing him back into the room so that he would witness his son's big moment, knowing that the party, the launch, was as much about that as it about anything else.

It had taken him a few seconds to note the starkly clean silver benches, the abandoned plates of food, and the fact that the space was devoid of kitchen staff, as if some dark wind had swept them from the room.

Then…sounds of a scuffle…movement. His father looming over someone trapped against a bench. And his father's voice, like gravel over a sore throat, with a level of aggression even he'd never heard before.

Which was when Ronan had seen *her.*

He'd noticed her doing the rounds earlier: one of the caterers, tall, graceful with spiky dark hair over a stridently beautiful face. But it was the cool gleam in her dark eyes, the way she'd intentionally avoided serving anyone who dared to chat her up, that had stuck with him.

Good for her, he'd thought, a big fan of autonomy, of temerity, of pushing against expectation—before adding *keep an eye on her*, her in this room full of entitled men, to his list of things to do to make sure the night ran smoothly.

And now she was pinned down in his father's arms. The part Ronan had never been able to process, even after all these years, was that for a microsecond he'd imagined it was mutual—his father being known for his bullish charm, for his tenacity, and for the women. Till her dark eyes had shifted when she'd seen him, searing him. They'd been filled with mortal panic.

Ronan's hands slipped on the steering wheel at the memory, a sheen of sweat having sprung up all over him, and he moved out of the fast lane, easing back on the accelerator.

His father was a classic bully—in the work place and at home—an absolute master of quick, cutting, emotional abuse. For Ronan, it was all he'd ever known. It had been the foundation of his childhood. But until that moment Ronan had never seen evidence of *sexual* violence.

Ronan had left his own body then; his breath had sapped from his lungs at her fury and her fear. And the shell that had protected him his whole life, protected the familial connection to his father, had snapped free. *He'd* snapped free.

A fury had filled Ronan that night, primal and painful, as he'd flown across the room and hauled his father away. The older man's arms had flailed, pots clattering, the sweep of salt and pepper hair falling messily over his eyes. Dull eyes. Rotten eyes. Eyes that had once been the exact colour of Ronan's before drink and age had seeped in.

When his father had fled, Ronan had swallowed down the bile filling his throat and faced the stranger in their midst.

Her gaze—*Hadley's* gaze—had been pure energy. And rage—as if she'd been a second away from kneeing the old man in the balls, had Ronan not intervened. She might have managed it too. And yet, for all the trauma of that moment, the family mess that had ensued, not a day had gone by when Ronan did not feel deep relief that that he'd walked into that kitchen when he had.

Slowing to a stop as the light turned amber, Ronan ran a hand over his mouth. He and Hadley did not talk about that night; at least, they hadn't for years. And yet it coloured every conversation, every disagreement, every moment they were alone.

Was it that way for her? He'd been there when it had happened. He'd witnessed her in her most vulnerable moment. Was it possible, when she looked at him, she sometimes saw his father too?

He'd asked, "Are you okay? Can I help in any way?" When he'd got nothing, "What's your name?"

She'd glared at him then, all spit and fire. "Why on earth would I tell you that? I'm done with this job, so no point trying to get me fired."

"Fired?" Ronan had reared back. "I'd never…" His father—his monster of a father—had no doubt told her exactly that, as some kind of leverage against resistance. *Hell.*

He'd placed a hand on his heart then—at least on the region where a man's heart ought to be, a non-Gerard man—and said, "I only want to help. If I am able. If you'll allow me. I'm Ronan Gerard."

"I know who you are," she'd spat. "Your photo is on every screen out there."

Ronan had winced. Right; of course: the launch. Speeches lauding his education, his ambition, his connections, were no doubt happening right then. It had all suddenly felt so self-serving, incestuous—old money calling on old money—as if he'd been swept up in the way things had always been done rather than how they could be done. It was a mistake he'd never make again.

Then she'd begun to pace, fists clenched, shoulders up around her ears, raging at the sky, making it clear she was angry at *herself* for what had happened.

Which had been enough to bring Ronan's focus back where it needed to be: on *her*.

Riding a wave of pure instinct, he decided she was tough enough to handle difficult truths. He'd explained who his father was, how the man worked—that Constantine would find a way to blackball her, so she should be prepared.

Then Ronan had offered her whatever help she needed—a car to take her home, a glass of water, a Scotch—or to follow her in a separate car to the closest police station, where he would back up her account all the way. If she needed a recommendation for whatever job she wanted, she could count on him.

That night, she'd refused it all. Had made it clear that she didn't need or want anyone's help. That, unlike everyone else in this ivory tower, she was more than capable of looking after herself. She'd found it in her to thank him for his intervention, then she'd ripped off her apron and the ID badge on her shirt, tossed them on the bench and was gone.

Leaving Ronan shaken, sickened, emotionally spent, empty to the core…and done with Constantine Gerard.

Then the following Monday, Hadley Moreau had walked into the Richmond warehouse in which he and the boys had been renting a small space at the time.

How she'd found him, he had no idea. The guts, the daring, the determination it must have taken for her to turn up there the way she had… He'd never seen anything like it.

Ted and Sawyer had actually been in situ that day and Ronan remembered it had been almost comical—the laughter, the clatter of laptop keys and even the creak of the exposed plumbing had gone quiet at the intrusion of the lanky stranger.

"Hey," he'd said, his voice raw as Hadley had walked up to his desk, her knuckles white where she gripped the handle of her bag, highlighting the first of a range of delicate tattoos he'd learn over the years she sported—a forget-me-not string around the base of a finger.

The relief at seeing her again had given him a rush of adrenaline that had pushed him back in his chair.

Then he'd remembered himself and stood, his hands in his pockets so that she'd feel safe. "Is everything okay…?"

He'd paused; remembering her name, having seen it on her catering uniform ID, but not presuming to use it till she gave it to him willingly.

She'd nodded, chin lifted, jaw tight. Then she'd held out her hand. "Hadley. Hadley Moreau."

Ronan remembered nodding, as if her name had already been etched into his psyche. As if all roads had led to this moment. And, when he'd taken her hand in his, a spark had shot through him, spearing him, earthing him.

Change was coming.

Scratch that: it had been right there in front of him.

She'd told him she'd been listening at the party and—if it hadn't all been smoke and mirrors—she liked what she'd heard. That she needed work, after having had to leave her last job. She'd told him that she was a hard worker, a fast learner and that she took no crap. Then she'd asked what she could do to help.

And help she had, more than any one of them could have imagined. She'd fast become the glue that held them all together through the exponential growth of the company, administering billions of dollars of investment and spending and dealing with three big stubborn personalities.

Now she was leaving…for good.

Talk about change coming. It had been nipping at his heels for a while now, with Ted working from home half the time while looking after his daughter, Katie, and Sawyer away with Petra's work almost as much as he was off spreading the Big Think word.

Nipping at his heels? More like taking the legs out from under him.

If Hadley stayed, he could deal with the rest. If she left…

She *couldn't* leave: it was that simple. If he couldn't have *this one thing*, then what the hell was all of his money, honour and influence even worth?

Even as he thought the words, he knew it was discomfort talking. It felt as if the company he'd given his life to was getting away from him. He'd tied his identity to its ethos, its triumph, and, without the grip he'd had on the place from inception to prosperity, who the hell was he?

Eventually the quiet whir of the engine humming beneath him, and years of practice maintaining control over his emotions, took the edge off the unspooling thoughts that were not taking him to any place good.

The truth was, he and Hadley were now very different people from they'd been that night. They'd both worked hard to put it behind them. But, even while they never spoke of it any more, that night had stuck to them like a wound that had not quite healed.

For Ronan, it was the guilt at not having been brave enough, strong enough, to call his father out and to cut him off long before that night. And he knew Hadley had never come to terms with having had to rely on him to give her the leg up to the life she had now, even if she didn't know it herself.

Perhaps she did know it. Perhaps that was why she was leaving—because she realised didn't need him anymore. That she never had.

Ronan swallowed down the lump in his throat and zipped through traffic once more till he took the turn-off towards home.

If he was the only one still committed to Big Think with the same ferocity with which they'd all started, then he'd simply have to go up a notch.

"Call Holt Waverly," he commanded his car display and, while the phone rang, he prepped in his mind the message he would no doubt be forced to leave when the man did not pick up.

But he would not stop trying. While things might be changing—and all too soon things might be completely unrecognisable from those early days—he was still Ronan Gerard: ambitious, steadfast and inevitable.

CHAPTER THREE

HADLEY HUMMED ALONG with the Nirvana playing in her ear buds as she entered the code to let herself into Ronan's house.

She dumped the mail she'd fished out of his letterbox by the security gate into a bowl on the hall table—mostly flyers despite the custom brass sign on the letterbox requesting otherwise. She noted in her tablet that the flower arrangement needed replacing, then headed down the wide hall, her Doc Martens clomping against the marble tile.

The first time she'd seen Ronan's house—seen the high ceilings, the vast rooms, the darkly elegant décor, the golden chandeliers and the opulent antique furniture—her eyes had nearly bugged out of her head. For she'd never imagined such luxury existed outside of movies.

And she'd seen nice houses. Between "boyfriends," her mother had cleaned houses for a while, back when Hadley had tagged along before she'd been old enough to go to school. Till her mother, desperate and broke, had been caught filling her pockets with hidden cash, and they'd been off in the car again.

That was where she'd first learned to bargain—with herself, with the universe, with any gods that might be listening. Had vowed to work herself ragged, to make smart choices, to leave behind no mess, if the universe agreed not to mess with her for fun.

Now Hadley walked through Ronan's home with ease, humming, making notes on her tablet as she went, checking Ronan's wine cellar—a light-and temperature-controlled room off his kitchen—so she could tick off the required bottles he wanted for his table at the ball. It was not a job she'd delegate, even to Kyle—not quite yet.

A flutter of anxiety kicked at her belly. There was so much information to pass on before she left—not just about the job, but about Ronan. How to support him. How to push him. How to *handle* him.

She could just leave it up to them to find their own way. Ronan might actually find relief in the absence of their niggly fights. Of the tension that crackled between them. Of her insistence on having complete autonomy in her role.

He might also miss the ease of their shorthand. Miss the way she never let him coast. Miss *her*.

Was that even possible? Anytime they'd teetered towards anything even resembling closeness, intimacy, he'd pulled back. Sent another wall crashing down between them. As if he was still trying to prove to her that he had infinite self-control. That she was safe where he was concerned.

When "safe" was never a word she'd use to describe her feelings for Ronan. She felt hungry, exasperated, enlivened, valued. He made her *feel*. Period. The song in her ears hit a cacophonous crescendo, thankfully cutting off *those* thoughts before they got their claws into her as she entered the huge kitchen, her favourite room in the house. It was far too big for a single man with a private chef, with cleverly canted skylights sending shards of buttery dusk sunlight over the creamy surfaces, the bronze fittings and wood-panelled walls.

She plucked a grape from a bowl of fresh fruit on the corner of the bench, tossed it in the air, caught it in her mouth and…

"Hadley?"

Hadley coughed as she swallowed the grape whole, the rubber of her soles screeching against the floor. Her gaze tracked the room frantically, to find Ronan standing half-in half-out of the doorway leading to the pantry.

"What are you doing here?" Hadley asked, running a hand through her messy waves and down the casual, swishy and rather short mustard-yellow dress she'd thrown on, because after this she was heading to a movie night with Adelaid and Petra, which they'd forced her to attend upon pain of death.

A beat slunk by, as if Ronan was tracking her every move, before his deep voice rolled her way. "I live here."

"Could have fooled me," she muttered. The man spent all his time these days in his apartment at Big Think Tower, like a beast holed up in its gothic castle. "Didn't you have—?" her mind went to his calendar "—an osteopathy appointment this evening?"

"I cancelled."

She pulled herself upright. He *never* cancelled. She cancelled for him. It was her job. For a few more weeks, at least.

"But your neck…" she pressed.

"I came home for a swim instead."

"Of course you did," she ground out, for she'd wasted more time than she really had sweet-±talking her way to getting a last-minute appointment with an impossible-to-land practitioner.

"Why are *you* here?" Ronan drawled, his voice low and warm from the shadows.

A sharper memory slipped through—the rich lady asking the same of her mother, the stolen cash gripped in her fist, the understanding that her mother had done something bad and, by association, so had she.

Hadley stood taller.

"It's my job," she said flatly, "To check your cleaner is doing their job, to organise, to have your front gate serviced, to keep your cellar stocked. None of which you'd do otherwise."

"True," he said, with a slight lift of his mouth.

"For the next three weeks at least," she added, knowing it was a low blow. But she needed him…needed him to *say* something, anything that told her he realised this was for real.

Ronan came out of the pantry, shut the door with a soft snick then proceeded to move round the bench towards her. Was this it? Were they finally going to talk about this like grown-ups?

Which was when Hadley realised he was wearing nothing but a towel draped low on his hips.

Late-evening sunlight slanted through the kitchen windows, tracing his chest—golden-brown and rippling with muscle. His shoulders were broad and strong. His appendicitis scar caught the light when he breathed, slashing above one hip, the operation from before her time.

His feet were bare. One toenail was black as if he'd kicked it at some point or dropped something heavy on it. She found herself grateful for the imperfection.

He lifted a hand to his wet hair and raked it off his face. A drop of water made its way over his shoulder, over his pec, curling round a bare nipple before sliding down his abs and losing itself in the arrow of dark hair leading…

She was staring. Staring and *salivating*. Hadley lifted her gaze to his to find his dark-blue eyes glinting. And it had nothing to do with late sunlight and everything to do with the fact he'd caught her checking him out.

This was when he'd usually stiffen, sniff in a breath and look away, as if such a heated moment had never happened. Only this time he stayed, his smile growing. And Hadley felt a wave of warmth rush through her, sweeping into her cheeks and burning her thoughts to a crisp.

At which point *she* spun on her heel and walked out of the room. What the hell had that been about? And why—why now?

"Hadley," he called, only this time his voice was rich and thick, lit with the full understanding of every thought bouncing about inside her head.

She stopped and squeezed her eyes shut. She took a deep breath, steadied her features and turned. "Yep?"

"Where are you going?"

"Movies."

"I meant, why the rush?" A beat then, "You have a date?"

For a second she considered lying. She'd do it too, if it meant saving her skin. The niceties were for those who could afford it.

"I do," she said, watching his expression, the flicker in his jaw, the fist tightening at his hip. Then she added, "With Adelaid and Petra."

At which point she saw it dawn on him that she'd been messing with him. Deliberately, knowing she could.

His smile this time was different. Harder, somehow—lit with understanding and intent. He took another step her way.

She swayed a little, as if having less than five metres' distance between them while he was dressed—or undressed—like that was a dangerous thing.

What did she think might happen? That she might leap on him? Or melt into a puddle of lust? Sure, she'd managed, by the skin of her teeth sometimes, not to step over that line as yet; surely she could hold out now?

Hadley pressed her toes into her boots, held her tablet to her chest and ambled round the island bench towards him. Her eyes were on his face, not…the rest. Not that that helped. For it was that strong, beautiful, masculine, perfectly carved face that starred in her every fantasy.

She held out her tablet and showed him the page she'd brought up with the bottle of wine she'd chosen. "I was making sure you had enough. For your table, at the ball. You do."

He nodded. "Anything else I can help you with?"

So many things…such as the tickle at the back of her knees, the dryness of her mouth and the heaviness at her centre.

For a moment, a sliver of time, Hadley wondered what he might do if she said those words out loud. But, where he'd spent the past several years proving himself a safe person for her to be around, she'd spent them protecting herself emotionally. So she didn't say a thing, and with that came a jolt of soul-deep regret.

She hugged her tablet to her chest and looked him in the eye. "So, the Billion-Dollar Bachelor Auction. Great idea, right?"

A muscle in his hard jaw clutched. "Please tell me that's not what you're calling—"

"Of course not," she said, a quick grin flashing across her face. Ah, how she enjoyed goading him. Poking and prodding till she was gifted flashes of the man behind the mask. "Just between us."

"Wonderful," he murmured. "And, yes. It's a fine idea."

"Great," she said, deflating with relief. "I've tweaked it a little more. I want to encourage regular benefactors who already have access to you guys to have the ability to bid on behalf of groups who'd never be able to afford such an opportunity. To give a leg up to those who'd usually never see the chance." *People like her.*

By rights, considering where she'd come from, she ought never to have found need to set foot inside the front door, much less have an access-all-areas pass to the entire kingdom. But, after losing her catering job the night everything had gone to hell, with rent due and prospects lean, she'd seen her chance and taken it. And together they'd flourished.

Which was why she adored Big Think so very much. The piles of money, the fancy balls, the namesake tower were all set dressing: the glitter and sparkle that lured in investors so that Big Think could help as many people as humanly possible.

Something in Ronan's gaze made her wonder if he knew why she felt so motivated about this idea. If he too was thinking back to that fateful night, the dark shadow that both bound them and kept them apart.

Then he leant against the bench and his towel slipped. He caught the towel at one hip with a scrunch of a fist, but not before Hadley's breath hitched, the gasp echoing around the huge space. When his gaze snapped to hers, electricity arced between them like a living, breathing thing.

Their gazes tangled, hot and hungry. If her chest was rising and falling as deeply as his own, then a few more breaths and she might well pass out.

She was not alone in this…this purgatory. She knew his tells, and for once he was doing a terrible job of hiding them.

They were alone, in his house. On a warm, dusky evening. And he was already half-naked. What might he do if she closed the distance, placed her hand on his chest and felt the give of his warm, hard skin? How might he react if she grazed her teeth over that spot where his neck met his shoulder?

Would his chest lift beneath her hand as he dragged in a ragged breath? Would he tip his head, giving her better access? Would he tremble as his effort at keeping her at arm's length finally crumbled? Would he let go of the towel and wrap his arms about her, hauling her close?

Or would he even allow her to get that close before finding some reason to move? Would he bring down the metaphorical wall that continually slammed into place between them?

Then Ronan said, "I do hope you're not imagining I might dress like this for your meat sale."

Hadley blinked and realised her gaze was on his flat belly, drinking the jut of his hipbone, the hunk of muscle by his clenched fist.

Her gaze shot to his, expecting to find a smirk tugging at the corner of his mouth. But instead his face appeared grim, haunted even, as his eyes slowly roved over her. He took in the kick of the short skirt halfway up her thighs. Her ankle-high Doc Martens. Her legs in between.

By the time his eyes made their way back to hers, her breath was tight in her throat. For that face—rough-hewn, dark-featured, carved by the gods—was so beautiful, so heart-breaking, so deeply private. And for a few long, heady breaths she was so filled with yearning, with want, with barely banked flames seeming to lick inside her chest. Before they shot down the backs of her thighs and back up again, till she could feel the molten flicker at her core.

Then he shut it down, hard, like a door slamming over his features. The very same door he'd used when she'd resigned and he'd not tried to stop her.

"Found what you came here for?" he asked, his voice raw, cavernous, pained.

She nodded. For she had—and so much more.

"Good," he said, then moved to walk past her. Right past her, tightly past her, considering how spacious the kitchen was.

The knuckle of his clenched hand brushed hers, a handful of skin cells barely making contact. And her senses scattered and sparked at the rare touch.

And then he was gone, padding out of the kitchen and into the house.

Somehow Hadley made it out of the front door and to her car on legs made of jelly.

She made it down his driveway and out onto the road. With distance, she felt more confused than ever. More messy, wretched, frustrated and confused, sure that in the great balance she was right and he was wrong.

About what, she wasn't as sure.

"Realising I sound like a broken record but...do we wait?"

Ronan looked up from his phone to see Sawyer straddling a chair, a hand ball twirling on the tip of his finger, his eyes looking towards the doorway of the Founders' Room.

"We wait," Ronan insisted.

Sawyer flinched dramatically. "Sheesh. And there I was, thinking perhaps you'd finally admitted to yourself that Hadley is leaving."

"She still works here. So we wait."

He'd been away the past couple of days, a last-minute trip to Sydney to meet with some long-term benefactors. The kind of trip Hadley would usually join, but he'd used it to give himself some breathing space, in the hope of coming up with a plan that didn't end up with him aching for her, in his kitchen, half-naked.

And a plan had come.

Stay: that was all he had to say. One simple word. Only, every time he thought it, it took on connotations he didn't mean. Or, more to the point, connotations he'd prefer not to highlight.

Stay...because I need you.

Stay...because I can't imagine doing this without you.

Stay...for me.

Ronan pictured her in his kitchen the other night, dressed in that floaty yellow dress with its loose V-neck, the skirt flirting with the tops of her thighs and, below, those fifties-era silk stockings she favoured with the fine vertical lines dissecting the backs of her long legs as she'd walked away.

He'd watched her for a long moment before she'd seen him, floating around his kitchen to the music in her ears, no walls up, no worries, no pretending to be anyone other than who she was. He'd let himself imagine them in another life, if they'd met some other way, with no dark history between them, and it had made his heart thunder with unspoken possibility.

Then, in the moment she'd realised he was not exactly dressed for visitors, her gaze had turned liquid-brown, her tongue darting out to touch her bottom lip as she'd looked at him as if she wanted to lick him up and down.

It had hit him—this was no crush lapping back and forth between them. It had been building from a much deeper place. It was innate, earthy, simmering for such a long time that, if let loose, it could consume them both.

And he could not allow that. For he was born of a rotten heart. For all that he'd managed to use that knowledge to forge a business that had gone against all expectations, beneath that bolshie, tough exterior Hadley was far too precious, too hopeful, for the likes of him.

"Got it," said Sawyer, snapping Ronan back to the present.

Sawyer gave a double thumbs-up, then moved to lie back on his couch, lift his damaged leg to the arm rest, and put a cushion over his eyes.

While Ted frowned at Ronan as if something had just occurred to him.

"Problem?" Ronan asked.

Ted said, "Anyone had any luck getting her to change her mind?"

Sawyer shifted the cushion just enough to see over the top.

Ted went on, "Because I can't imagine a non-AI, actual living human being who would be able to do what she does." Then, belatedly, "For you."

"Without being reduced to a quivering puddle in the corner," Sawyer added helpfully.

"Exactly," said Ted. "It's as if the two of you were made for one another."

At that, Sawyer coughed out a laugh; Ted's non sequitur clearly tickled him greatly.

"And," said Ted, warming up now, "Have we ascertained *why* Hadley is leaving?"

"Not as such," Ronan admitted.

"There was that night, years back. The broom closet…?" Ted looked at Ronan as if he was something interesting he'd just found in a Petri dish. "Or was it a cloak room?"

"You're right," said Ronan, shifting on his seat. "Let's get on with the meeting."

But Ted's focus was honed now. "In the past you've tried to convince me I am mixing up my memories which, granted, has been known to happen—nerd brain. But I can *almost* swear I saw the two of you a few years back, at the first Big Think Ball, coming out of a cloak room together—or was it a broom closet?—looking…"

The room held its collective breath, till Ted said, "Dishevelled."

"How much coffee did you drink this morning?" Sawyer

asked Ted as he pulled himself up to sit, shooting a glance at Ronan which told him Sawyer knew way too much. "Not sure I've ever heard you say this many words in one sitting that didn't have 'genus' and 'family' involved—"

"It was the cloak room," said Ronan. And Ted and Sawyer turned to stone. Ronan sat forward slowly, till all the air in the room built with such pressure it felt as if they were in a balloon fit to burst, then said, "But nothing happened."

"But..." said Ted, like a dog with a bone, or a scientist with the sniff of evidence in his nose.

Ronan held up a hand. "You do remember how Hadley and I met?"

With Hadley's permission, Ronan had filled them in on the bare bones about that first day. He'd assured her they would be discreet, but also determined that as his business partners they deserved the whole story before taking on an unknown.

Ted nodded.

"Then you understand why nothing happened in the cloak room. Or any other time. Nothing untoward has ever happened between Hadley and me. *Ever.*"

Ted nodded again. But then his nostrils flared and he held out both hands in front of him, as if about to explain some complicated chemical equation. "I understand what you're saying. But I can't see the correlation. And it's just... I love you guys and want you to be happy. And I wonder if something happening in a cloak room is what you both need in order to be happy."

Ronan rubbed a hand over his jaw, wondering how the hell he'd ended up in the middle of this particular conversation.

"I can't..." he said, then stopped. "We can't..." Nope, that wasn't it. "What if leaving is what Hadley needs in order to be happy?"

And that was the kicker. The one great stumbling block that had kept the word locked in the back of his throat.

Ted's mouth opened, then closed, his shoulders slumping, defeated. While Sawyer gave Ronan an understanding half-smile. At which point Ronan grabbed his phone and pretended to be wholly engrossed in its contents. All the while, his mind tripped back in time and place to a certain cloak room.

It had been the first Big Think Ball. They'd all been on a high at how well it was going. The money had been coming at them thick and fast, meaning their first big project, Ted's pet project, would be funded for the next decade and they'd have more to spare for further projects.

He remembered the laughter in Hadley's eyes, the wide stretch of her lush mouth, as she'd dragged him into the cloak room so that they could avoid a particularly boorish benefactor who'd been trying to convince the two of them to join his wife and him for "a little swing session" once the ball was done and dusted.

When suddenly, enclosed in the darkness, their breaths loud, their laughter ricocheting off the close walls, they'd realised how close they were. And how alone.

In the dark, all his other senses had felt heightened. Her body heat had been just within reach, the taste of her perfume on the back of his tongue.

Then either he'd moved, or she had. Likely both—drawn together by that nameless, sightless, irresistible impulse they'd managed to keep locked away in the light of day. His hands had unerringly found her waist. Hers had slid up the back of his neck before sinking into his hair.

Then he'd felt the tremble in her fingers, felt a frisson of vulnerability, and it had taken him back to the moment they'd first met. When he'd found her in a hotel kitchen, his father's rough hands on her, her lovely face contorted in fear.

And he'd pulled away from her as if burned. One moment his desire for her had been a living, breathing thing—beckoning, calling, screaming at him to take his damn shot with the woman who filled his head day in, day out. The same woman who was pressed up against him, clinging to him, sighing for him.

The next, he'd felt drenched in shame.

It was then he'd finally had to admit, if only to himself, that his attraction to her was real. That it existed outside their first meeting, outside the work they achieved together, and lived within him every damn day.

It was also then that he'd promised himself that he would never act on it—never. For he'd never forgive himself if he took advantage, in any way, of the situation in which they'd found themselves. The one thing that truly separated him from his father was his complete self-control.

Now, it was as if her leaving had torn something open inside him—some place in which he'd buried every feeling, every rush of attraction and every *"what if?"* until every waking moment had been consumed with such feelings, such longing, he'd have had to leave the state in order to feel some relief.

Was *that* why she was leaving? Had she worked out, before he had, that distance would be the only answer?

Hadley. *Hadley, Hadley, Hadley.* Maybe she was right. If he didn't hear her name in his ears, taste her scent on the back of his tongue, see her face every time he looked up from his desk, maybe he could get over it. Over her.

Over it all.

He glanced up to see Ted and Sawyer in deep, whispered conversation. And, despite himself, he listened in.

"He's clearly *not* happy," said Ted. "He seems miserable. Has done for months."

"He's okay," said Sawyer. "A lot is going on, that's all. He'll figure it out."

"But we could do something about it," said Ted, his stage whispers getting louder now. "Adelaid thinks he's one eye-twitch away from turning to ash. She has friends. She could set him up."

Sawyer seemed to consider this. "You might be onto something. I wasn't kidding the other day—the love of a good woman would do him no end of good."

When Ronan's glare felt so hot it was in danger of burning the insides of his eye sockets, he rubbed both hands over his face and let loose. "I can get my own women, or woman, if and when I so desire. What I need right now is a proficient assistant who's not intent on selling me off like I'm a hunk of meat, and who can do the damn job without arguing about every little damn thing!"

At which point, Hadley stepped into the Founders' Room and froze. Her eyes were wide. Her lush mouth was pulled tight. Her dark hair was gloriously mussed—*dishevelled*, even—sending Ronan's synapses into a mass of sparks and blinding light.

Then a slickly dressed young man moved in behind her, lifting his hand in a sharp wave. "Hi," he said, expression unfazed despite the tension rippling through the room.

"Hi...?" said Sawyer, a small smile on his face, the only one of the group who thrived amidst chaos.

"Sawyer Mahoney, Ted Fincher, Ronan Gerard..." said the younger man, pointing each of them out. "It's an honour."

"And you are...?" Sawyer asked.

"Jonas St Clair," said the young man, before sweeping his hand across the sky and saying, "Aka, *The New Hadley*."

Hadley, colour high on her cheeks, chest rising and falling while she looked at Ronan as if she'd like to flay him where he sat, said, "Looks like you just got your wish."

Hadley sat knock-kneed on a pale-pink velvet ottoman in the middle of the ladies' bathroom on the twentieth floor of Big Think, her teeth wrapped around her thumbnail as she tore it to shreds.

So many emotions roiled through her, she struggled to pin down which to deal with first. Embarrassment at Jonas's first impression of Ronan, no doubt having heard his declaration just before they'd walked into the room. Hurt from the words themselves. And the ache of knowing that Ronan didn't mean them, and had clearly been lashing out because it was finally hitting him that she was leaving, for real.

In the car, on the way to the movies after the altercation in Ronan's kitchen, she'd called Emerson Adler—the founder of the Pitch Perfect employment agency and asked if she had any leads as to her replacement.

Turned out Emerson had been just about to call. While she knew any number of brilliant candidates, she'd been struggling to find one with just the right skill set to take on Ronan Gerard. She'd admitted she'd been beginning to wonder if he might be her white whale, till she'd hit on Jonas St Clair.

The next day, after discovering Ronan had gone to Sydney without her, without even telling her he was going, Hadley had instantly set up a lunch meeting with the mysterious Jonas at a café off Collins Street.

"Ms Moreau?"

Hadley had looked up to find a guy in his late twenties dressed in a sharp suit with a lavender tie and matching pocket square. On his feet, he wore spats.

"Hadley, please," she'd said, lifting off her chair to offer her hand.

"Jonas St Clair," he'd offered.

His handshake had been perfect—strong, but not a power move. Ronan would like that.

"And may I say, before I am forced to slip into professional mode, you are a vision of sartorial splendour." Jonas blew a chef's kiss then let his hands drop, as if swiping the moment away.

Hadley had laughed, liking him instantly, and not only because he'd liked her outfit. She liked his gumption. He instantly came across as sharp, bolshie, forward, focussed and unafraid. A frisson of destiny had come over her.

Two affogatos and a spate of stories about his mean, rich

old grandmother later, she'd offered him a one-week trial on the spot.

"Hadley?"

Hadley looked towards the door of the bathroom. "Mm-hmm?"

The door bumped before opening a smidge, and Jonas's face sneaked into the gap. "Are you decent?"

"I try."

Jonas opened the door a little more. "I've been around enough money people in my life to not be surprised by anything. Is it okay if I come in?"

"Sure," she said.

Jonas sat on the edge of the ottoman, leaving a perfectly respectful amount of space. "So, that was a heck of an introduction."

Hadley deflated. "I should have warned you that you might not be welcomed with confetti and home-made cake. My leaving has not yet quite sunk in with the powers that be."

"By that you mean Ronan?"

Hadley nodded.

"Making me even more sure I'll have big shoes to fill."

"So, you're not coming here to say 'thanks but no thanks'?"

"I'm the middle child of five kids with filthy-rich parents, both of whom are completely self-obsessed. Messieurs Mahoney, Finch and Gerard? I can cope with their whims and vagaries because that's my normal. And will, for the chance to work here." Jonas glanced around, taking in the décor and the elegant fittings. "For as long as I get the chance."

Hadley knew exactly how he felt.

She reached out, squeezed his arm then used it to pull herself to stand up.

For all that Hadley had felt overwhelmed with how much information she'd have to impart to her replacement, in that moment she realised there'd never be enough time to tell him everything. So she told him the big stuff.

"Don't pander, ever. Be yourself. Push back if you disagree—they'll cope. And never forget where you are. This place…what we do here…it's beyond special. More than you can even imagine."

"Done," Jonas said. Then pressed himself up to stand too. "And, if I feel the need to hide or kick something, I now know the place to go."

CHAPTER FOUR

AFTER THE MEETING was done—the three partners somehow having achieved less than before they'd started—Ronan headed straight to his private office, preparing to lock himself away and make decisions that would change the world, on his own if he had to.

Yet he couldn't settle. Every part of him felt twisted in the wrong direction as he tried to unpick how everything had gone so very wrong.

Learning Sawyer had clearly been onto him, and for some time, had been a jolt. But Ted? Ted who rarely saw anything past the edge of his glasses unless it lived in his house or wriggled under a microscope? So much for keeping his conflicted feelings for Hadley under wraps.

Then there was Hadley herself. Two solid days apart and he'd been itching to see her, to hear her voice. So much so, it had taken everything he had not to call in on his way back from the airport to hash things out, once and for all.

Only the fact that he couldn't imagine her opening her front door and him not wanting to pull her into his arms and kiss her had sent him to his apartment at Big Think to lose himself in work instead.

The look in her eyes when she'd walked into the Founders'

Room as his words had reverberated around the small space, the hurt: he could still feel it like a fist lodged between his ribs.

He was losing control more and more, when control was his base state, his foundation. This wavering was proving difficult to accept.

Thoughts roiling, pulse beating hard in the side of his neck, Ronan started at the disruptive knock on his office door. His *closed* office door that he usually left open so that he could see Hadley at her desk.

The knock came again—succinct, but resolute.

Hadley.

He breathed out hard, swiped a hand down his tie, rolled his neck and said, "Enter." And found himself sitting up straighter, bracing, as ever, against all that she was.

A swift swish of the door, and in she came, looking heartbreakingly beautiful in a loose white shirt tucked into high-waisted cream trousers. Her usual sharp silhouette seemed to soften more each day, as if she was unhitching herself from some character she'd been playing at Big Think and morphing into her true self.

She was also looking at anywhere but him as she walked up to his desk, as if she too was braced against all that he was.

Ronan sat forward, hands steepling on his desk, conciliatory, not combative.

Her gaze finally found his. She was fire and ice, heat and hurt, and concern for him. As if she knew his outburst had been the result of the fact that he was struggling too.

Then with a soft laugh, more of an exhausted outshot of breath, Hadley looked up at the ceiling and said a silent prayer to whatever gods might be listening. Then she looked back at Ronan and demanded, "Be nice."

Ronan opened his mouth to ask why.

But then she shouted, "Jonas! Get in here."

And in wandered the young man in the sharp suit. With his neat hair, manicured nails, good posture and confidence to spare, he took a quick sweep of the room, as if memorising everything he saw, before he moved to stand next to Hadley.

"Since we didn't get the chance for a formal introduction…" said Hadley, alluding to the fact Ronan had ordered the room cleared of non-essentials while they'd spoken of private matters, which had resulted in Hadley taking Jonas by the elbow and dragging him from the room a minute after they'd entered. "Ronan Gerard, this is Jonas St Clair."

"St Clair," said Ronan, his voice low.

"Pleasure to meet you, Mr Gerard," said Jonas, holding eye contact. Then, moving a step towards Ronan's lounge, looking at the bookshelves and artwork, he asked, "I assume that's a real Renoir."

"It is."

"My grandmother has claim on a couple. Though I'm certain at least one is a print she had framed after a show at the Met."

Ronan, surprised to find himself surprised, sat back in his chair and said, "St Clair—as in the shipping St Clairs?"

"That's us," said Jonas, swinging a charmed smile Ronan's way, alert, and deliberate. The kind that came with privilege, ease and a healthy dose of knowing it. The kind of smile Ronan had seen in the mirror his whole life.

Ronan's gaze slammed back to Hadley, to find her watching him, a small smile on her face. Her eyebrow lifted, a shoulder with it. Almost as soon as they'd started working together, they'd developed their own language, a kind of shorthand that went beyond words.

He'd miss that.

Refusing to let that thought move to its natural conclusion—that he would miss her—he forced his mind to settle.

This was his moment. His chance to put his foot down and stake his claim. But the mess of a conversation he'd had with Sawyer and Ted, in which *he'd* proposed that leaving Big Think might make Hadley happy, had made him realise what had been stopping him from stopping her from going.

Whatever Hadley wanted, he wanted for her, even if that meant saying goodbye.

As for Big Think, on that score at least, he had the final say. He could be a total arse and tell St Clair to get the hell out. That he would choose his own assistant, thank you very much. But Hadley would never have brought him here unless she was sure.

She knew she'd found her replacement. Not a new her, but a new *him*. Meaning this wasn't some game she was playing. This was *really* real.

Feeling himself spiralling, Ronan ground his feet into his shoes, pulled his burdens tight around him like armour, then pressed himself out of his chair and slowly made his way round the desk till he stood before this Jonas St Clair person. St Clair was, he noted, a good two inches shorter than his own six feet three inches—which he liked. He held out a hand.

Jonas kept eye contact, smiled and shook. It was steady, sturdy, strong, and then done. *Damn it*; it was the perfect handshake.

"Jonas," said Ronan, feeling at least one of the wide-open locks tumbling about inside him click back into place. "Welcome to Big Think."

Hadley's sigh was subtle. And, if Ronan wasn't mistaken, held the slightest hint of a shake, as if she too knew how real this had now become.

"Give me half an hour to show him around," said Hadley. "Give him the tour. Introduce him to as many people as he can handle."

Jonas, hands in suit pockets, smiled as if he had no limits.

"After which I'll pass him over to HR," Hadley went on. "Then I'm all yours for the rest of the day. Okay?"

"Okay," said Ronan, then leaned back against his desk as Hadley led Jonas out of the room.

Leaving Ronan attempting to get any work done with Hadley's voice saying *all yours* swirling around inside his head.

* * *

Hadley felt a sense of lightness she'd not felt in a long time, if ever. As if she'd swallowed helium or walked through a cloud of nitrous oxide.

It was partly due to Jonas and how well he already fitted in. Partly due to the fact that Ronan had accepted Jonas with such grace. But mostly due to the fact that she and Ronan were no longer circling one another like feral cats.

She'd left Jonas with Kyle, who was as anxious to make a good impression on Jonas as he was excited to have a new play mate. Then she'd headed back to Ronan's office to find him on the couch in front of his gargantuan bookshelves, feet up on the coffee table, talking to someone on the phone.

He beckoned her in with a finger and waggled the same fin-ger at the other couch. She sat where she'd been sent, dumped her tablet on the couch beside her and then, after a moment, kicked off her towering cream heels and put up her feet too.

Ronan stopped mid-sentence, gaze locked onto the sight of her wriggling toes and bare feet rocking back and forth. Then with a glance her way he shucked off his own shoes and put his socked feet beside hers, then went on with his conversation.

Hadley laughed, and felt lighter still. For this was far closer to the normal Hadley and Ronan than all the dreadfulness of the past few weeks: multi-tasking, manically productive, and intuitively making space for one another.

Though, rather than pull out her tablet and get work done till he was ready, Hadley took the rare chance to catch her breath. She slipped a little lower in the chair, let her head fall back against the headrest and closed her eyes. She let the smooth tones of Ronan's voice wash over her as he talked through a possible investment with one of their finances guys in a lab he'd toured whilst in Sydney.

When Ronan rang off with his usual, "Later," Hadley opened her eyes.

"You all right over there?" Ronan asked, the tip of the phone resting on his chin, his dark-blue eyes on her.

Having given into the light-headed lethargy that had come over her, she gave him a slow smile and said, "Yep."

Ronan's gaze darkened a fraction more as he let his phone drop to the couch. "Nothing you need? A cup of tea? A biscuit? A blanket?"

"Nope."

Ronan nodded. Then he breathed out hard through his nose, his gaze tangling with hers, a slight and very welcome smile lifting the corners of his mouth. "Where's Tweedledee?"

Tweedle...? Ah. The Big Think Ball the year before had been a Mad Hatter's Tea Party theme. Drowning their guests in wistfulness and whimsy made for higher donations, she'd found.

She tilted her head to see round her feet. "By that you mean...?"

"St Clair."

"Right. And Tweedledum would be...?"

"Kyle."

"And who am I in this scenario?"

"You're Alice, of course. Soon to be heading back through the looking glass."

Hadley's heart gave a little squeeze at how true that was. But she found a smile and said, "Does that make you the Queen of Hearts?"

"I think we've pushed this analogy far enough," he said, then tapped her foot with one of his.

"Fair enough," she said, tapping his foot back.

Only when her foot rocked away, his followed so that they sat, feet touching, with the room quiet, the heightened animosity and awful tension that had swirled around them the past weeks disappearing like mist in sunshine.

Then his foot started to rub against hers. Infinitesimally, but enough that there was no denying what he was doing. And she let him. Because it just felt so damn good not to be fighting or hiding. Just to be with him, this man who'd filled up so much of her life that she honestly couldn't picture what that life might look like once she'd left.

The thought of a week, a month, more, without seeing his face or hearing his voice, doing what they did so well, was suddenly so big a thing to face, she curled her toes to rub back against his. Friction, sweet and sensuous, sent sparks shooting up her leg till she felt as if her insides were filled with Christmas firecrackers.

Then Ronan's mobile rang, buzzing on the couch beside him. Which meant it was likely family, if they had that kind of access, as most calls went through her office. But he didn't even glance down.

Instead, he shook his head, once, twice, then smiled across the table as he blew out a hard, sharp, telling breath. A blatant acknowledgement, his first *ever*, that he was feeling what she was feeling. That there was something there between them.

Emotion clogged the back of Hadley's throat, and the backs of her eyes began to burn. For, while she'd *yearned* for such a moment, a sign that she wasn't imagining this mutual spark the way her mother so often had, she was just so relieved that they were actually talking again that she was terrified of screwing it up.

Hadley slowly pulled her foot away and dropped it to the floor. Then, with a tremble in her hands, she grabbed her shoes and shucked them back onto her feet.

"Get that call," she said, shooting him a quick glance to find him watching her, his gaze lit with understanding, with unchecked heat. *Oh, mercy.* "Then give me ten minutes to grab the proofs from the photo shoot, and the December projections, then I'll bring them back for your approval. Deal?"

He winced. He hated monthly projections. He thought them a waste of time, when his plan was always to exceed them. But she hoped it might help her get the proofs from the photo shoot past him. She'd heard from Adelaid's friend, Georgette, who worked in PR for Big Think, that Ronan had baulked at having to sit on a hay bale as opposed to being behind a desk, looking all Master of the Universe chic, which was how his shoots usually went down. But Hadley was certain she was onto something special with this one, so he'd have to deal with it.

He gave her a short nod, then reached for his phone and took the call.

"Ronan Gerard," he said as she walked the ocean of space towards the door of his office.

She felt his eyes on her the entire time, those warm, glinting yearning eyes, and it was a miracle her knees didn't give way.

"Shall I get cracking, then?" Jonas asked from his spot in the doorway of the Founders' Room. And, for all that Ronan had taken a liking to the kid, there was no denying the lingering sense of resentment that his presence meant Hadley's absence.

Right when they seemed to have found their way back to something close to normal, Jonas was stepping more fully into her role.

Ronan waved him away.

"Bright, that one," said Ted once Jonas had left. Then he dropped to his hands and knees to look for one of Sawyer's hand balls he'd tried to juggle in the middle of the meeting. Sawyer was in New York with Petra and his younger sister Daisy— something to do with art.

"He's no Hadley," Ronan grumbled. Then, hearing the pang of hunger in his voice, he pulled himself up. Since the truce they'd broached in his office, a meeting of feet in lieu of a handshake, he'd felt as if a hole had opened up inside him that he couldn't fill—not with food, not with work, not with grumbling at his co-workers.

"Unflappable," Ted added, now packing away the electronic gadgets he'd been mucking about with—something to do with new remote medical-treatment tech one of his teams was close to testing. "The fact he knew about competing tech in Germany—he might have saved us months and millions."

Ronan grunted his agreement and wondered where Hadley was. What she was doing. When he'd see her again.

His phone buzzed on the desk, snapping him out of the fog. A glance at it showed it was his mother calling.

He called her once a week, on a Monday when his father was at work, listening hard to her tone to see if maybe this was the week she'd had enough. If this was the week she'd finally hardened her heart to the man who'd terrorised them both throughout Ronan's childhood. Though, it had never seemed as if she saw it that way—for she clearly loved the man, accepting that her husband worked hard, needed to let off steam, and Ronan should be so lucky to have had the opportunities he'd had.

But she never called him. Not since he'd cut off his father. Bar the one time, after Big Think had taken off, when his father had used *her* to try to get Ronan to attend some event that would bring him caché.

It was no wonder he'd hardened his own heart enough for the both of them. If that was what love was, then he wanted nothing of it. Best to encase his heart in lead and leave the thing to petrify. Trusting in his head, and his gut, had served him well.

Till Hadley Moreau had waltzed into his tiny office in Richmond, so dauntless, so game, and he'd felt his heart smack against its constraints. Restraints he'd kept very much in place ever since. For, if his mother taught him anything, it was that his heart was the very last organ he should ever trust.

Ronan glanced at his phone again, and considered letting it go to voice mail, but could not. Just in case this was the day.

"Mother," Ronan said, running a hand over his forehead.

At that, Ted, who adored his own mum, looked up and gave Ronan an encouraging thumbs-up. Then he pointed to the door, in case Ronan wanted privacy.

Ronan shook his head. He'd make it quick. "All okay with you?"

There was a pause, then, "Of course, darling. Fit as a fiddle. It's about your father."

"What about him?" Ronan asked, his voice tight, gruff. "What has he done now?"

"Don't be like that, darling. I know the two of you do not see eye to eye, but some things are more important than silly old grudges."

Ready to spell out any number of "silly old grudges" he was happy to hold onto, he stopped when he heard a hitch in her breath. A hitch that clanged through Ronan as if his spine was a series of bells. Adrenaline spiked. His palms sweated the way they had as a kid when his father had come home from work asking for a Scotch.

"Mum, what's wrong?"

Ronan felt Ted move in closer, pulling a chair up beside him, quietly being there.

"I'm sorry," his mother said. "Sorry to be the one to tell you, but your father... He said he's been trying to talk to you, but you're so busy. And you're both so very stubborn. Your father is sick. Very sick, in fact. It's cancer. Darling, your father is dying."

CHAPTER FIVE

AFTER A RATHER fabulous morning during which Hadley had let Jonas run a brilliantly successful meeting between herself, Kyle and Georgette, as they finalised the winners from the Yellow Brick Road photo shoot, Hadley decided to check in on Ronan.

Enough time had passed since the footsie incident that, knowing their history, they could happily pretend it had never happened. Not that she'd forgotten a single part of it; not the relaxed way he'd shucked off a shoe, the rub of his foot against hers, nor the seductive smile. She might well dine out on that for quite some time.

Whistling as she walked—a little *Somewhere Over the Rainbow*—Hadley sashayed into Ronan's office with a quick rap on his open door. To find Ronan's chair turned towards the wall of windows behind his desk.

"Gerard," she said. "Question." When he didn't turn, she called, "Ronan?"

His chair squeaked, as if he'd only just heard her. Then his chair slowly turned.

Her stride faltered and her heart tripped and stumbled when she saw the look on his face. The hunch in his shoulders. The rock-hard set of his jaw. The redness around his eyes.

"What... What's wrong?" she asked, slowing.

Was it Sawyer? Ted? Ted's baby? Was it Big Think? Was it him? Was he…?

She was disaster planning, something her mother had been all too good at—figuring her way mentally through every possible terrible outcome so that she might be prepared. Hadley used to think that was simply what a person needed to do to survive. *What happens if I screw up? Have I saved enough money? Can this company truly be for real, or will it turn out to be some front and I'll have to be ready to disappear at a moment's notice?*

Time, the comfort of a decent wage, workplace respect and Ronan proving time and again that he had her back had helped Hadley realise that—for the lucky ones—it didn't have to be that way.

But now, seeing Ronan so distraught made her want to barricade the door then go to him, drop to her knees, take his hands in hers and kiss his knuckles till he felt ready to tell her what had happened.

But that wasn't her role here. A foot rub did not change that.

"Ronan," she said, and this time her voice was cool. *She* was cool. She could face anything. "Tell me what happened."

Then he blinked at her, *saw* her, and something in his face seemed to soften, just knowing she was there. And whatever thoughts she'd had about being *cool* fled in an instant.

Screw it, she thought, and before she even felt her feet moving Hadley went to him, She dropped into a crouch by his chair, taking him by the hand said, "Ronan, you're scaring me. Talk to me. Please."

"It's my father," he said, his voice like razor blades over ice.

And Hadley flinched—literally—her body reacting physically to his quiet declaration.

What the hell had Constantine Gerard gone and done now? Embezzled? Sure. Have a secret family on the side? She wouldn't put it past him. Arrested for sexual harassment…or worse? God, she hoped not.

She turned his hand over in hers and ran her fingers down

his palm in a way that used to keep her mother calm any time they'd lost yet another place to live.

Flashes of relief, then craving, then self-reproach flashed across Ronan's eyes—as if whatever had happened had stripped him of his ability to hide behind those beautiful, dark guarded eyes.

And while that hunger, and that rare showing of vulnerability, did things to her—warm, slippery, effusive things—she put them aside, compartmentalising. Another long-learned survival mechanism.

"Why are you leaving me?" he asked. But she knew he was deflecting—a survival mechanism of his own.

"Tell me about your father," she said.

"I can't."

"Why? Because of what happened all those years ago?" She shook her head. Old news. It had nothing to do with them, or with why she was leaving, if that's what was worrying him.

He swallowed. It was! It *was* worrying him—partially, at least. Because she'd given him no other reason, he'd gripped onto the big, bad one he'd yet to truly face. No wonder he'd been so elusive, so hard to read. If anyone would make Ronan lock down, as if the world was at DEFCON 1, it was his father.

"Families are complicated," Hadley said, her ankles starting to burn. She was wearing the wrong shoes for this. She pulled herself up to stand and let go of his hand, his fingers slipping through hers, leaving sparks in their wake. Then, knees a little wobbly now, she sat against the edge of his desk.

"I could have written my mother off a hundred times—the choices she made, the mistakes, the men she put her faith in to save her from herself…"

Hadley shook her head, wondering where on earth she as going with this. But the way Ronan looked at her, drinking in her words as if they were an elixir and he a man dying of thirst, meant she had no choice but to go on.

"Did *I* make the right choice, indulging her? Not putting my foot down? I'll never know. What I do know is that I was not responsible for her behaviour. She was the grown-up."

She kicked the edge of Ronan's chair. "Your father, his actions, were all locked in long before you came along. You are not, and never have been, responsible for his actions. Or for taking up the slack in the world by being right all the time. We do the best we can with the tools we have at the time. It's all we can do."

When she finally came to a stop, her words rang between them, echoing around the large space. She felt a lightness in her chest, a kind of giving, and a release, for some of those revelations had been new to her.

Ronan stared at her, as if struggling to believe that her thoughts on the matter could be true. He was struggling to see a world in which he was not striving, reaching, pushing to do better. To make up for the fact that Constantine Gerard was such an awful man.

"What's happened with your dad?"

Ronan rubbed a hand up the back of his neck, then, he gazed at her mouth, then her neck, then her eyes, then looked away and said, "My mother called this morning. He's dying."

Conflicting feelings rushed through her, and she gripped the edge of the desk. "Dying how?"

"Cancer. Stage four. Melanoma—spread to the lymph nodes. Liver. Brain."

"Oh," she whispered, imaging brutish, bullish Constantine Gerard succumbing to the ravages that must be going on in his body right now. And finding herself unmoved. Because she was a terrible person, with not an ounce of forgiveness in her body? Or because all the empathy she had was being given to the man's son?

"I'm sorry." Ronan sniffed lifting himself higher in the chair so that he was upright. Shoulders back, he shook off the doldrums. "You don't want to hear this."

"Yes, I do."

"But…" He stopped. His gaze was even more wretched, the conversation heading danger close to touching on how they'd met. As if he'd borne the weight of it all this time. Which he had, because she'd let him.

She couldn't let him do so any more. Not alone. It was long past time they talked it out.

"What happened to me that night," she said, "was awful. Humiliating. Scary. Your father had been trying it on for hours—whispers as I passed, hands reaching for me. I told him to stop. Made it perfectly clear. Yet it only escalated until he followed me into the kitchen, and demanded the others leave or he'd have them all fired on the spot."

She'd started out feeling certain that this was the right thing to do, but now her chest began to tighten as she forced herself to remember.

"Hadley…" Ronan said. Was he begging her to stop? No. His tone was different from any she'd heard before. As if he needed to hear it, to face it, to accept it. As if only then might he be able to move on.

"I faced him," she said, looking out of the huge windows of Ronan's office, Melbourne in all its gothic beauty displayed below. "Feet braced, like one of my mother's better boyfriends had taught me, thumbs untucked in case I had to take a swing." A swing! At Constantine Gerard. "But he had me against the bench before I could even raise my hand."

A shift rent the air as Ronan lifted himself from his chair slowly, taking care not to startle her. Then he moved to sit against the desk beside her, giving her space, but also putting himself in an equal position.

Of which she was glad because, now she'd started, it seemed she couldn't stop.

"His breath was hot against my face, his eyes wild, inhuman. And then he was gone… And you were there."

Hadley breathed out hard and looked sideways.

But Ronan was looking out of the window now, his own

hands gripping the edge of the desk. There was no sense of heroism in his expression. No, "you're welcome" in his posture.

"I'm so sorry," she said, remembering how the conversation had started. "Your father is dying and I chose this moment to—"

"I wanted to hit him so badly," Ronan said. "My fist was clenched, ready. I remember feeling so angry, I was surprised my skin wasn't tinged green. But then I saw the fear in his face, and felt my own fear reflected back at me. Terror was his move, not mine. So, I did the worst I could do, on my terms. I washed my hands of him. Told him I was no longer his son. Told him if he ever came near you, or if I even heard a *whisper* of him touching another woman against her will, I'd go to the press. I'd write a book. I'd tell the world every detail."

Hadley breathed out, knowing his truth as well as if it was her own. "Hell of a bluff," she said. "Though you'd never have gone through with it, in case it hurt me."

At that, Ronan turned to face her, only now he looked calm. As if he'd weathered the worst of the storm. And his eyebrows flickered north in agreement.

"Did we do the right thing that night, letting him go?" Hadley asked.

Ronan glanced at her mouth, then back to her eyes before repeating her own words back at her. "We do the best we can with the tools we have at the time. It's all we can do."

And Hadley could not remember a moment when she had loved the man more: his empathy, his strength, his determination to carry the weight of the world. He was such a good man, made more so by the fact he had no clue just how good he was.

Considering how combative they'd been of late, she couldn't be sure things had truly settled. She might not get the chance to be this close to the man again. So she took her fill of him, counting his lashes, the whirls in his thick, dark, mussed hair, the shades of blue in his dreamy eyes and the rises and valleys in his beautiful face.

"Can I do anything?" she asked. "Anything to help?"

Ronan's gaze, which had been searching her face as she'd been searching his, as if they were both too raw to hold back, tipped back to hers. Then a sad smile tugged at one side of his mouth. "This is helping."

She nodded. "It's okay to feel all kinds of things right now—conflicted, sadness, remorse. The wish that he might have been a different kind of man."

All feelings she'd had to reconcile when her own mother had passed away.

"Okay?" she said.

And he nodded. Then his hand moved, his little finger nudging hers in a show of solidarity.

An electric shock skipped up her arm, landing in her chest, making her gasp. It was like the firecrackers and the foot rubs, only a hundred times more. By the flare of his nostrils, the jerk of his arm, it was clear he'd felt it too.

In the past this was where one or the other of them would have made the smart choice and moved, deflecting with a joke or a grouchy demand. This time, the only movement came from Ronan's finger hooking over hers.

Desire flooded through her like a waterfall after a snow melt. When Ronan's gaze lifted to hers, a hot, hard blue, she couldn't have looked away, not even if the city outside the window had burst into flames.

"Hadley," Ronan said, his voice rough, her name a lament. His face was still ravaged by his recent news, but his eyes... They were lit with yearning, with heartache, with desire. For her.

There was no wall in place. No pretending this wasn't happening. There was just Ronan.

And, before she knew it, Hadley found herself leaning in towards him.

Or maybe he leaned in towards her.

Slowly, incrementally, the distance disappeared, as if both

were caught in some magnetic vortex, spinning inevitably into the space between.

Only to come to an inevitable halt, noses almost touching, breaths intermingling. The inimitable force of mutual desire held them close, the poles of their shared history still pushing hard to keep them apart.

Hadley's heart beat madly against her ribs and, like a disoriented bird fluttering against a window, her chest rose and fell so fast she began to feel light-headed.

Kiss the man! a voice cried in the back of her head. *You're leaving soon. Don't spend the rest of your life not knowing.*

When she lifted her eyes to his, he was watching her, his gaze warm and wild with want. And, unlike their near miss in the cloak room all those years ago, with the safety of the darkness enveloping them like a shroud, the wall of windows lit them up with sharp, summery sunlight.

Ronan lifted his other hand and used it to push her hair from her cheek. Then he moved in just a fraction, his cheek now brushing so close to hers, her eyes fluttered closed. She could feel his warmth, the prickle of his stubble, the sweep of his lips against her cheekbone.

She breathed him in deeply and felt him do the same to her. Her world all breath and warmth, and the burn of anticipation.

Fully clothed, leaning on an office desk, in the bright light of day and not even kissing—it was the single most erotic moment of her entire life.

Which suddenly made her want to cry.

What was she *thinking*? Her feverish brain managed to remind her he'd just learned his father was dying. She might as well have plied him with a bottle of tequila, for all that he was in a state to make sane decisions. She would not, could not, take advantage.

Hadley ducked her head.

Ronan groaned, as if in mortal pain.

"You're dealing with the most awful news, Ronan," she somehow managed to say. "Distracting yourself won't make it go away."

Only then did Ronan pull back—physically and emotionally. He ran both hands over his face. "You're right. You are. I'm sorry. I—"

"Stop." She was not going to let him apologise for something she wanted. Wanted with an ache that might never leave her. But she pushed herself away from his desk, turned to him and pulled him into a hug. Which, as his friend—and she was his friend, they'd been through too much to pretend otherwise— was what she ought to have done in the first place.

"Call him. Don't call him," she said, while trying not to swoon from the hard feel of him in her arms, "Whatever you decide to do, I'll have your back."

"Thank you," he muttered against her neck, his arms sliding around her till it was hard to know where she started and he began.

It hurt, physically, to pull back. But what choice did she have? Then Hadley somehow managed to walk out of his office on feet that felt like lead.

Hadley's foot bounced up and down, thumbnail caught between her teeth, as she watched Ronan work at his desk all the way across the hall from her own.

This was, officially, her last week as his executive assistant. The last week she could go *anywhere she liked* in this building she'd helped design. The last week when she would have access to the inner sanctum. The last week in which to pass on wisdom to Jonas. The last week in which to leave her mark on the place.

But all she could think about was Ronan.

She wondered if he'd called his father. If underneath the back-to-normal exterior he still felt as ragged and conflicted as he'd looked the other day. If he kept thinking about how it had felt to lean into her, skin brushing, breaths intermingling, millimetres, moments, from a kiss.

He sat back in his chair, lifted the end of his tie, gave it a look, then laughed at something said by the old university friend she'd patched through to his speaker-phone a few minutes before.

Even from that distance he was utterly compelling—dark, charismatic, exuding pure power. But the knot of his tie was just off-centre, which had her swallowing down a lump in her throat.

She shook her head, hard enough her hair caught in her lashes, then turned her chair so she was facing cool-as-a-cucumber Jonas instead. He lounged on her office couch, one foot hooked on the other knee, his phone to his ear, a hand waving nonchalantly through the air as he yakked it up with an epic new Big Think supporter who also happened to be his godfather.

Hadley had had to hustle hard to make those kinds of connections, especially in the early days. Jonas did not. And she was glad of it.

Jonas hung up then sat forward and noted down the promises made in the call, so that a contract could be sent out as soon as possible. Then he asked, "What next?"

What next? Great question. Especially on the heels of the second wind that had come over her.

She had a few days left to make that hustle. To do whatever was needed to leave Ronan in the very best place to do his job. For, with Sawyer away, Ted spending more time with Adelaid as her not-that-easy pregnancy progressed, Ronan's father's illness forcing him to face parts of his life he'd spent years putting aside, and her imminent departure, life had been pushing back in a big way.

Hadley stopped jiggling her foot as it hit her what she had to do.

Ronan and his father had been in a messed-up place long before she'd come along. A father figure, Constantine Gerard was not, not in the way Ronan had needed him to be. But there was one man out there who was. A man born of privilege who'd earned his true reputation by working hard but, most importantly, by putting his family first.

She turned to Jonas. "Do you know Holt Waverly?"

Jonas blew out a long, slow whistle. "I know *of* him, of course. The man's a legend. But the dusty, cowboy chic, father-to-daughters thing, it's all rather outside my realm."

That was just what Hadley had been thinking.

Ronan had been going after Holt like a bull at a gate—all chest-beating machismo. Hadley had tried, and failed, to convince Ronan there was another way—that, as a father of daughters, Holt Waverly might respond to a more feminine energy.

"Why?" Jonas asked.

Hadley had her tablet open now, the keyboard up, fingers tapping like crazy. "Because it just became my mission in life to make that happen."

"We are *built* on a promise of future proofing!" Ronan thundered as Sawyer's image on the wall screen of the Founders' Room, connecting from wherever he was staying in upstate New York, flickered and stuttered. "How is this even happening?"

Sawyer's face had paused, mouth open, brow furrowed, the connection clearly lost. Again.

Ronan grabbed the hand ball he'd been squeezing and tossed it at the wall next to the screen, right as Hadley walked through the door, missing her head by inches.

She ducked, before shooting him a look that said he'd better watch out. But he was already half out of his chair, hand hovering mid-air.

"Seriously?" she asked.

"Apologies. That ball was meant for Sawyer."

Hadley looked to the screen, where in the half-screen beside Sawyer's comically frozen face, sat Ted in his home office, arms outstretched as his daughter, Katie, came rushing in, before attempting to climb onto his shoulders while shouting, "Dada, Dada, Dada!"

Ronan slammed shut his laptop without bothering to say

goodbye, and the vision went to black before the Big Think Corp logo morphed elegantly onto the screen.

"Things going well?" Hadley asked.

Ronan growled. For all that he'd had the briefest sense of reprieve the week before, since his mother's phone call everything seemed to have unravelled all the more. Unravelling was not in his tool box. This was a serious company, with serious concerns, and he was not in the mood to deal with this circus.

The fact that he'd woken up on Monday morning, knowing it was to be Hadley's last week, had not helped.

Hadley, who'd crouched before him and taken his hands when she'd found him after his mother's phone call. Who'd looked him in the eye and insisted, vociferously, that his father's actions had nothing to do with the two of them.

Hadley, who'd lit up like a firework when his finger had touched hers. His finger, for hell's sake—his *pinkie* finger. After which she'd looked at him with such longing there'd been a fifty-fifty chance he might have self-combusted on the spot. Thankfully he hadn't, giving him the opportunity to discover her hair smelled of flowers, her skin felt like velvet and, when they were as close as they'd ever been, her crackling energy coursed through him as if it were his own.

Hadley, who'd been the one to pull back, to make the shrewd choice, right when he'd lost the will ever to deny her anything ever again.

Hadley, who—if he'd asked—would have sourced better Wi-Fi for Sawyer. And video-chatted with Katie so Ted could give the company five kid-free minutes. Sure, Jonas could probably wiggle his nose and make it happen too, but it wouldn't be the same.

Nothing would be the same again.

"You okay over there, boss?" Hadley asked, remote in hand as she switched off the screen.

He sat back and watched her—all spare movements and quicksilver energy as she shifted Ted's chair and tidied Sawyer's bowl of hand balls. The tips of her dark hair swung just below her chin, with that "just got out of bed", mussed quality that did things to his inside. He watched her heart-achingly lovely profile—those long lashes, full red lips, tip-tilted nose and that stubborn chin. The shiny dress that whispered at her waist and swirled about her ankles, making her look like a movie star.

Busy work done, she looked up and caught him staring. She stood up straight. And from one breath to the next the temperature in the room seemed to go up a degree, or three.

"Not even slightly okay," he grumbled, answering her question. Or was it some other questions rattling about inside his head? Who knew? "I need consensus on the Hobart deal, and Sawyer's connection was completely up the spout."

"Did he mention the snow storm?" she asked.

Ronan thought that perhaps he had, but it had bounced off the other thoughts filling his head. The "it's Hadley's last week" thoughts that had him feeling tetchy as all hell, even before the damned video call.

"Now," she said, clasping her hands together, a beatific smile settling on her stunning face, "How much do you love me?"

Ronan stilled so suddenly, his heart might have stopped for a second or two. For, while he knew she wasn't being *literal*, her words caught at some raw, unprepared place inside of him.

Grateful he was not actually expected to answer, Ronan sat back in his chair when Hadley went on.

"I've booked the jet, you see," said Hadley. "For this afternoon. To take you to Adelaide...for a meeting with Holt Waverly."

At which his heart restarted with a vengeance.

"You don't have to say anything," she said, wafting a hand over her shoulder as she ambled from the room. "Think of it as a parting gift, from me to you. Just be ready for the car to the airport in two hours. Oh, and Jonas will go with you on this one."

"Hadley..." he said, unable to hide his shock and awe.

"Don't argue," she said. "Jonas will be fantastic. Just think—lots of lovely bonding time for you both on the plane."

And with that she was gone, like a wisp of smoke. And if Ronan hadn't been in love with her before...

He stopped that thought with two hands around its neck, smothering it before it had the chance to take breath.

Holt Waverly.

He searched his ego, needing to ferret out any slivers of envy that he'd not landed the meeting himself before they took root, and found there was none—not a jot.

If he'd ever had a sign that he could not be more different from his father—a sign that, no matter what happened from here, that wound was healed—that was it.

And Hadley Moreau had gifted him that.

"You ready?"

Hadley looked up from her computer, her eyes taking a moment to focus on Ronan leaning in her doorway, hands in pockets, feet crossed at the ankle, pale-blue, button-down shirt stretching across his mighty chest.

"Ready for what?" she asked, her pulse leaping just because he was there.

"Work trip," Ronan said, his tie knot so far to one side, she'd have guessed he'd done it deliberately if she didn't know him so well. "Come on. Time to hustle."

She blinked. "I'm not going. Jonas is."

"Change of plan," he said, an eyebrow raised, cheeky smile flashing across his face with such suddenness, such utterly unfair gorgeousness, her lungs threatened to collapse in panic. It was as if the thought of finally meeting with Holt Waverly was akin to an iron infusion. "Let's do this, you and me, one last time."

Then he tapped the door frame and walked out of the door.

Of all the things they'd done, all the travel and glamour and success, their hustles, when they ventured off in search of locking in a new business partner, had been her favourite thing: packing light, staying in glamorous hotels, the private jet, the long, tiring and extremely intimate days when she and Ronan spent every minute together. And when a meeting went well, the two of them tag teaming in perfect sync, glittering with clever banter and the shiny lure of their beautiful Big Think brand, it was like nothing else.

One last time.

While the thought of it was like a shiny lure—especially considering how much admin she had to get through that day to make sure Jonas would be ready to take over—it was just not a good idea. Not after the footsie thing. And the nearly kiss. As for the fact Ronan had completely undermined her by changing the plans she'd made, well, that was just not how they did things around here.

Hadley belatedly hopped out from behind her desk, jogged to the door of her office and called, "Wait!" but Ronan kept on walking.

She passed Kyle, who was busy tapping away at his computer, and hissed, "Where's Jonas?"

Kyle shrugged.

"Ronan, wait," she called. "I'm far too busy. And Jonas needs to learn how to do this."

Ronan stopped, turned and said, "I don't care."

And something in his voice—the certainty, the pig-headedness—made her see red. "I'm not going."

"Yes, you are." Then, "You made this happen, Hadley, when I could not. Now you have a plane ride to explain it to me, in detail. Besides, as of this moment, you still work for me. Meaning I get to say what work is more important. And, right now, that is Holt Damn Waverly."

That glint in his eye, the fighting words, switched on her stubborn gene like nothing else. It called to the clash of wills that had fuelled the push-pull of their relationship for years.

Saliva filled her mouth and her heart beat hard but steady

against her ribs. And Hadley realised that ribald frustration was far easier to deal with than feelings, yearnings, and vulnerability. And maybe, just maybe, leaning into that was the only way she'd get through the next few days intact.

"Fine," she ground out. "I'll go."

"Great," said Ronan, turning so that his jacket swished around him as if he were a freaking musketeer. "This will be an overnighter, so book us a suite. Somewhere memorable for out last hurrah."

With that, he waggled his eyebrows before disappearing into his office.

"Yes, *boss*!" she yelled. "Whatever you say, *boss*!"

Then she looked around her, glad they were on his private floor so she didn't look like a lunatic to anyone but Kyle, who was grinning and shooting her a double thumbs-up.

CHAPTER SIX

"WHERE THE HELL are we?" Ronan asked as they ran into the lobby of the motel and shook off the rain that had already drenched them the moment they'd stepped off the Big Think jet.

Then, when their car had dropped them at their accommodation, they'd had to weave their way around big rigs filling the motel car park in order to reach reception.

Yep, *motel*. The Big D Motel to be precise—a single-storey, flat-roofed truck stop with its own service station attached, some way off Sir Donald Brandman Drive.

Hadley felt a frisson of pleasure at the shock in Ronan's eyes as he took in the dried flower arrangement, the yellowing lace curtains and the mission-brown laminate reception desk where sat a squat little Christmas tree, the edges of its fronds changing colour.

"This," said Hadley, her arms open before her, as if showing off something fantastical, "is our lodgings for the evening."

"I don't understand."

"Sure, it's not our usual kind of place…" she said, really feeling it now.

Their "usual place" meaning some opulent, two-bedroomed suite in some ridiculously expensive six-star hotel, including a welcome hamper they never opened. All paid for by Ronan, not Big Think, who was determined never to have anyone look his way and say, *Chip off the old block*.

She went on. "When you demanded I choose somewhere memorable, I remembered staying here once with my mum, when I was seven or eight. Having only ever lived in mum's car, if not her next new boyfriend's place, I'd never stayed in a motel before, and at the time I thought it was so posh."

When Ronan's gaze made its way back to her, she batted her lashes angelically. Knowing he wouldn't dare call her out, given the story about her poor mum.

His eyes narrowed, dark and penetrating, and if they'd been able to shoot lasers they would have burned her to a crisp on the spot.

Thankfully, a bump came from the curtains behind Reception and Hadley turned to find a woman shuffling in behind the desk.

Reading the woman's name tag, Hadley smiled and said, "Dorinda, is it? I'm Hadley Moreau, and this is my wonderful, forgiving boss, Ronan Gerard. I called ahead earlier to book two rooms in your fine establishment for tonight."

The woman blinked at Hadley's enthusiasm, before her gaze moved over Hadley's shoulder to find Ronan who was looking around the space as if he'd woken up in Oz.

Dorinda, on the other hand, had taken one look at Ronan and gone catatonic, forcing Hadley literally to wave a hand in front of the woman's face.

"Two rooms?" said Dorinda, cheeks flushed, hands fretting as she hastened to find their booking. "I'm sorry, love, but we have you down for one."

Hadley's own smile dropped away. "One?" she asked, her voice lifting rather terrifyingly at the end.

"One room, twin beds. If that helps?" Dorinda's eyes moved once more to Ronan, her expression making it clear she thought two beds would be a travesty.

Hadley's cheeks warmed as she felt Ronan move up closer

behind her. "If you could change the booking to two *rooms*, that would be great. They don't even have to be anywhere near one another. Opposite sides of the complex is just fine."

"No can do," said Dorinda, clicking the inside of her mouth. "It's Monster-Truck-a-Con week. Only way you got this room was a last-minute cancellation."

So much for her big protest move. Seemed they'd have to go six-star after all. Not a sentence she'd ever thought she'd utter, but such was life with Ronan Gerard.

Hadley opened her mouth to thank Dorinda…

"Not a worry, Dorinda," said Ronan, reaching past Hadley's shoulder, the cuff of his jacket scuffing her wrist as he accepted the clunky key.

Hadley turned, caught his eye, and found it hot and hard.

Then, "Come on, Hadley, time to get moving if we want to settle into our lovely room before heading off to that big, important meeting we've been trying to land for literally years."

"But…" Hadley looked at Dorinda, who was watching Ronan leave with love hearts dancing around her head. Then she held out a flat hand and, to Hadley, said, "So you'll be paying the security deposit, love?"

Hadley dragged the small overnighter she always kept ready to go in her office over the chunky door frame that led to her room—*their* room—to find Ronan had already claimed the bathroom.

She took in the pastoral paintings on the stuccoed walls, dark-brown carpet and ancient printouts of local menus in a hand-made folder on the bedside table. And the twin beds with their red-and-gold quilts and mismatched Christmas-themed pillows propped up against the headboards.

Exhausted from her devilish dealings, as well as trying to fit six months of work into the past few weeks, Hadley fell face-first onto the bed closest to the door. As always, preferring to have the exit within reach.

Wincing when it squeaked, she rolled onto her back and a spring dug into her shoulder, after which she started laughing. For it was all just preposterous: her job, her life, her leaving… so much drama. All to end up back in the Big D Motel, wearing a dress that cost more than the accommodation, the delicate fabric now stuck to her limbs like wet tissue.

The sound of a running shower had her whipping her head towards the bathroom. A shadow moved past the slit of light below the door. The thought that Ronan might be naked had her sitting back up.

Sharing a glam suite was one thing; this was a disaster in the making. She found the TV remote, turned it on then changed channel till it landed on some reality show she didn't recognise. And she turned it up, loud.

A few minutes later the bathroom door swung open and Ronan stood in the doorway. He filled it, all big, broad and fuming. Once again, he was wearing nothing but a towel.

She rolled her eyes and turned her back.

"You're on my bed," he grumbled, striding towards her.

"I didn't hear you call dibs."

"And yet. I'm taking the one closest to the door."

She was about to say, *"How about you take the one in some other hotel I can still book,"* but when she glanced back, and saw the deep furrow in his brow, she decided that was not the hill she'd choose to die on.

Instead, she hopped off the bed, walked around the end, and sat on the other—all the while trying her best not to get too close to all that warm skin gleaming with dampness. "So, we're doing this now?" she asked. "Just walking around half-naked?"

"Seems so," he hissed, grabbing his wet jacket from the back of a chair and showing her the creases. Creases which a six-star hotel would have steamed out for him in half an hour.

"Ronan…" she said, her tone apologetic.

He shot her a look over his shoulder while he rifled through his things, coming up with nothing remotely wearable.

"Ronan," she said again, standing, moving round the bed. Only he chose that moment to stride towards the other side of the room, where his trousers lay over the back of a plastic chair, and nearly bowled her over.

Feet planted, Hadley instinctively reached for him, both hands landing on his chest—his bare chest. And, when momentum tipped her backwards, one hand grabbed frantically for his shoulder and the other dove around his waist.

When the world stopped moving up to meet her, Hadley swayed to balance, only to find herself wrapped around her half-naked boss.

Ronan loomed over her, big, bold and discombobulated. His gaze was hard, his hair a mess. His mouth a thin line. Her hungry gaze took in sculpted muscles, a smattering of dark hair and meaty shoulders, hulking and rounded from the weight he bore every day of his life—all honest, brute strength. His pupils were the size of pennies.

"What the hell is going on with you today?" he asked, his voice like sandpaper rubbing over her skin as he raised her back to vertical.

"Fair question," she muttered. One she couldn't possibly answer without utterly giving herself away.

With that she slowly disentangled herself. Slowly. When the hand at his shoulders brushed along his neck, and through the curls of his hair, it was enough to send ripples of heat through her arm to her belly.

When she was free of him, and standing a good pace back, she found him breathing as if he'd just run a marathon. Eyes closed, expression grim, he looked feverish. He looked... *unmade*. A big, beautiful human mess.

Because she'd been a human limpet? Or because he was so angry with her he could barely find the words to tell her?

"Ronan," she said yet again, her voice quiet but strong, "Ronan, open your eyes."

Whatever he heard in her voice, it was enough for him to comply.

"Okay," she said, holding out both hands in conciliation, "So things have gone a little Wild West the past few weeks. And maybe, booking this place, I leaned into that a little more than I ought. But it is what it is, and we are where we are. And we have a couple of hours till we meet Holt Waverly, which I know is important to you."

His nostrils flared, the skin of his chest was blotchy and pink, the fist at his hip holding his towel in place rigid and white. As for his towel, well, it had a ridge where she was sure it had not had before. As if…

Oh, my.

Hadley's gaze shot to the ceiling, to the wall and then to a safe spot in the middle of Ronan's forehead. Because the man wasn't angry—at least not *only* angry; he looked as though he was about to implode with the effort not to…stand erect.

"So, this is what I suggest we do from here," she said, having to stop and lick her bone-dry lips. "Let's forget what just happened, with the all the gripping and the holding and the wet skin… I have somewhere in mind where we can grab lunch. And we can buy some dry clothes. And then let's go make Holt Waverly an offer he can't refuse!"

She finished her speech by punching the air, as if her skin wasn't zinging, her heart racing, her entire body scorching with the knowledge Ronan was hard for her. The fact that they were in a small, slightly whiffy room with rather low ceilings and the sound of truck brakes outside helped—just—to stop her from doing anything completely stupid such as asking if there was anything she could do to help his *situation*.

"Okay," he said.

And it was enough to set Hadley into action. She spun, bustled over to her suitcase, grabbed a clean outfit, then, eyes front, slipped past him to rifle through his bag. She came up with a pair of jeans and a T-shirt that brought with it the soft, warm, musky scent he exuded after a night's sleep. A little light-headed, she tossed them over her shoulder. "Put this on, for now."

"Yes, ma'am," he said, a smile in his voice, and she didn't dare turn in case he took her at her word.

Having gathered her own back up outfit, she slipped into the bathroom and closed the door, leaning back against the cool wood, eyes closed, legs shaking. Then she shook herself from top to toe, before changing fast enough to set some kind of record.

Once dressed, she called, "Ready?" while checking herself in the mirror, and wiping under both eyes, pinking up her cheeks with pinching fingers and ruffling her damp clumps of hair that would turn to wild waves by the time they dried.

A minute later, he knocked. "I'm ready."

She gave her reflection a good talking to before squaring her shoulders and heading back out into the main room, where Ronan stood near the door, looking painfully good in grey T-shirt and jeans. Everything was back in place, where it should be.

Pity, she thought. Then, *What? No! Be good. From now on, be good. This is your last work trip together to land his white whale. Nothing else matters. Nothing.*

"I'll call a car, then," said Hadley, her voice far too high. "We can do this. You and me."

His gaze was unreadable, as though he'd flipped some switch while she'd been in the bathroom that had put some invisible distance between them.

She nodded and grabbed her handbag, as he opened the door, only to look up as she reached his side.

He was looking down at her, feeling dangerously close, as he murmured, "As for forgetting the way you clung to me back there, all damsel-like? Never gonna happen."

With that, he gave her a little nudge out of the door and shut it behind them.

The rain had stopped. Ronan stepped onto the path in front

of the row of squat rooms, the sun now beating down on the wet ground, and stretched out his arms, breathing in the petrol-scented air as if he'd stepped into a forest glen.

That glint of excitement was back. The thrill of the chase was creeping up on him. The Ronan Gerard charisma was ramping up, and fast.

This was going to happen today. He was going to do the thing he'd wanted to do for as long as she'd known him. And she'd made it happen. Meaning, when she walked away, she could do so without feeling as if she'd left anything undone.

Then he turned to face her, a ferocious grin on his face, and said, "Come on, Moreau, let's get this thing done." If Hadley's knees gave way, just a little, she collected herself in time to hop in their waiting car.

Holt Waverly was as advertised.

Ronan took him in—he was tall, rangy, ruggedly handsome and spare in shape and movement. When he tipped his hat off his head, it left a crease in his hair. On closer inspection, the dint, perfectly matched on either temple, appeared permanent.

"Now, that's a man," said Hadley on his left, her voice low and more than a little awed.

Ronan's gaze shot to hers to find her watching Holt cross the glossy hotel foyer, but he knew, as a man knew such things, that she was messing with him. She was giving him something else to focus on rather than how badly he wanted this to work out—*needed* this to work out.

As if feeling his attention, she looked his way, all fierce, dark eyes, pursed red lips—a true vision of loveliness.

Her expression changed, eyes narrowing: *you've got this.* Then, as her certainty, her faith in him, gave him wings, she moved to stand in front of him, right up in his personal space as she reached up and fiddled with the knot of his new tie.

"There," she said after a few long seconds of yanking, twisting and smoothing, during which he had to grit his teeth and think about the dreaded monthly projections, so as to not find himself in the situation he had that morning beneath the thin, scratchy motel towel.

"Much better."

"If you say so," he ground out.

Across the foyer—the hotel far fancier than the place they were staying in—Waverly's gaze locked onto his, as if measuring him up in half a second flat.

"Holt," Ronan said, holding out a hand. The off-the-rack shirt and suit they'd picked up in a mall on the way were pulling at his shoulders, ever so slightly too small when compared with the custom-made—but dripping-wet—gear back in the motel. "Thanks so much for seeing us."

"Ronan." Holt nodded, grasping Ronan's hand in his, the grip all bone and sinew. And hard enough, if Ronan hadn't been expecting it, he might have winced.

But by then Holt's gaze had slipped sideways, a wide, sunny smile stretching across his weathered face.

"You must be Hadley," Holt said, his voice a growling rasp of a thing, as if it too had had too much sun. "I thought you said you'd not be joining us."

Then he opened his arms for a hug.

And Hadley—who, as far as Ronan had ever seen, was *not* a hugger—*blushed* as she stepped into the older man's arms and took it.

"Last-minute spot of good luck," she said, pulling back and gifting the man a wide, blindingly beautiful smile. "I even dragged this one to Jensen's for lunch earlier, and ordered the Waverly steak, exactly as you suggested."

Holt's famous bright-blue eyes creased into a thousand lines at both corners. "And...?" he queried.

"Utter perfection. Turns out it's not all cowboy boots and slow-motion rides through clouds of red dust—you know what you're doing out there on the station."

The older man laughed, clearly delighted.

While Ronan watched on, a downright third wheel, yet loving it. The things this woman could achieve by sheer force of will, the way she surprised him every day, gave him a hell of a thrill.

He must have made a sound, for Hadley glanced his way, giving him the final moment of that smile before she blinked furiously at whatever expression she saw on his face. And then it was gone, leaving him momentarily blinded.

"Now," said Hadley, "lunch was hours ago, and I'm famished. Shall we?"

Holt nodded and Hadley ushered the men after her, waiting until they were in step, then she dashed off on a pair of prohibitively high heels faster than they could keep up without hitting a jog.

Ronan noticed, with a flash of heat, that along with the little black dress she'd picked up along with his suit she'd sourced those stockings she favoured, with the fine black seam gracing the backs of her long legs.

He looked at Holt, in step beside him, to find the older man's gaze now laser-sharp, as if casing the room for predator and prey, and not quite sure how he'd ended up there.

Ronan laughed softly. "Why do I get the feeling Hadley flummoxed you into doing her bidding?"

Holt shot him a look, eyes narrowing. "Because you've been in my shoes."

Ronan laughed again. "*Touché.* You do know *I've* been trying to set this up for an embarrassing number of years?"

Holt smiled knowingly.

"So, how did she do it?" Ronan asked.

"She's a mercenary, that's how. Got onto my youngest, Matilda, via some common connection. Tilly is a total soft touch. Through her, she got onto me. And in a three-minute phone call managed to bring up the fact she'd never known her father, and admired my closeness with my own daughters, and how their futures must keep me up at night. Somehow tugging on the only three heartstrings I possess."

Holt shot Ronan a look. "Then, once I was putty in her hand, she talked about you. About your vision, your determination, how you put your money and time and energy where your mouth is. That beneath the slick facade, you are a good man and, if I didn't hear you out, then I wasn't nearly as clever as I thought I was. And so, here I am."

There was not a single thing Ronan could say to that which wouldn't make him look like an absolute goose.

"She's a keeper," the older man said as Hadley waltzed into the elegant hotel restaurant as if she owned it. She gathered a waiter and a bar tender, both of whom followed her as if in a trance while she chose just the right table in the corner of the hotel restaurant.

All Ronan could say was, "I'm well aware."

The fact that he couldn't keep her—that all too soon he'd be letting her go, and that she'd said all those things about him— tumbled him like a rogue wave, knocking loose every one of the thousand dangerous thoughts, warm feelings and intimate moments he'd experienced with Hadley over the years—the ones he'd resolved to keep locked down deep inside.

And, barraged by a tumult of emotions while wearing a too-small, shop-bought suit, that was how he had to nab Holt Waverly. If he pulled it off, it would be the coup of a lifetime.

In the end, Ronan didn't have to pull anything off at all, for he'd been invited to the Hadley and Holt Show.

While watching Hadley snare any man in her thrall had never been a comfortable place for Ronan to be, he knew that she was doing exactly what he paid her to do: smoothing the way, for him.

She asked after Holt's three grown daughters, and talked about different cuts of beef the way a sommelier would talk of wine, while Ronan sat back, watched and learned. For this was a master class. She did not leave any stone unturned. The student had become the teacher.

The bigger question was why? Was she going above and beyond as an apology for booking that ridiculous motel room? Because this was their last such trip? Or because she knew just how much he wanted this to land?

And she knew. Because she *knew* him—every flaw, every foible, every weakness. And yet she'd told Holt Waverly that he was a good man. She'd said those actual words. And…and he couldn't get past it. She *knew* him and believed he was good.

Just as he knew her.

No one watching her now, holding her wine glass just so, all panache and effortless cool, would believe she'd had such a tough start. But he could see it in how hard she worked, how she double-and triple-checked herself to make sure not to mess up, in the biting repartee that made her compelling company, but also kept people at arm's length.

He'd seen any number of men succumb to her beauty and try to match wits only to watch, with no small amount of enjoyment, as she'd squished them like bugs. Not that she'd been pure as the driven snow. She'd dated along the way—a couple had lasted weeks, if not months—but none had stuck. An outcome that had left him fiercely relieved, even if his dating history had sputtered much the same way. His job was so constant, so consuming, he'd needed her at his beck and call.

He'd needed her… He just needed her.

For all that he'd grown up with every advantage, she reflected the best and worst parts of him: slow to trust, hyperambitious and compulsively alone. It was almost as if they'd been destined to stand in one another's path, so as to be forced to face their own weaknesses. To own them, to use them for good. Without one another, they might both have suffered from arrested development.

Was that why she was stepping back? Had she evolved past all that? Was she finally at a point where she believed herself deserving of a different life? A life filled with time, daylight, space and breath? A life devoid of such relentless, unforgiving pressure?

Ronan breathed out hard, then did something he'd never once done, opening a sliver in the lead case around his heart. So that he might imagine a life without Big Think. He tried imagining long weekends, lazy mornings, and coffee for the sake of coffee, not as a life force. Tried imagining a life lived beside someone else.

But he could not. It was a big, grey blank. Normality a terrifying unknown. As if he'd guarded his heart against invasion, against tyranny, for so long, it was too late to be any other way.

He closed himself up quick smart and the lead casing around his heart held tight. His life's mission—the need for restitution—was unfinished. And he did not see a time when it would ever feel otherwise.

And yet the *feelings* that had earlier been knocked loose, all added up to one thing, one great, big, deeply hidden truth.

He'd never known anyone like Hadley Moreau—acerbic yet kind, unsettled yet strong, warm, engaging and spellbinding yet truly elusive. Her duality thrilled him, spoke to him, unnerved him, touched him. Hadley was under his skin, in his bones, wrapped around every part of him in ways he could not see himself to undoing.

He wanted her. He wanted her to stay. He wanted her in his arms. He wanted her so badly, his chest hurt. He wanted her so deeply, he dreamed of her and yearned for her.

All that with an emotionally stilted heart; a locked down, shut off, shrivelled thing. Despite all the years during which he might have evolved along with her, he remained ill-equipped, unworthy.

And she deserved far better—far better—than a Gerard. So, he would have Big Think, and he would lose her.

So be it.

"Ronan?" Hadley's voice broke into his reverie and he blinked to find her watching him, her voice loud, motioning with her eyes that Holt had asked him a question.

Holt, seeing that Ronan's gaze had been so steadfastly focused on Hadley, cleared his throat and said, "I was sorry to hear your father is unwell. How is he doing?"

Unprepared, the question hit hard. Ronan's mouth opened and closed; akin to a fish flapping on the shore. Heat rose up his spine, gathering in his throat, tightening till he fought the urge to loosen his tie.

A hand landed on his thigh—Hadley's hand, squeezing, pinching really, rather hard, till it yanked Ronan fully into the present moment.

He said, "It's no secret that my father and I have not been close for some time." Then wondered where the hell that had come from.

When he looked at Hadley, her eyes were sharp, questioning, then, after a beat, encouraging. Her grip softened; her thumb stroked over his knee.

Go on. You can do this.

Ronan went on. "We have wildly different values, my father and I, when it comes to business, politics, social contracts..." *Women. Family. Respect.* "And yet it's been difficult, knowing he's unwell."

Holt grunted.

While Ronan wondered if opening his heart for that tiny sliver of time had rent some permanent change. Had it let something in, or let something out?

Either way, path chosen, Ronan followed the flow. "I envy you—how close you are with your family. I think that's what partly led me to create a kind of family at Big Think."

Hadley's hand jerked, before it slipped away.

"I also know," said Ronan, "that your legacy is important to you, Holt. Not your public legacy—" that was his own father's *raison d'être* "—but what you leave behind for your family. The example of a life lived with passion and purpose, as well securing opportunity, comfort, and health for them all. That is why I believe you and I are such a good fit. Your goal is our goal, only on a global scale."

"To save the world," said Hadley, stating Big Think's simple yet ambitious mission statement.

"A hell of a big call," said Holt, leaning back in his seat. If he crossed his arms, Ronan knew they were doomed. But his fingers danced on the table top—thinking fingers, curious fingers.

Ronan smiled and said, "Gargantuan." Then, "Care to help?"

When Hadley once again squeezed Ronan's thigh this time, it was a manic *squeeze-squeeze-squeeze* of excitement, as good as a high-five. Only far too close to sensitive nerves that were sitting up and begging for more.

His hand landed on hers and stilled it just as she turned her hand so that her palm slid against his, fingers tangling, a perfect fit.

They had been a phenomenal partnership, enjoying unheard-of success. A crack team. All of which felt diaphanous and transitory, compared with the warm, strong, tangible fingers curled into his.

When Hadley's gaze caught on his, a slice of heat cut right through him, bringing with it a wave of inevitability. And he felt his heart thump once, then twice, against the seam he'd opened earlier, pushing hard against its decades-old constraints. Knocking, wanting to be let out.

So, he let her go, dragging his hand away and steepling his fingers on the table. Hadley's fingers curled against his thigh another second then slowly slipped away.

Holt picked up his glass and swirled it a moment before lifting it in front of his face.

Ronan lifted his own glass. "To legacies to be proud of."

After a long, laden beat, Holt sat forward and touched his

glass to Ronan's, then Hadley's. "To our families, both born and made, and their futures."

And Ronan knew—as truly as he'd known anything—that Holt Waverly had just decided to get into bed with his company.

CHAPTER SEVEN

HADLEY WAS BUZZING.

If success was an aphrodisiac, it was no wonder she'd spent the past several years with a near-constant itch when it came to Ronan Gerard.

Now, in the back of the car taking them up the motorway, Ronan filling up the back seat beside her, she flinched every time he breathed. Her body rolled towards him every time he shifted. Even the tips of her fingers vibrated with the need to flick away all her excess energy.

Was she really ready to give this up?

Not the hyper-awareness of the man beside her, for that was exhausting, and destined to continue shredding her heart until it was nothing but dust, but the rest? Having a plan, planning a plan and achieving a plan—that stuff was addictive. It was like a happy-ever-after every time.

When the car pulled into the motel car park, the Big D sign sending blue and red light over the windows, Hadley had the door open before the car had even rocked to a stop.

"Wait up," Ronan said.

But she had too much energy. And she was within sight of their room, key in hand, and couldn't wait to get out of this scratchy dress.

A hand clamped down on her wrist.

She stopped, a high heel scrunching on the gravel, and turned to find Ronan, his gaze on the place he held her. His was jaw tight, his nostrils flaring, his thumb cruising over her wrist.

"I said, wait."

"Well," she said, her heart suddenly in her throat, "I didn't want to wait."

He looked up then, light spilling over his back creating shadows in his hard-cut cheeks, the dip of his throat, the bulk of his shoulders pressing against the confines of the cheap suit, and she couldn't quite see his eyes.

She flicked an eyebrow in question. "Well, I'm waiting now. What's so important you have to tell me in a motel car park?" she asked, her voice miraculously cool, considering how warm she felt, how electric.

He watched her a moment longer before he seemed to realise his thumb was running up and down the edge of her wrist. He let her go as if burned. Hot and cold; it was always like this—the two of them sparking like crazy, then…the icy chill of rejection.

And that was why she could happily give up the rest. Because there was only so much of that a woman could take before the constant waves of expansion and shrinking made her crack.

She was about to turn, when he said:

"Thank you." He looked up. "Thank you."

Hadley's next breath hitched in her chest, then caught, pressing into her collar bone like a fist. "You're welcome. But, while I warmed him up for you, you're the one who caught him. And it was beautiful, Ronan. Because it was real."

He watched her, rubbing at the hand that had held hers. "I didn't only mean for tonight."

"Oh."

"I meant for all the nights. And the days. And the weekends. For the years you gave to…" A beat, then, "The years you gave to Big Think."

Hadley swallowed. Ronan might often be brutally efficient

with his words, having been taught that words had power—that they could cut as easily as they could lift–but he'd also been raised to be polite.

But this felt weightier than mere courtesy. It felt thick, heavy and deliberate. It felt like goodbye.

"Of course," she somehow managed. "It's—it was my job."

Ronan's gaze darkened; she could tell, now her eyes were getting used to the contrasts of the light. He dropped his hands to his sides as he took a couple of slow steps her way. She felt herself sway towards him, as if caught in his magnetic wake.

His voice was deep, rough, as he said, "Waverly told me what you said."

"Said?"

"That convinced him to meet us." He glanced up at the sky, which was clear now the clouds had moved on, but there were no stars to be seen, considering the light pollution of the Big D Motel sign. "He said you told him that I was a good man."

Hadley's chest tightened. *Oh, Ronan.* So much was happening to him; the shape of his business, and the family he'd built, changing faster than he could keep up with. And now his father was unwell, adding old poison to the mix.

"You want to know what I actually said?" she said, taking a step his way.

He dragged his gaze from the sky and looked down at her. His eyes were dark, his jaw tight. His chest lifted and fell. His eyes moved back and forth between hers, as if he wanted to know the truth—her truth—and would stand right there, in the motel car park, till she'd laid it all at his feet.

A small shiver wracked her body at the intensity in his gaze, and at the fact she was really about to say this out loud, no sarcasm or safety net.

"I told Holt Waverly that he might like the world to think he was a tough old cowboy, but anyone who looked hard enough could see he was a conservationist at heart. A man who wanted the outback air to be as fresh and wholesome for his future grandkids as it was for him."

She took a breath. *In for a penny...*

"Then I told him that, in just the same way, he might imagine you're a sharp, intense, fiercely competitive businessman who happened to focus on future-proofing technologies in order to make a pretty good living. Yet the only reason your name meant anything to you was if it helped you help people. That your motivations are pure. And whether you had a hundred dollars, or a billion dollars, you'd find a way to do the most good with it that you could."

Hadley finished with a small shrug and wished that the lights beaming down on his back were less...motel-bright.

"Hadley," Ronan said, his voice rough. The air seemed to shift between them, to thin. As if whatever wall he'd kept between them for all these years had simply dissolved away.

"Ronan," she said, her voice husky in the night air. "I know you want us all to think you're bullet-proof. But you're as much of a mess as the rest of us. Only rather than wallowing, or fighting it, it's your superpower. Once you realise that, then you'll truly be unstoppable."

Had he moved closer, or had she? For suddenly his finger was at her chin applying the gentlest pressure. Lifting her face so that she had no choice but to look at him.

His dark brows had lowered over his deeply soulful eyes. But not in confusion, or frustration; there was sweetness to his expression, a kind of pained acceptance as his gaze roved over her face.

Hadley's next breath in was a gulp as she struggled to contain the feelings flooding through her. Her heart ached for him, and because of him. The base state of being that came from loving him.

Loving him.

Because she loved this man. How could she not? It went all the way back to that first night. It hadn't been the way he'd leapt to her defence, or offered whatever help she'd needed, it had been the fact he'd trusted she was strong enough to decide for herself what was best.

If she'd never met him, she'd have been okay. She'd have hustled and worked hard, scraping out space for herself in the world. But *with* him, she'd flourished. Flourished from his trust in her, the lack of pretence in the way he treated her, the acceptance of her oddities, the ease with which he'd let her into the inner sanctum, gifting her a place in the family he'd created. With him, she'd been able to stretch her wings. To make mistakes, certain she had a cushion to fall back on.

She hadn't been a slave to her circumstances—she'd had the luxury of choosing exactly who she wanted to be.

If he was now a better man because of how much she'd pushed him, she was a better woman because of the belief he'd had in her.

"Thank you" wasn't even close to enough.

Hadley looked into Ronan's face, that bold, beautiful face, then she lifted a hand to his chest. She felt the hard, steady beat of his heart against her palm. Her fingertips found the edge of his tie and she curled it into her hand and used it to tug him closer, while she lifted up onto her toes and pressed her mouth to his.

She'd imagined kissing this man so many times. Imagined them coming together like two storms—the hardness of his jaw beneath her reaching hands, the clash of teeth, heaving breaths, all lust and speed, thunder and lightning.

But the moment her lips met his, the whole world seemed to gentle. Her thoughts slowed. Her heartbeat became a whisper.

While his finger at her chin shifted. Was he pulling away? *Please, no.* No, he was moving so that his hand, that big, strong hand, could cup her face, his thumb sweeping over her jaw, tilting her face so he could better angle the kiss.

And, oh, that angle as he kissed her back; slanted, warm and mesmerising. His lips slid over hers, lifting away then tasting her anew in a sweet, lush, quiet exploration. Savouring, luxuriating and gentle, so gentle, her body feeling as if it was filled with stars.

Her fingers curled harder around his tie, her knuckles brushing against his shirt. And her breath caught, the sweetest hitch, as he slid a slow arm behind her back, pulling her close.

A whimper cracked the silence—his? Hers?—a deepening of the kiss the only answer.

She slid her arms around his neck as she pressed higher, her body curving against his. She tipped her head so they were like quotation marks, tucked perfectly into one another's shapes.

And as his hardness brushed against her belly, and the whimper became a moan, Ronan's hands began to move over her, diving into her hair, fingers digging luxuriantly into her waist, sending waves of liquid desire washing through her.

Needing breath, needing air, she pulled away with a gasp against his ear. And it must have set something off in Ronan, as he lifted her bodily and carried her backwards towards their room, all the while kissing her anew in lush, drugging sips and licks as he took her down, down into some hot, molten, boneless place.

Then she was on her feet again, and there was the clink of keys as they stumbled into the room. The heavy slam of the door snapped them apart.

Hadley stepped back, the ugly brown carpet catching on her heels. The sound of traffic was muted by the soft furnishings, the room lit by a sliver of light coming through the blinds and a big red-fringed desk lamp they'd somehow left on.

Ronan looked a right mess; his shirt askew, his hair all over the place. His tongue ran back and forth over his lower lip, as if missing the taste of her already, a move she was entirely certain he had no idea he was making.

And a single spark of self-protection flared inside her. She was in charge of her own destiny. She could still put a stop to this. She could walk away in one piece.

Meaning she'd leave without knowing this, knowing *him*. A travesty big enough to swallow every other worry whole.

And so she made herself a bargain.

One night—one night to let go, let loose, let out all the feelings and wants she'd kept trapped inside her all these years. One night of not worrying about how the universe might trip her up for daring to want things she couldn't have.

And she wanted one night with Ronan Gerard more than she wanted air.

She shucked off her heels, kicked them across the room, then reached for the zip at the back of her neck, only for it to catch on the cheap fabric. She tugged again, but it wasn't going anywhere.

She swore blue murder and Ronan, a deadly-serious expression on his face, came to her, turned her on the spot then worked at the catch till it yanked down a few inches, enough so that he could he pull the dress off one shoulder.

His mouth came down on the tender tendon where neck met shoulder, before his hand followed, sliding over her collar bone and dipping below the neck line to trace the curve of her breast. As if he'd imagined doing just this so often, he could have done it with his eyes closed.

When his fingertips brushed the swell once more, she reached back, hooking her hand behind his head, and held on tight so that when his fingers brushed lower, sliding beneath the lace of her bra to whisper across her nipple, she didn't melt into a puddle at his feet.

Knowing that was imminent, she pulled away and turned in his arms, gripping his cheeks as she kissed him, harder now, more frantic. There was nothing gentle about it anymore. He made his way down her neck, scraping, lathing, till his teeth were tugging at the loosened neckline of her dress.

When the scratchy fabric and the heat rolling threw her threatened to turn her into flames, she reached back, grabbed the edges of the zip and yanked. The zip opened enough that she could shimmy free.

Her dressed pooled at her feet and she stood before Ronan, in her black lace bra and matching underwear.

The world seemed to pause for a moment to take it in before, with a growl, Ronan had her back in his arms. He tugged at the lace edge of her half-cup and leaned her back as he took her nipple on his mouth. Her leg wrapped around his, her hands clawing for him as he feasted on her as if she was all that was keeping him alive.

Her mind spun; her senses were in an uproar. Every part of her clamoured to get closer to him. Hadley yanked at Ronan's shirt while he tore his jacket from his back. Then his hands were on her while hers were on his belt, tugging it free, loosening the fly while his hands moved to her backside, cupping her and hauling her to him.

The feel of that hard length had her moaning, mumbling for more…and, please, now…just as the backs of her knees hit one of the beds and she fell backwards with a bounce. The old springs bounced her back up, so that her eyes sprang open, to find Ronan standing over her.

There was no towel this time. His shirt flapped open, a couple of buttons missing, by the looks of it, and his trousers were low on his hips, the fly wide open. The jut of him against his underwear had her coughing in shock.

Which brought on a smile. Pure devil. Then Ronan reached down, slowly, and rearranged himself while she flopped back on the bed, arm over her eyes lest she literally pass out from lust.

The bed dipped at her feet as he walked his hands along the sides of her calves, stopping to touch, to feel, to trace the bones and muscles, with hands and mouth, sending goose bumps springing up all over.

When she opened her eyes it was to find him on his knees, his eyes on her belly as he kissed his way down her sternum, watching in rapt concentration, his gaze hungry, as her body followed his touch, rising and undulating as his hand moved lower.

Humming now, as if in his happy place, Ronan's finger ran along the edge of her underpants, dipping below the trim before pulling out, again and again as his finger moved from hip bone to hip bone. He teased her till she began to writhe under his touch. Then his cheek lifted in a smile as he lifted the elastic and let go with a soft snap.

She hissed, her skin so sensitive, it was all pleasure and pain. Till Ronan hooked his thumbs into the sides of her underwear and without finesse yanked them over her hips, down her thighs, over each of her feet, before tossing the scrap of fabric over his shoulder.

But his gaze never left hers as he settled lower, moving so that his breath was a warm puff against the neat patch of curls between her legs. His hands on her hips, thumbs tracing the bones in small circles, before moving down her inner thighs and gently encouraging them apart.

Shivers swept up and down her body. Shivers that threatened never to stop. Hot and needy, she let him move her where he pleased, marvelling at the fact that this was happening, while also marvelling that it had taken this damn long.

Ronan's gaze travelled up her body, his expression wondrous, worshipping, taking in every centimetre as if committing her body to memory, before his gaze found hers.

"May I?" he asked, his thumbs now tracing the fine, sensitive skin at the very tops of her inner thighs. Up and down, back and forth, whispering against her curls before moving away. And only the fact that she was panting now stopped the laugh from escaping her mouth.

"Yes!" she said, for it was not the time for quips. She knew he'd not go further without a clear directive. "Yes, a thousand times, yes!"

And that was all it took as, with a growl, he buried his face between her thighs. His nose bussed that most sensitive of spots, again and again, his fingers moving ever closer, parting her slowly, before his tongue took over with tender laps, then long, luscious licks, dipping inside her then circling her centre, not quite touching—a deliberate dance that was pure agony and ecstasy.

And all the while the vibration of his happy hum only added to the intensity as his deep voice trembled through her, his lips clamping over her, and he began to suck.

Her body bucked, her hands reaching to hold his head in place. Her nerves pulled taut, as if a single twang might snap her in half. But instead the pleasure within her only built and deepened as Ronan's mouth moved over her in deep, consistent draws, pleasure coursing through her with hot, hard, flashes of pure joy.

When she made to sit up, to move, to slow him…anything but this agonising intensity…his palm pushed her back to the bed, his thumb brushing over the tight nub of her nipple again and again, mimicking the tempo of his mouth.

"Ronan," she said on a sob, on a sigh, on a rush of pleasure that pierced her core.

"Tell me what you want," he said in warm rush of air over her centre, before he was back, doing what he did so well only faster, harder.

What did she *want*? What bargain had she made? She barely remembered her own name.

"You," she managed after a second, an aeon…who knew? "I want you."

With that, Ronan's tongue licked up her centre in a long, slow, hot stroke. And then everything tightened, the entire universe contracting to the base of her spine, and held there a moment, for the whole of existence, before the second big bang spiralled into the ether in waves of heat, light and blessed relief.

* * *

Ronan paced the cracked concrete outside the room, finishing off the phone call.

Once Hadley had fallen asleep, snoring lightly, as if succumbing to deep psychic exhaustion, his watch had alerted him to a missed call from his mother.

He'd gone outside to listen to the message, which was as much and as little as he would allow himself to do for now. For he was doing the best he could with the information he had.

He then listened to the half-dozen other messages that had come in—for it seemed life had gone on as normal while they'd been holed up in their dodgy little room. Then he stared at his phone for a long while, twisting it over and over in his palm as he tried to reconcile those two worlds. The pleasure and the pain.

Then he slid his phone into the back pocket of his too-small suit pants and headed back into the room.

Where he found Hadley lying on her stomach, the sheet covering her from hip to toe, one arm flopping over the side of the bed, the light from the dusty red lamp warming one side of her face. A lock of dark hair lay over her cheek, curling about her mouth.

Ronan pressed the heel of his hand to his chest when his heart gave a great, big kick. As if it was no longer knocking on the encasement but trying to kick the thing down.

He sat on the edge of the bed, the mattress dipping under his weight, and reached for her. Then, remembering he'd been outside for some time, he pulled his hand back and rubbed it till his fingers were warm.

Only then did he trace a light finger over her cheek, sweeping her hair aside, then down her back and along the edge of her ribs, the swell of her breast. His chest tightened as she rolled into his touch.

The eye not pressed into the bed fluttered open, narrowed, then widened, then shut tightly.

"Hey," he said, laughing.

Smiling a soft, sweet, unfettered smile that hit him right between the ribs, an armour-piercing arrow denting the encasement round his heart, Hadley lifted her head and tucked her chin on her forearm. She was so beautiful, he could barely breathe.

"Hey," she said, her voice rough. Her eyes fluttered closed when his hand swept down her back, fingertips tracing the fine bumps of her spine and the curve at the top of her backside where the sheet draped, but not quite, till goose-bumps scattered over her skin.

Then he leaned over her and pressed a kiss to a mole between her shoulder blades and she let out a soft moan.

He slid to the floor then, to his knees, so that his face was level with hers. She blinked languidly, her eyes pitch-dark. He leaned in, waited for her to lift her head and kissed her until heat gathered at his core. Kissed her till she moaned again.

Then she rolled onto her side, and what could he do but kiss the breast she'd presented to him?

Her hand dipped into his hair, tugging as he spent a good deal of time getting to know her left breast before he licked his way along her ribs. Then she fell back onto the bed, face down, with a hearty sigh.

While he'd gone hard as a rock. He could have spent all night licking her skin, kissing every part of her and then doing it all again, for the taste of her remained on the back of his tongue and he wanted more. He was addicted, for life.

So he grabbed the edge of the sheet and whipped it away to find her naked, completely and utterly. Her long, lean curves were like a dream. His dream. A dream he'd never, ever thought would be made real.

He shifted his knees apart, the growing urgency pressing against the zip near the point of pain. But he didn't want to leave her, to stop touching her, stop kissing her. Not yet.

He kissed his way down her side, a groan lodging in his throat when he reached her backside. The twin cheeks were soft and pink in the low light. His body now thrumming, his ears whumping from the rush of blood within, he grazed her, learning her taste, every taste, in the hope he'd never forget it.

Mouth moving lower as she began to roll under his touch, sweet, heady sighs escaping her mouth, he smoothed his hand down the dark vertical line of the vintage stockings she preferred. Only...

"What the hell?" he rasped, lifting up. For those weren't stockings: they couldn't be, for she was arse-bare.

His fingers gently pinched, searching for silk, only finding nothing there.

"Ow," she said, alert enough now to lift onto one elbow and look down at her legs. Her breasts were level with his mouth, warm and pink from the blanket on which she'd been lying. "Pluck all you like, but that's a tattoo."

He laid his hand flat on the back of her thigh, then ran a finger down the thin vertical stripe, then back up again, stopping at the small black bow tattoos that sat just under each butt cheek.

Hell. All that time she'd been walking around with those bows, right there, and he'd never known. If he had...

If one day he found out Hadley Moreau had been put on earth to keep him in a kind of emotional purgatory, then he'd believe it. Only this wasn't punishment. This was nirvana.

"Are there more?" he asked.

One eyebrow kicked north.

"Show me," he said, grabbing her hips and turning her over.

She fell back on the bed, all husky laughter, and he'd literally never heard a sound he loved more. Then he leaned over her, face close, as if studying her scientifically. He knew about the string on her right ring finger. Taking her hand, he ran his tongue along the raised black mark.

After which she pointed the way to the tiny, fine-lined steampunk dragonfly between her breasts, and he pressed a sucking kiss to the spot, which had her fingers digging into his hair.

He kissed, licked and ran his thumb over the several more

she pointed out—all dainty and private; all stories, he was sure. Stories he still hoped she might one day tell. Till once again he found the small bow inked into the back of a thigh and he kissed her there, feeling the slight raise of it against the tip of his tongue.

Her intake of breath—sharp and hot—was enough for him to continue. He ran the tip of his tongue down the long line of her leg till she rolled fully onto her stomach, her hands gripping the sheets, her backside lifting off the bed.

When his mouth moved to her thighs, she reached back, her hand running own the hard ridge, pressing against his zip. "Ronan," she begged.

He didn't have to be asked twice. He moved off the bed and found his bathroom bag with the pack of condoms, then, having held himself together as long as he possibly could, whipped off his trousers and sheathed himself, then moved onto the small bed as best he could.

"Are you *now* thinking a suite would have been better?" he asked, his knees barely fitting on the bed as he slid his hand beneath her belly, then lower, tracing her centre till she gasped.

"Not for a second," she said, lifting to her knees and guiding herself back. Her chest flat to the bed, her face turned sideways. Her eyes closed, her body flushed, warm and pliant, as if he'd turned her boneless.

"Now, stop talking and take me," she said. "Now."

Holding on, mentally and physically, for all he was worth, lest the mere sight of her had him spilling over before he was even inside her, Ronan's hands spanned her hips. He guided himself into place, sending waves of insane pleasure up his thighs and into his balls. He rubbed his tip against the notch, caressing her, circling, till her mouth was open and gasping.

When the scent of her hit the back of his throat, warm, sweet and ready, a wave of the most brutish pleasure gripped him. Self-control at its limit, he pressed forward, just as she pushed back, and filled her to the hilt.

And there they stayed, breaths held, lost in a moment of pure pleasure, surprise and utter reality. They were here; this was happening. And Ronan could have died in that moment and believed he'd lived a pretty darned fine life.

It took every ounce of self-control to pull out in a long, slow sweep. She cried out at the lack of him, before he lodged himself deep inside her once more. Then he did the same, again and again, feeling more inside his own skin than he ever remembered feeling before.

He thought not with his head, but with instinct, feeling as if he could hear the movement his blood and feel the path of every nerve.

When she began to roll back against him, her fist clutching the sheets, her breath hastening, he matched her movements. The pink of her skin matched the heat rolling through him. The tension in her face matched the pleasure gripping him, searing him, turning his spine to fire.

Needing to feel her in every way possible, he curved himself over her, a hand sliding between them to roll his thumb over her nub in gently insistent circles that had her gasping. His next stroke angled differently and stars sprang up on the edges of his vision as pleasure built like a coming storm. With the next slide her body stilled and quaked beneath his, and he kept on, not stopping, holding her there, holding himself back, until her shivers subsided.

Then she reached between them, her fingers sliding over his, holding him there as she came again, a bucking orgasm that had her inner muscles tightening around him. And nothing could have stopped the light spiralling through him, slamming him towards some place high, hot and tight, before he shattered into a thousand pieces.

He came down to find them both breathing hard, their hands still touching, their bodies still quaking.

He eased himself free then laid her down, tucking himself against her back, curving his arm over her ribs, his heart kicking madly when she reached for his hand and tucked it into her chest.

The sweetness, the intimacy, rocked him. It was like nothing he'd ever known. Had never known he wanted. And now... now he knew there was no other way.

When she let go of his hand, it took everything in him not to grab it back. But then she turned, facing him, their noses almost touching.

He counted her tangled lashes and the creases in her full lips, which he salved with a swipe of his tongue. Then she kissed him, lushly, wantonly, with everything she had.

They kissed for some time, saying things with taste and touch that neither of them seemed able to say with words. Then afterwards they both washed, made their way back to the same small twin bed and fell asleep in one another's arms.

A pre-dawn mist had descended over the city as the car took them back to the airport the next morning, adding to the unusual quietness in the back of the car.

Ronan had woken that morning to Hadley's hand stroking him, long, leisurely sweeps of her hand that had had him bucking into her grip before his eyes had even opened.

After which she'd rolled him onto his back and straddled him, one of his condom packets between her teeth. She'd sheathed him with protection, then with herself, and they'd rocked silently, hands moving over one another, reaching for soft, wet kisses before spiralling over the edge as one.

Now Hadley flicked through her tablet, moving appointments, editing her notes on the Holt Waverly meeting, prepping bullet points for a press release for when their deal was finalised, before sending it to Jonas with a contented sigh. As if nothing had changed at all.

Ronan sat back and watched her, a growing certainty leeching into his bones that if they landed back in Melbourne without talking about it, without making sense of it, that would be it. A night out of time, never to be spoken of again. They had a history of avoiding the hard stuff if they could, after all.

But what to say? Why now? *What* now? *Now that that's happened, I can't imagine a world in which it never happens again?* What, exactly—motel sex? Or was this a chance to re-define things between them, given they'd never actually de-fined them at all?

He ran a hand down his face, imagining her response—the glint in those clever dark eyes, the tilt of those unforgiving lips. He'd be as good as begging for rejection. Willing it—after hav-ing been treated as an afterthought his entire childhood by a father who only saw Ronan as a mini-version of himself, and by a mother who only saw his father—would be nonsensical.

He was not a man who begged—not ever—and he wasn't about to start now. She'd already said all the pretty words about him being a good man, but it still wasn't enough for her to want to stay. *He* still wasn't enough.

Suddenly they were pulling into the private tarmac, the Big Think jet appearing out of the thinning gloom, and Ronan's chest felt tighter still.

He *willed* her to look his way. But instead she looked out of the car window as they slowed, then slid her phone and note-book into her bag and readied herself to alight from the car as it slowly cruised towards the wing of the plane.

Right, if she *didn't* look back before hopping out of the car, that would be it. He'd spent the past several years telling him-self he didn't have feelings for her; he could do it again, surely?

And if she *did* look back… Ronan's heart kicked so hard, it took his breath away.

Her hand moved to the door handle.

Then her fingers pulled back and she turned and looked at him over her shoulder with a swing of her dark hair and an up-ward tilt of her red lips. The memory of their night together, was alight in her eyes. She was so damned lovely, it physically hurt to look at her.

This was it. A chance to do better than he had before.

"Don't go," Ronan said, his voice rough.

Hadley blinked, then glanced towards the jet. "But they're waiting—"

"Don't go," he said again, his voice rough. "Don't leave Big Think. Don't leave…" He was going to say "me", only that wasn't what this was about, was it? Damn it, he needed to get his head on straight.

"Ronan," she said, an understanding smile kicking up at both corners of her mouth. "If we'd wanted our last trip together to be a memorable one, I'd say we succeeded, but it's time for us to go."

Then she was out of the car, door slamming as she headed towards the jet.

Ronan was out of the car too, running after her, his original jacket flapping at his sides, crushed and still slightly damp. "Hadley, wait."

She stopped and turned, exasperated now. "The engine is running." But there was something else: tightness about her eyes, a melancholy.

"I decline your resignation."

She held a hand over her eyes, blinking against the weak sunlight. "Because of *last night*?"

"What? No. Of course not." Not the falling into bed part, at least, but all that it had exposed. "Hadley, you know how valued you are by the company. By me…and Ted and Sawyer. I know I should have said it sooner—instantly, in fact—but your announcement… To say it was unexpected is a massive understatement. I didn't handle it as best I could. If there's something you're missing, something you want…"

This time both eyebrows rose.

And Ronan held out his hands in frustration. "This has nothing to do with last night."

Hadley shook her head, then looked out across the tarmac as

though searching for the right words. "I think you'll find you have that backwards."

"Meaning?"

"The only reason last night happened is *because* I'm leaving. You'd never have let it go that far otherwise." She watched him then, waiting to see if he might deny it.

But he could not...because it was true.

Disappointment flashed across her eyes, and something akin to pain, before she turned her back on him and headed for the steps leading up to the jet.

Ronan ran a hand over his jaw, finding it tight enough to crack bone. This wasn't going the way he'd wanted. None of it was. But he was where he was in life because he never backed down.

"Hadley," he called once again, jogging to catch up with her.

"Ronan!" she said, throwing up a hand even as she upped her pace. "You cannot purport to want to save the world while wasting this much jet fuel."

Then she stopped, spun on him and said, "Look, this trip was about so much more than Holt Waverly. It was about you struggling with what must be deeply challenging feelings regards your father's news. Me taking one last chance to push back when you tried telling me what to do. Our last night together..." She swallowed. "It was just one night."

Her voice was strong, but her eyes... They were dark, misty and awash with more emotions than he could rightly name. Then she shook her head hard, turned and jogged up the stairs and was inside the plane.

Ronan followed, locking down the emotion roiling inside him as he greeted the crew, dumped his gear and found his usual seat. He turned to look over his shoulder, finding Hadley across the aisle and back one seat, already back to frowning at her tablet.

Only as the plane rattled its way through the low-lying fog before smoothing out once they breached the clouds, did it occur to him that Hadley had said the only reason they'd fallen into bed together was because she was leaving. That *he'd* never have let it go that far otherwise.

What was her excuse?

CHAPTER EIGHT

HADLEY HAD NEVER ONCE, in the entire time she'd worked at Big Think, finished her day at five o'clock.

She'd not wanted to—she'd been desperate to learn everything she could, to prove and improve herself, and then the place had become a part of her.

After their flight back from Adelaide, Ronan had taken her at her word and let her be. Meaning she could spend her last days reliving their night away—the scrape of his teeth over her collar bone, the feel of him between her thighs, on the tarmac, him asking what he had to do to get her to stay—or she could lose herself in the work. Now on this, her last official day as a Big Think employee, her desk was tidy by five o'clock, her to-do list complete.

Now what?

Sit there a while and pretend she had things to do? Or go home, watch *Grand Designs* and eat a party bag of Twisties then go to bed, blaming the ache in her belly on overindulging.

She let her head fall to her desk and groaned. The bargain she'd made—one night… It was laughable that she'd believed that would be enough. That scratching her seven-year itch would put an end to all her feelings. Now her mind was filled with the man, trying to think up ways she could twist her bargain, but every outcome ended up with her heart dying a slow death.

She would not be that woman, taking scraps, building castles in the sky. Her poor mum had tried that—looking for a man to save her from herself, again and again, as if expecting a different outcome—only to become smaller and smaller with every romantic failure.

So, no. Just, no. No bargaining required.

Hadley pressed back her chair, picked up her small packing box with Cactiss Everdeen balanced atop, and made her last ever trek to her office door. When her legs began to shake, as the gravity of what she was doing really took a hold, she reminded herself she was not *leaving* leaving, not quite yet.

She'd sequestered a smaller room in an empty wing on a lower floor to use until the Big Think Ball was done, but this beautiful space, that she had designed so meticulously, now belonged to Jonas.

The man himself was sitting on the corner of Kyle's desk, which had been draped in copious amounts of Christmas tinsel, Christmas music playing lightly from his speaker.

"Leaving already?" Jonas asked.

Kyle moved out from behind his desk to take the box, and his eyes flickered when he saw how little it contained.

"I'm all done," said Hadley, her voice huskier than she'd have liked.

"Great!" said Kyle, slipping a hand through one elbow, Jonas the other. "Then, you're coming with us. We have plans that include multiple cocktails."

"No, I have to…" She looked towards Ronan's door to find it closed. If that wasn't a kick to the heart, what was?

If she went home, she'd just relive her night with Ronan over and over again. The way he'd watched her in the car to the airport, the confusion in his eyes as he'd run after her on the tarmac.

"You know what?" she said. "Plans sounds perfect."

* * *

Ronan turned down a hallway on a floor of Big Think he was sure he'd never seen. The lights lit up as he moved through the space, thus saving power, as the area was mostly empty; the rooms built in order to cater for future bright minds they would invite to use the space rent-free.

If Hadley had deliberately chosen an office as far from his as possible from which to project-manage the upcoming Big Think Ball, she'd succeeded. If she thought that would stop him from looking for her, well, there she'd been mistaken.

After their conversation on the tarmac and how certain she'd been on leaving things be he'd had to respect that. He'd given her space, and time, to settle into her new role.

He'd also not wanted to look like some desperate sixteen-year-old with a crush, even though that's how he felt: moody, caught up in daydreams, and in a near constant state of arousal.

It was untenable. Not at all congruous to running a multi-billion-dollar company. Meaning he had to do something to take the edge off. Seeing her the only fix.

Nearing the end of the hallway, he heard music—sultry, smoky jazz that might have had a holiday theme. He saw light under a door, picked up his pace and, once there, slowly pushed open the door to find…

"Whoa."

A jewel-blue office chair with a caramel-coloured jacket slung over the back sat oblique to round glass desk covered in papers and fabric samples. On a side cabinet sat a bunch of plants in bright pots, including a strangely familiar cactus. A speaker pulsing notes into the air sat atop a top-notch coffee machine, alongside a small fake Christmas tree laden with rose-gold tinsel and tiny pale-blue lights.

"Ronan?"

Ronan spun to find Hadley in the hall behind him, holding a small carton of milk. A pair of glasses were perched on the end of her nose—those were new. Her hair was pulled back in a squat ponytail—that was new too. As was her outfit—skinny jeans and a loose, floral top that seemed to verge on translucent but not quite.

"Hi," he said, his voice rough. In fact, every part of him felt slightly wrong, as if seeing her again after a few days apart had knocked him sideways.

While she appeared perfectly cool, chilled, unfazed to the point of nonchalance. As if she had settled into her new role without a single speed bump. Which was *just great*.

"Did you need me for something?" she asked, eyebrow raised.

Hell, yes, he needed her for something. For many things. Standing there danger close, drinking in her fine features, breathing in her perfume, he could think of a dozen ways he needed her.

Not that he would say any that out loud, having taught himself the art of self-sacrifice far too well.

"Nothing in particular," he said. "I just happened to be in your part of town so thought I should swing by. See if you needed *me* for anything."

Her nostrils flared the slightest amount, but it was enough for him to wonder. To imagine if maybe he wasn't alone in missing this…this energy he gleaned simply from being near her.

"I have all I need here, thanks," she said. Then held up the carton. "Bar milk, which I borrowed from my new neighbours down the hall. A small start-up Sawyer brought on board. Nice guys."

She moved to slide past him, the brush of her elbow against his shirt setting off a shower of sparks in his belly.

Eyes rolling internally at his own ineptitude, muttering to himself to pull it together, he followed her into the room—feeling a little dizzy from the knowledge of how much he missed having this in his life every day.

"Coffee?" she asked, holding up the milk.

It yanked him back to their first year working together, when getting him coffee was something she did. Then one day she'd told him he was a big boy and could get his own damned coffee, and from that point the lines had been drawn. From that point, their past had seemed as if it had been finally put behind them their working relationship had been more partnership than boss and employee. Or so he'd thought.

"I'm fine," he said.

Hadley set to making herself a cup. "Jonas and I have been in touch several times a day, and he seems to have everything in hand. I truly think he might be some kind of savant. Or a robot, built specifically for that job. I'm sure he's much easier to work with than I ever was."

Ronan grunted his assent. Jonas was doing fine; better than fine. He was instinctive, efficient and happy to work all hours. He'd also been coping with Ronan's moods with an easy smile, as if he knew Ronan would wake up one day and decide he was done with being a grouch.

"And how's...? How's your mother?" Hadley asked, choosing the easier route.

"As expected," he said, her last call carrying an urgency that Ronan visit. That any chance of reconciliation was depleting—fast.

But that wasn't why he'd tracked Hadley down. Wasn't why his pulse beat in his neck, and his mouth felt too dry, or—

"What took you so long to come find me?" she said, her hand pausing on the dial of the espresso machine. Her head was down, as if she'd tried to stop herself from asking, but the weight of it had become too much.

And he heard it, like an angel's song: the wanting, the missing. The slight flare of her nostrils assuring him he was not alone in feeling the sensory bombardment that being in the same room together.

The song changed, a slow number that brought up images of speakeasies, smoky basements, and people wrapped around one another in dark corners. Or maybe that was all him—his desire for her like a living thing crawling over his skin, tugging at his clothes. Making a mess of his voice as he said, "You knew where I was."

He knew, almost instantly, that it was the wrong thing to say. "Hadley—"

But she cut him off. "One of the start-up guys down the hall is from Amsterdam, and it got me to thinking of the first trip we took together. With Ted. To visit your new lab there."

Ronan breathed out. "I remember."

"Do you remember the dinner at that hole in the wall? So much food. So much wine." Her lips quirked at the memory.

"I do," he said, his gaze dropping to the movement—to that mouth. He remembered how it had felt against his. The heat of it trailing over his chest. His belly. Lower.

"Do you remember the walk back to the hotel?" she asked, turning to lean back against the cabinet, her fingers gripping the edge. "When we stopped on the bridge to watch the barge make its way down the river?"

Ronan remembered. He remembered the breeze playing with her hair, though it had been shorter then. He remembered thinking how incredibly lucky they were to have her on their team. He remembered thinking he'd have gladly given that up if it meant he could wipe away the way that they'd met.

Ronan pushed away from the door. "You wore a red dress that night, first time I'd ever seen you in a dress. And these earrings—long, gold—that brushed your neck when you moved."

Hadley's chest lifted, her tongue swiping quickly over her lower lip.

And he felt himself go hard all over. As if, despite all those years spent using some freakishly competent inner strength to hold himself back, he'd lost the knack completely.

For he also remembered her turning to look at him, a smile in her eyes that had soon been overtaken with heat, with invitation. All of which he'd no doubt returned in kind. Because he'd wanted her, even then.

Yet it was a fraction of the want he felt now. This felt urgent, as if it was tied up in his very life force. He took a step her way, then another. Till he was close enough she had to look up to hold eye contact. Then he reached up to take her by the chin, tugging his thumb over that full bottom lip.

"What took you so long?" she said, her breath washing cool air over his damp thumb. And he knew she was no longer talking about the past few days, but about their entire relationship.

"I didn't trust myself to know when to stop."

"But I trusted you," she said, then her tongue darted out to touch his thumb. Before she leaned closer and took it into her mouth.

Skin shocked by a thousand pricks of sensation, brain a cloud of need, Ronan pulled his thumb free and cradled her face in his hands.

Where their first kiss had been a beautiful surprise, this felt decided. There was no heightened emotion, no adrenaline kicking them into gear. This was Ronan, holding Hadley, because it was something they both very much wanted to do.

When his fingers brushed her cheekbones, she sighed. When he leaned down to kiss her forehead, her eyes fluttered closed, and he pressed a kiss on each eyelid, velvet-soft, a promise to be gentle with her. To repay that trust.

Then her hands ran up the front of his shirt, her body lifting, her head tilting, and he pressed his lips to hers. Sparks, heat and a sense of something new poured through him. Like New Year's Eve in slow motion.

Her hands, making their way over his shoulders, up his neck, into his hair, made a slow exploration that matched the languorous pace of the kiss. A kiss built on sensation and instinct, longing and connection. A kiss he wished could last forever.

His hands moved into her hair, catching on the hairband holding it back, dislodging it so that her waves spilled over his fingers, and her moan as his fingers found her scalp turned things slow to needy quick-smart.

All pressing bodies, and needy hands, he lifted her thigh to his hip. To roll against her centre, so she could feel just how much he wanted this.

She gasped against his mouth. He smiled at the sound. Then he nipped her full bottom lip before sucking it into his mouth. The heat roiling between them deepened, till he could barely see past the fog in his head.

The coffee machine whirred angrily as it turned itself off and Hadley jerked, turning towards the sound. Ronan took advantage, turning her all the way, his hand sliding across her belly, drawing another gasp.

Nudging her hair aside to kiss the back of her neck, he slipped a finger beneath the beltline of her jeans, then another, before opening the button with a snap as he pressed his hand into her trousers, her zip opening for him as he dipped his fingers between her legs to find her ready…for him.

Her arm slid around his neck, using it as an anchor as she opened herself to him, warm and wanton as he gave her all that he craved.

A finger slid along her seam, parting her, finding that nub then circling, circling, consistent, relentless. Even as she jerked away he found her. Even as she curled into his hand, chasing the relief, he didn't let up.

He would give her anything she wanted, all that she needed. She only had to ask.

When he bit down on her shoulder, then gave her neck a long, slow lick, mirroring the move of his hand, she cried out his name.

Then there was no more finessing, just long, sure, deep strokes as she came and came and came. He held her to him through it all. Till finally, she stilled, her mouth open, her face contorted in the most beautiful vision of pure ecstasy before she broke, waves of pleasure wracking her body.

But he kept on stroking, luxuriating in the way she trembled, her joy soothing the ache inside of him. When a sob escaped her mouth at the same time as her hand gripped his neck harder, he let her set the pace. And she rocked against his hand, gentling, slowing, caressing, hunting those final flourishes till she was limp in his arms.

As the fog slowly cleared, Ronan found himself braced against the cabinet, legs apart, Hadley a rag doll in his arms, soft jazz floating from the speaker, with the door to her new office wide open.

None of which had registered from the moment his mouth touched hers.

"Ronan?" she said when he moved an inch, her voice husky, holding none of its usual mettle.

"Can you stand?" he asked gruffly.

She straightened up. "Kind of." Then she turned, her hand reaching between them.

But Ronan moved back, rearranging himself as best he could. The speed with which he'd lost track of his surroundings, of any consequences, sat uncomfortably in his gut. That, and he felt so over-sensitised, one touch and he might blow.

Hadley's eyes questioned him: still dark, a little wild, and vulnerable in a way he'd never seen in her. All of which only added to his sense of unease, none of which was her fault.

So he stepped in, took her chin and kissed her again. Thoroughly.

"Next time," he said, shifting to give the hard ridge between his thighs a little room, if not relief. Because more than relief he needed to know there *would* be a next time. It was get him through.

As it turned out, it was the exactly right thing to say, for Hadley grinned before laughter escaped her lungs in a burst of pure joy. "I can live with that," she said, then shook her head, as if she too was happy to have a promise of more. Then she said, "Off with you, then. For I am a busy woman and I have work to do."

Ronan ran a hand over his hair and straightened his shirt, while Hadley watched his movements with a hunger he'd remember till his dying day.

Moving to her door on less than stable legs, he shot her one last look. One that had her teeth biting down on her bottom lip. Walking away from her then, with her hair a mess, her jeans still snapped open, her shirt half-hanging off one shoulder, was the hardest thing he'd ever done.

But he knew that the work he'd done, the self-sacrifice he'd perfected, had led to this, had led to her.

He knocked his knuckles on the door frame in goodbye—for now. Then he took his time making his way down the hall, glad now that she'd chosen a room so far from the rest of the world.

Not only because he needed time to make himself decent, but because it made this…whatever it was…feel as if it was private, untouched by all that they had once been.

How long it might feel that way, he couldn't possibly know. How long before he saw her again was up to the universe. But, for now, he'd take it.

In the end, he didn't have to wait long, for that night Hadley came to him, late, once the building had emptied. His staff having long since gone home, the only sign he wasn't alone in the world the whir of the cleaning staff somewhere nearby.

He heard a sound and looked up to find her in the door of his office, holding the heels of her shoes in one hand, twirling her security pass with the other, the one that still gave her access to every part of the building.

He hadn't told her to keep it because he'd hoped this might be the result, but because as far as he was concerned, she could go where she wanted, do as she pleased, and hold the keys to his kingdom for evermore.

"Hey," she said.

"Hey, yourself."

She padded into the room, closing the door behind her, then kept on coming, dropping her shoes, one by one.

Ronan made to stand, the need to be near her, to touch her, taking him over. But she shook her head and he settled back in his chair. He was glad to be sitting, as his legs might well have given way when she pulled her shirt over her head, letting it trail to the floor. Then she snapped open his very favourite pair of jeans in the history of jeans, stopping only long enough to step out of them before letting them pool where they landed.

The low light of his desk lamp poured over her, mixing with the twinkle of city lights behind him. He was dying to kiss her lean curves, the swell of her breasts, the edge of her nipples just peaking over the top of her half-cup bra, the dip at her waist, the dark shadow showing through the soft floral underwear at the apex of her thighs....

Pulse trumpeting in his neck, his belly, *everywhere*, he dared not blink as she rounded his desk, pressed a hand to his chest and straddled him. Then asked, "Is now a good time?"

He swore his response before lifting up, a hand delving into the back of her hair and pulling her to him for an open-mouthed kiss that had him fast forgetting his own damned name.

It was a good while later—spent, drenched in sweat, his shirt open, his trousers at his ankles, his tie somehow half-hanging off his neck—that Ronan came back into his own skin. His toes strained to hold his weight, his body bent over Hadley who was splayed out naked on his desk and his own primal, rawness still ringing in his ears.

The cool of the office must have trickled over her skin, as she shivered, goose bumps shooting up over her arms.

He reached down, and lifted her into his arms. He kicked his trousers from his ankles, carried her to the lounge chair, then sat with her curled in his lap.

Body loose, skin slick and pink, she lifted her head and looked him in the eyes. And the emotion there was so raw, so rich, it should have shocked him to his core.

But instead it seemed to meet something inside him. Some twin emotion that he could not name, only feel. A rush, a roar, a truth he'd been avoiding rose inside of him, but he stamped it down unsure that he could handle it. Unsure that he deserved it. A familiar smoky darkness rose inside him then, the kind that all the spectacular sex in the world could not quite snuff out.

Till she lifted a hand to his face, her eyes wide, telling him to stop thinking so hard. then she kissed him on the mouth once, hard, then pulled herself up and away. She found her clothes and stepped into them. When she found her underwear, she was already dressed, so she tucked it into her back pocket.

Then she shot him a glance, taking in his rakish tie, his socked feet, the jut of his erection ready to go again after having watched the way she put herself together, her movements so spare, so elegant.

She whistled through her teeth before biting down on her bottom lip in a way that said, "next time", without her having said a thing.

Then she picked up her shoes and walked out of his office.

And so it went, over the next few weeks.

They had no trouble finding one another—in stairwells, in the car park, in her office or his—as if they each had in-built compasses, permanently seeking one another out.

Sometimes it was quiet and slow; sometimes a raw, fast coming-together. Other times there was laughter and whispers in darkness. Ronan liked those times best, for it harked back to late nights in his office in the *before*, trips they'd taken to a hundred cities the world over, drunk on exhaustion and success. But not enough to act on the underlying sexual tension that had seasoned their relationship from the beginning.

When Ronan discovered she liked it when he talked, he articulated the feel of her skin beneath his hands, the taste of her on his tongue, how much he loved the flush on her neck as he touched her there... He couldn't believe he was saying the actual words he'd been thinking for so many years. He wondered why the hell they'd wasted so much time. And quieted the niggling, questioning voice, asking what he might yet to do to ruin it all.

Then, suddenly, it was the week of Christmas. And, just around the corner, the Big Think Ball.

CHAPTER NINE

IT WAS STILL a week until Big Think Ball—or, as the rest of the world called it, Christmas Eve. The whole crew—bar Petra, who was still in New York—had gathered at Ted and Adelaid's new Mount Martha home—a glorious, woodsy gabled mansion with the most beautiful outlook over the bay beyond.

"Drink up!" said Adelaid, forcing after-dinner eggnog into Sawyer's hand, then rubbing her lower back.

"You're not going to pop, are you?" Sawyer asked of Adelaid, before happily downing the drink. With Petra away, he was sleeping over. Then, *"Are you?"*

"Relax, Ted's a doctor," Ronan growled from his position by the fireplace, frowning at his phone as he tried to change the *Christmas for Kids* playlist crooning through the hidden speakers to anything else.

"Of *chemistry*," said Sawyer, slight panic in his voice.

Ronan's laugh, all deep and husky, sent shivers down Hadley's spine. As if he knew she was watching him, he glanced over to where she leant against the door to the kitchen. The heat in his gaze so sharp, so focussed, she felt it pierce her heart.

She spun into the kitchen, where she bumped Adelaid away from the sink and took over loading the dishwasher.

"Thank you!" said Adelaid. "I have to pee so bad." Then she was off, waddling to the bathroom.

Hadley took a moment to grip the cool of the kitchen bench, because the evening had been a lot. Wonderful, yet bittersweet. For once she left Big Think, it might well be the last such gathering she would ever be invited to attend.

Then there was the constant fear she and Ronan would give themselves away. Despite Adelaid's earlier attestation that *everyone* had been walking around eggshells for ages, waiting for Hadley and Ronan finally to crack, the others had never seemed to notice. And Hadley wanted to keep it that way. Her final week was going to be emotional enough without having to deal with any extra noise.

Besides, no promises had been made, no plans. Only short trysts. Lovely trysts—hot, sweet, tender and delectably intimate. As if, having known one another so well for so many years, they had nothing to prove and nothing to hide. But only inside the walls of Big Think Tower.

All of which made the whole thing feel beautifully tenuous. Like sunlight refracting through droplets of morning mist clinging to a freshly made spider's web, a single shake of a foundation branch and...it would be gone. As if it had never been.

"Okay," said Adelaid, sweeping Hadley out of the kitchen and pressing her back into the sitting room. "Ted can finish this up later. It's party time."

Scooting around the humungous Christmas tree, laden with wildly inappropriate ornaments Adelaid had collected over the years, Hadley waited for Adelaid to get comfortable on the plush ten-seater couch before finding a place at her side.

When toddler Katie made a beeline for her mum, Ted, standing behind the couch, swept her up and over his shoulder till she giggled uproariously.

"Thank you," Adelaid mouthed, her gaze sparkling with love.

Hadley's heart clutched. Ted's and Adelaid's tenderness towards one another was so obvious. They just let it all hang out, as if there was no fear that one day they'd blink and find it had all been a beautiful mirage.

Was that why Hadley was so fearful of anyone finding out about how she felt, Ronan included? Her mum had put so much faith in love being some ultimate answer, only for it to side-swipe her again and again. And again…

"Hadley," said Adelaid, and Hadley flinched.

"Hmm? Yes?"

"I've been meaning to say. The *Wizard of Oz* photo shoot— genius. Truly."

Hadley smiled her thanks. It had come together even better than she'd envisaged. Forgoing the boys' usual corporate spit and shine for unexpected whimsy, had led to fantastic media take-up.

"What *Wizard of Oz* shoot?" asked Ted, now holding Katie on one hip.

Adelaid gaped affectionately at her husband. "To think how I've been educating you as to the wonder of vintage films. You, Sawyer, Ronan…hay bales…."

"Ah. How was that related to the *Wizard of Oz*?"

"Did you not see it?" Adelaid asked. "You, my big, beautiful, clueless, brilliant, tawny bearded wonder, were the lion. Which is spot on. You took one look at me, and *bam*! Instant courage."

A smile tugged at the corner of Ted's mouth. "True, that."

"While you…" Adelaid reached out with a foot and lightly kicked Sawyer in the shin.

"The Scarecrow," said Sawyer, clicking his fingers at Hadley. "I did wonder when they gave me a tartan shirt and torn jeans."

Adelaid grinned. "People have always underestimated you, Sawyer. They think you're all biff and buff. But our Petra always knew you were razor-sharp."

Sawyer's smile was a mix of "aw, shucks" and fierce love for his absentee girl. Hadley's heart kicked so hard against her ribs, she winced.

"As for *you*, Ronan Gerard," drawled Adelaid, waggling a

finger at him as he stood near the fireplace. "Hadley nailed you best of all."

At that, Hadley stilled, while Ronan did a full spit-take into his drink before coughing into a closed fist.

Sawyer, showing exactly how sharp he was, glanced from Ronan to Hadley and back again, before saying, "Ronan's the yappy dog, right?"

"Toto!" said Katie.

"That's my girl," said Adelaid, reaching back to grab her daughter's foot. "But, actually, Uncle Ronan is the Tin Man. The one with no heart."

It took Adelaid a little longer than the rest to get the sense that all the air had been sucked from the room. While Hadley's throat seized up. For she'd meant the exact opposite. But how to tell him, without giving herself away? How to assure him that his heart was the best part of him?

"No, no, no! Wait." Poor, sweet Adelaid, famous for speaking before she thought, blanched as her hand fluttered to her chest. "You know full well that's *not* what I meant."

"So, I'm *not* heartless?" Ronan asked, raising a single eyebrow.

"Gosh, no! I meant you do present as a gruff, alpha, silver-spoon tycoon, figurehead of a behemoth company."

Ronan raised both eyebrows at that, comically so, and he crossed his arms dramatically, clearly playing with Adelaid now. She knew it too, by the colour that returned to her cheeks, and the gusts of breathless laughter she struggled to contain.

And, while Hadley knew that those words had pressed hard into soul deep bruises the man carried like a badge of honour, in that moment, Hadley had never loved him more.

"I do hope there's a 'but'," Ronan encouraged.

"But..." said Adelaid, now deep into a mass of giggles, giving the occasional, "Ow, ow, ow..." as she held a hand to her side. "Beneath the shiny exterior, you, Ronan Gerard, are *all* heart. *That's* the point. Right, Hadley?"

Hadley stilled as the group turned to face her, waiting for her response. Of course that was the point. But if she said yes...?

Ears buzzing, she turned to Adelaid. "I'd thought I'd been more subtle than that. This being my last ball, I've wanted it to be special. To really say something. For me, the shoot says that while Big Think has been a place dreams are made of—you guys didn't land the road to some magical place, you built it."

The silence that came over the room was different this time. It was thick, warm and fuzzy, and Hadley had no idea what to do with the emotion coming at her from all corners.

"Oh, Hadley," said Adelaid, hauling her in for a half-hug, her belly somewhat getting in the way.

While Ted placed a hand on Hadley's shoulder and gave it a squeeze.

Sawyer shook his head. "Why are you leaving us, Hadley?"

"Leave her be," said Adelaid, as she alone knew how conflicted Hadley was. "She just gave the perfect Big Think family Christmas toast, so let's raise a glass."

Adelaid grabbed her glass of pineapple juice from the coffee table then lifted it in the air and said, "To bravery and bright minds and big strong hearts. And to friends who become family. To Big Think."

Hadley lifted her glass of bubbly, and only when she took a sip did her eye line shift, finding Ronan.

He was watching her, his expression fierce.

Only it wasn't his heart she was thinking about in that moment—it was her own. And the fact that it had been in his hands for so long, she wasn't quite sure how it would cope when she finally took it back.

What if she didn't take it back? What if she braved up and stopped getting in her own way? If his heart was as strong and as capable as she knew it to be, wasn't it just possible he just might surprise her?

Later, once Katie had been put to bed with the promise of dreams of sugar-plum fairies and reindeer bells, and after Petra's surprise arrival at the door in a whirlwind of happy cheer—

a true Christmas Eve miracle—Hadley ducked outside, needing air not quite so thick with all that loving, happy emotion.

The warm summer wind tugged at her hair. The fairy lights pinned to the wrought-iron lace of the porch eaves scattered golden light over her arms as she leaned against the railing, watching moonlight twinkling off the bay beyond. Voices, song and laughter hummed inside the house behind her.

"The Tin Man. That's one I've never been called before."

Hadley didn't turn. She didn't need to. She'd felt Ronan coming long before he announced himself.

He shut the door behind him. Then moved in beside her, resting his elbows on the railing. "Though I'm sure it's not the first time you've called me something no one else would dare."

Hadley shot him a look.

Ronan's gaze landed on hers, deep, dark blue: her favourite colour in the whole world. He shifted, crossing his arms on the railing, so that his fingers of one hand were near enough to touch, before he asked, "So what's next for the Wizard?"

"The…?"

"The one behind the curtains who really makes the magic happen."

Hadley breathed in deeply, taking in the night air; Ronan's assertion knocking about inside her like a pinball. "I have options. Emerson, from Pitch Perfect, has sent through a dozen interesting offers."

"I bet."

"But I think I'm going to cave-dwell for a while. Sleep in, garden, see a movie at an actual cinema—the kinds of things I imagine normal people do for pleasure."

He hummed with understanding. "Is that why you're leaving? To have a 'normal' life?"

She shook her head, but he stopped her with a finger brushing against her arm. A light caress, in contrast to his hard gaze as he watched the place where their bodies met.

This man with his hard, shiny outer shell and his warm, kind, generous heart. The heart he refused to acknowledge, as if it made him weak, instead of it being his greatest asset. He'd seen her naked, he'd seen her cry, he'd seen her enraged and giddy with joy. Hell, the moment they'd *met*, he'd seen her at her very worst and had told her he was on her side.

Not only did he deserve to know the truth, he could handle it. After the last few weeks that they'd spent together, she was sure of it.

The muffled voices in the house lifted, and a new song began. Hadley thought of the joy in Petra's eyes when she'd seen Sawyer coming at her like a steam train, and Adelaid's expression as she'd tucked herself under Ted's arm, his hand resting protectively over her pregnant belly.

Then she angled a little Ronan's way and said, "When I started working for you, I barely knew myself. I was so desperate—for security, for comfort, for independence. I'd have fought for those things, tooth and nail. Only, with you they came so easily, and in such abundance, and I just stopped fighting. Stopped fighting for what I wanted next, in case I lost what I had."

"What was it you wanted?"

Hadley lifted a hand to Ronan's face, cradling his hard jaw and running her thumb over his cheek, the rasp of his day-old stubble sending goose bumps up her arm. Then, heedless of who might be watching, she leaned in and pressed her lips to his.

His hesitation was brief, before his eyes slammed closed and he kissed her deeply, like a man drowning. He turned to pull her into his arms, as if he'd been craving her all night long.

When they finally pulled apart, lips clinging for a tenuous final moment, Hadley's eyes fluttered open, their breaths loud in the night air.

"I wanted that," she said simply. "I've always wanted that. Only wanting and not having does tend to wear a person down. And I didn't want to be worn down. I want to…garden, and see movies, and sleep in on Sundays."

And here was the kicker. Oh, the lies she'd told herself in

an effort at not making the same mistakes her mum had made. When the truth was she wished she could have her mum back, long enough to just hug her. And tell her she was enough.

"And I want to have a family, or at least *be* a family. Not because I work with someone, but because we chose one another, and made promises to one another, and meant it."

She took a deep breath.

"What I want is to love. And be loved." Rather than making her feel weak, saying it out loud made her feel invincible.

"I'm in love with you, Ronan," she said, unable to help the catch in her voice. "And that's why I had to leave."

There—that was it. That was all of it. Having shed the load she'd been carrying for so long, she felt limitless. As if she might float up and away. But she didn't want to float away. She wanted Ronan to respond.

He did, by leaning back, just enough for moonlight to spill between them. Enough to let in the warm night breeze where before there had been only him.

Well, she thought, *that's a response all right*. Cheeks warming, stomach churning, she reached out for him, curled her fingers into his shirt and gave him a shake. "Say something, damn you."

It worked.

"You've got me wrong," he said. "You've got me *all* wrong. I can't."

"Can't what, exactly?"

"I just… I can't."

And that was it. That was all she got.

While in the background voices sang loudly, joyously, *I Saw Mummy Kissing Santa Claus*, Ronan's jaw turned to granite, his blue eyes onyx dark. She wasn't even sure the man was breathing any more. It was as if he'd morphed from a potent, decided, hot-blooded man into a suit of armour, impenetrable and cold, before her very eyes.

What had she *thought* would happen? Honestly? That he'd fall to his knees and declare his undying love for her? He'd known how she felt. He'd had to—some semblance of it at least. The rich vein of sensual tension coursing between them, teetering on the border between flirtation and vexation, had been the keystone of their relationship.

And now he *"couldn't"*? Couldn't what? Couldn't *love her*? Why not? What was wrong with *her*?

No, that wasn't it. She'd been with him, *really* been with him. He worshipped her. What he meant was that he *wouldn't* love her. Wouldn't even allow for the possibility. Because that would mean he'd stopped fighting against all the demons in his own damned head.

Which made her not worth *stopping* fighting for.

Hands shaking, insides crushed, she took a step back, then another, distancing herself from Ronan, from the yearning that still curled inside her. For, while her heart felt pummelled, her feelings all awash, there was pride there too.

Pride in how she'd taken the leap. Pride that she'd stopped hiding from herself. And she wasn't about to lose that by begging.

While Ronan might be brilliant, might be deeply committed to being a better man—might well be the love of her life—she wanted more. And, no matter how many times she failed, she'd not stop reaching. Because she was her indomitable mother's daughter, after all.

Hadley said, "Merry Christmas, Ronan. I hope you get whatever it is that you do want."

Then she stepped in to press a kiss to his cheek and felt him expand towards her. Felt the tension in him, as if he was struggling not to haul her close. Because wanting her had never been his problem—believing he deserved her had.

Heading inside, she said her goodbyes to a chorus of, "No!" and, "Stay!" She hugged each friend, a little harder than she usually might have, then headed out into the sultry midsummer's night.

With no plan, no destination, no driving goal—only herself to hang onto.

* * *

She had him wrong. Hadley had him all wrong.

Ronan knew he had a heart…it was just a battered, bloodied mess of a thing. Beaten into submission young, his parents' example of what relationships looked like having sent it cowering into the deepest recesses of his chest.

What was left of it, he kept under lock and key, protected and safe, so that he might eke out just enough empathy and hope to do the kind of work he had to do. Until there was nothing in reserve for anything else. Anyone else.

Not nearly enough to give Hadley what she'd asked of him. To give her what she deserved.

Hell, he'd been so selfish, taking all that he could of her these past weeks.

And all the while Hadley had loved him. *Loved* him. She'd said the actual words. Hadn't she? The more he replayed her declaration inside his head, the more it began to feel less and less real.

Attraction, yes—God, yes. Understanding, intimacy, friendship built over years of knowing one another—absolutely. The truth was, he adored her. If he had to be stuck on planet Earth with a single person, he'd choose her, hands down.

And there *had* been a moment, a pause in time, after she'd said those words and an explosive warmth had bled the hairline cracks in the iron casing around his heart. The same cracks that being with Hadley these last weeks had brought on.

But *love*? Surely she knew him better than that. For, to him it might as well be a cyclone, the kind one had no hope in hell of curtailing. The kind that made a person feel helpless, out of control. Was she surprised he'd shut down? Tin Man? Try Fort Knox-level bank vault.

"Hey."

Ronan flinched hard, his neck pinching. Then he turned to find Ted ambling up to him, hands shoved into his pockets, feet bare on the wooden porch.

Ronan rolled out the tension pulling at his shoulders, breathed into the ache in his gut and managed to say, "Hey."

"I've been sent to find out if you're planning on coming back inside any time soon. Or are you keeping an eye out for Santa?" Ted leant down to see out from under the roof, where starlight poured down on the dark greenery between their house and the bay, creating an eerie glow.

Voice ragged, Ronan said, "I think it's best I head off. Can you give Adelaid my apologies?"

Ted gave Ronan a look. "Not in the mood for sing-alongs? Now Hadley's left?"

Ronan's instinct was to deflect. To self-protect. But his armour had taken a beating and he found himself saying, "Something like that."

"Mmm. Can't be easy for you, mate, with her gone, me working from home, and Sawyer away with Petra a lot of the time. You could have made it hard for any of us to make the changes we did. And, considering the investment we've all ploughed into the business, you'd have had every right. But you've been a prince among men—Adelaid's words, not mine."

Ronan breathed out, the weight of Ted's words gushing through the cracks in his armour—bigger now, and too many to mend.

Ted glanced at Ronan. "I'm sorry if we've let you down."

At that Ronan baulked. Did they really think that? Was that what his descent into gruff moroseness over the past couple of years had led them all to believe? Did Sawyer think that?

Did *Hadley*?

"Ted," he said, his hand landing on his old friend's back. "Big Think was my breathtakingly ridiculous dream. When you two lumbered into my life, I lured you into my plan. *Any* time I've had with you at my side has been my fortune."

Ted's mouth crooked into a smile. "I think you'll find we were happy to be lured. Without *you*, we'd have both flubbed about in mediocre careers."

Ronan's mouth twitched, but more out of habit than any feeling of mirth. For his whole body ached, as if he'd come down with a sudden flu. "Highly unlikely. But thank you for pretending otherwise."

Ted's smile grew, for he knew his worth. His work would have been ground-breaking with or without the others. Just as Sawyer would have found stratospheric success in any field he'd tried. While Ronan...

Ronan's instinct was to claim brilliance regards the scaffolding he'd created, and the clever people he'd forced to join his cult. Except Hadley's earlier words, regarding the Big Think dream, and the family he'd built, forced him to acknowledge that he was more than the sum of his parts.

Ted reached out and slapped a hand on Ronan's back. "Now come back inside when you're ready. And stick around. It's nice in there."

With that, Ted ambled indoors, ducking to fit under the door frame. Leaving Ronan feeling freed. As if he'd been holding onto a lead balloon his whole entire life, and had finally let it go.

After the horror show with Hadley, he *also* as if his insides had been hollowed out. But he'd rebuilt himself from less before. He could do it again. So long as he stuck to the promise he'd made himself all those years ago—to protect those under his care—at all costs.

And protecting Hadley meant compelling her to see that loving him would never be in her best interests, then so be it.

CHAPTER TEN

THE NEXT WEEK went by impossibly fast. As if Hadley had clicked her heels together three times and it was the night of the Big Think Ball.

"Holy Dorothy," said Jonas as together they stood in the entrance to the ballroom at the Elysium Hotel. It was not long before the guests were due to arrive and the gang was all there, taking in the custom-made light show of creamy dappled light shimmering and shifting over the walls, ceilings and floors—images of trees, fields and floating orbs of witch-light drifting in and out of focus. While at their feet golden swirls of light—less yellow brick, more buttery dreamscape—swept from the entrance, through the ballroom then up onto the stage.

A rush of satisfaction slid through Hadley, warming the edges of her still stone-cold insides, like the tiniest flame still trying its best to survive an ashen fireplace.

"Oh, Hadley, it's perfect," Petra, a world-class art curator, pronounced.

"That's saying something," said Sawyer, drawing Petra in to kiss the top of her head.

"I assume proper measures have been taken to ensure no one will experience vertigo?" Ted pondered as he watched the lights move across the high, gilded ceiling.

Adelaid smacked her husband on the arm. "Stop being Science Boy and just appreciate the gorgeousness."

Kyle laughed. "Good luck besting this next year, Jonas," he said, before dragging Hadley's replacement off to do a final tech check.

The others followed, moving into the ballroom, pointing out all the deeply charming touches.

While Hadley breathed out, suddenly deeply exhausted. Since driving back to Melbourne on Christmas Eve night, she'd been keeping herself going by willpower alone. Now the end was here, and there was nothing more she could do, she could quite happily have found an empty room and cried.

A rush of tingles skittered over her skin and a moment later Ronan moved in beside her, his gruff voice scooting up her arms and into her chest as he said, "Hadley. This is phenomenal."

"Thank you," she managed, the first words she'd said to him since Christmas Eve.

Not because she regretted telling him how she felt. That had been a revelation. The tough, insular young woman who'd been ready to scratch and fight the world for her place in it, had found such faith in her own decision-making ability, she'd let herself fall in love. And that was a hell of a thing.

Which didn't mean it didn't hurt like hell not to have all those big wonderful feelings returned.

Hadley braced herself and turned to face him. Her heart stuttered when she saw how hard he looked. His gaze tight, his stance rigid. It was as if he'd clad himself in new heavy-duty armour, several layers deep.

But this wasn't the time to worry about Ronan, or herself. Tonight was about raising funds to pay for projects Big Think had not yet even dreamed of.

Holding her tablet in front of her like a shield, she said, "Okay, report time. As it stands, donations have already exceeded projections. We've sold more tables than ever before. And, once the Founders' Auction goes ahead, I honestly believe we will have raised more money than we did the first and second years combined."

Ronan finally looked her way. And as her eyes met his, the one place he couldn't hide no matter how hard he tried, she saw *him*. His sorrow and his struggle. His desire and his demons. His obstinance and his aspiration. And, as if some flood gate had been accidentally left open, her love for him swept through her like a rogue wave.

It was too much. She didn't even bother making up an excuse, merely spun and walked away. But where could she go? The She the hordes were gathering at the front door. And she had actual important work still to do. So, she turned back, only to stop again.

"Can I help you?" a soft voice asked.

Hadley looked to her right to find she'd stopped outside the cloak room, of all places, considering what had happened—or nearly happened—the night of the first Big Think Ball.

That moment swept over her with such aching clarity. She and Ronan, tossed together into the dark. Her hand running up his lapel, the rampant thudding of his heart proof that she wasn't alone in her desire. The way, even in the near-darkness, she'd felt his gaze drop to her mouth.

Even though nothing had happened, that moment had unlocked the possibility. It had been the tipping point after which everything had changed, leaving her in a permanent state of yearning.

"Hadley?"

Blinking her way out of the fog of memory, Hadley looked up to find Ronan standing a few feet away, brutishly handsome, all potent power constrained beneath the confines of his sleek tux.

When he walked towards her, desire sprang to life inside her, curling and unfolding throughout, as if all it needed was the mere hope of rain to bloom.

Unless... What if she stayed? Let him speak? Maybe he'd just needed more time?

"Hadley," he said again when he neared. His voice was low, intimate and ragged. His gaze was hot and hungry.

She couldn't breathe for the anticipation.

He took another step towards her, his hand reaching…

"Oh, brilliant!" a voice called out. One of the young photographers—all of whom had been recommended by Sawyer's little sister, Daisy—hired to cover the event.

And the moment was shattered, like a pebble hitting a pane of glass.

"Photo op!" said the photographer, lunging towards them, holding an old-school flash camera to his eye.

"Wait," Hadley said, needing a moment to collect herself.

For this was not Oz; it was real life. There would be no magical transformation in the Tin Man. Ronan would remain the king of stubbornness. "We should find Sawyer and Ted, while you're all nice and pressed. Before you get food on your ties."

Then she glanced at his bow tie, to find it was crooked—infinitesimally, but still. She felt Ronan notice her noticing in the way his body stilled, his chest lifted. In the way he held his breath, as if waiting for her touch. Waiting for her to turn into him, step between his shoes, breathe deeply of his warmth and his skin, her fingers brushing his shirt as she fixed his nearly perfect tie. It was the same sweet foreplay dance they'd been performing for years.

She glanced up to find him watching her, an eyebrow lifted.

Then, fingers tingling in disappointment, she left his tie alone, and turned to face the photographer. "Second thoughts, take the photo."

"Great!" said the photographer. "Scoot in. Nice and close."

Hadley scooted in, a ripple of awareness shifting through her as Ronan's hand landed on her lower back.

"Now, smile!"

For some reason she could never explain, rather than grit her teeth and force a smile, Hadley looked up at Ronan, to find he was looking down at her. Her emotions went into freefall.

Time tumbled over itself. Multiverses, what-ifs, chances missed and opportunities avoided coalesced into that moment. Their shorthand went haywire as she read so much in his eyes that he didn't have the language, or the capacity, to say.

Click-click-click.

"Gorgeous!" the photographer declared, then bounced off towards the ballroom.

"Gerard!" a voice called.

Hadley blinked back into the moment, and looked up to see the doors at the far end of the long entrance hall had opened, the first of their guests arriving in a wave of glitter, sparkle and black tie.

As if they shared the same consciousness, Hadley and Ronan stepped apart and the Big Think Ball began.

The rest of the night flew past like a beautiful dream until it was mere minutes before the Billion-Dollar Bachelor Auction. The big finale. Hadley's last hurrah.

She checked the account on her tablet, a wad of emotion lodging in her throat when she saw that in the past half-hour they'd reached her blue-sky target and exceeded it by over a million dollars.

Scrolling down the lists of donors—most anonymous, some not—she stopped. Her throat closed up at the sight of one name in particular. She looked up, searching for Ronan, her instincts finding him in an instant.

Miraculously, he was alone, standing at the side of the room, watching the evening unfold. While she'd managed to avoid him for much of the night for her own mental health, there was no way she could now.

"Ronan," she said, as she approached.

He turned, his dark-blue eyes lighting up.

Telling her heart to calm the heck down, Hadley held up the tablet. When he saw the total, he coughed out a husky laugh. "Seriously?"

She nodded, a smile catching at her mouth.

The smile turned to laughter when he suddenly reached for her, picked her up and spun her round. Those nearby looked and laughed, surprised and delighted.

When Ronan slowed, Hadley slid down his body, her hand running down the back of his neck and over his shoulder. As her heels hit the floor, their gazes caught, locked in a private moment, heat and history coursing between them.

Stronger now, Hadley was the one to step away. "There's one more thing. The donation that put us over the edge…it was from your father."

Ronan reared back as if slapped. "What the…? No. He'd never."

"He did." She showed him the relevant donation in bold: Constantine Gerard and Associates.

Ronan lifted a hand and ran it over his face as he peered out over the crowd, as if looking for hidden danger. "I can't accept it."

"You can," said Hadley, reaching out and taking him by the arm, squeezing till his gaze returned to hers. His armour now gone, as if that had been a mirage and it had taken too much energy to keep it in place. Then, "You *have* to."

"But why?" he said. "Why now?"

"An olive branch? An apology? His way of finally telling you he sees value in what you are doing? The only way to know is to ask him."

It was just as likely Constantine Gerard was messing with his son, as he always had, but this moment was not about *him*. It was about Ronan giving himself permission to make peace— with his father's actions, his father's past, his father's blood running through his own veins—so that he could truly move on.

Maybe then he could could allow himself to love. But not until he loved himself.

Hadley traced her hand down his arm till she took him by the hand. His fingers curled instantly, protectively, around hers.

"You are not your father, Ronan."

"I know," he said, his voice deep, ragged.

"You are not your father," she said again.

"I know," he growled, louder this time. Loud enough that the air from his words tossed her hair from her cheeks.

"Then you know that this money is bigger than all of that. Take it and do good with it. Because you can."

The orchestra struck up a chord and Hadley glanced distractedly towards the sound, to find couples moving around the dance floor, eyes to the sky, laughing and cheering as the light show changed to make those dancing appear as if they were being rained on by golden dandelion dust.

When she looked back, it was to find Ronan looking down at where their hands were joined. He turned her fingers over till her palm faced up and he ran a slow thumb down the centre, sending a hot flush up Hadley's arm.

Then he used that hand to tug her closer and said, "Dance with me."

"But the donation…"

"Will be put to good use, as you rightly proposed. Now, put work aside and dance with me. In this amazing space that you created."

Slipping her tablet into the pocket she'd had built into the voluminous skirt of her designer dress, she nodded and let Ronan draw her closer still. Then he led the way to the dance floor. His hand was tucked over hers, as if he never wanted to let her go.

But he *was* letting her go, in every sense. She no longer worked for him, and he refused to give into his feelings for her. Which meant this moment, this dance, was to be their full stop.

Which was why she refused to read anything into the heavy glint in his eyes. Or the thud of his heart as he turned her into his arms. Or how tightly he held her—one hand tucked between them, the other low on her back as they swayed to the strains of *Moonlight Serenade*, dandelion dust floating down on them from above.

Hadley let her eyes drift closed, and let herself love him, one last time.

A smatter of applause brought Hadley back to the present far too soon, to find they were still swaying while everyone else was facing the stage, cheering as the MC made his way to the podium.

The MC's velvety voice crooned into the microphone. "Now, for the moment we've all been waiting for. It's time for the Founders' Auction!"

The crowd—dappled in gauzy light, giddy with money, and warmed by excellent booze—cheered uproariously and made their way back to their respective tables.

"Hadley," Ronan said as Hadley too began to move away.

She tilted her chin towards the stage. "Go on," she said. "You're on. Go charm their socks off. Time to bring it home. For Big Think."

Ronan looked to where Ted and Sawyer—looking dapper, dashing and winningly chagrined—were making their way onto the stage. Hadley drank the man in while she had the chance: his thick, dark waves, that strong jaw, those languid, deep-blue eyes, and that big, strapping frame built to hold up the entire world.

She loved this man. She had done for a very long time. Only what she'd come to realise these past weeks was that she wanted to be loved with the same intensity, the same certainty, the same vulnerability. There was no half way. No wishing and hoping it might turn into something more.

And, if Ronan couldn't give that to her, then she had to let him go.

"Go on," she said, giving him a light shove. It toppled him off-balance but he caught himself quickly. He turned back with a glint in his eye, a flicker of the fight she'd been waiting for, before the crowd swallowed him up, the surge of enthusiasm pressing him towards the stage.

Hadley didn't wait to see if he made it.

She turned on her heel, the crystalline colours refracting off the moisture in her eyes, the music, the laughter, bouncing off the bubble she created around herself as she floated towards the exit.

Plucking her phone from the other pocket, she sent a quick text to Adelaid and Petra, letting them know she was okay. She wished them both Happy New Year. Then she walked down the long hall, past the cloak room, through the wide front doors of the hotel and into the night.

Ready to start the New Year as she meant to go on—her Big Think era behind her.

Spending the day after the Big Think Ball—known to the rest of the world as New Year's Day—on *Candy*, the Big Think yacht, had been a tradition for the men. A chance to ease sore heads and reflect on the year they'd put behind them, before starting the new one with bigger goals than ever before.

It was also one of several traditions that had fallen by the wayside as first Ted then Sawyer had found others in their lives to consider first.

So it was somewhat of a surprise when Sawyer had knocked on Ronan's front door at the crack of dawn. "Great. You're here. Worried you might be sleeping it off in the Tower."

Fair, Ronan had thought, since he'd practically moved in there. But spending the night in that building, after the way Hadley had left without even saying goodbye? He couldn't have thought of anything he wanted less.

Heading out to sea, Sawyer at the helm, Ted lay back on the plush couch that ran the length of the cabin below, nursing a rare hangover due to the number of people who'd insisted they drink to the health of the baby near-bursting from Adelaid's belly. While Ronan sat upright, eyes ahead, head thumping from a frown he just couldn't shake.

"How long has he been like that?" asked Sawyer, after dropping anchor and joining them below deck.

Ted said, "A while."

"You think he might be broken?"

"I'm not *broken*," Ronan growled, his voice rough. Then he blinked and squinted against the brightness, to find Sawyer leaning back against the bar, arms crossed.

"Okay. Then you look like crud for no reason at all."

Ted sat up slowly and looked at Ronan. "That's putting it nicely."

Ronan felt his lip curl and glanced at the windows, wondering how long it might take to swim back, only to find they could no longer see land.

Sawyer grabbed three bottles of some healthy green sludge from the fridge, handed them over then took a seat, putting himself at the point of a triangle: the three corners of the Big Think empire.

Only Ronan very much felt as if he was hemmed in. "Why does this suddenly feel like an intervention?"

"Are you in need of an intervention?" asked Sawyer.

A muscle flickered under Ronan's eye.

"No?" said Sawyer. Then he lifted his drink in salute and the others followed suit. "Then, let's drink—to a hell of a year."

"Hell of a few years," said Ted.

Ronan winced as he tasted the health drink—no more beers, like in the early days. Everything had changed. Ronan made a sound, like the sound a man might make if he was quietly losing his mind.

He sat forward and let his head fall into his hands. He could sense Sawyer and Ted mouthing things at him over his head.

"Okay," said Sawyer. "So, now seems like as good a time as any to bring up the elephant in the room."

Don't say Hadley, Ronan begged inside his own head. *Please don't say Hadley.*

Sawyer didn't in fact say Hadley. "We've been limping along for a while now, pretending our original business model was still sustainable. But the truth is, you've been taking up far more than your share of the slack, and that's not fair."

Ronan didn't deny it. How could he? He was exhausted— emotionally, physically, and psychologically. He'd been stretched so thin, he'd somehow let the best thing that had ever happened to him slip through his fingers.

He ought to have refused Hadley's resignation the moment she'd offered it. Put an end to the ludicrous idea then and there. Instead, they'd fallen down some interminable rabbit hole that had led to this.

To him walking into on Monday morning and her not being there. Ever again.

"Big Think belongs to all of us," he managed. "Always will."

"It will," said Sawyer. "But you have to give yourself the same grace you've shown us. You need time and space, room to find a life outside of the company. What you do is important, but so are you."

So was he.

Not merely as the co-founder of a multi-billion-dollar company, or the son of a man he was trying to best, but just Ronan, the living, breathing, human being.

"You're right," said Ronan before he even knew it to be true. For Big Think had never been just about the work. It had been about community and friendship, the urban family they'd built. It had been about giving each of them the chance to shine, whatever that had meant for them.

The others had taken that chance and flourished, while he'd deliberately, forcibly, lived within the margins, the grey in between. Holding on tight to that safe space, while the brightest, most vociferous, pushiest, punchiest creature on the planet did her all to yank him into Technicolor.

He pictured her office, all the jewel-bright colours, under her glinting gold ceiling, Hadley deliberately creating a space that felt bold, and luminous and decadent. A space for talking, arguing, sharing. Big things, small things, things that only they'd cared about.

He pictured her lying back on the bed at the Big D Motel eating crisps from the mini-bar, watching some old movie with the sound of truck brakes screeching outside, the light from the red-fringed lamp making everything look a little naughty.

Hadley.

"What did he say?" said Ted.

Ronan looked at Sawyer to find him smiling. His eyes were wide, as if saying, *Jump on in, the water's fine.*

"He said 'Hadley'," said Ted, clicking his fingers. "So that's why he looks like crap."

Sawyer mimed his brain exploding.

Hadley.

Hadley, who wasn't a founder but had been in the inner circle all the same.

Hadley, who was the sole reason their big ideas came to fruition.

If Ronan was the brass, Sawyer the brawn, Ted the brains, then Hadley had been the core. The soul. The strong, steady, consistent, heartbeat that had kept pressing them forward all this time.

But, more than that, she was also *his* core. *His* soul. *His* heart. He was smitten with her, he respected the hell out of her, and he adored her. He *wanted* her so badly, it physically hurt, which he'd worn as some sort of badge of honour. If he could feel that way, and go without her, then didn't that mean he was a better man than his father could ever hope to be?

But he'd only been punishing himself, and punishing her, when all he'd ever truly wanted to do was support her, enjoy her, work beside her and admire her. To live alongside her.

But, instead of telling her all that, he'd been so terrified of showing a chink in his famously formidable armour, he'd stood there while she'd carved out that heart and handed it to him on open palms.

And he had said nothing.

"Hadley," said Ronan, her name on his tongue like water for a man dying of thirst. "Hadley loves me."

Sawyer breathed out long and slowly. "You think?"

"I know it. She told me so."

"She did?" said Sawyer, and that time he looked genuinely shocked. "Wow. Good for her. And what did you say?"

"Nothing."

"What do you mean, nothing?" Sawyer asked.

Ronan shot him a look. Only for Sawyer to sit back in his chair, his hands on his head, his eyes wide with shock. "How can a guy as smart as you be so stupid?"

Ronan wondered the same thing.

But a sense of clarity was finally coming over him, like cloud clearing over a calming sea.

She'd not left because she loved him, but because she loved him but couldn't be sure he'd ever come to realise that he felt the same.

When the very thought of *not* loving Hadley now felt incomprehensible to him. How could a person know her—know her street smarts, her sincerity, her warmth, her curiosity, her ferocity—and *not* love her?

Ronan felt time stretch and contract, swirling around him like the tornado. He'd spent the better part of his adult life believing that he was fuelled by the determination not to be anything like his father. He'd martyred his life to the mission, as if it was an act of moral excellence. But he'd achieved that the moment it had even occurred to him to try.

"Damn it," he said, launching to his feet. Then, louder, "Damn it!"

"Is he okay?" asked Ted.

"He'll get there," said Sawyer.

"Should we do something?" Ted asked, concern now edging his deep voice.

"Like what?" Sawyer asked, sounding far more chipper.

"A cold compress to the back of the neck? I don't know, I'm not that kind of doctor."

Feeling as if lightning had hit his veins, Ronan declared, "I'm in love with Hadley."

"We already knew that, right?" Ted whispered, while Sawyer put a finger to his mouth.

"It's why we niggled and snapped and drove one another crazy. Why I stayed at work so late all the time. Why her office mirrored mine. She left because while working for me it would never happen. She quit so we could…"

So that they could *be* together. Which was incredibly unfair to her. Why shouldn't he have been the one to leave? Well, he couldn't, because it was his company, but then it was hers too, as much as it was anyone's.

"You done?" Sawyer asked.

"Hmm?"

"You've been standing there, looking like you're in the midst of the rapture, for a few minutes now. Just let us know when you're done so we can get the heck back to land."

"Oh, I'm done. In fact, I think I know how to fix it all."

"Great!" said Sawyer, sweeping to his feet, only to wince when his leg old injury made itself known. Then he was off, taking the steps a little more carefully.

Then came the distant sound of the anchor winching back into place, the rev of the engine and off they went, in a tight circle that sent Ronan and Ted rocking sideways before the boat shot off, back towards shore.

"Can't he go any faster?" Ronan ground out.

For, when a man like Ronan Gerard realised what he wanted the rest of his life to look like, he was not about to sit back and wait for it to happen.

First to Big Think Tower, so that he might put things in order there. He did not want to leave anything to chance.

His feet took him to the Founders' Room, only to pull to a

screaming halt in the doorway. For Hadley was sitting on his "throne" at the head of the table. His hungry gaze drank in her denim overalls over a black tank-top, her face free of make-up. Her forehead creased, her thumb playing over the bow tattoo on her finger as she stared out of the window to her right. A big box of stuff on the table at her elbow.

She looked soft, unguarded and utterly lovely. How he'd managed to go this long without falling to his knees and declaring himself, he had no idea.

And yet, Ronan didn't move, didn't even breathe, standing in *her* spot in the doorway, trying not to blink funny in case she disappeared.

But something alerted her to his presence anyway. That something that had always meant they knew where each other was in any room.

She sat up, blinking furiously. A finger wiped under each eye. Had she been *crying*? *Hell*.

"Hadley…" he said, moving into the room.

"Ronan," she said, standing and fussing with the packing box. "I'm sorry. I came in to clean out my makeshift office, thinking no one else would be here. I'll finish up and get out of your hair."

"It's no problem," he said, his voice calm, his movements slow; hyper-aware of how easily, and how quickly, he could screw this up. He'd proven himself more than capable of that already. "Take your time. Truly."

"What are you doing here?" she asked.

"I had some pretty important business to attend to," he said.

"Oh," she said, trying to act as if it wasn't her business now, but he could see she was itching to know. Because his business *was* her business and had been from the day she'd walked into that old warehouse and demanded he give her a shot.

He reached into the back pocket of his jeans and pulled out the handwritten document—the one he'd just scrawled, then copied and sent to their in-house lawyer—and slid it along the table. It spun as it moved, stopping so that she had to walk a step closer to pick it up.

"What's this?" she asked, bending to look but not touching, as if it might bite.

"It's a partnership agreement. Go on," he said. "Read it."

She watched him a moment before her eyes dropped back to the paper. Curiosity won out, as always, and she unfolded the paper and read the words.

Words offering her a quarter share of the company.

Ted, Sawyer and he had agreed, without reservation, on the ride back to shore to give up equal portions of their own shares in order to bring Hadley into the fold, if she was amenable. With remuneration going back to day one of her tenure with them.

He waited for her to absorb it. For Hadley, he'd wait as long as it took.

When she looked up, her eyes flickered with shock, confusion and a good measure of disbelief. "I don't understand. How is this possible? *Why?*"

Ronan knew she meant *why now*. Once she read on she'd find the arrangement as not dependant on her actively working for the company if she still decided to leave. It was merely the agreement they ought to have put before her all those years ago, if he'd not been so intent on treading carefully, carefully, when it came to impeding on her autonomy.

He moved slowly down the edge of the table.

"Why the offer?" he said. "Because Big Think was not Big Think before you came on board. It was a collection of egos and promise, of talent and gumption. Then you walked in the room, took one look at us and knew exactly what we needed in order to coalesce. You brought form and finesse. And without that, without you, we might never have found our way out of that Richmond warehouse."

He swallowed, needing to have every wit about him to get the next part right.

"As for why *now*? Because I've come to realise that I've spent the past several years not letting you know how deeply I value you, in case you saw through me and saw everything. Which was unforgivable. And unfair."

"Everything?" she asked, pink rushing into her cheeks, her fingers gripping the agreement till it crinkled. When she noticed, she quickly set to straightening out the page.

Which gave Ronan a burst of hope. It wasn't an instant yes, but it might not be a no.

"Every thought," he said, "Every feeling. Every secret wish. Every ounce of longing. You knew that you riled me, you knew that you pushed me, you knew you made me want to be a better man. But I couldn't have you know that I adored you. That I dreamed of you. How despairingly I wished we'd met under different circumstances so that I might have asked you out, come to know you over a glass of wine, taken you home and kissed you senseless under your porch light. The way normal people go about such things."

A small sound escaped her mouth, halfway between a sob and a sigh. He'd put her through the wringer but she was strong enough to take a breath, to think, to decide for herself.

She looked down at the document. "This offer…" she said.

"Is without conditions. A quarter-share, if you want it. We are all in agreement. We all think it's way past time."

Ronan forced himself to stop moving towards her when she was just out of reach even though he wanted to touch her, so badly. But this was business, and he needed her to know that one had nothing to do with the other.

"Initial thoughts?" he asked, his voice miraculously dry, even while his heart felt as if it were beating in his throat.

"There goes early retirement," she muttered, a glint of fire bursting behind her dark eyes.

And Ronan laughed. It was as if a valve had burst open, and once he started laughing he couldn't stop. He laughed so hard his cheeks hurt. So hard he bent over and gripped the table, the relief akin to being filled with helium.

And Hadley joined him. She gave a short gasp of laughter at first, then great rolling barks that had her clutching her side as if she had a stitch.

Then their laughter eased, falling away to soft sounds on both sides, till their gazes tangled and the room filled with a sizzle of electricity. As if they'd just realised it was the two of them alone in the room. The only ones in the entire building, in fact.

Then she said, "Why? Why couldn't I know that you dreamed of me?"

"Because then you'd have to examine your own feelings and surely decide that you couldn't waste your time on a man such as me. A Tin Man with a useless heart."

Hadley blinked. Then she took a step his way, the first since he'd entered the room. Then she took another step, and another, then lifted the hand holding the sheet of paper and placed it on his chest...up and a little to the left.

"Not useless," she said, her voice low, quiet. "Bruised. In need of time to heal." Then she took his other hand and placed it over her heart. "I know, because like calls to like."

He curled his fingers around hers, before lifting her palm to his mouth and dropping a kiss on the soft cushion of skin.

Her head dropped back and she sighed. Which he took as a good sign, and kissed his way down her wrist, following a row of freckles inside her forearm before he reached her elbow. He ran his thumb into the bend, over the constellation tattooed into the soft skin, and she bit her lip.

"Hadley," he said. "Look at me."

She did something truly rare then; she did as he asked without questions. And he saw it in her eyes: her love for him, radiating like a moonbeam. How had he never seen it before? Had she hidden it that well, or had he been too stubborn, too scared, to see it for what it was?

He pulled her hand back to his chest and said, "I'm going to tell you something now. And I want you to promise me, in advance, that you will forgive any blunders, because I'm running on gut instinct here. Okay?"

She squinted at him, head shaking back and forth. "I make no such promises."

Fair enough, he thought with a grimace. She was far too savvy for that. So, he started with the hook.

"I love you, Hadley Moreau."

At that she ceased shaking her head. Her eyes opened wide. "I'm sorry, but did you just say...?"

Ronan held up a finger and said, "Let me get through this."

She snapped her mouth shut and nodded, her eyes big, dark and focussed on his. Her body now trembled under his touch.

"I remember the day you walked into my office, so clearly," he said. "Skinny jeans, Doc Martens, several earrings glinting up one ear. Like Audrey Hepburn had had a baby with a biker. Serene yet utterly terrifying, practically daring me to turn you away. It wasn't just that siren face of yours that gripped me through the middle, or that core of steel that glows, fiery hot, from within. It was the way you refused to be wholly impressed by us. As if we had to earn your respect. Exactly what I needed before I knew I needed it."

Hadley laughed then, a cough of joy that she couldn't contain.

He took a breath. "But there was that whole thing with my father..."

She shook her head. "You know where I stand on that score."

"I do," he said, "But it took me a really long time to accept that. Likely because, every conversation we had from that day on, I could hear my heart clanging in my chest any time you neared. And I knew how lucky we were to have you. So I chose to park those feelings, as wild and unexpected and new to me as they were, to a man who prided himself on being contained."

"Ronan, I..."

He placed a finger over her mouth. "Nearly done."

Hadley was really trembling now. Or maybe it was him. Either way, so long as they held one another up, he knew they'd be fine.

"Then you kissed me, outside the Big D Motel, and invited me into your world in a way I'd never dared hope possible. Right when I was on the verge of losing you."

He shook his head. "I never claimed to be a smart man when it came to matters of the heart; in fact, I'd quite happily state that on that score I'm a complete dunce. I'm sorry it took me this long to own how I felt, how I *feel*, about you."

He lifted both hands to cradle her face. "I love you, Hadley Moreau. I've loved you for longer than I remember loving anyone or anything. And if I'm not too late, if I haven't acted in such a way that means you can't trust my words…"

Hadley curled her fingers into his shirt, yanked him to her and kissed him hard. Then her eyes squeezed shut and she threw her arms around his neck and kissed him harder.

And Ronan knew this was it for him. He'd never love anyone the way he loved her. He was done, gone, smitten. He was hers. For ever more.

He pulled back and kissed her once more, a place marker, then said, "Marry me."

"Ronan," said Hadley, rearing back and shaking her head, all laughter and joy. But again it was not an outright no.

So, again, he said, "Marry me."

She pulled up the piece of paper still clutched in her hand. "How do I know you don't just want me for my money?"

Ronan pulled her closer, her softness sinking into his hardness, and her eyes glazed over as she felt it too. "I guess you'll never know."

She smiled, her eyes flitting between his. And he saw it— the moment when they were finally, *finally*, in complete sync. Her breathing evened out, her gaze lit with a healthy measure of *about time, you damn fool*.

Ronan said, "This my pledge—I am yours, if you'll have me. Yours to organise, to bait and debate, to nudge and mould and push, so that I never rest on whatever laurels I might think I have. Do with me as you please."

Her eyes narrowed as she leant back, trusting him to catch her if she fell. And her smile…her smile was like an arrow right through his now fully unencumbered heart.

"So, who's going to tell Jonas that he has to move out of my office?" she asked, her eyes sparkling.

Ronan was as relieved as he was glad. The rightness of it flowed through him like breath. "I'll leave that up to you."

"Fine, but I'm keeping him for myself, meaning you'll have to find yourself another assistant."

"Is that right?"

"Already regretting your offer?" she asked.

"Not even slightly," he assured her.

She settled herself against him, the trembling having stopped now that they were wrapped around one another. Now she felt strong, supple and warm. Now she was shifting subtly, back and forth, rubbing herself against him, the friction making it hard for him to… Well, hard, basically.

"Does that mean you accept our offer?" he asked.

"I do."

"And you're coming back to work?"

"I am. But not only because you gave me part of your company," she said, her fingers now playing in his hair.

"That's fine. I didn't give you part of my company in order to make you stay."

He leaned down then, arms wrapped around her waist, and kissed her, sealing the deal.

"I love you, Ronan," she said simply when she came up for air.

"I love you more."

"Not possible."

We'll see, Ronan thought as he turned and lifted her onto the table.

And gave in when she pulled him down over her. For when a man tells the woman he loves that she can do with him as she pleases, it behoves him to follow through.

EPILOGUE

"Come back here," whispered Hadley, taking Ronan by the hand, before looking around, and dragging him into the nearest room, which happened to be a cloak room.

He didn't complain. In fact, he rarely complained these days. Having this woman in his life, truly in his life, made that life a rather wonderful thing.

In the semi-darkness of the cloak room, several things occurred to him at once; the fact that the first time they'd nearly kissed had been in such a space, and that on this day, their wedding day, did tradition not state that he wasn't meant to see his bride until the big moment? Both of which were soon smothered by having her near.

He hauled her close, figuring *why not*. But she pressed her hand to his chest, stopping him at the last.

"Here," she said, then reached up and fixed his tie. His gaze drifted over her face, that heartbreakingly lovely face, while her fingers fidgeted at his neck.

"I do have attendants you know, either of whom could have told me if my tie was not straight."

"Pfft. As if they'd notice. And in all the years I've known you, you've never been able to get a tie right," she said, giving the knot a final yank.

Ronan slipped his arm around her waist slowly, so as not to startle her, his voice dropping a note as he whispered against her ear, "Did it ever occur to you that I might be completely adept at tying a tie? I just liked the way it felt having you near, fussing over me."

Hadley's hands stilled, her dark gaze locked onto his. "Is that true?"

Arm now fully around her, Ronan spun her till she was backed up against the wall of coats. And she didn't stop him. She was too busy calculating. When her eyes once again found his, they were glinting.

"You are such a rogue," she said.

"And you are such a bossy-boots," he shot back.

Fight flared in her eyes before she said, "You love that about me."

"More than words can say," he agreed, his voice a growl, his need for her sweeping over him.

And when she began to melt in his arms, he had the feeling searching him out to fix his tie was as much a ruse for her as it had ever been for him.

But then she tilted her head away. "Do you hear that?"

"Hear what?" Ronan asked. Her hair was longer now, meaning Ronan was forced to gather it in a twist and toss it over her shoulder so he could press his nose to her neck.

"Knocking," she whispered.

"Ah, guys…" Sawyer's voice came through the door. "The guests are getting restless. We might want to get the party started."

Hadley bit her lip, then gave in and said, "Coming!"

"Not yet, you're not," Ronan affirmed, hand moving over her backside.

"Later," she said, pushing her hips back, laughing and shaking her head at the same time. "We have something more pressing to do right now."

Ronan pulled himself together. "Promise?"

"Today, in this dress? Let's just say I'm a sure thing."

Several minutes later, Ronan stood beneath an ivy-covered arbour at the end of an aisle scattered with soft white rose-petals. Ted and Sawyer stood by his side.

Sawyer and Petra, having secretly married while on a quick trip to Florence, had their bouncing baby boy Claude in tow. Sawyer's mum was currently cradling him in the front row, while Petra's mother, sitting beside her, made kissy cooing noises; neither woman paying attention to the proceedings at all.

One of Adelaid's many brothers was chasing Katie around, which Katie clearly thought was the best game ever, if her screams of laughter were anything to go by, while baby Cary slept in another of Adelaid's many brother's beefy arms.

Ronan caught *his* mother's eye and she gave him a watery smile.

When his father had died, Ronan had attended the private family funeral, standing up beside his mother, holding her hand when his father's surviving brother had presented a eulogy as unflinchingly damning as it was kind. Leaving the world with a fair picture as to the complex man Constantine Gerard had been.

And while he remained stoic throughout, that night, curled up in Hadley's arms, Ronan had cried.

Something that might well happen again today, if the ball of emotion lodged in his throat was anything to go by.

Then the harpist perked up, playing Pachelbel's *Canon in D*. Adelaid and Petra appeared, looking teary, smiley and delightful in dresses of pale green, walking solemnly down the aisle.

The music changed, going up a notch, or maybe that was Ronan's heart thundering madly in his ears as Hadley appeared. Her dress a column of creamy white, the material hugging her in a way that had Ronan picturing monthly projections for all he was worth. Her face was serene, her lips freshly slicked with

red. Her hair, though, was somewhat dishevelled. No doubt due
to their recent shenanigans in the cloak room.

Fine with him; dishevelled was his favourite look on her.

Ronan breathed in and wriggled his toes so that the vastness
of this moment, all that had led up to it, did not take him out.
Besides, Hadley was out there alone, all eyes looking her way.
Nobody was giving her away, as she'd been adamant that the
only person with the right to do that was her.

Which also suited Ronan just fine, especially as she was
willingly giving herself to him. And he to her. Which they had
been doing for some time now. They didn't need any legal papers to make that a reality—they had, after all, been known to
do just fine till now without contracts to bind them.

And yet, here they were, about to promise their lives to one
another in front of friends, family and a flock of seagulls flying over the Finchers' beautiful Mount Martha house, no doubt
hoping to score some crumbs once the party moved to the grand
marquee overlooking the bluff.

Ronan stepped out onto the grass and held out a hand. He
waited for Hadley to take it before helping her up onto the dais.

"Hey," he said. "Long time, no see."

Hadley shot him a look, the kind that levelled him smack,
bang—a kick to the heart. He'd do whatever it took to keep
those looks coming as long as they both did live.

"Ready?" he said.

"Born ready," she answered, though her fierce expression
showed him the thought of promising herself to him was filled
with meaning that went beyond a single day.

Best friends at their sides, the sun shining down from above,
Hadley and Ronan turned to face Jonas, who of course had a
marriage celebrant's licence to go along with every other quali-
fication he had up his sleeve.

Ronan, who still had Hadley's hand in his, used it to pull
her close till they were shoulder to shoulder, side by side. A
matched pair.

When Jonas said the words, "Dearly beloved, we are gathered here today to see these two lovebirds finally tie the knot," the crowd went wild. There was cheering and whooping, making Hadley laugh so hard, she leant against him for support.

When she looked up at him, he stole a kiss. And she let him, lips lingering till they pulled away as one. A little breathless. A whole lot happy.

Certain it would only get better from there.

* * * * *

Beauty And The Prince

Justine Lewis

Justine Lewis writes uplifting, heartwarming contemporary romances. She lives in Australia with her hero husband, two teenagers and an outgoing puppy. When she isn't writing, she loves to walk her dog in the bush near her house, attempt to keep her garden alive and search for the perfect frock. She loves hearing from readers, and you can visit her at justinelewis.com.

Books by Justine Lewis

Billionaire's Snowbound Marriage Reunion
Fiji Escape with Her Boss
Back in the Greek Tycoon's World

Visit the Author Profile page
at millsandboon.com.au.

Dear Reader,

Thank you for picking up (or clicking on) *Beauty and the Playboy Prince* and embarking on a little fairy-tale escapism.

We often use the term "fairy tale" as synonymous with a happy ending, but traditional fairy tales often had darker sides (the Brothers Grimm, Hans Christian Andersen, I'm looking at you). Bad things often happened, especially to women and children, and the stories were later sanitized to resemble the ones we are familiar with today.

Being a royal these days is a little like a fairy tale—in all senses of the word. There might be castles and luxury, but there is also a darker side. Royals enjoy extreme privilege, but it often comes at a high price. Your life and privacy are no longer your own.

Royal status is my hero Ed's burden and destiny, but he is happy and willing to serve. His best friend, Simone, has experienced the darker side of royalty and fame and it isn't a path she wants to choose for herself. Instead, she is happy living above her secondhand bookshop in Paris, away from the public eye. But fate has other ideas for Ed and Simone. I won't give more away. I hope you enjoy their story.

Happy reading,

Justine

For Robby and serendipitous meetings.

Praise for
Justine Lewis

"Justine Lewis will capture every reader's heart with
her poignant, intense and dramatic contemporary
romance, *Billionaire's Snowbound Marriage
Reunion*. A beautifully written tale...this affecting
romantic read will move readers to tears and have
them falling in love with both Lily and Jack."

—Goodreads

PROLOGUE

The Cursed Kingdom
Florenan Fairy Tales, 1786

ONCE UPON A time there was a beautiful kingdom, high in the Alps. In the summer the valleys were green and lush. In the winter snow capped the beautiful peaks. Perched in that kingdom was a beautiful palace and in that palace lived a king.

But the King took all his subjects' money and spent it on cards, dice and horses. His wife left him, taking all the crown jewels. The kingdom was almost bankrupt.

A witch placed a curse over the kingdom saying that the kingdom would be destroyed if the King's sons followed their father and put their own base desires before their people. The witch prophesied that the kingdom could only be saved by a prince who was brave and true and who put his family and his people above himself.

The first Prince loved wine so much he ignored his wife and neglected his country. His wife died of loneliness and a giant earthquake shook the country nearly causing it to crumble into ruins.

The second Prince thought that he had evaded detection by the witch and her curse. He secretly loved many women who were not his wife until one day when he became so distracted by his lovers that the kingdom was invaded. The war ripped the country apart and the Prince had to flee.

And the third Prince? The third Prince vowed to break the curse by always putting his duty first. By staying true to his country and not his base desires.

The third Prince vowed never to marry.

CHAPTER ONE

SIMONE SAID *AU REVOIR* to her last customer, closed the door to the bookshop and slid the steel lock across with a satisfying clunk. In the small office behind the counter, she turned on the television to check on the tennis scores and got to work reconciling the day's accounts. She needed to be quick if she was going to meet her friends, Julia and André, at the bistro down the street.

Tallying the days' takings was thankfully taking longer these days. Business had been steadily picking up over the past few months and she was back on track working towards her savings goal to enable her to, hopefully, buy the bookshop within the next few years.

The bookshop, The Last Chapter, was situated in Simone's favourite part of Paris, the Latin Quarter. Also known as the Fifth Arrondissement, the Latin Quarter was characterised by the sound of bells from churches small and large, the thick wooden doors hiding secret courtyards and the narrow laneways, all winding their way up the gentle hill to the Pantheon.

It was home to black ironwork decorating the windows, flower boxes with blooms of all colours. At street level, it was home to the tempting boulangeries, patisseries, fromageries and wine shops selling world-class wines that even students could afford.

This was a place of students, intellectuals, readers, dreamers with hundreds of years of learning. And, when you were particularly lucky, the smell of baking croissants.

Simone didn't even mind the tourists. They came from all over the world, bringing their own experiences, thoughts and dreams to Paris as they had been doing for centuries. Besides, tourists made up half of her customers.

Simone's boss was a British investor named Mr Grant. He owned the building and the business and spoke regularly about closing the bookshop and opening a convenience store instead. Simone had worked in the bookshop for nearly eight years and had managed it for five. She also lived in a studio apartment on the sixth floor of the same building.

'The bookshop is over a hundred years old,' she'd reminded Mr Grant. 'Think of all the history!'

It was the history of The Last Chapter that had convinced Mr Grant to keep the business operating for a while longer, while Simone saved enough money to be able to purchase it from him.

She glanced at the small television, looking for the tennis scores, but the headline on the ticker tape across the bottom of the screen made her suck in a sharp breath. *Mon Dieu.*

A woman was claiming to be pregnant with the King of Florena's child. The claim might have made some people express shock, but most would simply shrug. If Florena had been any other small European kingdom Simone probably would have done the same. However, Simone had spent the first sixteen years of her life not only in Florena, but in the royal residence, Castle Villeneuve, itself. She knew the King and his family. While she didn't return to Florena often, it was still her home. Her mother still lived there, working for the royal family. Simone could only imagine what they must all be going through.

King Edouard and Queen Isabella had always given the appearance of being, if not a happy couple, at least a functioning one. Their union had resulted in just one child, Prince Edouard, known to Simone as Ed, born exactly nine months after their wedding.

The marriage hadn't been arranged, but it had been beneficial to both. Isabella was the daughter and sole heir of one of the richest men in the world. The royal family of Florena had been struggling financially and reputationally after King Edouard's father, Old King Edouard, had wasted the royal family's private fortune with his reckless spending and womanising. Queen Isabella's fortune had meant the royals did not have to seek assistance from Florenan taxpayers, which had settled the republican cries from certain politicians.

Isabella gained a title and status, the country benefited from the money and connections she brought with her, and the kingdom gained peace and stability.

Young and good-looking, the King and Queen had probably hoped that love would grow.

It hadn't.

But this hadn't been merely indifference. The King had been having an affair and had fathered a child that wasn't the Queen's. Simone's thoughts went to the Queen, but her heart went out to Ed. Her childhood friend and companion.

She grabbed her phone to search for more information than the television was offering her. A twenty-six-year-old woman, Celine, claimed to be in a two-year relationship with King Edouard, who was thirty years her senior. She was now pregnant with their child. The King, or indeed any member of the royal family, was yet to comment. The Queen was reportedly in the Caribbean. The King was in Florena, but hadn't left the palace. And the Prince?

No one knew.

His last official engagement had been in New York as part of his duties as the Florenan trade envoy to North America. Ed's position as trade envoy might have seemed nepotistic, until you learnt that he spoke five languages and held degrees in economics and international relations. Few other thirty-year-olds were as qualified as he was to represent his country.

There was a knock at the door and she groaned. The *Closed* sign, written in seven languages, no less, was clearly visible. She contemplated pretending she wasn't there, but the customer knocked again, hard enough that she worried about the old glass pane shattering.

She poked her head out of her office.

The customer was a taller than average male. He was wearing a baseball cap and, despite the unseasonably warm autumn day, a coat and scarf.

She could have let him in, a customer was a customer after all, but his insistent knocking made her pause.

'Simone, it's me. Let me in.'

Simone moved around the counter and to the door. The man cupped his hands around his face to block out the streetlight and pushed his nose against the old glass to look inside. Their eyes met and she stopped. Green eyes that could still, despite much wishing otherwise, make her heart stop.

It was really him.

Ed.

'Sim, please.'

What was he doing here now? Just when her life was going smoothly. When she was doing just great, thank you very much.

She slid the lock back, but before she turned the knob she paused, took a deep breath, and repeated the mantra she had perfected over the years.

Don't fall. Don't fall.

His palms were pressed against the glass and above them his green eyes pleaded. She pulled open the door and he fell inside, almost landing on her.

'Oh, Sim. Thank goodness.'

'Ed! What on earth are you doing here? Haven't you heard?'

'Why do you think I'm here?'

Ed pulled his cap off, revealing the same mass of light brown curls that had always topped his head, now cut short at the sides and slightly tamed. She wasn't sure how she felt about that.

It's not any of your business how handsome he looks or how he's chosen to wear his hair.

Simone locked the door behind him, still confused. Befuddled. Shocked. And no less clear about what was happening. Ed clearly wasn't in a hurry to enlighten her. He looked around the bookshop.

The Last Chapter was older than any of Simone's grandparents. It covered the ground and first storeys of a narrow slice of the street. Its two floors, along with a substantial part of the narrow staircases, were covered in second-hand books written in several different languages. The previous owner had liked to tell customers that F Scott Fitzgerald, Ernest Hemingway and Gertrude Stein had visited the bookshop—claims that Simone had long ago decided never to try to verify in case they proved false.

Ed put his hands on his hips and surveyed the small room as though he were surveying his vast estates.

'So this is the famous bookshop.'

'I don't think it's famous,' she replied.

She'd made The Last Chapter thrive since she'd taken over the management, but it wasn't yet Shakespeare and Co.

'In the palace it is.'

Simone winced at the idea that they might talk about her at the palace.

'It's great to visit it at last.'

Implicit in his comment was that in the eight years she had managed the bookshop he had never bothered to drop in for a visit.

Though why would he? Even though they had grown up together they had seen very little of one another in the past decade, ever since she was sent away to school and banished from Florena.

'Ed, I don't understand. What's going on?'

'It's lovely. Cosy, rustic. And you've perfectly captured that ancient book aroma.' He picked up the closest book, an old copy of *Florenan Fairy Tales*, thumbed the pages and made a show of breathing in the scent.

An exasperated groan escaped her throat. 'Edouard. Please. What's going on?'

At the sound of his full name Ed's shoulders tensed.

Ed replaced the book from exactly where he had taken it, but still didn't speak.

He walked along the nearest shelf and ran his finger along it, as though searching for something. She didn't know what he was looking for, but doubted he would find it in her small section of German crime novels. He stopped and sighed, but still didn't turn.

Her heart swelled and broke at the same time. Ed was in her bookshop. His beautiful hands touching her books. His tall frame only just fitting under the low ceilings. He was in the same room as her, breathing in the same air, for the first time in years.

'You've heard?'

'Yes. Just then. On the news. But—'

'I expect everyone's heard.'

She might have seen the headline, but she had no idea what Celine's pregnancy would mean for Florena. The country was a small, progressive constitutional monarchy, but still. She had no idea how the royal family would navigate an illegitimate child. Apart from anything, the news must be personally devastating for the Queen. And for Ed.

'Ed, is it really true? It's really your father's child?'

A half-sibling for Ed.

'I assume so.' He shrugged. The attempt at nonchalance didn't hide the stress on his face, which in turn couldn't mask the heartbreak in his eyes.

'When did you...? I mean how long has it been going on?'

'A while.'

'You knew?'

'I knew he was seeing her, yes.'

She tried to keep her expression neutral, knew she'd failed. 'Your mother? Does she know?'

He laughed. 'Celine called her two days ago to tell her.'

'Oh.' Simone didn't even want to imagine how that phone call might have gone. 'But what does it mean? For your parents? For Florena? For Celine?' Simone was a little ashamed that Celine came as an afterthought. She didn't know her, but still.

'Who knows?' Ed threw his arms up to the low ceiling. 'That's what everyone at the palace is tearing their hair out about. If this had happened two hundred years ago Celine would've been given a house, a generous pension and the child would've been given a title. But now?'

Ed glanced out of the window. It was dark outside now and with the lights on any passer-by could see inside the bookshop.

'Is there somewhere more private we could go?' He nodded to the back room. 'I'm trying to keep a low profile.'

'Wait in my office for a moment and let me finish up. I'll be two minutes.'

Simone turned off the television and her computer, checked the alarm system and picked up her phone and keys.

She showed Ed through the storeroom and to the back door.

'It's very rambling, isn't it?' he said.

'I hope that's a compliment,' she grumbled.

'Of course. It's lovely.'

His attempt at flattery grated more than it should have because it highlighted the gulf between them. He would inherit a palace that she had merely lived in as the child of a cook.

The back door led to a staircase that took them up the five flights of stairs to her attic.

'Is there an elevator?' he asked at around the third flight.

'Yes, but I thought you'd like to work on your figure.'

She knew he'd get the joke. Ed was in as good shape as ever.

No one could miss his strong, lean legs, washboard stomach, and shoulders that could rival those of a champion rower.

She wasn't in bad shape herself. After all she walked up and down these stairs several times a day. She still felt self-conscious, though, with him walking behind her, unable to miss the sight of her legs and bottom ascending the stairs, even if he'd wanted to. Not that he had ever, in the twenty-five years they had known one another, shown the slightest interest in her physically.

Once they reached the sixth floor, she slid her keys into the lock and paused before pushing open the door. She shouldn't be ashamed. She loved her apartment. It was perfectly big enough for her and her cat, Belle, and she was proud to be managing her own business.

But she couldn't help looking at her apartment through Ed's eyes. It wasn't vast or stylish. It was most definitely quaint. Too bad. If Ed couldn't see its charm then he could just leave.

She pushed open the door to her one-room apartment.

He placed his small black backpack on her sofa and looked around. One half of the room was her living quarters, with a soft, cotton-covered sofa, a table just large enough for two chairs, some plants, bright prints on the walls and a small bookshelf—because you still needed books, even if you did have an entire bookshop downstairs.

In the other half of the room, behind a gauze curtain that psychologically separated the spaces, but didn't provide much actual privacy, was her double bed.

The kitchen was basic, with only a small fridge, a single sink, an oven and small bench space. Despite being raised by a chef, or maybe because of it, Simone didn't often cook. The bathroom was large enough to fit a sink, shower and toilet, but not much else.

'Is this all? Is there another room?'

She made sure her glare was withering. 'It's an attic in the

Fifth Arrondissement and I manage a second-hand bookshop. I'm doing very well to afford this.'

'I meant, isn't it charming?' he said.

'Were you expecting Versailles?'

'No, Simone. It's lovely. Truly.' He sat on her small sofa, lay back and spread out his arms, making himself quite comfortable. She looked at him, at a loss of where to begin.

Once upon a time, as the fairy tale went, they had been close friends. Friends who squabbled, but adored one another at the same time. He was a year older than she and had been in her life for nearly as long as she could remember. Simone's father had died when she was only four and she and her mother, Alea, had been invited to move into one of the small apartments in the back of the palace, where Alea worked as a cook.

Ed was the only other child who lived in the palace and, even though Ed was the Prince, and she the daughter of one of the staff, the two children had found one another. When Ed hadn't been at school, or doing what young princes did, he'd always sought her out.

Simone had attended day school, and had certainly not done any of the aristocratic activities he had, like horse riding or skiing, so she'd always been around in the palace somewhere. In the kitchen with her mother, in the garden with the dogs, or riding her bike around the beautiful grounds.

The two of them had squabbled and teased each other, but they'd always had one another for company on the weekends when he was home from school and during some of the holidays.

Being with him now was familiar, almost like going home.

She told herself her feelings for him were only platonic, because of their long friendship. Because he reminded her of simpler times. Because he'd been with her through some of the saddest times of her childhood.

Not because the sight of him made her heart race. Or because catching a breath of his scent could make her head swoon. Or because she trembled just thinking about pressing her body up against his and…

Platonic. That was all her feelings were. All they ever would be. She might have had a childish crush on Ed once upon a time, but she had well and truly moved past that. She'd had to.

'Wine?' she asked.

'I thought you'd never ask.'

'It's not fancy.'

'Thank goodness. I plan to drink it quickly.'

She hid her smile. They would be fine. Two old friends catching up over a drink. She could manage this without getting any ideas that it might be something more. She took a bottle of cheap Bordeaux from the rack and uncorked it before sitting on the sofa next to him, being careful not to brush against him.

She poured two generous glasses and let him take a few sips before saying, 'I'm so sorry again. What a shock.'

He shrugged. 'Yes, but also no. The thing I can't get my head around is that I'm going to have a half-sibling. At thirty!'

Ed was at the age where he might have been having children himself, but he was the Playboy Prince. Unmarried. Unattached. And seemingly proud of it.

'Have you spoken to your mother? How is she?'

'Furious. He's always been much more discreet.'

'What do you mean? Always?'

'About all his affairs.'

'*All* his affairs? There've been others?'

Ed gave her another quizzical look. 'You must have known.'

'I mean… I guess I didn't think he'd been faithful. But two years is a relationship.'

'I mean, *you* must have known.' He stared at her, waiting for a response.

'I've never had an affair with him!'

He burst into laughter. 'That's not I meant.'

What did he mean? What did any of it mean?

'Ed, what's going on? Why are you here?'

He put his glass down. 'I was actually hoping I might be able to stay.'

CHAPTER TWO

'STAY? HERE?' Ed watched as Simone looked around her apartment, such as it was. If he'd realised she lived in a studio he might have thought twice. But his need to see Simone had overwhelmed everything else. When he'd received the phone call from his father, telling him he was going to have a baby brother or sister, one of his first thoughts had been of Simone. Growing up, she had always been there for him. And now he needed her more than ever.

Ed had jumped on the first plane from New York to Paris as soon as he'd received his father's order to come home. But in the seven hours it had taken the plane to cross the Atlantic further developments had caused his father to call again and say, 'Stay where you are. Lie low.'

When his father had said this, Ed had thought of Simone again and how fortunate it was that he had flown into Paris. She was safety, security and home.

His parents' marriage had always been unhappy. His home not filled with love, but with tension. From his early childhood Simone and her mother, Alea, had provided the home he craved. Even though they had drifted apart over the years, Simone was still the person he trusted most in the world. The news that he would have a sibling had made that suddenly very clear to him. He'd *needed* to see her.

He realised now he'd put his own selfish feelings above any thought for her reality. The apartment, which was really just one room, was barely large enough for Simone. If she lived here with someone else then they must share a very intimate relationship. He looked at the bed, possibly the smallest double he'd ever seen. The idea of sharing a small bed with Simone sent an unexpected jolt through him. The tabloids might say that he, the Playboy Prince, was happy to share a bed with the nearest warm body, but the tabloids exaggerated. And Simone wasn't like any other woman. She was his oldest and dearest friend.

The sofa where they sat was on the same scale as the bed: cosy. He and Simone sat hip to hip on the sofa, which wasn't unpleasant, but the warmth of Simone's leg against his was certainly distracting. Two years it had been, maybe three, since they'd seen one another. And she was different, though he couldn't pinpoint why.

'I know it's sudden. Celine spoke publicly before the palace got their story straight and a plan in place. Press are camped outside the palace, with more flying into Florena each hour. Father told me to stay here and lie low. It'll probably just be one night.'

Simone drew and released a deep breath before saying, 'Yes, of course. But don't you need to be there?'

'You'd think,' he mumbled, mostly to himself.

While it would be years—decades, even—before he became King, he was still the Prince. The King's only child. He wanted to be there to help. The matter involved him too. Most of all he wanted to help his father decide on the plan of action. The King had several options, but there was one in particular Ed really didn't want him to choose.

'Maybe he wants to spare you from it?'

'It's his scandal, not mine. Doesn't it look worse if I'm not there? Like I don't support him?'

'I don't know.'

She shrugged and looked as confused as he felt. In the craziness of the past day it was such a relief to be here, with her. She lifted her feet and tucked them under her bottom. He liked her hair. It was even longer than when he'd seen her last. Dark blonde, and falling in messy waves down her back. Her face was shaped like a heart and her eyes as brown and bright as ever.

She had been adorable as a kid, with big eyes, blonde curls and chubby cheeks. He wasn't quite used to her seeing her older. Grown up. He still sometimes saw the four-year-old he had unexpectedly stumbled across one day in his garden. He hadn't been much older. No one had told him another kid was moving in. Discovering her playing with his dog had been like magic. A friend he'd always wanted. A playmate who would play hide and seek and all sorts of games with him. A confidante who, despite their different backgrounds, still understood what it was like to live in the beautiful yet secluded palace.

He also remembered her as an uncertain teenager. The friend he'd seek out when he returned from school every holiday. Simone and Alea's apartment in the palace had been an oasis away from his cold parents. Alea's kitchen always warm and welcoming. His parents didn't even love each other enough to bicker, but Simone and her mother had always shown unconditional love and support. When someone mentioned the word 'home' his thoughts always flickered to Simone's apartment before duty focused them back on the palace proper.

Now, sitting on the sofa next to him, he saw child, teenager and woman all at once. The chubbiness of her cheeks had vanished, leaving cheekbones. Her bright blonde curls were darker and heavy with the weight of her thick, long hair. But her beautiful big brown round eyes remained the same. And they were looking at him now with concern.

'What do you think will happen? With your parents…?'

'Divorce? Probably. But then there's the issue of Mother's money. Her fortune has been paying for the running and the upkeep of the palaces and the family's expenses. Mother's father left me some money, but it is nowhere near the same amount. Besides, I don't know if she'll give Father the satisfaction of being able to marry Celine. It could get messy. I don't know if he even wants to marry Celine.'

'What about the baby?'

'I'm sure he'll look after it. He'll have to acknowledge it.'

A baby. A sibling. Twenty-four hours later he was still struggling to process the news. Ed couldn't think of another monarchy that had faced such a crisis in modern times. Sure, there were monarchs who had kids out of wedlock. But usually not when they were still married to someone else.

It would be a good enough reason, he thought, to get rid of the monarchy altogether.

The Florenans were generally proud of their independence, but there were always those who argued that the country would be better off if it were subsumed into another larger country. Like France or Italy. The current Prime Minister, Pierre Laurent, was in favour of making closer ties with France, the country of his birth. Ed had tried to raise his concerns about Laurent with his father, but the King had laughed them off.

'Nonsense. The people will never agree to that. I've seen off six Prime Ministers. Besides, the people love us. The House of Berringer has been around for five hundred years and we'll be here long after Pierre Laurent.'

Simone poured him another glass of wine and topped hers up. 'I don't have anything much to eat, I'm afraid. I could order something in.'

'Whatever you were going to have would be fine,' he said.

She looked down. 'I was going out.'

He was an idiot. He should have realised that she had a life. Plans.

'I'm sorry. A hot date?'

'No, just dinner with some friends.'

The relief he felt when she said that was almost physical, but he still said, 'You should go. I'll be fine here.'

How would he have felt if she had said she had a date? Uneasy? Sad? And that was silly. Simone was his friend.

She's probably had many boyfriends you don't know about. Look at her, she's gorgeous.

He was trying not to look at her, because each time he did his body tensed and his head became lighter.

Exhaustion. That was all it was. Nothing more. This was Simone, and he didn't get tense or lightheaded around Simone.

'No. It's okay. I see them all the time. I haven't seen you in...'

Two years.

She'd seemed to avoid Florena more and more the older she got.

'You didn't visit last Christmas.'

'Managing the bookshop...it's too hard. I open every day, except Christmas.'

'You work seven days a week?'

She shrugged. 'I'm saving up to buy this place one day.'

'Really?'

'Yes.' She sat up straight. 'What's wrong with that?'

'Nothing, it's great. This apartment?'

She nodded. 'And the bookshop. And I'm on track.'

'Wow, that's great.'

'You sound surprised.'

He was, but that was on him, not her. They hadn't spent much time together at all in the past decade, and without him realising it she'd become a grown-up. Not just a grown-up. A successful, impressive, beautiful grown-up. Who was about to own a bookshop and an apartment in the middle of Paris. She'd flourished since leaving Florena as a sixteen-year-old.

'I'm impressed, but not surprised.'

She gave him a crooked grin. Even when she made a face she was gorgeous.

Something inside him twisted. She didn't have a hot date tonight but was there someone special around? If there was he wanted to meet him.

And yet he also didn't.

'So, is it just you living here?' That sounded casual enough.

'Oh, no. My five flatmates are out.'

He stared, open-mouthed, long enough for her to laugh.

'Of course it's just me. There's barely room enough for you!'

He felt his face warm. 'I meant, is there…? That is, are you seeing anyone?'

Now it was her time to pause and study his face before answering. It was none of his business if she was seeing someone, but as her friend he wanted to know. He needed to know that she was all right. That whoever she was with was not someone like his cheating father.

She tilted her head to one side, delaying her answer even longer. With every moment the pause lasted a knot grew tighter and tighter in his stomach.

She was seeing someone. And it was serious. She was about to tell him she was engaged. Or about to be.

And he realised he didn't want that. That was…wrong. Simone married to some Parisian.

'No. There's no one.'

He exhaled. More loudly than he'd expected. Why had she taken so long to answer? More to the point, why had so much seemed to hang on her answer?

He and Simone were only friends. Besides, Ed had no plans to enter into a serious relationship—now or ever. Royal marriages were rarely happy marriages. They had even less chance than celebrity matches. Edouard Henri Guillaume, Prince of Florena, was the latest in a long line of Princes Edouard, none of whom were known for their fidelity. His father's scandal was just the latest in a long line. Ed was not going to risk his country's future on a royal marriage that would likely end the same way.

While Ed's faithfulness had never been tested—he'd never had a relationship that had lasted long enough to give it a serious stress test—he was the Playboy Prince. Everyone knew that. And Playboy Princes didn't magically change their stripes just because they were married. Genetics were not on his side. The best way to prevent another royal divorce was simply not to get married in the first place.

Which meant no wife and no children, and he was content with that. One of his cousins, or one of their many offspring, could inherit the throne. He also had no wish to bring into the world a child who would endure the same loveless, stilted childhood that he'd had. Who would watch one parent flirt with every female staff member. Watch the other slowly drink herself into oblivion.

Simone got up and moved around the small kitchen. He studied her back as she assembled a plate with some bread, cheese and hummus. Her movements were fluid, her curves hypnotising and very watchable. Though that could have been the transatlantic trip catching up with him.

She put the plate on the coffee table.

'A feast,' he said.

'Don't joke. I wasn't expecting to eat here myself, let alone entertain royalty.'

'It's great, and honestly I'm not very hungry.'

She looked at him as if she didn't believe him. She knew him too well.

'We can order something in if you like. This isn't exactly up to my mother's standard.'

Alea, an acclaimed chef, had stayed working for the King even after everything that had happened between the two of them. Ed had never been able to work out why, but he conceded there were many things he was destined never to understand about romantic relationships.

They ate the food and drank the rest of the wine. 'The bookshop is great. Truly. Why a bookshop?'

'I've always loved reading. But more than that I've always loved sharing books. A big part of my business is helping people track down out-of-print books. The bookshop is just one part of the business. Much of what I do is online.'

The certainty she had about her ambition was inspiring. He'd had no idea growing up that this was her dream. 'When did you realise this was what you wanted to do?

'Not long after I was sent away. Banished.'

'You weren't banished.'

'Yes, I was.'

'You were sent away for your own protection.'

She scoffed. 'My protection? It was a bit late for that.'

'Yes. Your protection. In case anyone found out.'

It was strange that she didn't remember, but it had been a strange and stressful time. His father had grown very close to Simone's mother gradually over the years. As their affair had developed the King, Alea and the other staff had been anxious to protect Simone from any fallout and his father had paid for Simone's boarding school fees. Ed suspected that having Simone out of the apartment had suited his father as much as his professed motive of protecting her from scandal.

Simone had jumped at the chance to leave the palace and study in Switzerland, and Ed hadn't realised at the time that it would mean that Simone would never return to live in Florena again.

'But they did find out. The video got out,' Simone said.

'What video?'

Ed's stomach dropped. It had been a day of earth-shattering scandals in his family, but he was sure he'd have remembered a video of the King and Simone's mother.

'What video? The one of me embarrassing myself in front of everyone at your seventeenth.'

Ed rubbed his eyes. It was early afternoon in New York and he'd missed a whole night's sleep. But he must be more exhausted than he realised.

He didn't remember any video from his seventeenth, but when he saw Simone's mouth fall open he stopped and, fortunately, had enough sense not to blurt out the first thing on his mind.

Was it possible that Simone didn't know about the affair his father and her mother had conducted for at least a year?

No. That would be absurd. She must have known.

Simone had been sent away to school. Not only to protect her from any fallout if the affair became known but also to hide it from her. Was it possible her mother—nor anyone else for that matter—had never told her? Was it possible she'd never figured it out?

CHAPTER THREE

WAS HE SERIOUS? How could he have forgotten about the video? *What video? The* video. The one that had ruined her life. Shaped the course of everything that had come after it. The single most embarrassing, frightening and heartbreaking moment of her life.

'This is not the time to joke,' she said.

He held up his hands. 'I'm not joking.'

'You're seriously telling me you don't know about the video of me making a fool of myself at your party?'

He looked genuinely pained with confusion, his green eyes wide and innocent.

'I honestly have no idea. What video? Please tell me.'

'I don't want to talk about it.'

She crossed her arms. If he didn't remember she didn't want to enlighten him. That would be like reliving the whole horrible experience again.

She had devised a plan. To her deluded, infatuated, teenage brain it had seemed like the perfect plan.

Ed had been about to turn seventeen and in one more year would go abroad to university. His head was beginning to be turned by the glamorous young women who had constantly been thrown into his path. He'd been growing particularly close to a girl called Morgane, the daughter of friends of his parents.

Morgane had always been finding some excuse to visit him at the palace.

The world had been at Ed's feet. If he was ever going to love Simone she had known it had to be then. Before he saw too much of the world and realised that she, provincial Simone, who had never even left Florena, was not good enough for a prince. It had been then or never.

Her dilemma had been that if she told Ed she loved him and he didn't feel the same way she'd jeopardise their friendship. So she had devised a way to let him know she loved him without actually making a declaration. Plausible deniability and all that. She'd decided she would sing to him, and if he loved her too he'd think the song was about him. He'd come to her and they would fall into each other's arms and be together for ever and ever.

Simone had helped Ed and his assistant organise the party. They'd chosen a nineteen-eighties theme, with arcade games, glo-sticks and, most importantly, karaoke.

Her plan had been much more subtle than actually coming straight out and saying, *Ed, I'm in love with you*. But if he felt the same way surely he'd understand what she was saying.

Best-laid plans and all that... The sound system hadn't been terrific. And it hadn't helped that she'd chosen a song that stretched even the best singers in the world—*I Will Always Love You*, the Dolly Parton/Whitney Houston classic.

It had turned out that Simone's voice sounded different in the summer house than it did in the shower.

There had been laughter and sniggers. Ed hadn't laughed, but he hadn't said anything either, being too busy talking to Morgane all night.

He hadn't returned her feelings. But, she'd reasoned, as she'd cried into her pillow that night, at least she hadn't come right out and told him. Heartbreak was bad enough without the other person knowing how much they'd hurt you. At least she hadn't had to face the pain of having him reject her to her face.

She had decided she would get a good night's sleep and in the morning Ed would have forgotten all about it.

But the next day it had been everywhere.

All over social media and the front page of the newspaper, the *Daily Florenan*. She'd been made into a hashtag, for crying out loud.

And cry she had. Alone in her room. All that day and into the next.

And the things they'd written about her. The comments on the video had been merciless. All of them mean. Some dark. A few telling her to end her life.

She'd been a sixteen-year-old kid.

The next day her mother had come to her room and asked how she felt about going to school in Switzerland for a semester. Simone had never heard a plan that sounded so good. She'd known she was being sent away in disgrace, but she hadn't cared,

One semester had turned into six, and she'd never had to live in Florena again.

She swirled the stem of her wine glass, hoping Ed would change the subject.

But he pressed on. 'Do you know why you went to boarding school?'

She scoffed. 'Of course I know. Do *you* know?'

He nodded.

'Then I don't know why we're even talking about this.'

She tore off a piece of bread and loaded it up heavily with hummus. Two hours ago she'd been happily going about her life, but now Ed was making himself at home on her couch, digging up old memories and picking at her emotional wounds.

'So tell me,' she said. 'Why do you think I left?'

'No, no. You first.'

She took a swig of wine. She might as well tell the story first. Her way.

'You remember your seventeenth birthday?'

'Yes, I was there.'

The grin he gave her almost made her stop talking. He was impossible. Gorgeous and utterly, completely impossible. She looked at the spot on the wall where the paint was peeling rather than looking at his sparkly, teasing green eyes.

'There were lots of people at the party. Friends of yours. Friends of your parents.'

'And you.'

'Yeah.'

Did he remember what she'd been wearing? A red dress chosen specially that had been at the absolute top of her budget. Still not as fancy as the couture worn by some of the other guests. Did he remember how her hair had looked? Sleek and straightened and shinier than it had been before or since.

No. He did not.

Still, if he didn't remember the dress or the hair, maybe he didn't remember the singing.

'It was in the summer house...' she said.

'Nineteen-eighties theme. We hired Space Invaders machines,' he added.

He did remember. Some of it at least.

She drew a deep breath. 'And I, being a stupid sixteen-year-old, thought it would be a good idea to sing.'

He didn't speak. He just let her keep talking.

'I chose the wrong song. And I made a mess of it.'

'It wasn't that bad.'

'Thank you for saying that, but we both know it was. And I was destroyed.'

'Destroyed? By whom?'

'By the world! Everyone on social media. I was a hashtag.'

His eyes were blank, jaw slack.

'You don't remember?'

'Of course I do. I just didn't think it was that bad.'

'Not that bad?' Ed might have been oblivious to what her

gesture meant, but the rest of the world hadn't. They had all deduced correctly that she'd been trying to serenade him.

'Sim, sweetheart. I had no idea you felt this way about it.'

'Well, it was awful. I was hashtag *palaceserenade*.'

'Please don't think for a second that I'm trying to diminish or dismiss what you went through, but I do understand.'

She crossed her arms.

Ed leant towards her, his green eyes holding hers in a caring gaze. For a moment she thought he might lift his hand and brush her cheek. Simone pulled her gaze away from his.

Don't fall. Don't fall.

'As someone who's been the subject of many hashtags, and more than his fair share of memes, I do understand. And what I've learnt is that the rest of the world never thinks as much about you as you think they do. I bet no one in Florena even remembers it.'

'Oh, they do.'

Each time Simone visited Florena the trolls would somehow find her. Once a photo of her in a supermarket had made it onto social media. Another time a photo of her and Alea in a café had done the rounds. With the usual number of hateful messages, comments and threats.

She wasn't a celebrity. She had been a sixteen-year-old girl at a private party. The trolls still came after her. She'd been such a liability to the palace she'd been sent away to boarding school. Ed could be blasé about it—he was always in the public eye—but he could handle it. She didn't have that kind of strength.

'Really? I'd almost forgotten.'

He had completely forgotten. Because he'd barely noticed in the first place. He'd forgotten because his life had moved on. But that video was still on the internet. With all the vile comments.

'It's different for you,' she said.

'Why? Because I'm a prince? Does that make me immune from mockery? Laughter?' He placed his wine glass down and stood. 'Maybe I should go.'

Oh, no. This wasn't what she'd meant.

She stood too and reached for his arm. 'Ed, no. Please. I'm sorry. It was insensitive of me.'

It was only then, once he was looking down at her hand gripping his, that she realised how close she was to him. And how outrageously strong his biceps felt under her grip.

'Ed, please stay.'

He nodded. 'I know you didn't mean it. I know it *is* different for me. I have the protection of the palace. I've been trained to cope. And you were only sixteen. Besides, you should've been safe in the palace. It was meant to be a private party.'

She nodded.

Growing up, he had confided in her many times about the intrusiveness of photographers. About how it felt to have his every move scrutinised. He was fortunate that his parents had made sure he had been supported, counselled and given techniques to manage the peculiar psychological stressors that came with being a prince.

'I'm sorry.' She gave his arm another gentle squeeze. Damn, it felt good. If only she could slide her hand up to his shoulder, slip it around his neck and…

Ed shook his head. 'No, I'm sorry. I didn't realise how much it had affected you.'

'Well, yes, one stupid song changed my life. But I suppose if I hadn't been filmed I wouldn't have had to leave Florena and then I wouldn't live here.'

She threw her arms wide. She loved her apartment, her bookshop and her life in Paris.

The look he returned was unreadable, but the way he twisted his body just enough to free himself from her touch spoke volumes. They were both upset but he couldn't leave. And she didn't want him to leave like this.

She poured them both another glass of wine and he sat. They settled in for an evening of chatting about his travels and work and her bookshop, the books they'd been reading, the podcasts they had been listening to. Avoiding talk of palace gossip and their teenage years.

Eventually, when her eyelids were drooping, he said, 'You should go to bed. You have to work tomorrow, I assume.'

She nodded. 'Do you want the bed? I'll take the couch.'

'I won't accept it. You're the one doing me the favour.'

'But the couch is tiny. Barely big enough for me.'

'Which is exactly why I won't let you take it.'

He could share your bed.

And what if her hands had a life of their own in the middle of the night? What if her unconscious self couldn't help sliding over to his side of the bed? How would she explain that?

'Wait a minute. Do you have any bags? Were you travelling with anyone?' Simone asked.

'I left the airport right away—as soon as I saw the message from Father. My valet took everything and went on to Florena.'

'So you have nothing?'

He looked down at his backpack. 'A toothbrush but not much else. It'll be okay. I'll have a call to return home by the morning.'

It would only be one night.

'We could share?'

The air was suddenly as thick as her voice sounded.

Her heart beat hard in her chest several times before he answered, 'Are you sure?'

'We've slept together before.'

His mouth dropped.

'When we were kids,' she said. 'Sleepovers, sleep-outs!'

'It's not quite the same thing.' He spoke slowly, carefully.

She'd gone too far. 'We're just friends. We might be a little older. But we're still just friends.'

If she kept saying it enough it might eventually become true.

He didn't speak for a very long time—so long that she was sure her cheeks must be the colour of a stop sign.

'Are you sure?' he asked.

She exhaled. 'I think I can manage to keep my hands off you,' she joked.

He leant towards her. Close enough that she could feel the heat from his body. He stared at her. Raised one eyebrow.

'What if I can't?'

He didn't smile, and a whoosh swept through her body.

The thought of Ed not being able to keep his hands off her was absurd. So why wasn't he laughing?

She looked into the depths of his eyes, so closely she could see the flecks of gold. And something else. Suddenly each breath felt as if she was dragging bricks into her lungs. There was no oxygen in the air, and something was pressing on her chest.

He turned his head and cleared his throat. 'I'm just worried your snoring will keep me awake.'

He smiled and the spell was broken.

Simone bumped his upper arm gently. 'I doubt you'll be able to hear my snoring over your own.'

She grabbed her pyjamas and changed in the bathroom. She washed her face and brushed her teeth—her usual evening routine, but it felt so strange with Ed being just outside the door. Ed Berringer was in her attic. His tall, athletic frame was sprawled on her small bed.

Oh, Ed... It was so much easier to forget him and push her feelings to one side than it was to face them. She managed when she wasn't near him. When he was simply an idea, not a living, breathing man. But tonight he was a living, breathing, beautiful man who was going to sleep in her bed.

No. She'd got over Ed once before. She was not going to put herself through that again.

Climbing carefully into bed so as not to bump him, she said, 'Will you be able to sleep?'

'Eventually. I need to get back onto European time anyway. Thanks again.'

'You don't have to thank me. You're welcome any time. I'm glad you felt you could come to me.'

The smile he gave her melted every single muscle in her heart.

Don't fall. Don't fall.

It was just a childish crush and she'd made herself get over it once before.

She was about to turn and begin what would surely be a restless night when she remembered.

'Wait. Why did you think I was sent away from Florena?'

'Oh, just that… The song. The video.'

'Really? But you mentioned an affair?'

'Yes. The hashtag *palaceserenade* affair.'

She sighed. That was all he meant.

She could feel him shuffling next to her, trying to make himself comfortable. She turned out her bedside light and the room fell into darkness.

'Goodnight, Ed.'

'Goodnight, Sim. I hope the foxes don't get you.'

She smiled. They had camped out a few times in the palace garden one summer. They had put up a tent and toasted marshmallows on a small camp stove. They had made a pact to stay up all night, but they'd fallen asleep in the early hours, exhausted. They must have been nine or ten maybe.

'Do you remember when we camped in the garden?'

'Of course. We did it a few times. I was so lucky to have you growing up. And now. I know we haven't seen much of each other lately, but I really do think of you like family,' he said into the darkness.

She sighed.

He thinks of you as a sister.

Eventually his breathing became steadier and deeper. She knew he was asleep.

He wasn't in her bed by choice, only by circumstance. She didn't want something to happen between them simply because she was the nearest warm body. Besides, her and Ed was impossible. The last thing she wanted was to return to Florena and its hateful press. The last thing she wanted was to face the scrutiny that would come from dating Prince Edouard the Playboy Prince.

She chanted this to herself over and over, before she finally fell asleep.

CHAPTER FOUR

ED OPENED THE windows and the sounds of the street floated in. Snatches of conversation, cutlery clinking on plates, a television in another language and over it all the contented hum of the city. Below him the street was already bustling with Parisians going about their day. Including Simone.

He wasn't sure when she had left as he'd been in a deep, deep sleep. Exhaustion, jetlag and maybe one too many glasses of wine had thankfully, meant he'd slept soundly. Now he was awake the real nightmare began again.

There were no messages from either of his parents and neither answered his calls.

He located the coffee machine in the small kitchen, and brewed himself a cup.

He scrolled through his tablet as he drank his coffee and searched for the most recent press about his father. He'd tried calling his father's advisers, but those who answered told him they knew nothing. He should be back in Florena, showing support for his father. Being the respectable face of the monarchy.

Ha! Respectable! No wonder his father wanted him to stay away.

Ed was far from innocent. Though he was hardly as promiscuous as the tabloids would have people believe. Maybe about a tenth of their reports about him had any substance.

Still, his name was almost never printed without the words 'The Playboy Prince' preceding it. Ed enjoyed a party as much as the next single thirty-year-old, but he wasn't amoral. He'd never cheated on anyone because he'd never stayed with any woman long enough for it to be an issue. If his father couldn't stay faithful, if his grandfather couldn't stay faithful, what made Ed think he could? It was much simpler not to marry.

He wasn't the falling in love type. Just like his father and grandfather. Ed's duty was to his country first and foremost. While he was young Ed was travelling the world promoting Florena and its economic interests. A life in the air left no time for serious relationships. And in the future—hopefully many years in the future—he intended to fulfil his role as King alone.

That way he could avoid the type of scandals that had plagued his forefathers. Loveless marriages inevitably led to infidelities, unhappiness and scandal. Not to mention unhappy children who didn't understand why their parents only spoke to one another sarcastically, if they even bothered to speak to one another at all.

Apart from dating, which as far as he knew wasn't a crime, he was a respectable person. He'd studied diligently and worked hard. He treated everyone with respect and avoided trouble. He had done everything expected of him as a prince. And he'd done it well. Which was why it went against every fibre of his being to stay here and not return home to help figure out a way through this mess.

You could just leave. Get on the next flight.

He could, but his father had ordered him to stay away. His king had told him to stay where he was. So he must.

Besides, going home would mean leaving Simone. He wasn't ready to do that. His instinct to come here had been spot-on. Last night had been calm. He could relax with her. Say exactly what he was thinking and feeling. With her, the troubles and worries seemed that much further away. If he couldn't be in Florena this was where he wanted to be.

He flicked on the small television. The news channel had his father's news rotating across the ticker tape every five minutes or so, simply described as 'a disgrace'.

Ed held degrees in government and international affairs. He spoke several languages. Why didn't his father want him in Florena?

He looked down at his clothes. The same outfit he'd been in for over twenty-four hours now. He looked up 'clothing delivery Paris'. If he bought a change of clothes and other supplies his father was bound to summon him home immediately. He ordered some clothes and pyjamas from his favourite designer and paid for an urgent delivery.

But the call from the palace didn't come.

A noise outside the window caught his attention. A black cat was on the window ledge, meowing to come in. Belle. He opened the window and the cat jumped inside. She weaved between his legs and he stroked her behind the ears.

To his mind, there were three main ways this could play out. First, his father might decide to divorce his mother and marry Celine and weather the fallout. Second, Laurent might insist he put the question of the monarchy to the people as a vote. Ed wasn't sure how that would play out. Even a narrow win for the monarchy would still feel like a loss.

But there was a third possibility. The worst possibility of all. One he didn't dare think about.

Abdication.

Ed knew he would be King—he'd been training his whole life for it and had made his peace with it. But not yet.

And not like this.

The journalist on the television was interviewing a woman who was saying that the most important person in the whole royal scandal was the unborn child. Once upon a time he'd wanted a sibling, and then Simone had come along. That little

222 BEAUTY AND THE PRINCE

girl he'd stumbled across one morning in the garden, tossing a
ball to Suzette, his dog. They had played for hours and later he
had thanked his parents for getting him a sister.

They'd laughed mercilessly. 'Oh, darling. She's with the staff.
She's not your sister.'

But if they'd thought she was beneath him they hadn't seemed
to mind that Simone had kept him occupied. They hadn't seemed
to notice the hours and hours he'd spent with her in the palace
kitchens, or in Simone's apartment, eating with her, watching
television, playing games, because neither of them had seemed
to notice anything he did unless he got into trouble.

Ed had seen Simone irregularly since she'd gone away to
school, because of his study, travels and work. He shouldn't
have taken her friendship for granted. He should have visited
this apartment before now. Made more of an effort to see her
whenever he was in Paris.

He had been busy with his studying, his job and other official business. And other women. But it was also true that he
had taken her, his oldest and dearest friend, for granted.

It was hard to shake away the guilt. While neglecting his
best friend wasn't as bad as anything his father had done, it still
wasn't the behaviour of the man he wanted to be.

Ed pulled out his phone and searched for the video she had
claimed was the reason she'd been sent to boarding school. A
video he had pretended to remember, but in reality had no rec-
ollection of.

He searched for hashtag *palaceserenade*, certain that there
would be no results. But there it was. There *she* was. A sixteen-
year-old Simone, belting out 'I Will Always Love You'. She
didn't have a bad voice, but it was a difficult song for anyone.
Let alone a kid in a room full of people whom he saw were jeer-
ing her. But she held her head high and kept going through it all.

His heart ached for the sixteen-year-old. She was gorgeous.
She looked different from the way she usually had back then.

Her blonde hair was straightened and sleek. The red dress showing more skin than he thought a sixteen year old should.

What had possessed her to sing that song? Other people had been singing, but he didn't recall anyone taking the karaoke as seriously as Simone had. He hadn't thought about that night in years. As far as he was concerned his seventeenth birthday had been much like his sixteenth. A palace-sanctioned party with as many of his parents' friends as his own.

He watched the video a second time and then read the comments. They were pretty horrible, and would have been devastating to read as a sixteen-year-old. But those comments and that video were not the reasons his father had paid for Simone's boarding school fees or her university tuition. Did she really think he would have done that over one video?

He watched it a third time and smiled. Sixteen-year-old Simone might have been mortified, but he'd bet if she watched it now, at twenty-nine years old, she'd marvel at the courage of that girl. At how gorgeous she looked.

He paused the video and looked at the frozen frame.

She doesn't know about the affair my father and her mother conducted. She probably thinks her mother paid her school fees.

He could understand Simone not knowing at the time, his father had been discreet, but surely at some point someone would have told her.

He looked at sixteen-year-old Simone, frozen in time. Saw the dreamy look in her beautiful eyes.

Was it his place to tell her about the affair? Probably not. It wasn't his secret to tell.

The only thing he did know was that he wanted to see her. Not the sixteen-year-old, but the beautiful twenty-nine-year-old woman downstairs, going about her day. Running her own business in one of the most beautiful parts of the world.

You could go downstairs.

And be seen? No. He pulled out his laptop. There was a day's worth of emails to catch up on. He was still the Crown Prince and Trade Envoy and had responsibilities. He set to work.

Simone didn't know what she'd expected to find when she went back upstairs that evening. But it wasn't baking.

Her apartment smelt of her mother. Of home. The source of the aroma—a plate of madeleines fresh from the oven—sat on her kitchen table.

'Are you trying to make me homesick?'

'Why? Have I?'

Simone turned her head so he wouldn't see the tears welling in her eyes. She closed her eyes and breathed in deeply. To steady herself and banish the tears. The madeleines reminded her of her mother. She missed her deeply. So much it made her ache. They spoke most days, and Alea came to Paris whenever she could. She loved it as much as Simone, and not living in the same city was hard.

'I take it you haven't heard from the palace?'

He shook his head.

'I'm sorry.'

Simone reached over and touched his shoulder. He was wearing a soft cashmere sweater and felt warm and delicious under her touch. Her hand tingled and the sensation spread up her arm. He lifted his own hand and placed it on hers, rubbing it slightly.

If only she could move closer and slip her hand all the way across his shoulders. Slide into his lap and...

'I'm sure they know you care,' she said, trying to string a sentence together even though her body was bursting with sparks.

'You're stuck with me a little longer.'

'I told you—you can stay as long as you need.'

She took her hand away with regret, because if she didn't do it now she just might slide it up to his neck, into his soft hair and...

She had to change the subject. 'I can't believe you baked. And madeleines!'

He passed her one and she took it gratefully. Sweet, with just the right amount of softness and chewiness.

'It's the only thing I know how to bake. Your mother taught me.'

Simone remembered a twelve-year-old Ed, always begging for the biscuits and watching Alea make them. Simone marvelled that Ed had actually remembered how to bake them. Just like her mother's.

You're older now. Stronger. You can do this.

He looked up, their eyes met, and her stomach swooped. This was bad. Very bad. As a kid her affection for him had been innocent. She'd adored him, but when her mind had leapt forward to what might happen if they should ever actually kiss she hadn't known what would happen next. Everything after a chaste, Disney-movie-like kiss had been unknown to her.

She hadn't experienced deep physical desire until she'd come to Paris. Since then she'd gravitated to men who looked nothing like Ed, and had several fulfilling physical relationships. She'd convinced herself she was really physically attracted to a different sort of man, and that her feelings for Ed were platonic only.

'You got some new clothes,' she remarked. 'Thank goodness. I didn't want to say anything, but the smell…' She held her nose and waved her hand.

He laughed—as well he might. Despite his wearing the same outfit for twenty-four hours, there was nothing she found offputting about his scent at all. And now, with fresh baking and a freshly showered and changed Ed, her apartment had never smelt as good.

Careful, Simone. Careful.

This was good. Banter. Teasing. Like when they were kids. Before she'd been swamped with adolescent hormones and decided she had a crush on him. If she teased him he wouldn't realise how close she was to burying her face in his neck.

'And there's more.'

Ed stepped to one side and revealed an eclectic feast. Fresh bread, cheese and a bottle of Burgundy. He lifted the lid off the casserole dish on top of the stove to reveal a simmering chicken casserole.

'You made coq au vin? How?'

'Is it still your favourite?'

'Do you expect me to believe you cooked this?'

'Why couldn't I cook this?'

She levelled him with a look.

'Okay, you've got me on the casserole. It was pre-prepared. I didn't think you'd thank me if I made it.'

She laughed.

'But I did bake.'

She nodded. That she believed.

'I wanted to thank you. For letting me impose another night.'

Another night. In the same bed as Ed. It was just as well he'd shown some appreciation for what he was putting her body through.

Before she realised what was happening, his large hand enveloped hers—warm and secure. His thumb brushed against her wrist and her body swayed.

'I'm very grateful. I know we haven't seen much of one another lately, and I know I'm putting you out. But I'm very glad I'm here with you.'

She looked into his eyes. They were earnest and serious. Deep and soulful.

Don't fall. Don't fall.

'It's been an awful few days and there is no one else who understands me quite like you do.'

Their faces were a mere foot away from one another's. If she didn't move now she'd reveal too much.

She shook her head and turned, so she didn't make a fool of herself.

As she turned she noticed the vase on the coffee table.

Flowers. The vase on her small table was filled with pink peonies.

It's a centrepiece for a table. He hasn't bought you flowers.

But it felt as if he had. And he'd baked her madeleines. And bought her wine.

Ed pulled out her chair. It hit the bookcase behind, but she didn't mind. Sitting in her cramped apartment with her prince was the only place in the world she wanted to be.

CHAPTER FIVE

BEING A PRINCE was not the endless lark everyone thought it was. On days like this it was positively tedious. Did anyone else have to worry so much about public perceptions that they would agree to be trapped in a Parisian turret for twenty-four hours?

The only communication he'd had from either of his parents in the past twenty-four hours had been a brief message from his father's private secretary thanking him for his patience and telling him his father would speak to him soon. He'd tried to get some work done, even attempted a video conference, but he hadn't been able to concentrate. His thoughts kept drifting to his father and his mother. And then Simone.

Baking was a type of procrastination that was entirely new to him, but it had worked. And, best of all, he'd made Simone happy.

Simone sat, closed her eyes and groaned as she breathed in the food. The sight did something strange to his chest. The steam from the coq au vin rose around her face, leaving a gentle glisten across her skin.

She grabbed a handful of hair from the nape of her neck and twisted it back from her face so she could eat without it falling in front of her, revealing the smooth skin behind her ears. He bit down the desire to kiss it.

How had he never noticed how gorgeous she was? They hadn't seen a lot of each other in the past few years, but even so. Now that he'd noticed it was difficult to believe he hadn't before.

Maybe it was just familiarity. She reminded him of happy times. Of childhood. Of feeling secure.

She was a best friend.

Except…not.

Now she was an independent woman, running a business in one of the world's most popular cities. The woman sitting across from him now, with her eyes half-closed, groaning gratefully as she ate the meal he'd procured.

You've actually never noticed her lips before. Pink. Plump. Perfect…

He shook his head.

'How was your afternoon?' he asked.

'Good. We had lots of traffic. And I managed to track down some sought-after first editions for some buyers.'

'Do you have any help in the bookshop?'

'A few casuals. My friend André helps out if I get really stuck.'

André. Ed's back straightened.

'His girlfriend, Julia, is my best friend.'

Ed felt his muscles relax.

'But you still work seven days? That's a lot.'

'I want to own this place, and that takes hard work.'

He drew breath, about to ask her how much money she needed, but she raised her hand before he could get half a word out.

'I need to do this by myself—and I can. Mum's offered to help, but I don't want to accept. She's done so much for me, especially putting me through school, helping me out when I first came to Paris.'

'Your mum's terrific. But did she really pay your school fees?'

He had to tread carefully. But he also had to know what she

knew. While it wasn't his secret to tell, it didn't feel right that he knew something like this when Simone didn't.

Simone looked up. 'What do you mean?'

'It was an exclusive school. Your mother did well to afford it.'

'Who else would have?'

'I… That is… I wondered if my parents might have.'

The creases on Simone's gorgeous face deepened. 'Why would they?'

'Can you not think of a reason?'

She laid down her cutlery and crossed her arms.

'No. And I don't think Mum would have accepted. Besides, my father left her some money. Not a lot. But enough. We're not royalty, but she's not poor.'

He was now certain that Simone didn't know about the affair. But she was certainly suspicious.

'Ed… What do you know?'

'Nothing. I'm sorry. It was very rude of me to question you. I've had a strange and privileged life and sometimes I make assumptions I shouldn't.'

And sometimes I don't shut my mouth when I should.

Their parents' affair wasn't his secret to tell, but not telling felt as if he was betraying her. Half the palace or more knew about his father and her mother. Was it right that Simone didn't?

'My business is great. I don't need any help.'

He frowned. 'But you're working seven days a week.'

'Because I want to! I love my job,' she insisted, in a way that indicated the conversation was over.

They ate in silence a while longer. He tried to think of something else to talk about, but drew a blank.

He looked out of the window at the city lights. He hadn't expected to be staying a second night here and had assumed he'd be back in Florena by now.

'I'm sorry for imposing on you.'

'I've told you I don't mind.'

'I didn't mean to imprison myself in your apartment.'

She laughed. 'You're not a prisoner. Not really. You're free to leave any time. It's your loyalty to your father that's keeping you here.'

She smiled at him, and her compliment warmed his chest.

There were worse places to be trapped. Though it would've been nice to be somewhere more spacious. Maybe with a pool. Or some sunshine. But at least he was trapped with Simone.

'I'm sure it won't be for much longer,' she said.

He shook his head. The silence from the palace said so many things. Was his father contemplating a press blackout or something else entirely?

A prisoner. The look on Ed's face was heartbreaking. Ed had never really struggled with his destiny or his duty. He saw it as an honour, not a burden. Simone had no idea how Ed would cope if his role were taken away from him. Some people were suited to a life of duty and Ed was one of them.

Simone was not. As a child she had adored living in the palace. Adored catching glimpses of the Queen all dressed up for a night out. Or even a night in. Young Simone had once thought it was the life she wanted. But that had been before hashtag *palaceserenade*. Before the worst of the internet had rained down on her.

'I don't know how you do it,' she said now.

'Do what?'

'Put up with everyone knowing who you are and commenting on you.'

'I wouldn't wish it on anyone.'

Her heart dropped. She knew she would never even date Ed. Let alone marry him. Her body shouldn't be reacting like this to something she'd always known was true.

Besides, apart from proving to her that Ed didn't love her, the whole hashtag *palaceserenade* nonsense had shown her that she didn't have what it took to be in the public eye anyway.

'But some people don't choose to be famous,' she said. 'It just happens because of circumstance.'

He looked at her closely and she felt her skin burn. Did he know what she was saying?

'You have to learn to get used to it,' he said. 'Or you break.'

'Yeah.'

She understood that. The few weeks when her video had been all over the internet had been the worst of her life. Physically leaving Florena had helped, but blocking social media had been more important. The problem was every time she'd thought it might have died down she'd check to see if people were still talking about her. She'd go online to check, and all the horrible things—the really toxic comments—would come across her screen.

'You can't worry over what other people say about you. You have to have a clear sense of yourself. What is real and what is not.'

They were wise words. But easier said than done.

'Do you always manage to do that?' she asked. 'To have a clear sense of yourself?'

He pulled his 'I'm thinking' face before replying, 'Mostly. I don't go looking for clips about me. My staff tell me what I need to know. Otherwise I block it out.'

It was easy when you were a prince. And when you had staff to monitor your social media presence and advise you about it. Ed had been raised with the confidence of knowing who he was and what his role in the world was. He was also being given the support to keep doing it.

'Maybe you should too,' he suggested, leaning into her.

The words were no use to her now, but would have helped when she was sixteen.

She had been a kid. She hadn't had the training he'd had. No one had explained to her how to deal with the trolls.

How had she got through it?

The school counsellor had been amazing. A wonderful

woman who'd tried to instil in Simone exactly what Ed was talking about. A clear sense of herself and a disregard for what other people thought or said.

Her best friend Julia, who was not only good at hugs, but also gave great reality checks, was wonderful too. 'He's not the one for you. And you know that.'

But looking at Ed now, reclined on her couch, twirling his wine glass, she knew a small part of her wished this was her life. Their life. Working in the bookshop in the day and sharing their evenings together. Eating, drinking, talking. And later she would take his face in her hands and....

It wasn't fair that he was still her favourite person in the entire world.

Before she realised it was almost midnight. They had been talking, laughing and reminiscing about their childhoods. As the evening wore on her thoughts became more muddied, her inhibitions lowered. She stood to get them both a drink and when she returned to the sofa her weight pushed the soft cushions closer and their hips touched. Nothing like a bit of self-torture.

But when she looked at him he was smiling. Contentedly.

'There's nowhere else I'd rather be imprisoned,' he said, and lay back.

Now their shoulders were touching. The sofa really was too small for both of them. Or she'd sat too close to him. She inhaled to clear her head, but breathed him in. He smelt of her own shampoo, and damn if it didn't smell good on him.

Even if Simone did still have feelings for Ed—which she didn't—they could never go anywhere. He thought of her as a sister. Besides, she certainly wasn't going to marry a prince. Not when she'd already experienced the kind of vitriol that was reserved for women who did.

He was finishing a story about a friend he had in New York and she was only half listening. Her thoughts were preoccupied in thinking about how close their shoulders were. The way his hair curled around the back of his ear. The light stubble that was now apparent on his cheeks.

It was lucky she was holding her glass in her hands, otherwise there would be nothing stopping her placing one of them on his knee.

Giving herself a mental shakedown, she tried looking for his flaws. His annoying habits.

He sucked on his thumb when he was thinking. He blinked when he was lying. He often lost track of what he was saying and stopped speaking mid-sentence.

Damn. Even his flaws were adorable.

Simone came back from the bathroom after changing into her pyjamas. Ed tried not to study the loose fabric skimming gently over her curves. He ran his tongue around his mouth, which had suddenly gone dry. She eyed his new pyjamas—another of today's purchases.

'You'll be wanting your own cupboard space soon,' she said.

He was glad she kept joking. It was what they did. They *didn't* stare into one another's eyes for long, uncomfortable moments.

They climbed into their respective sides of the bed and when they were settled she reached over and switched off the bedside light. Ambient light crept in from the street but otherwise they were in darkness. They lay on their backs, looking at the ceiling.

Last night, exhausted from his trip and with more than enough wine in his stomach, he had fallen asleep easily. But tonight… He wasn't sure how he would fall asleep as long as he could feel Simone's gorgeous weight in the bed next to him. They weren't even touching, but he could feel her in his bones and in his pores.

What if he pretended to sleep and accidentally rolled in her direction? What then?

She'll push you back to your side of the bed or get up and go to the sofa.

Simone had invited him into her bed platonically. He couldn't throw himself at her.

'What if I can't keep my hands off you...?'

Last night he'd said it as a joke. Tonight it didn't feel like a joke at all.

Each time one of them moved he was careful to keep the space between them. For her sake more than his. He knew that if their bodies collided he'd be at risk of coming completely undone.

So he endured. As still as he could. Wound tighter than tight. Listening to her breathing become heavy and regular. But even then sleep evaded him.

His thoughts of Simone were confusing, to say the least. Upsetting at worst. Had she always been this beautiful and he'd just failed to see? Or had she been transformed somehow because he was trapped with her.

Excuses aside, he knew the truth. She was beautiful and always had been. He just hadn't noticed because she was his friend, and friends didn't think about friends like that. But now he had noticed the pink of her lips, the blush of colour across her cheekbones, the sound of her laugher.

It was seeing her here—in her home—in Paris. Thriving. Planning to buy her own business and apartment. He realised, with an uncomfortable lump in his chest, that she belonged here now and not in Florena. A sense of loss swept through him. He longed for her to be by his side. And not just as his friend. He longed to be even closer to her than they were now, with their bodies lying mere inches apart.

No. He told himself that he was being silly. The sensations his body was experiencing when he thought about Simone were happening just because of the immense amount of stress he was under.

The longer he lay awake and pondered, the more he realised that it didn't matter why he was seeing her differently. The better question was what he was going to do about it.

The answer, he knew, was absolutely nothing. She was his best friend. The person he was depending on. The relationship he most wanted to treasure and nurture.

Rolling over and sliding his palm over her soft curves was not even an option. Putting his arms around her and pulling her to him was out of the question. Taking her rosy lips against his and tasting their sweetness was unthinkable.

Not to mention arrogant.

What made him think she would even welcome such a move? She was happy in Paris. He was a friend from her past and had no role to play in her future.

And this was hardly the time for him to do anything that would get his private life into the public realm.

So these new feelings and desires were just a blip. An aberration. Once he was home and no longer trapped here their lives would go on as they were meant to.

Separately.

Besides, he wasn't here as Simone's prisoner, but as her guest. If anyone was keeping him prisoner it was his father.

Around two a.m. Ed carefully reached for his phone, in the vague hope there would be a message, but his home screen was blank.

Simone rolled over and a wave of her scent reached his nose. She smelt like summer in the garden at the palace and his muscles clenched even tighter.

She was comfort and home all rolled into one. That was all it was, he told himself as he lay stiffly in the dark, trying his best to keep still. He hadn't anticipated the longing he'd feel to roll over and pull her close. Hadn't anticipated how many times he'd come so close to doing so.

He contemplated getting out of bed and going back to the sofa to cool down. But his limbs were heavy and the thought of leaving Simone was even less appealing than the risk that he might roll into her.

He brought his breath in time with hers and finally fell asleep.

* * *

Ed had no idea how many hours later he woke up. The curtains were flung open and the sunlight streamed in brightly, exposing everything.

Simone handed him a cup of takeaway coffee.

'You're a goddess,' he replied, eagerly inhaling the smell of the fresh brew.

The words escaped his lips before he could think twice, but he wasn't wrong. Her golden hair caught the morning sun and his breath with it. He couldn't read the look that passed across her face. Confusion? Annoyance? He should probably try to rein in these new strange feelings. Especially since he was already imposing so much on her. On her life. On her bed. He couldn't repay her generosity by hitting on her.

'I'm afraid you might need something stronger than a coffee,' she said. 'You need to watch this.'

Simone picked up the television remote and turned on the news.

'What is it?' he asked.

'It's better if you just see.'

It didn't take long for the report Simone was referring to to come back through the news cycle. The Prime Minister of Florena, Pierre Laurent, was giving a press conference. He was standing on the steps outside the Parliament building. While the crowd of journalists was not massive, it was big enough.

'The citizens of Florena have had enough. This is not the behaviour we expect or deserve from our monarch. This isn't the Middle Ages. This is the twenty-first century. The way in which the King has disrespected his wife, Queen Isabella, is not the way we expect our sovereign to treat women.'

Ed couldn't help snorting. Prime Minister Laurent had been divorced a few years ago after having an affair with his secretary. For him to throw allegations of inappropriate behaviour against the King was a little rich.

'But we know it isn't just the King. We know his brother left

Florena several decades ago after embezzling funds from the Government. And the King's father, the former Prince Edouard, whose premature death was notorious...'

Ed groaned. His grandfather had taken a drug overdose at the age of thirty-five, before Ed had been born. He had been in a hotel in the Bahamas with two young women who were barely out of their teens.

The allegation against his uncle was fair, but Uncle Louis hadn't set foot in Florena for years.

The allegations against Ed's grandfather were, unfortunately, true, but he'd been dead for nearly forty years.

The money the Queen had brought with her to the marriage had restored the private fortune of the royal family, and Ed's father had spent the last four decades reigning over and representing Florena with success. This was his father's first indiscretion. His first public one, at least.

'The stench of this family runs deep,' Laurent continued. *'Every Florenan knows the story* The Cursed Kingdom, *but this royal family has not learnt anything from that fairy tale. They are determined to ruin us all.'*

The Cursed Kingdom! Now he was citing an old children's story. This man was the limit.

'Dignity—that's all we expect from our monarch. He's not expected to run the country. He doesn't have to make the hard decisions.'

The Prime Minister straightened his own jacket as he said this.

Ed had feared the election of Laurent as Prime Minister would be bad for the country and he was not happy to be right.

'I think it's time Florena joined the twenty-first century.' Laurent continued.

'Oh, spare me the republican speech,' Ed yelled at the television.

Simone shook her head. 'It's worse than that.'

'We could be stronger if we joined with another, larger coun-

try. We need to have a serious discussion about whether it is sensible or viable to do this. I have been having discussions with the French Government...'

'What?' Ed stood quickly, nearly spilling his coffee.

'It doesn't make economic sense to keep our nation as a microstate...'

'Microstate!' Ed yelled. 'We're nearly as big as Belgium.'

'The geopolitical reality is that we need the protection of a larger country.'

Simone stood back, her face creased with worry. Ed grabbed his phone and pressed his father's number. To his enormous relief the King picked up right away.

'Edouard,' the King said.

'I have to come home.'

'No. Definitely not. You have to stay there. Are you somewhere safe? Somewhere private?'

'I'm with Simone. In her apartment.'

'Perfect,' replied his father.

'No! I'm no help here. I need to come home. I need to show that I support you.' He spoke too quickly and loudly, but this was the first chance he'd had to plead his case—he needed to go home.

'That's just it,' the King said. 'You need to distance yourself from me.'

'Having an affair is hardly in the same league as what Grandfather did. Or Uncle Louis.'

'That hardly matters. I don't want you getting dragged into this as well. Just stay where you are and in a few days everything will have blown over.'

Ed raked his hand through his hair. His father was in denial. What would happen with Celine? The Queen? They needed a plan.

'No, it won't blow over. Laurent clearly has a broader agenda,' Ed insisted.

He wished he were having this conversation face to face

with his father, so he could see the expression on his face and his body language.

'He's all bravado. Why would he suggest joining France when he'd just be doing himself out of a job?'

'I agree it doesn't make sense, but that's his plan.'

There was silence on the other end of the phone. And then a deep, resigned sigh. 'I wish... I wish I'd planned this better.'

You should have done a lot of things better, Ed thought.

His father had been reckless, but it was hard to blame him. He was human. Ed had known for years that his parents' marriage wasn't happy. But he'd never expected his father to be indiscreet. He'd certainly never expected his father to be caught impregnating a woman who was younger than his own son.

'The last thing we need—the last thing this country needs—is you being photographed with me.'

'But—'

'Don't argue with me, Edouard. Stay where you are. This isn't about you so don't make it about you.'

With a few words the King made him feel like a teenager again. He remembered another long-ago conversation. The one where he'd begged his father not to let Simone leave Florena.

'It's for her own good. Don't argue with me. If you care about her you will let her go.'

Ed had argued then. Pleaded with him to let Simone stay. Losing her then had been a wrench. The feelings of that day came flooding back. Pleading, arguing, and then the strange emptiness he'd felt when she was gone. A feeling that would creep up on him at unpredictable times during his adult life. A feeling he was missing something, but couldn't quite figure out what it was.

Now, knowing there was little point arguing with his father, all he said was, 'Please don't make any major decisions without talking to me.'

'You have my word.'

Ed held the silent phone in his hand. He had his father's word, but what was that worth?

'Did you hear that?' he asked Simone.

'I'm sorry. It was hard not to listen.'

He looked back to Simone, looking awkward in her own home. He wanted to go to her, pull her tight, but wasn't sure if it would be for her comfort or his. He stayed sitting on the couch.

'He wants me to keep away from it all but it feels disloyal.'

'I know it goes against every instinct you have. You want to be there. You want to do something. And it's frustrating being stuck here in this shoebox.'

He did want to be doing something, but when the time came to leave Paris it would be with trepidation. And sadness.

'It's a nice shoebox,' he said.

She gave him a sad half-smile. 'I see where your father's coming from. If you go home…if you make some kind of statement supporting him…it could backfire.'

'How?'

'Because at his next press conference Laurent will say that since you support your father you can't be trusted either. And that Florena should sack the entire House of Berringer.'

'But how can I not support him? It looks worse if I don't, doesn't it? He's the King and he needs to stay being the King. For the sake of the country. Otherwise Laurent would have us become the smallest *department* in France.'

Simone turned and unpacked a shopping bag. She placed pastries, apples and strawberries on the small bench. 'Trust your father. I'm sure he has a plan.'

Ed wished he shared her optimism. If his father did have a plan, why would he not share it with Ed? He wasn't a kid any longer—he was trusted to manage Florena's trade relations with the United States. Why not the royal family's response to this crisis?

His muscles felt as if they might snap. First a sleepless night next to Simone and now feeling helpless and that his father didn't trust him.

'He's right, though. Laurent's plan to join France doesn't make any sense.'

'He was born here, wasn't he? Maybe he thinks it will give him a shot at running a bigger country. He thinks that if Florena is part of France he'd have a chance at being President of France.'

Ed buried his head in his hands. The man was ruthless and ambitious, but it hadn't occurred to Ed that Laurent would be so ruthless as to essentially destroy his own country to achieve that ambition. But Simone's theory made sense.

He turned back to Simone, who was preparing some of the fruit for her breakfast.

'That's quite perceptive of you.'

She laughed. 'You sound surprised.'

'I'm sorry if I do. It's been a long while since we spent so much time together.'

She shrugged. 'I follow the Florenan news.'

'You do?'

'My mum still lives there.' She drew a deep breath. 'And you.'

Her back was turned and for a moment he let his gaze rest on her. Her blonde hair was tied up in a messy bun. Her shirt dipped just low enough at the nape of her neck to reveal the soft creamy skin at the top of her back. He wanted to taste it. Lick it. He pressed his lips together.

'It's not the first time someone has discussed getting rid of the monarchy,' she said, not quite putting an end to his illicit thoughts.

The whole situation was strange. They were discussing the end of his country and all he could think about was what the skin on Simone's neck would feel like against his lips. He had to get a grip.

'Talking about a republic is one thing, but he's talking about getting rid of our whole country.'

Simone turned, putting an end to his opportunity to study her surreptitiously, and passed him a bowl of fresh fruit. Then she sat on the armchair, tucking her feet under herself, and hugged her coffee. He took the fruit gratefully. It wasn't what he would have chosen. Left to his own devices he might have taken a cap off a bottle of Scotch, but the breakfast was just what he needed. Sitting here with Simone was just what he needed. It was so much better than hearing this news alone.

'What do you think of Laurent?' he asked.

'Me?'

'Yes—you've been following the news.'

'Sure, but I've never met him. What do you make of him?'

'Ambitious. Slippery. Like most politicians. What do you think?'

'Ambitious, yes. And he likes to travel. He always seems to be visiting somewhere. And he's dating one of your old friends.'

'What? Who?'

'Oh, you know… What's her name?'

'No. I've no idea who you're talking about.'

'I thought…that is…maybe you dated her for a while? Morgane Lavigne.'

'Oh, her? I haven't seen her in years. Really? They're dating? Aren't you the fount of Florenan gossip.'

Simone shrugged. 'I keep in touch with people.'

'I'm impressed,' he said.

Simone continued to surprise him. The singing. The calmness and security of her flat. Her quirky bookshop. And her insight.

None of those things alone should have been surprising. What was rocking him, though, was the way he felt breathless when she brushed past him. The way his mind kept drifting to her. Just like his gaze, which now rested on her lips as she carefully sipped her coffee.

He knew he needed to get home to Florena as soon as possible, but when the time came he wasn't sure how he'd be able to tear himself away from Simone.

CHAPTER SIX

IT WAS A relief to get down to the bookshop and away from Ed.

How embarrassing to mention Morgane and know she was dating the Prime Minister when Ed didn't even know that. Simone wasn't proud of it, but she did occasionally look to see what Ed's old flames were up to. Or any woman he was currently linked to.

Morgane Lavigne had often visited the palace with her parents, and had gone on several holidays with the royal family. Like Simone, Morgane had known Ed since they were children. Unlike Simone, Morgane had shared a brief relationship with Ed in their teens. She had been the person Ed had spent most of his seventeenth birthday party with. The two of them had been wrapped up in each other. Morgane had been sultry and glamorous, even as a teenager, and each time Simone had seen her she'd been monopolising Ed and Ed had never seemed to mind.

Stalking Ed's exes on the internet was not in line with Simone's strict 'No Ed' diet, but at weak moments she did relapse. Which was how she'd known about Morgane and Laurent—from some photos Morgane had posted and her vague comments about being the 'other' first lady of Florena. Morgane owned the public relations company that completed work for the government.

If she couldn't get the Prince she'd go for the Prime Minister, Simone had thought cattily, then hated herself for it and immediately shut her laptop.

The morning started off relatively busy, with several customers, including some needing help with rare finds. A tap on her shoulder made Simone squeal in fright, stand and spin, her heart rate propelling her upward.

'Gah!'

The figure behind her was dressed in a black fedora, a red bow tie and thick-rimmed glasses.

'Are you trying to scare me to death?'

'Sorry. I was trying to be inconspicuous.'

'Looking like that?'

'I dialled 1-800-Disguise.'

'Seriously?'

'Seriously. You can get anything delivered these days. I've decided to help you out.'

'Ed...'

'It'll be fine. I need something to do. I need distracting. There were no emails waiting for me this morning. The video meetings I had today were cancelled.'

'Oh, Ed.' She didn't know what that meant but it didn't sound good.

'I'm sure there's some other explanation. The government's busy...'

Ed frowned. Something was happening in Florena's inner government circles and its trade envoy to North America was clearly not supposed to know what it was.

'There must be things you need to do. Away from the counter. Away from the bookshop, even.'

There were. She needed to shelve the new books and take some online orders to the post office, and she had no idea when she was going to manage to do that. André was due for a shift later that afternoon, but in the meantime she was alone.

'There are—thank you. I do need to go to the post office.'

'Go out for an hour or so. I'll be fine.'

'What if you're recognised?'

'Firstly, the further I am from Florena the less recognised I am. Secondly, who is going to believe that the silly man in the fake glasses and the bow tie in a Paris bookshop is me?'

'*I* don't believe the silly man in the fake glasses and the bow tie in a Paris bookshop is you.'

'See? I've fooled you, and you know me better than anyone in the world.'

His words made her heart pause. Even after all these years he still thought of her like that.

'Ed, there are plenty of people who know you. Who could recognise you.'

'It'll be fine. Besides, depending on how things go, I might need to ask you for a permanent job, and customer service experience will look good on my CV.'

Her heart broke for him. And his family. And everyone at the palace. 'It's not going to come to that.'

'There's no need for a crown prince of Florena, or even a trade envoy from Florena, if Florena doesn't exist.'

'Ed…' She slid her hand up his arm and squeezed his shoulder, but stopped just short of pulling him into a full embrace. Feeling the warmth of his body under her fingertips, she felt her heart get caught in her throat. She finally managed to say, 'Your father will take care of it. The Florenans won't stand for it. There are so many things standing in Laurent's way.'

He scoffed and she sighed. She wasn't going to be able to convince him. But he was right about one thing. He needed to be doing something other than watching the news and spiralling into despair.

'I need to go to the post office. If anyone wants something in particular that you can't find, take their details and I'll get back to them.'

'I can do this, Simone.'

This time he touched her arm. It was only to reassure her, but it felt as though he'd kissed her.

Kissed? Your heart rate couldn't handle it if he kissed you.

She gave him a quick explanation of the payment machine and gathered the parcels. As she walked along the street, dodging the tourists and breathing in the crisp autumn air, she was glad to have some space, but couldn't shake him completely from her thoughts.

Something was different about him. The casual comments. On their own they were nothing, but they were adding up.

'You're a goddess.'

'You know me better than anyone else.'

'What if I can't keep my hands off you?'

What was going on with him? He'd never been flirty like this with her before.

But the last time they'd spent this much time alone together they had been kids.

They'd seen each other since childhood, but usually there had been others around. Her mother or palace staff. They emailed one another occasionally. And he'd send her the occasional text message, usually to show her where he was in the world. Those messages would delight her and break her heart just a little as well. They only highlighted how their lives were on different paths.

This was different.

He was different.

He's stressed. He's going through a crisis and you're his oldest friend. He is relying on you and only you. He's just grateful and appreciates your friendship. That's all.

Once she'd posted the parcels and her hands were free Simone dialled her mother's number and was relieved when Alea picked up straight away.

'Darling. How are things? Did you see the press conference?'

'We did.'

'What a mess! How's Eddie?'

Simone smiled at her mother's use of her old name for him. 'Stressed.'

'Of course he is. But there's nowhere better for him to be right now.'

'He really wants to go home. I'm not sure how much longer he'll last here.'

'I honestly don't know what the King's long game is. There are rumours, but...'

'What sort of rumours?'

'Oh, just silly rumours. I'm sure things will quieten down soon.'

'Rumours about the Queen? Do you really think they'll divorce?'

'I don't see how it could be otherwise, to be honest.'

Simone stopped walking in the middle of the street, to the annoyance of the couple walking behind her. She stepped into a doorway.

'Ed hasn't even heard from his mother yet. I suppose that makes sense.'

'Don't say anything to Ed. As I said, we don't really know.'

Simone doubted she'd be telling Ed anything he hadn't already thought of. A royal divorce, a royal wedding and a royal baby seemed to all loom on the horizon.

Poor Ed. Having your parents' marriage disintegrate was bad, no matter how old you were. And having to go through it in the spotlight was even worse.

'I'd better get back to him. Let me know if you hear anything at all.'

'Of course. You too. Mwah.' Her mother blew her a kiss and ended the call.

Simone looked up at the great sky. Autumn was coming to its end and she could feel the change in the air.

Ed had spent the morning in the bookshop. He wasn't sure if he was helping or making a nuisance of himself, but it was better than staring at his phone or the four walls of Simone's apartment. Being in the bookshop, spending time with Simone, helped keep his mind off other things. When he was near Simone it felt as though everything would be all right. Somehow.

Around midday Simone went out to pick up some baguettes for lunch, and after that Ed went upstairs, to see if anyone had sent him any work. They hadn't. And the video conferences scheduled for the next day had disappeared from his calendar.

He groaned. He hated feeling useless.

The King didn't answer, but Ed was no longer surprised. He tried his father's secretary, who told him the King was in a meeting and would call as soon as he could. The King should change his voicemail message to say that and spare everyone the time.

He was used to this distance between him and his father, but still found it ridiculous that they had to communicate through a third person. If Ed ever had children they would always be able to reach him, whenever they wanted.

Not that he was going to have children. He'd told his parents as much. It was the one royal duty they couldn't ask of him. He'd do the job, but he wouldn't subject any woman to life in the fishbowl that was the palace of Villenueve. His parents had looked at one another, but not argued. How could they? They knew they were the very reason their son would never walk down the aisle.

Besides, his cousins had children, and now he was going to have a younger sibling the royal succession was hardly in danger.

Ed had no intention of marrying so he would not have children. He was always very careful about that. Unlike his father, he thought bitterly.

Besides, living a single life wasn't a problem. He'd never found someone he knew he could trust enough. Or someone he wanted to spend time with when the initial rush of seduction had worn off. He'd never been obsessed by a woman. Never been ready to chuck in his whole life for her.

Ed tried to read some reports but unsurprisingly he couldn't concentrate. He stretched and attempted some sit-ups and push-ups, the only exercise possible in the tiny apartment, though that too failed to clear his head.

What would happen to him if Laurent got his way? Presumably, his family would have to leave the palace. But could he still live in Florena or would he be an exile? He could come to Paris. Find a place—a bigger place, near to Simone. He could see her every day. They could be neighbours just like they'd used to be.

His body relaxed instantly at the thought. If Simone were fully in his life again he would be able to cope with whatever came next. The realisation was both surprising and comforting.

Would it be the end of the world to be an ordinary person? He knew other princes and princesses often longed to shake off their titles, but he never had. Apart from playing a few child-hood games, he had never wanted to be anyone else.

Childhood games. The memories made him smile. Once upon a time, when they were very young, he and Simone had loved to play make-believe. They just hadn't always agreed on what to pretend to be.

'I want to play kings and queens,' she'd say.

He'd groan. 'But that's not pretending.'

'You're not King. I'm not Queen. It's still make-believe.'

'Detectives.'

'We always play that.'

'Okay, you can be a princess and I'll be a superhero.'

'I want to be a superhero too. A superhero princess.'

Simone had pretended to be a princess disguised as a super-hero and they had run around the garden chasing Suzette, who had apparently robbed several banks.

He smiled. He'd have to remind her of that tonight.

But if he wasn't a prince he wasn't going to be a superhero either. Who would he be? Plain old Ed Berringer, former prince?

No. Laurent was not going to get his way. Abolishing Florena was inconceivable.

Tomorrow the news cycle will have moved on and I can go home. Everyone will forget what Laurent was saying and get on with their lives.

Yeah, that's what you thought yesterday.

Ed walked over to the bookshelf. Only a special kind of person would have two storeys of books downstairs and then have another bookshelf in their shoebox apartment. He glanced at the titles, but his eyes were drawn to the shelf with a collection of framed photographs. He picked up one that looked as though it had been taken on a night out or at a party.

Simone wore a strappy red dress, not unlike the one in that video. She wasn't looking at the camera, but at the man next to her. Her smile was magical, uninhibited. Ed felt as though he'd been punched in the stomach and put the frame down as if it was on fire.

The woman in the photograph—the woman downstairs— was beautiful. Grown up, sophisticated, self-assured.

He sighed. If his family were kicked out of Florena, living in Paris, being near Simone, would have its benefits.

He should stop moping and do some work. He was still the trade envoy to North America—for the time being at least.

CHAPTER SEVEN

ED WAS WAITING when she got to the top of the stairs. He was wearing the fedora and the silly glasses. 'Do you have dinner plans?' he asked.

'I thought we could order something in,' Simone replied.

'How about ordering something out?'

'Go out? But, Ed…'

'Not to a restaurant…maybe just have a walk. It's dark. We can go along the quieter streets.'

Her heart leapt. She'd love to go out with Ed, and could tell he was bursting to leave the apartment.

'Are you sure?'

'If you can bear to be seen with me?'

He did look slightly ridiculous. In addition to the hat, glasses and bow tie, he'd found an old black coat of hers.

'In that get-up? I wouldn't miss it.'

He smiled.

Simone bought a bottle of Burgundy with a screw top from the shop across the road and they picked up a box of pizza from her favourite place down the street. They made their way to the Seine. The light had gone and they found a section of the bank with no one around and sat, with their legs dangling over the edge, taking turns to drink the wine straight out of the bottle.

Ed seemed relaxed, but Simone kept looking around.

'Relax. There's no one. I have a sixth sense for photographers. Besides, we look like students down here, with our wine in a brown paper bag.'

'I am surprised you came to me,' she confessed, taking a sip of the wine.

'I was in Paris. You're my person in Paris.'

Of course. That was all. She was convenient. The nearest warm body.

'I was just wondering...' The wine had loosened her tongue. But he'd probably be gone in the morning, so she might as well ask her question now. 'Are they pressuring you at all?'

'What about?'

'To find someone. Get married. Produce an heir and all that.'

Her mouth was dry when she asked. She'd never been quite so direct with him. They talked about other things, not relationships.

'Always.'

'Is there someone?'

'Are you asking if I'm dating someone?'

'Well, I suppose so. Yes.'

He laughed. 'No, Sim. I'm not dating anyone. I would've told you long before this if I was.'

He leant towards her, close enough that she could see the crinkles around his eyes through his fake glasses when he smiled, and said, 'Simone, I'd always tell you something like that.'

'You would?'

'You're my person.'

'Your person *in Paris*,' she clarified.

'No. My person. Full stop.'

The muscles in her chest tightened. 'Really?'

'Yes.'

Despite the cool air, her face was warm. His eyes were too serious. She closed the lid to the pizza box and brushed invisible crumbs from her lap.

He just means you're his friend—that's all. You've always known that. It's not a surprise.

But the way her heart was beating so fast at his declaration was a surprise.

They were best friends. It should be enough. But one day Ed would marry a beautiful princess. Or a movie star. And Simone would be back to being his person in Paris.

'But if they're pressuring you? Your parents?'

'They've been throwing heiresses in my direction for the past decade.'

'And?'

'I keep ignoring them. Delaying. It's not something I plan on doing. I told you this, didn't I?'

'Yes, when you were twelve.'

'It's still the plan.'

She'd never have to stand in the royal cathedral in Florena and watch him get married to someone else. It was something at least.

'But what about the monarchy. Having an heir?'

'Not you too!' He pushed himself back, making to stand.

'No. I don't care. Honestly.' That was a big fat lie. This was one of the most significant conversations she'd had in years. 'I'm just curious. Your parents must have said something?'

'Yeah, well, I try to avoid their questions. It only leads to arguments. But now that I'm going to have a sibling it's worked out great. I'm about to have a younger brother or sister. They can inherit after me. As far as I'm concerned it's the one good thing to come out of this mess. They'll have to stop hassling me for an heir. Father's done that for me.'

'You can't be serious?'

'Why can't I be?'

They sat in silence, watching the lights reflecting in the river and the boats slowly passing by.

After a while she couldn't help herself. 'Can I ask why? As a disinterested bystander not as your parent.'

He looked at her again, his eyes narrowed in sharp focus. That look of his made something inside her flip.

'Sorry. It's personal. You don't have to tell me,' she said quickly.

'I'm happy to tell you. It's not a secret.'

She held her breath.

'I'm a playboy looking for the nearest warm body. Everyone knows that.'

Something inside her twisted. 'But that's not true. Not really.'

'It's what the tabloids say.'

'But…it's all exaggeration? Lies to sell papers?' She held her breath, and her heart seemed to stop as she waited for his answer. She knew Ed's reputation, but she also knew Ed. He wasn't a womaniser. Or was he?

'Yes, it's lies…mostly. But…'

'But what?' Simone felt sick, waiting for his answer. What wasn't he telling her? Had he really slept with half the models in Europe?

'I don't think I have what it takes. Besides, I don't believe that love lasts. Certainly not long enough to sustain a long marriage. If anything, the events of this week just prove it. My parents hate one another. They've made one another miserable. Mine wasn't a happy childhood home. You know that.'

It had been barely a home. Ed's parents had often been away, and when they'd been around, Ed had just seemed unhappier.

'But not every couple is like that. My parents were happy.'

He looked as though he were considering his next words carefully. 'Everyone falls out of love eventually.'

Her heart cracked. If only that were the case…

'You didn't know my parents together,' she said.

'Did *you*, though?'

He probably meant that she must have only vague memories of her parents together, but you only had to see how Alea still spoke about her husband to know that love could last years and years—even beyond death.

'Your parents might be unhappy. That doesn't mean every couple is. Have you ever been in love?' The question was out before she realised she didn't actually want to know the answer.

'No.'

She exhaled. Of course he hadn't been in love. If he'd really felt the exquisite pull and pain of true love he wouldn't be saying this.

'Have you?' he asked.

If her face hadn't been red before, by now it would be setting off fire alarms.

She looked at her plate and considered her answer.

'That's a yes,' he said.

'I didn't say that.'

'It's a yes—otherwise you wouldn't look like that.'

'Like what?' she squawked.

'Like you don't want to answer the question. And it ended badly, didn't it?'

It didn't even begin.

She pressed her fingers to her burning cheeks to cool them.

Ed raised an eyebrow, but he must have noticed her discomfort because he didn't ask anything further.

They watched the boats a while longer, and when they had finished the wine Ed stood and offered Simone his hand to help her stand. She took it hesitantly, anticipating the jolt that would race through her. Yep—there it was. As predictable and inconvenient as ever.

They walked along the bank, up the river and then climbed the stone stairs to cross the Pont d'Austerlitz.

Halfway along Ed stopped.

The middle of a Parisian bridge looking up the Seine must

surely be one of the most romantic places on the planet. Why was he doing this to her?

Ed turned his face to the sky, giving her a moment to steal a glance at his beautiful torso and then his face. Free to study him, she let her gaze follow the line of his strong jawbone, move over his cheekbones and rest on his soft brown eyelashes. Even in the silly glasses he was still heart-stopping.

'Have you been in touch with your mother?' he asked.

'Yes. She doesn't know much.'

'Has she seen my father?'

'Apparently no one has apart from his private secretary. And Laurent.'

'Laurent's been at the palace?'

Simone nodded. 'At least once a day, apparently.'

'Checking the joint out?'

'Meeting with your father, they say.'

'Did she say what the mood's like?'

'Tense. Sad.'

She didn't want to tell him everything her mother had said. It would just make him worry. Everyone was very concerned about their jobs, about Florena, but also about the royal family.

'Mum knows you're here. I couldn't lie to her. But she hasn't told anyone except to let them know you're somewhere safe and loving.'

Loving? She couldn't believe that word had come out of her mouth. It was the word her mother had used, but Simone hadn't expected to repeat it.

Ed studied her through narrowed eyes. It was that new, strange look she had seen a bit lately. As if he was puzzled by her.

Great.

He wasn't attracted to her. He was puzzled. It was a step up from 'I think of you as a friend', at least.

'Do you remember we used to play pretend?' he asked.

'Of course. Detectives and superheroes.'

'You always wanted to play kings and queens.'

'Yeah, but we had to play superheroes because you said, "Kings and queens isn't pretending." Even though I was definitely not a queen. And we had a palace to pretend in and everything. But no, we had to investigate who had taken Suzette's dog toys. I knew all along that you had hidden them.'

Ed laughed. 'I'd forgotten that.' He looked thoughtful for a moment. His green soulful eyes stared, unfocused, over the water.

'We did play kings and queens once.'

A memory long forgotten, dreamlike, surfaced into her consciousness. They'd been in the palace, had sneaked into the throne room one evening when his parents had been away and the staff distracted. Ed, who'd felt comfortable in the room, had run around with Suzette. Simone, who had not shared his ease at being in the throne room, had entered the room carefully and with awe. It was lined with gilded mirrors and portraits of past kings and queens of Florena, and they had looked down at them with disapproval as Ed had chased the dog until she barked.

Her chest warmed—as much from the memory as from the fact that he had remembered.

No one knew her like he did.

'You told me to sit on the throne,' she said.

'And I crowned you with my baseball hat.'

She laughed. 'Why?'

'Because you wanted to be crowned and that was all we had.'

'I was eight. I probably did.'

The baseball hat had felt precious and serious while they were pretending. Now she shuddered. A crown would be an impossible weight to bear.

Which was fine, since Ed was never getting married and didn't believe in love. And since she was never going to return to Florena.

A boat full of drunken revellers passed underneath them.

They were waving, as boat passengers often did. Ed waved back and she laughed.

'What if they recognise you?'

'In my brilliant disguise?'

'Even in that. Those glasses are ridiculous.'

She reached for them, as if to pull them off, but her hand froze. Ed's hand had wrapped around hers, preventing her revealing his disguise to the world. He was meant to be incognito. But she wanted to see his face without them.

They were so close. She knew she should let go, but it was like trying to separate magnets. He pulled her hand away from his glasses, but far from letting it go he drew their clasped hands into his chest.

They mustn't be seen. It would be bad if he were recognised—worse if she were seen with him. But still she was stuck. Ed didn't let her go and she didn't pull herself free.

She could hardly breathe. Tonight the rest of the world had fallen away. Tonight the only thing stopping her standing on her toes and kissing him was the wall she had built around her heart. And that wall was starting to feel less like stone and more like paper.

Thin tissue paper.

That could be blown away with the merest breeze.

Like the air that escaped Ed's lips as he sighed. 'Simone...'

He didn't sound hesitant. He sounded tortured. He sounded like her heart felt.

Just as she was about to step back his lips were on hers. It was quick. Even though Simone had been thinking of kissing Ed, the surprise nearly brought her knees out from under her. It might also have been the perfect way Ed's lips fitted against hers. The way his fingers tilted her head to the precise angle needed to send blissful sparks shooting through her.

She pulled herself back. What was he thinking? This was madness.

'I'm sorry... I thought you wanted... I misread.' He looked at the ground.

This was ridiculous. He wasn't to blame any more than she was.

'No, you didn't misread.'

He lifted his gaze back to hers. Through the clear lenses of the glasses she could feel the gravity in his next question. 'You wanted to kiss me?'

'Want. Present tense.'

She lifted herself up onto her toes, feeling his body rub against hers as she brought her lips to his mouth.

The sensation of his hard body pressing against hers only blew that wall further into oblivion. Had she gone too far? Would they be seen? No. They wouldn't be identified out of all the other couples making out on all of Paris's beautiful bridges.

His broad hands slid up her back and into her hair. He gently held her head in place while he covered her with kisses. From her lips to her neck. Behind her ears and back again.

Ed is kissing you. His tongue is currently in your mouth. You can feel him. All of him. What does it mean? He doesn't believe in love, so what is this?

She ordered the voices in her head that were telling her to be careful to stop. Not to ruin what could be the most perfect moment of her life. She wanted to live in the moment. Savour each kiss, each caress, each heartbeat.

His tongue, tasting of red wine and hope, slid past hers. His muscles slackened and then tensed under her hands, which for the first time had the freedom to roam where they wanted to over Ed. She slid one hand over his shoulders, around the soft nape of his neck into his thick hair.

It was something she'd only dreamt of. The feel of his skin. The taste of his mouth. She'd rehearsed it in her head so often as a teenager, but the sensations coasting through her body still caught her off guard. There was no way she could have prepared herself for the way her muscles shivered when he slid his hand down her back, rested it on her bottom and pulled her firmly against him.

When the desire pooling inside her was about to overflow, the voice of reason became louder and she pulled her mouth back from his. She caught her breath and saw he was doing the same.

His face was flushed and his breath shallow, and it took every last ounce of her sanity to ask, 'What's going on?'

CHAPTER EIGHT

SHE EXHALED WITH a half-sigh, half-groan, and Ed trembled as he answered.

'I don't know. Maybe we could make it up as we go along.'

His lips travelled past her ear, down her neck to the low neckline of her dress and she wobbled on her stilettos. He held her tight and steadied her. He checked that she was all right, then he closed his eyes and kissed her again.

'Is that okay?' he murmured into her neck.

There was no roadmap where he was going. This was uncharted territory. Off-road into the unknown.

But what if he got hopelessly lost?

You're already lost. You may as well see where this leads.

This was a far better way to be spending his time than fretting about his future. Simone's kisses were sweet and soft, and after trying just one he was completely, hopelessly addicted.

That's probably why you never kissed her before. You knew it would be impossible to stop.

'Are you sure this is a good idea?' she asked.

He couldn't remember being more certain of anything. Kissing her. Wanting her. It was like gravity. The sun, the moon and the tides.

There were probably good reasons why they shouldn't be

doing this, but with Simone in his arms they paled into insignificance.

'For starters we're friends,' she said.

That was the very reason he wanted to kiss her and slip this dress off her gorgeous body. To feel every inch of her. Because she was Simone. His oldest friend. His beautiful, amazing friend.

He guessed that must be what she meant. Friends sometimes didn't want to sleep together because they were afraid it would ruin their friendship. The thought hadn't occurred to him. This would only deepen their relationship. Make it even more special.

'Our friendship won't change. It's too old for that and too strong.'

He layered kisses along her low neckline, nudging the fabric down even further as he went. Maybe she did have a point. If he lowered his mouth much further maybe everything would change between them. The taste of her skin and the warmth of her pressed against him caused another thought. Their relationship might change, but only for the better. He'd never felt so close to her. That had to be a good thing, didn't it?

He'd never slept with his best friend before. He'd never slept with a friend before. So how did he really know?

You know that Simone will always be in your life. You know that losing her isn't an option.

He felt her body lean into him, her desire matching his, letting him know she agreed. The skin of her hand was unspeakably soft. He had to keep going back over it with his fingertip to see if it really was as beautiful as if felt. Soft and warm. Alive.

'But not here,' she said, thankfully being sensible enough for both of them.

It was dangerous enough for him to be out and about, let alone losing himself like this in public.

He wanted her. All of her. And it was threatening to overwhelm everything else.

He grabbed her hand and pulled her in the direction of her

apartment. They walked fast, but each time they had to stop to cross a road they would kiss again, and inevitably fall back into the kisses. He wanted to get back to the apartment, but he was enjoying the lingering and anticipation nearly as much.

They stopped to kiss on every street. They stopped to kiss in front of the bookshop. On the stairs, on the landing. And finally they were inside her apartment, jackets being pulled off and shoes kicked away.

He trailed kisses along her collarbone and felt her shiver.

Then a buzzing startled them both, and Simone's limbs froze beneath his hands.

'Is that your phone?'

Leave it, he was about to say. But he knew it was hopeless. He couldn't give his whole self to her while he wondered what the call was about. Who it was.

'Check it. You have to check it.' Simone untangled herself from him.

He wasn't sure if his decision to leave his phone behind had been accidental or deliberate, but it had been serendipitous. Because there were many missed calls.

Calls that would have disrupted his evening with Simone.

Calls that he needed to return.

'My father,' he said.

'Should I leave you?'

'No. Stay. Please.'

Ed didn't bother listening to the messages. He wanted the news straight from his father. He sat on the couch and motioned for Simone to sit next to him.

He dialled his father and placed the phone on speaker. Simone's eyes widened, but he simply picked up her hand and squeezed it.

'Ed. You took your time.'

'Sorry, Father. I was caught up.' Ed squeezed Simone's hand again and she squeezed back.

'I've made a decision. It is mine alone to make. I've abdicated the throne. I signed the papers just over an hour ago.'

'You're abdicating?' The words felt strange on his tongue.

'I have already—Your Majesty.'

It sounded like a joke. A cruel, cruel joke. Made all the worse by the timing. He could hardly bear to look at Simone, sitting next to him. She rested her head on his shoulder.

'There should be a car arriving for you shortly. It will take you straight to the airport. We can talk more when you get here. I'm about to speak to the press.'

Ed couldn't answer—not even to argue. He knew, as well as his father did, that there was no point. It was done.

His father ended the call.

Don't make any decisions without me.

Ed wanted to throw up. He was now the King of Florena. King Edouard the Fourth of Florena.

He focused on his breathing, hoping the news would start to sink in if he did.

Another day, another night, and they might have a chance to figure out what was happening between them.

'That's all? It's done?'

Simone was as shocked as he was at the swiftness of the King's actions. At the brevity of the phone call.

Ed laughed. 'He didn't even ask how I was.'

'You're not even there. He didn't wait for you to get back.'

'That's been the point all along.' He could taste the bitterness in his voice. 'That's why I had to stay—so that I wouldn't be standing next to him now. So that I wouldn't talk him out of it. So that I wouldn't have a choice.'

She nodded. 'He should have talked to you. Should've involved you.'

'But that would have been too hard for him. Over these past few days my father's hardly proved himself to be a man of courage or honour.'

Simone stood to get them both a drink. She pulled a dusty

bottle of Scotch down from her top cupboard and poured them both generous glasses. Then she turned on the small television and they waited. The tickertape announced that the King of Florena would be giving a live address at any moment.

Ed wondered how long they had before the knock at the door came and he was taken away.

The screen changed to a shot of the palace of Villeneuve and then to the King.

Except he's not the King any more. You are.

His father looked tired as he sat behind a desk and looked down the camera.

'Thank you all for joining me this evening. It has become apparent over the past few days that I am not the best person to be serving this country. I have allowed my personal life to distract me from my duties and I have not been the King you deserve or the man I want to be.'

The Scotch burnt Ed's throat on the way down, but he still took another large sip.

'The most appropriate person to be serving our beautiful country is my son, Edouard, who as of one hour ago became your sovereign. Edouard is devoted to this country, and I know he will dedicate his entire life to your service.'

'He was talking about you like you aren't a real person,' Simone whispered, once the King had finished.

'But from now on I'm not. Not really. I'm the sovereign. The head of state. The embodiment of Florena.'

He had to go back to Florena and save his country.

Simone clenched her fists and paced the room. It only took four steps in each direction, so she was pretty much going in circles.

How would he get through the next few days without her? How would he get through the nights? Less than half an hour ago they'd been undressing one another. Now...? Now he was lost.

'Come with me.'

If he couldn't stay, she could come.

She shook her head and kept shaking it. As if she was convincing herself it was the right decision.

He knew what she should do. 'You could come with me—please.'

'I can't leave the bookshop.'

'I'll pay for someone to look after the bookshop. Please.'

'Oh, no, no, no. That's not how things are going to work.'

'What do you mean?'

'I mean… I just can't.'

'Is it about the money?'

'It's the whole damn thing! Ed, this is happening so fast.'

She didn't need to tell *him* that. He'd been the monarch for ninety minutes and hadn't even known for most of that time.

He needed her. Couldn't imagine going back to Florena and getting through the next period without her. He didn't want to return without her by his side.

The realisation was almost as overwhelming as the news his father had just delivered.

He wanted Simone.

He needed her. As he needed air.

What had happened between them on the bridge hadn't been an aberration.

'Come with me. Please.'

He stood and went to her, grasping her shoulders with his hands and stopping her pacing.

She looked up at him, but her expression was pained. 'Ed… What would I be?'

'What do you mean?'

'You know what I mean. If I came with you, what would I be?'

Ah, right…

Why couldn't they just be Simone and Ed? Best friends? Surely not everything had to change at once.

'You would be my friend.'

She grimaced. 'And I'd just sit in the palace all day as your *friend*?'

Would that be so bad? She was his best friend, and now they were exploring whether she might be something more.

She looked at him, as if waiting for him to catch up. Would she be his *girlfriend*? Did kings even *have* girlfriends? He knew the answer to that. Kings had wives. And they had mistresses. And Simone would be neither his wife nor his mistress.

Bringing a new, unsteady relationship into the mix at this point would make things in Florena go from bad to worse. There was no room for exploring their new relationship now he was the new king. There was no room for missteps, break-ups, gossip or rumours. There was no room for them to see how this new side of their relationship developed naturally. Privately.

She was ten steps ahead of him. She'd already seen the problems that he wanted to ignore.

'The absolute last thing you need is gossip and speculation about your personal life,' she told him.

'I see what you mean. It's complicated.'

But how was he going to get through this without her?

Simone couldn't be more than his best friend because he didn't believe in love. And throwing a nascent relationship into the mess that was the current saga of the Florenan royal family...

He couldn't do that to her. And he couldn't do it to his people. *His people*.

'Ed, I want to be with you. Please know that. You are one of the most important people in the world to me. And I want to help you. But do you really think me going with you...as things are now...is that the best thing for Florena? For you?'

He picked up her hand and turned it over in his, steadying his breath and his thoughts. Her skin was soft. Her nails short and clean. He wanted to know these hands as well as he knew his own.

Damn, why could he taste salt in the back of his nose?

Because you're going to miss her. Because standing up and walking out of this room is going to be the hardest thing you've done in your life.

He looked at her and almost broke—but didn't. He wasn't being fair on Simone. It wouldn't be fair to drag her into the circus of which he was now the ringmaster.

This is what you always knew, isn't it?

It wouldn't be fair to subject a woman to the scrutiny of the Florenan royal family. He couldn't do it to anyone he really cared about. Least of all Simone.

He choked out a rueful laugh. It was either that or cry.

'Is there nothing I can say to make you come with me?' he asked, though he already knew the answer.

'You know as well as I do that having me there will just make it worse for you. And my life is here. I can't just abandon it for a few months.'

'A few months?'

'Well, yes... Until you find your feet. Until...'

She didn't need to finish the sentence. *Until we break up.*

Because he didn't believe in love. Or marriage.

He looked back down at her hands, still wrapped around his. Keeping him anchored. He was afraid to let them go. Afraid that when he did she would float away from him.

There was nothing else to do but say goodbye.

He cupped her chin in his palm and tilted her mouth towards his. He opened his mouth and pulled her in, making sure that every taste, every shiver, every sigh was marked indelibly onto his memory. But as he did so he felt his eyes fill with water.

He pulled back and saw his own tears glistening on her cheeks. He brushed one away with the back of his thumb. She jumped back as though she'd been scolded.

'Goodbye,' she squeaked, before pulling away and moving to the door. 'Good luck.'

She grabbed her coat and closed the door behind her before he could catch his breath to reply.

CHAPTER NINE

THE ENGRAVED INVITATION arrived for her just before Christmas.

> *The presence of*
> *Simone Auclair*
> *is requested*
> *at the coronation of*
> *King Edouard the Fourth of Florena*
> *on 31st January at 11 a.m.*
> *Dress: full morning dress.*
> *The coronation will be followed by*
> *a state dinner and ball.*
> *Further instructions will be provided upon*
> *your acceptance of this invitation.*

With the invitation, or summons—she wasn't sure which—was a handwritten note.

Dearest Sim,
I know it might be hard for you to come back to Florena,
but I can't imagine getting through this day without my
best friend.
All my love, Ed.

She turned the card over and slipped it under a book on her desk. Go back to Florena? Not just for a quick flying visit to her mother but to go to the coronation? And a ball? To be seen and photographed?

You don't have to go.

It was true. No one would tie her up and force her to attend. And once the coronation was over she would be free to leave.

She didn't have a choice. Not really.

I can't imagine getting through this day without my best friend.

My best friend. After everything, he was still her best friend, and this was probably the most important day of his life. As hard as it would be for her, it would be unforgivable not to be there for him.

To go as his friend.

He'd said that on that wonderful and horrible evening two months ago, before he'd been whisked away to assume his duties. He might as well have asked her to go as his sister.

'Friend' was something, though. It wasn't nothing.

But even after their kisses he was still thinking of her as just his friend.

That time on the bridge had nearly ripped her in two. There was no doubt in her mind that if the phone call from his father had come later they would have made love and their relationship would have changed for ever.

She sighed. It didn't matter what either of them had thought or felt on the bridge that night.

She couldn't have gone to Florena as anything *but* his friend. Now that he was King there was really no possibility of them being together. Friendship would be all they were allowed to have. No matter how much their bodies might wish otherwise. Ed knew that. Her heart just had to realise too.

To be fair to Ed, he hadn't meant to hurt her or insult her by asking her to go to Florena as his friend. He really did want his friend there by his side. And she wanted to be there for him too—as his friend, apart from anything else.

She ached when she thought of him in Florena on his own, facing his new life. Alone.

Once it's over you will leave.

CHAPTER TEN

SIMONE HADN'T BEEN back to Florena for over two years. Her mother always joined her in Paris for a week over Christmas, so Simone did not have to leave the bookshop. It had been a decade since Simone had called the kingdom home, and now she could see the country as any visitor might.

The palace sat on a high peak, keeping watch over the city and the great valley of Florena. In summer the valley was green and lush. Now, in midwinter, the slopes were covered in their famous powdery snow.

The small country was picturesque.

Her heart began to soar when she saw it, but she caught it and pushed it back down again. Florena might look as if it had been ripped from the pages of a fairy tale, but she knew better. She knew that looks were deceiving and fairy tales were most definitely not real.

The apartment where Simone had grown up was two storeys above the palace kitchen. The building was nearly as old as the main palace, but in the last century the upper levels had been converted into comfortable and spacious apartments for the senior staff.

Their living room overlooked the ancient cobblestoned courtyard that palace staff criss-crossed all day, going about their lives much as they had for centuries. Doing laundry, gardening and cooking. Simone's old bedroom had a view of one of the palace's private walled gardens. The manicured grass where Ed and Simone had once played with Suzette was now covered in snow.

She was privileged to have grown up there and to be able to return when she wanted to visit Alea, who had now been given the security of a lifetime tenancy in her apartment—one of the last things the former King had done before abdicating.

The old King Edouard might have deeply hurt his son in the way he'd abandoned the crown without consultation, but Simone could not help being grateful for the way he'd thought about his loyal staff at the end—especially with everything else on his mind.

Simone understood that the King—that was the former King, now styled as the Duke of Armiel—was living in southern France with Celine, awaiting the birth of their daughter in the coming May.

The Queen, who still held that title, had only returned to Florena briefly and quietly, and was now dividing her time between the Caribbean and New York. She had agreed to a divorce, but the negotiations over property were fraught. Simone understood from her mother and from general rumour that the Queen would keep half her fortune, leaving the remaining half with Ed. Ed had some money his maternal grandfather had left directly to him, but the Queen's fortune was so large that even half of it still left both of them on most rich lists. The new Duke of Armiel would have to rely on his own funds, which were believed to be small, along with generosity from Ed.

Ed... She sighed.

He had been in touch since he'd left Paris, with occasional messages and phone calls that were memorable for all the wrong reasons. There'd been either long pauses or they'd spoken over one another. Even their messages had been polite and perfunctory. Neither of them had dared to mention that night in Paris.

The morning after her arrival back in the palace, Simone sat looking out of the window at the activity in the courtyard with a cup of hot coffee warming her hands.

'What are you doing today?' her mother asked as she ate her breakfast.

'Relaxing here, I think.'

'Do you have plans to see Ed?'

Simone shook her head. Ed knew Simone had accepted her invitation to the coronation, but she hadn't told him exactly when she would arrive. He'd be busy with preparations and with being King. He wouldn't have time for her.

'I think he'd like to see you. He'd appreciate seeing a friendly face.'

Simone wanted to pump her mother for further information, but didn't want to risk giving anything away. She wasn't even mentally prepared to answer questions about Ed, let alone to see him.

They'd kissed. Made out as they'd wound their way across Paris like teenagers or tourists. And if that phone call hadn't come from Ed's father they would, she was ninety-nine per cent sure, have ended up in bed. Any reservations she might have had had been shattered as he'd held her and she'd felt how much he'd wanted her too.

'Never mind,' her mother said. 'Do you have an outfit for the coronation?'

Simone nodded. 'An advantage of living in Paris.'

She'd spent some of her precious savings on it, but she was determined to look amazing.

'And for the ball?'

'I don't think I'll go.'

'What? You must come. All the long-standing staff have been invited.'

Simone winced. She knew she couldn't miss the corona-tion…but the ball? It was a social event and she would feel completely out of place. Besides, her mother's comment confirmed what Simone had expected. All the long-term staff of the palace were invited. Simone's invitation was by virtue of her mother's position only.

'So I take it you don't have a dress?'

'No. So, you see, I can't go.' She shrugged.

'Not so fast, *mademoiselle*. I may have something... It might need taking in, but we're a similar size.'

Alea disappeared into her room and returned with a large white box. She lifted the lid and Simone gasped. The box was overflowing with raw silver silk. Her mother lifted miles of fabric out of the box, revealing a bodice with a sweetheart neckline. The bodice was embroidered with intricate flowers and swirls.

It was a work of art.

'When did you get this?'

Simone had thought she was aware of most of the formal wear in her mother's wardrobe, and was sure she would not have missed something like this.

'Oh, I'm not sure.' Alea waved the question away. 'Try it on.'

Even without make-up or her hair done, Simone was transformed. She wouldn't be inconspicuous if she wore this dress. Her plan for her stay in Florena was to fly under the radar. She wanted to avoid press attention at all costs.

'It's a statement piece,' her mother said.

'But what sort of statement would I be making?' Simone mumbled, mostly to herself.

'It says that you belong. It says you are regal.'

'But I'm not regal—and I don't think I should pretend I am.' She had no intention of pretending to be royal.

'Regal is a state of mind,' Alea said.

'I'm not sure I can back up whatever this dress is saying.'

'Why not?'

Simone shook her head. Any answer would only invite more questions.

Since arriving back in her childhood home, she had been struggling to supress her sixteen-year-old self. The naïve, uncertain parts of herself. In Paris she was confident, worldly and strong. Back here she was constantly expecting someone to remember her as the girl who had tried to serenade the Prince.

Paris, she realised, was also a state of mind. She needed to channel some of her inner Parisienne to make it through the next week.

'But you'll wear it?' her mother asked.

Simone nodded only to placate her. She would decide later if she really could subject herself to the scrutiny of a public ball.

'Great.'

Her mother kissed her and left for work, leaving Simone standing in the dress in front of the mirror. She swayed her hips and watched the fabric swirl around her legs.

Make-believe.

It wasn't real.

Just as what had happened between her and Ed wasn't real.

Oh, it had happened. She hadn't dreamt it. They had really kissed and spent an amazing evening wandering the streets of Paris together.

But her feelings were pointless, hopefully temporary, and maddening. She'd fallen for Ed once—a childhood crush, certainly, but still devastating in the way only first love could be. She wasn't going to make the mistake of falling in love with him as an adult. She'd worked too hard to overcome her heartache the first time.

And Ed's feelings for her...? They were fleeting at best. Most likely already non-existent. She'd caught Ed at a vulnerable moment. He'd been under stress because of his family problems. Trapped in her apartment. In the ordinary course of things he would never have kissed her. Much less said he wanted to sleep with her. Simone *knew* that.

Fairy tales were not real.

What *was* real were internet trolls, threats on social media and online harassment. She'd already had a taste of that, thank you very much. Now that Ed was the King, the scrutiny on anyone he dated would be intense. She wasn't up for that, emotionally or psychologically. It was part of the package Ed came with, so she needed to keep a firm lid on any feelings that threatened to rise up in her again. Like they had when she was a teenager.

So she wasn't about to drop in on him today or any other day she was here. She wasn't going to bombard him with messages that would only distract him from his duties. Or, worse, make him feel that he had to come down here and explain to her that what had happened between them in Paris had been a mistake.

Two days after the coronation she'd leave. The next time she returned to Florena would be next Christmas, and by that point the time she and Ed had spent together in Paris would be a vague memory. Something that had happened in the crazy time before the old King's abdication.

André had offered to run the bookshop while she was away and she had gratefully accepted. In the meantime, she would stay in her mother's apartment and catch up on some screen time. Watch some movies by the fire. She might help her mother out in the kitchen, but she was unlikely to cross Ed's path.

She probably wouldn't even see him. He was the King now. He'd be too busy to see her, much less anything else.

She unzipped the dress, climbed out of it, and went for a shower.

Ed hadn't thought it would be easy leaving Simone in Paris, but he hadn't expected it to be as hard as it had been. He'd walked away from women before, and even though Simone was different from the others he hadn't expected this.

Constantly looking around for her.

Starting to speak to her.

Reaching for her and always finding she wasn't there.

He hadn't expected to go to bed hoping to dream about her.

He hadn't expected to feel so devastated each time he woke to find she wasn't next to him. That he had to face another long day alone.

The past few months had been the most stressful in his life. The abdication, defending the country against pressure from Laurent and now preparing for the coronation… It had been enough to push even the most resilient person to the brink.

Was it any wonder his feelings for Simone were so confusing? She was his oldest friend, and now a woman he'd kissed and been minutes away from sleeping with. That didn't have to mean anything, did it? The dreams? Talking to her when she wasn't there? The longing that rippled through his body when he thought of her? That was all just because of the stress, wasn't it?

The one thing he knew for certain was that she was back in Florena today.

Last night, to be precise. Alea had told him she would arrive late. He'd figured she needed some time with her mother, but it was now the morning and Alea would have left for work. He couldn't wait another moment.

He'd wanted to call Simone every day, and each time had had to stop himself. Partly because hearing her voice wasn't the balm he'd hoped it would be. Only a further reminder of what was missing from his life. And also because what if she got the wrong idea and thought that his intentions towards her were more than they could be?

Because they couldn't be together. She lived in Paris, had a life there—a life she was rightly proud of—and he couldn't ask her to give that up. Besides, since his father's abdication, the very future of his country depended upon Ed staying out of the tabloids.

A relationship wasn't in itself a problem…but a break-up? A scandal? That would be just the sort of thing that would send his people to the polls and end the independence of his country.

That was not going to happen while Ed was King. He'd devoted his whole life to this country and he wasn't about to see it swallowed up to fulfil the political ambitions of Pierre Laurent. His role might be largely ceremonial, but that wasn't nothing. His job description stretched from diplomat to charity worker and many things in between. The monarchy gave Florenans pride in their country and in their history. It gave them stability.

It was a lot to put on one person's shoulders. Which was probably why sometimes—after the dreams, after he spoke to her when she wasn't there—he forgot all the reasons why they couldn't be together. Because he wanted her. It was selfish, but he needed her.

She should be here with him. She belonged here. She should be with him. Should share his bed and share his life.

Then he'd remember.

Duty. Fidelity. The future of Florena. The fact that no King Edouard had ever managed to stay faithful to his wife. The fact that one more scandal might spell the end of the entire country.

Ed drew a deep breath and knocked on Simone's apartment door.

Duty. Fidelity. Florena.

Simone threw open the door and said, 'Did you forget your key—? Ooh!'

Ed forgot all those things. At that moment he wasn't even capable of remembering his own name. Simone was wearing only a white towel, her skin still bright and glistening from a recent shower, her hair tied messily on her head.

Ooh! indeed.

He wanted to reply with a witty retort, but he'd forgotten every word he'd ever known.

'Ed, I'm sorry. I thought you were my mother.'

Ed. She'd called him by his shortened name. His nickname. She was the first person in three months not to call him 'Your Majesty' and he wanted to kiss her for it.

He wanted to kiss her for many reasons.

When he still couldn't respond, she said, 'You'd better come in, just in case anyone comes past.'

He followed her inside and as she reached behind him to close the door he caught her scent. Flowers. Summer.

'I'll just get dressed,' she said.

'No,' he said.

The first word out of his mouth since he'd walked in and his voice felt strange.

She gave him a questioning look.

'It's good to see you, Simone.'

He stepped towards her and leant down to kiss her cheek, breathing her in. The scent of her bodywash mixed with the steam from the shower and swirled around him. His knees weakened.

He felt a sweet sigh escape Simone's mouth—and that was the end of him. He pulled her into his arms, wet towel and all, and kissed her lips. Properly. Without hesitation or restraint. Picking up exactly where they had left off before the phone call telling him about the abdication had come.

She melted into the kiss. Paris came back to him in flashbacks: her smiles, her soft skin, their bodies pressed against one another's. His body remembered hers as if it had been yesterday. And hadn't it? Hadn't everything else in the world stopped when she hadn't been around?

'Ed!' she gasped as she pulled away. 'Is this…? Should…?'

'You're having trouble with your words too,' he said.

Her brow furrowed.

'Your mother's downstairs.'

'My mother's the least of our worries.'

'I'm not worried.'

And he wasn't. They were in private, and he trusted Simone with his life. For once his feelings were completely certain. He wanted her. As soon as possible.

'I am!'

He reluctantly let her go. As he stepped back her towel dropped, exposing a beautiful bare breast and a very erect pink nipple. He grinned, and Simone pulled the towel to her. Muscles inside him that had been inert for the past few months suddenly woke up.

'They don't deserve to be covered up,' he said.

Her flushed face turned ever redder. 'I'm only here for a week,' she said.

'Do you mean, *I'm only here for a week so I shouldn't let that towel drop*? or do you mean, *I'm only here for a week so I may as well let the towel drop*?'

His throat went stone-dry as he waited for her answer. Just when he thought he might crack, the shadow of a grin appeared across her beautiful face.

'Maybe the latter?'

'Maybe?'

He stepped towards her. Ready to pull the towel away. Ready to rip his own shirt off his back as soon as she told him she was sure.

'What if someone finds out?' she said.

'I'm not cheating on anyone. We're two single consenting adults. We're not doing anything wrong.'

'I don't want to do anything that will jeopardise your job... the country.'

'It's unlikely anyone will ever find out. No one knows about Paris.'

He reached out and rubbed the back of his thumb over her bare shoulder. There was no one in the world he trusted more.

'Is that all you're worried about or is there something else? Say the word and I'll walk away now.'

She swallowed hard.

'Okay. I won't walk away. I'll leave the room while you get changed, and then I'll ask you to come and have a coffee with me and a walk around the garden. Which was, by the way, my original plan. You greeting me warm from the shower and wearing only a towel that doesn't seem to be able to stay up was a happy accident, but not part of my plan.'

She laughed, and he knew it would all be okay. Whatever happened.

In a rush she moved towards him and lifted herself to his lips. The surge of relief and emotion that ripped through him made him groan. Simone was in his arms. Warm, soft, wet. Smelling like soap and heaven. Tasting like coffee and home. Their lips pressed together. Their muscle memory from Paris knew exactly how to angle their heads to mesh their mouths perfectly.

She slipped her arms around his neck and pushed her fingers through his hair. His knees almost gave way. This woman was magnificent. Her sighs asked him for more and he was only too happy to give it. It was more wonderful and more satisfying than anything he'd felt since the last time he'd held her in his arms.

The towel dropped away again, this time to the floor. Simone was utterly naked, utterly gorgeous, and utterly in his arms. Suddenly his own clothing was too hot and way too tight. He shrugged off his jacket and it landed with her towel. Simone's pretty fingers dug his shirt out of his waistband and the sensation of her fingertips stroking his stomach made every muscle south of his waist tighten. She kissed him passionately as she undid his shirt buttons, one by one. He wanted to help, but his fingers were currently busy trailing their way down the smooth skin of her back to her perfect bottom.

It was a dilemma. Every second he spent undressing himself was a second he couldn't hold Simone, and he was quite sure he never wanted to let her go.

She tugged his shirt away from his body and threw it to the floor with a force that suggested she was as pleased as he was to see it gone.

Skin on skin was magical. The feeling of her bare body against his brought every sensation in his body to the surface.

'You have no idea how much I've missed you,' he murmured against her neck.

'I have some idea.'

'I've thought of you every hour… I've missed you every minute…'

Simone pulled back and looked at him. Her expression was dumbstruck. Her eyes were open wide and her jaw slack. He'd said too much and was in danger of saying even more. He didn't know how he felt about Simone. His feelings were confusing. Overwhelming. He didn't know how to describe them to himself, let alone how to explain them to her.

Except to say that he'd missed her so much that it had ached. A physical pain in his body that wasn't relieved by exercise or work, sleep or alcohol.

Her mouth found his, again and again. All his words left him. There was only Simone and skin and warmth and this room.

Coronation? What coronation?

Constitutional crisis? What constitutional crisis?

Her fingers were at his waistband again, expertly undoing his belt and his trousers.

Manoeuvring his trousers at this stage of his arousal needed a gentle touch, and when her fingers touched him he reached down and held her hand.

He'd been waiting so long he knew that if she touched him there he might just come apart.

'Is everything all right?' she asked.

'Everything's wonderful.'

He wriggled his way out of his underpants and then pulled her back to him. For a brief second he thought about slowing down and taking their time. This was the first time they'd made love. They should be savouring, lingering... But maybe she felt, like him, that they were already making up for lost time. This hadn't been five minutes in the making. It had been three months. Their lives had been on pause since their last kiss.

Things were building inside him...sweet and, oh, so strong.

He felt himself being nudged in the direction of her bedroom, but her mouth didn't leave his. They were having a new type of conversation with their lips. No less meaningful than any they had had with actual words in the past.

I want you. I need you. Don't stop. Yes. There. Please.

She kicked the bedroom door closed with a satisfying bang and they tumbled onto her bed. His lips sought out her breasts and took a hard nipple into his mouth. She moaned, and he could feel her sighing. She was barely holding herself together, just like him. His tongue and her nipples were a magical, combustible combination.

Her hips bucked beneath him and the sheets bunched in her hands. She was as ready as he was, and it made him feel more powerful than any title they might bestow upon him.

'Ed… Ed, for the sake of your kingdom, please tell me you've got protection.'

Her question momentarily snapped him back to reality. The royal family already had one unexpected child on the way— they did not need another.

'Yes,' he panted, and dragged his body away from hers. 'Wallet.'

He hadn't come to see her with the intention of seducing her, but a part of him clearly hadn't ruled it out entirely.

Simone sat up on her bed with her blonde hair tousled around her flushed face. She grinned at him, temporarily halting his mission. He knelt back on the bed and kissed her again. He couldn't get enough.

A low murmur escaped her lips and she pushed him away. 'Have you forgotten what you were doing?' she asked.

He climbed off the bed and opened the door, hearing Simone whistle as she watched him from behind. With relief he saw that the living room was still unoccupied. He grabbed his trousers and went back to the bedroom. He found his wallet and the protection it contained. Ripped the packet as he rushed back to her.

She took his hand and the packet. 'Let me…' she murmured.

He had to bite back a moan as he watched her delicate fingers sheath him, trying his hardest not to come apart in her hands.

'I want you…' She nuzzled his neck.

'I want you.'

All of you. Always.

But he didn't say that to her. He barely acknowledged the thought to himself. It was too big, too much, considering the task that now lay before him. Not falling apart before she did. Not making a right royal mess of their first time together.

He must have paused too long with the thought, because Simone tugged at him, took his face in her hands and looked him straight in the eye. Then she adjusted herself, guiding him into her.

Her eyes half-closed, mouth half-open, she surrendered herself completely to him. There was a thin sheen of perspiration on her forehead. Her lips were swollen as he brought her to the brink.

Once they were as one, he didn't want it to end. This was his true destiny.

The rest of the world stopped and it was just them. Nothing else mattered. Not duty. Time. Nothing but Simone. They wound each other so perfectly tight and reached a perfect peak before they both found release. They held each other as they tumbled, fell, and came completely undone.

CHAPTER ELEVEN

IT WAS AS if she'd just woken up from an erotic dream. Disorientated, breathless, hot. And very confused.

Because this wasn't a dream.

It was a very real encounter.

Ed was next to her, also catching his breath, warm and trembling.

She rested her head against his chest and he pulled her against him, each anchoring the other as the waves of pleasure continued to wash through them.

She brought her breath in time with his and enjoyed the feeling of his firm chest against her cheek.

You've just made love with the King, a little voice whispered in her head.

But she dismissed it easily. He might be the King, but he was still just Ed too.

You've just made love with Ed.

She was incapable of moving even an inch because of the happy chemicals still thumping through her body.

And the shock.

And Ed's arm, flung across her, trapping her where she'd fallen.

His breathing was heavy, his face sweaty. His head tipped back and he looked up at the ceiling as he groaned.

'Oh, Sim. I can't believe we've only just realised we could do that.'

She was in real trouble.

Over the years Simone had often sought solace in the thought that maybe Ed wasn't very good in bed. That maybe they weren't physically compatible. It hadn't been a silly thought. They were relaxed in one another's company, and ease in public didn't always translate into heat in the bedroom. It might just as easily lead to something very bland. Maybe Ed, under his suits and underwear, was really not that much...

How wrong she had been.

Not only was Ed really all that and more under his clothes, he had also been at constant pains to please her. She shouldn't be surprised. He was her kind and caring friend. But, strangely, she had expected him to be more selfish in bed than he was. And Ed had most definitely been generous. Over and over again.

Her heart was in more danger than ever.

Ed isn't going to marry, and you aren't going to marry a prince.

No one, least of all Ed, was talking about marriage. This was just a one-off. Completing what they had started in Paris. That was all. A fling.

Can you really have an emotion-free fling with Ed?

She was about to find out.

'You know what I said in Paris?' he murmured.

He'd said so many things in Paris, but she knew what he meant.

'Do you think we've just ruined our friendship?'

'No, I don't feel differently about you,' she said honestly.

So many things had changed between them in the past few months. She cared for him as much as ever, but her emotions were closer to the surface, instead of being safely locked away.

He made a face. 'Really? Then I needed to try harder. Can I have another go?'

She laughed, but he didn't. His face was still calm and serious.

'Do you…feel differently about me?' she asked.

'I've felt differently since Paris,' he replied.

Her stomach swooped. 'What do you mean?'

She was afraid she wouldn't hear his answer over the roar of blood rushing past her ears.

'We haven't seen much of one another over the years.' His gaze fell on her bare shoulder and on his thumb, stroking it. 'I forgot…or rather…maybe I'm seeing you for the first time.'

She couldn't speak. They were words she'd dreamt of him saying. Ever since she was sixteen and had stood up in front of a room of people to sing to him. To tell him she loved him without saying the words.

'And for you? Was this too much of a surprise?' he asked.

'Definitely a surprise.' *You have no idea.* 'But a good one,' she added quickly.

A surprise. In the same way that winning the lottery was a surprise. Something you dreamt of, but never expected to actually happen.

'I'm glad to hear it.'

Ed tipped his head towards her and pressed his lips to hers. Pleasure slid down her spine. Not just because it felt wonderful, but because of the ease with which he did it. As if it was the most natural thing in the world to be kissing one another. Lying here, with him, placing languid kisses on one another was like a dream. Literally. She'd had this dream several, sweaty, discombobulating times in the past few months.

'What's it like?' she asked.

'Being with you? Wonderful.'

She swatted him gently.

'I meant being the King.'

'Oh, that. Not nearly as fun as what we just did.'

She smiled against his chest. For a moment he was hers. Just hers.

'I'm serious, though. Now I'm here you can tell me. How's it been? Really?'

'Busy. Stressful. Lonely.'

She tightened her embrace around him. For this moment at least he wouldn't be lonely. At this moment everything was as it should be.

They lay like that for a while. Talking, laughing, touching one another. The distant sound of a trumpet playing somewhere in the palace reminded her.

'Don't you have a kingdom to run?' she asked.

'Do I? I'd forgotten.'

His joking was sweet, and for a few precious moments she felt like the most important thing in the world to him.

But they both knew it couldn't last.

'You can't forget,' she said.

'I know, but it would be nice, wouldn't it?'

She propped herself up and looked at him. 'Yes, but it's just a fantasy. We both know it's fun to think about from time to time, but you have your life and I have mine.'

Ed's eyes darkened as he held her gaze. 'How long are you here for?'

'A week. I leave two days after your coronation.'

He grimaced, as if she'd reminded him of an execution and not of what should be one of the proudest days of his life.

'I'd like to see you again,' he said.

Again. The word shocked her back to the present and the reality they had forgotten for the past few hours.

Simone spun her legs off the edge of the bed and grabbed the nearest piece of clothing—her pyjama top, discarded hours earlier—and pulled it to her. The happy hormones had worn off and she'd hit the cold wall of reality with a thud.

She tugged the top over her head.

It was all very well to let herself get swept away with Ed and how wonderful it felt being with him, but they had to return to the real world. The one where he was the King of a country in crisis and she had built her own life and her own business in Paris.

Ed sat up. His gorgeous bare torso taunted her from her messed-up bed. Begging her to slide her hands over it and feel its hard magnificence.

'What's the matter?' he asked.

'It can't happen again.'

She searched her bedroom floor for some other clothes. Something to cover her bottom half. Suddenly she was feeling too naked. It was all very well to walk around the apartment naked when they were in the throes of passion, but now that they had to redraw the lines of their relationship she was feeling too exposed.

Protecting her heart was now her first priority.

'As wonderful as this was, you know we can't do this again.'

For a heartbeat, part of her hoped he'd argue with her, but he didn't.

'Can we see each other as friends?'

'I don't know.'

It was an honest answer. She didn't know how she could possibly sit across a table from him or on a sofa and talk to him while not thinking about what they had just done. She could still feel his mouth on her most sensitive parts. Her mind was still full of the memory of him moving so strongly and beautifully inside her. Her muscles were still trembling.

The answer on her lips was, *No. We can't. Because if we do I won't be able to push these feelings back down again. You are so close to breaking me completely.*

It hurt to even think it.

'Simone, I'm not just going to walk out of here without a plan to see you again. I don't want us to do the awkward silence thing again. The last few months…not knowing if I should call you or not…have been awful.'

She put her face in her hands so she wouldn't have to look him in the eyes and see the pain written across them.

Could they be friends?

Can you imagine not being friends with Ed?

And that was it, wasn't it? She couldn't really conceive of a future that he wasn't part of in some way.

'Tonight?' she said.

'Tonight I have an official government dinner.'

And there it was. It wasn't his fault, but his duty would always come first. As it should. She hung her head.

'Tomorrow, though. I can cancel my plans tomorrow night.'

She shook her head. 'Ed, this is hard enough as it is. We both know this is impossible. *We're* impossible. I don't think we should make things any harder than they already are.'

'I have a few hours tomorrow afternoon, I think.'

She laughed. 'Ed, face it. Your life isn't yours any more. I don't want to make things harder for you.'

Or for me.

'You don't even want to spend time with me?' he asked.

It was so hard to explain that she did want to be with him, but she also didn't. It sounded foolish, but there it was. She was torn in two.

'Of course I want to spend time with you. But things just got complicated, didn't they?'

She looked down. She was wearing only her pyjama top and her panties from yesterday. She couldn't even dress herself, she was in such a state.

'You said nothing had changed,' he said.

'What?'

'A moment ago, you said your feelings hadn't changed.'

A moment ago her body had still been flooded with endorphins. Now reality had broken through.

'I spoke too quickly. Besides, it doesn't matter how I feel. The world has changed. The situation is different. You're the King.'

'I'm still me.'

His voice was small. Not at all regal. And it broke her heart.

How could she reconcile this monarch, the figurehead of his country, with the boy she'd always known?

It didn't matter if she could or not. She simply had to. They both had to.

And they both had to realise that this thing between them—whatever it was—belonged to their old lives and not their new futures.

'I know.' She knelt on the bed and took his face in her hands, cradling it. God, he was beautiful. 'I know. But we can't change what's happened. You have your duty and I won't let you jeopardise that for me. Besides, we both know I don't belong here.'

'Sim…'

His words petered out and they both knew there was nothing left to say. She left the bedroom and him to go and get dressed.

A few minutes later he emerged from the room, fully dressed and ready for a day of official duties. Looking as if nothing had just happened.

He kissed her quickly on the cheek. 'We'll figure something out. I promise.'

She nodded, but didn't believe him.

It was late morning—not even lunchtime—but to her body clock it felt like the middle of the night. She felt as if she'd lived a thousand hours, yet in real life it was no more than four.

That was the effect Ed had on her.

She wandered around the apartment, looking at her mother's things. Ceramic figurines that had belonged to Simone's grandmother, a framed photograph of Simone's mother and father on their wedding day.

She picked it up and held it closer to study it. It was slightly yellow, older than Simone herself. They looked happy. They had loved each other. And if cancer hadn't taken her father too soon they would still be together. Simone was sure of it. After all, Alea had never remarried. Until the last two or three years Alea hadn't even considered dating anyone.

Simone put down the frame and picked up the next photograph. It was of her and Ed, posing with Suzette. They couldn't have been older than ten. She didn't remember the photo being taken, but she remembered the jeans and bright stripy sweater she'd been wearing.

This was why she didn't come back here. It felt and smelt like her childhood, and those memories were overwhelming. Because they were all memories of Ed.

Happy memories, to be sure. Her happiest. Of waiting for Ed to come by. Of playing in the garden with him. Of sitting on her couch—this very couch—watching television with him. Of playing video games. Of playing with Suzette.

Suzette the cocker spaniel. She'd been a deep golden brown that had faded as she'd got older. She had been one of the first beings to meet her here when Simone had first arrived, still reeling and confused after her father's death. Not quite understanding the enormity and significance of their move, she'd been excited to be moving to an actual palace. She'd loved her new bedroom at first sight, and then she had seen the garden from her window.

She'd rushed down and found Suzette.

A puppy! She'd always wanted a dog.

The palace really had seemed like a fairy tale. And then the boy had come along. She hadn't known he was the Prince at first. In fact, she hadn't realised that for a while. He'd just been Ed. A boy about her own age who had told her where the balls were, to throw to Suzette, and shown her all the secrets of the garden.

Simone fell asleep on the sofa. But even her dreams were about her childhood.

Another memory. She was fourteen. The last day of the school year. She'd come home from school, sad to be saying goodbye to her friends for the summer, but glad that Ed was returning from boarding school. And there he'd been, in the palace kitchen, talking to her mother. And eating. Because that was what fifteen-year-old boys did.

And no wonder. When he'd stood up she'd seen that he was nearly a foot taller than he'd been in the winter. Clean, soft face. A jawline that was starting to firm up. Shoulders that were broader and straighter than when she'd seen him last. But still the same deep green eyes that reminded her of the evergreen trees that grew in the garden. When he'd smiled her stomach had flipped. A new and strange sensation.

I love him, her fourteen-year-old self had thought.

She might have been young, but she'd *known*. She'd known in her heart that she loved this boy like her own soul, and would never stop loving him.

And then suddenly they were in the summer house, and everyone was laughing and pointing at her. Mocking her singing. She tried to get out of the room, but people kept blocking her way. And laughing. Laughing. Laughing...

CHAPTER TWELVE

ED HAD HIS dinner with the French Ambassador moved to lunch, and then cancelled some other appointments, saying he needed to preserve his energy for coronation day. It wasn't a lie, exactly. He was doing something for his own mental health by seeing Simone that night.

She didn't want them to sleep together again, and he not only respected that decision but reluctantly agreed that she was right. She was stronger than him. She was saving him from himself. Making sure that this thing between them—he didn't know what to call it—didn't get any more difficult than it already was.

He had to put his job first.

Duty first.

Wasn't that what being the King was really all about?

His father had spoken to him throughout his life about sacrifice—sacrifice for his country, his people, the greater good—and Ed had never understood. Being King would be an honour and even a pleasure, he'd thought. He wouldn't be giving up anything. Anonymity? He'd never had that anyway.

Now he understood. Now, not only did he understand in his head, but he felt it in his chest—the true meaning of sacrifice.

Simone would leave Florena after the coronation. Things would return to how they had been and it would get easier. It always did. Any time he said goodbye to a woman it hurt for a while and then it got better.

Simone's been the last thing you think of each night and the first each morning since you got back from Paris.

He conceded that might be true, but that was just due to their unfinished business in Paris. The rude interruption of his father's abdication. Now that they had scratched that itch—so to speak—things would return to the way they had been. Simone had made it clear there was no other choice.

And as usual she was right.

This brought him to Sara. His stylist, hairdresser and sometime make-up artist. Because, yes, he occasionally wore make up. For television appearances, mostly. Or official photographs. A light dusting of power to stop the glare of stage lights. Or some concealer to hide the effects of a big night.

He was a figurehead. If he didn't look healthy people talked. If he looked hungover they talked even more.

But now Sara paused when he made his request. 'Are you sure?'

He nodded and she set to work. In fact he was shocked with the enthusiasm with which she tackled her assignment. A few times she even laughed. She was enjoying herself way too much. And when he asked for recommendations as to where he could take an old friend for a night out she was equally obliging.

When she'd completed her handiwork, she even helped him choose an outfit and pad out his shoulders to complete the look.

When he stood in front of the mirror she cackled, patted him on the shoulder and wished him luck. 'I'll be keeping an eye on social media.'

'What?'

'Kidding. I'll resign if someone identifies you. I'd consider it a professional failure.'

Ed turned from side to side in front of the mirror. He was quite proud of his new nose. It was large. Any larger and it would be too distinctive. But it was balanced out by the wrin-

kles she'd given him. And the wart. He was less keen on the
wart, but Sara had insisted.

She'd definitely got too much pleasure from making him look
as if he was forty years older than he was, but he had been prepared to let her. She was doing him a favour. He wanted to show
Simone that even after yesterday morning they were friends,
first and foremost. No funny business. He wasn't taking her out
to seduce her, but so they could have a friendly night together.

Simone would not be attracted to him looking as he did now.
Like a seventy-year-old man with a gigantic nose and a wart
on his chin. When he arrived at her door looking like this she
would know that he was serious about their friendship. That he
could accept that friends were all they would ever be.

Either that or she'd laugh.

It was very strange, walking through the palace made up as
he was. No one bowed, but they did give him puzzled looks.
Still, no one stopped him to ask who he was and what he was
doing. Something he ought to bring up with his head of security.

Simone opened the door to the apartment and didn't speak
for a long time. He didn't want to be recognised, but this was
Simone! If she didn't recognise him he'd know that he was safe
to go out in public.

But he'd also be strangely disappointed.

A few heartbeats passed before a smile crept over her face.
'Your Majesty.'

'What gave me away?'

'What do you mean? You look exactly like you did yesterday
morning. Only now you look like you had a good night's sleep.'

'Ha-ha.'

'What on earth are you doing?'

'I've come to ask if you would like to go out for a drink
with me.'

She laughed. 'With you looking like that?'

'It's my disguise. The glasses might have worked in Paris,
but here I need something a bit more.'

'That's definitely *more*. Who did you get to do it? Jim Henson?'

'Again, you're hilarious. My stylist—Sara. She was surprisingly happy to do it for me.'

Alea poked her head around the door, did a double-take, then laughed.

He stepped into the room and did a spin. 'What do you think?'

Alea was kinder than her daughter. 'It's only your voice that gives you away. If you don't speak, no one will know who you are.'

'Thank you.' He turned back to Simone. 'So, will you come with me?'

Simone turned to her mother, said they'd been planning on spending the evening together, but Alea waved her out through the door.

'Go—have fun. You've been hanging out here all day. Go and have a good night.'

'I'm in my pyjamas,' Simone said.

Ed recognised the lovely curve-skimming silk set from Paris. He swallowed.

'So go and change!' Ed and Alea said in unison.

Simone pulled on some fitted black trousers and a soft, loose white sweater. She examined herself in the mirror. It was just a casual night out. There was no need to go overboard. But then she remembered the last time she'd gone to one of Florena's bars and she pulled down a box from the top of her wardrobe.

It was her old dressing up box. Full of odd but fun items that she and Alea had collected over the years. She took out the short dark wig she had worn to a fancy dress party when she had gone as Lois Lane. She tucked her long blonde hair up inside it and put on some lipstick.

She hardly recognised herself.

'Hey, why do *you* need a disguise?' Ed said when she emerged from her room.

'It's hardly the same as yours,' she said, as they made their way to the back door of the palace.

'But still… Why?'

She should be honest with him. This was still Ed.

'Once, a few years ago, I went out in the old town with Mum. I was photographed. And…well, they linked photos of me with that video and piled on the abuse. I know it isn't anything like what you have to endure, but I'd rather wear the wig.'

And if Ed was recognised her name might be published next to his.

She didn't tell him that, though, because it would sound as if she was ashamed to be with him. Which she wasn't.

She was protecting them both.

Ed frowned, but picked up her gloved hand and squeezed it. Simone looked around the quiet street. There was no one around. For a few minutes they walked along the road like any normal couple.

The moment ended when they reached the old town. Despite the cold and the late hour, the cobblestoned streets were still full of people and Simone dropped Ed's hand. The Christmas decorations had been taken down and replaced with bunting for the coronation. Flags of red and white—Florena's national colours—hung in strings across the streets. Fairy lights adorned half the houses. The other half were strung with garlands of evergreen branches.

The shopfronts were decorated too. A string of bejewelled paper crowns hung in the window of an old sweet shop. The next shop was a cake shop, with a large cake shaped like a crown in its window and a display of cupcakes making up the Florenan flag. It seemed every shopfront on the cobblestoned street was preparing for the coronation.

'It's amazing,' Simone said.

Ed nodded.

'This is all for you,' she whispered. 'Can you get your head around it? I'm not sure that I can.'

'No, I can't. It's like there are two of me,' he said. 'The King and Ed.'

She nodded and turned. 'Duty first.'

He reached for her hand again and drew her to him. Even that small, innocent gesture felt risky, standing where they were.

'Don't forget, Simone. I'm still Ed. I'm still your Ed.'

She nodded, though she didn't agree.

Ed showed her into a nearby old-style pub. It was small, with low ceilings and a roaring fire. Simone ordered their drinks, both judging it best if Ed did as little speaking to others as possible, and they found a quiet table near the back.

Candles lit the table, but even in the low light she could still make out the sparkle in Ed's eyes.

Even with the make-up he was still handsome.

You will still adore him when he's old. There will never be a time when you are not attracted to him.

She shook her head.

'What are you thinking?' he asked.

She sighed. 'I'm thinking how unfair it is that you will probably still be handsome when you're seventy.'

Ed smiled, but then looked down. 'Do I look like my father? I'm worried I look like him.'

'Honestly, no. You don't. You look like your mother.'

He grinned. 'I'm sure she'd love to hear you say that right now.'

'Not now, silly, but in general. You have her eyes and her hair.'

'I feel I'm destined to be like him.' Ed's words were soft.

'You aren't like him.'

'Edouard the Fourth. Philanderer. Cheater. Playboy.'

'You aren't any of those things.'

Simone wanted to reach over the table and pick up his hand, and for a moment it felt as though she could, but she kept her hands tightly in her lap.

'You are your own person. A good person. And you will

show everyone that. You will do your duty. You won't make your father's mistakes.'

You will not get involved with the palace crooner.

Simone continued. 'And your plan is the best one. Stay single. Stay loyal to your country. You will be like Elizabeth the First of England!'

Ed looked sombre. 'I really didn't ask you out tonight to talk about that. I simply wanted to have a night out with my best friend. Truly.'

They ordered another drink each and he told her about his parents and feeling trapped between them and their lawyers. He asked about the bookshop and about Paris. She told him about the TV shows she'd been bingeing, the books she'd come across. Everyday mundane things. For a moment she forgot where she was and why she was there. They drank, they laughed, and they pretended for a few precious hours to be just Simone and Ed.

But soon they made their way back through the streets and to the private gate of the palace. Entering without being noticed, they walked along an ancient colonnade that bounded one side of a small quadrangle at the side of the palace.

'Thank you for this evening,' he said.

'You don't have to thank me.'

'I do. Thank you for giving me a few hours of normality. For letting me pretend.'

'Oh Ed…'

A wave of emotion rushed through her. She wanted to make everything all right for him. She wanted to spend many evenings with him as they just had.

Before she could say anything he had slipped his arm around her waist and pulled her towards him. Their lips, cold at first from the walk, quickly warmed one another on the outside and from within. Her knees wobbled and he pushed her gently against the nearest wall for support.

It was exquisite.

It was tender.

It was too much.

'We shouldn't be doing this. Not here!'

His lips tugged on her lower lip and he let out a tortured groan. 'I know…but it feels so good.'

She felt so good.

Complete.

Home.

She dipped her head. *No.* Home was in Paris.

'Stay,' he said.

The word hung in the air. She was waiting for him to take it back. He was waiting for her answer.

'Not for ever,' he said.

She exhaled.

'Just a little longer…'

'I have to get back to the bookshop. To Paris. I can't come back here. You know that. Nothing's changed. If anything, it would be harder for me to stay here.'

'Why not just try it for a while? A month or two? That's all. Your mother would love it.'

The mention of her mother and the look in his pleading eyes made her chest ache.

'You know I don't feel at home here.'

'But this *is* your home.'

She sighed. She hated having to talk about that video. The mockery and the trolling.

'Ed, please, you're not being fair. Not to me. Or to yourself.'

He couldn't promise her for ever and she respected that—because she couldn't promise it either.

'Is it really about the video?'

'Yes, partly.'

'You shouldn't be worried about that.'

She cringed and stepped away from him. 'Stop joking. It isn't funny.'

'I'm not joking. You sounded fine. It's a difficult song and you weren't awful…'

'Wow, thanks.'

'Sim, you looked lovely. Beautiful. It was really sweet.'

A horrible uncomfortable thought crept over her. 'When was the last time you watched it?'

He bowed his head. 'Recently…'

She narrowed her eyes.

'Okay, maybe yesterday.'

'Yesterday! Why? It was the most embarrassing moment of my life and you're still watching it?'

She set off along the colonnade.

'Simone, I love watching it. I'm sorry, but I do. I love looking at any photo or video of you. I'm quite addicted.'

She stopped and looked across the courtyard at the towers of the palace. He liked her singing. It had taken thirteen years, but she'd finally charmed him. She let out a rueful laugh.

'Have *you* seen it lately?' he asked.

She shook her head.

'You should watch it. I think you might find that it isn't as embarrassing as you remember.'

But whether it was good or bad wasn't the point. The fact that it had made its way to the smartphone screens of everyone in Florena was mortifying. The fact that the photo of her clutching the microphone, mouth wide open and eyes half closed, had launched a thousand memes was enough to make anyone want to emigrate.

And then the online abuse… It had come right off social media and into her own inbox. Trolls, going out of their way to tell her how ugly she was. How stupid she was. How pathetic she was for throwing herself at the Prince. How she should probably end her own life.

'So it was embarrassing?' said Ed. 'We've all done drunk karaoke. We've all had embarrassing photos of us published. Join the club. Remember those photos of me with the Spanish models?'

She nodded. She remembered those photos all too well. 'It looked like you were enjoying yourself.'

'I'd had too much to drink, and I *was* enjoying myself, but the photos were out of context. It made it look like I was a second away from ripping their bikinis off with my teeth.'

She raised an eyebrow 'And were you?'

'No. Someone just took the photo at the wrong moment.'

She didn't want to think about Ed and the trio of Spanish models he'd been partying with. She also didn't want to think about the video. And what had followed.

She pulled her coat tight against the cold. 'They hate me here.'

'No, they don't.'

'They mocked me. Laughed at me. Some of them told me...'

Some of them had told her to die. She couldn't even say it aloud.

The messages had continued for weeks. At first she'd changed her email address, and then her phone number. But the trolls had still found her. She'd eventually given up all social media. For a sixteen-year-old away from home that had been hard.

It had been weeks before she'd been able to sleep properly again. And all she'd done was to sing a song at a party. If people knew she had slept with the King... Then what? What sort of attacks would await her?

Even if she wanted to stay and put herself through that kind of humiliation again, she wasn't sure she physically could.

'I'm constantly worried that someone will make fun of me, but I've had to learn to rise above it or I'd be paralysed,' Ed said.

'It's different for you. You're the King.'

He blinked. A long, confused blink.

'I'm nobody,' she clarified.

'You're not nobody.'

'But I'm not your Queen. Or even your girlfriend.'

She held her breath while she waited for him to answer. Half hoping and half dreading that he'd contradict her.

You could be my girlfriend. You could be my Queen.
But he didn't.

'I could protect you,' he said.

She sighed deeply. 'You couldn't the last time I hit the front page. No one could. I was sent away. Banished!'

Ed frowned. 'I was a kid then. I didn't know what had gone on. This time I'll protect you.'

'I was sent away. I was such an embarrassment to the palace that I was *sent away*.'

She was one more word away from breaking down.

'Is that what you think?' he asked.

'It's what I *know*. And you even think your father paid my school fees. That's how much they wanted to get rid of me.'

He groaned. 'That's not why you were sent away.'

'Then why?'

He looked at her for a long while before saying, 'I can't tell you why.'

She tugged on her gloves and tightened her scarf, which had been dislodged by their kiss. 'Because that *is* why. I was sent away in disgrace. Even though your father isn't around now, having me here would just give Laurent more ammunition. I have to leave for your sake.'

Ed laughed loudly. 'Bad karaoke singing is not scandalous enough to destroy the country. Even yours.'

Rage built inside her and it took every ounce of control not to scream at him. *Hysterical woman screams at King!* She could write the headline herself.

'The country turned on me—'

'It wasn't the entire country.'

'I wasn't welcome and...'

Her throat closed over. The things they'd said to her... She didn't want to stay and be abused again. Even for Ed.

They reached the door that led up to her apartment.

Ed stepped towards her with his hands out. Perfectly earnest. 'Simone, I'll protect you. It wouldn't be like last time.'

'It doesn't matter. My life's in Paris.'

It was lovely that he wanted to try, but they both knew that her fear of the spotlight was only one of their problems.

'I just wish you'd feel comfortable spending more time here. I don't want to upset you, but I want to keep talking about this. I understand there are many reasons why you wouldn't want to come back, but I don't want you to think that banishment is one of them.'

He leant down and kissed her cheek. His lips lingered and they breathed in each other's scent, as if to carry the memory away with them. Every time she had to say goodbye to him her heart broke a little more.

She turned and began to climb the stairs before she could change her mind.

Back in her room, she tugged off the wig and rubbed her itchy scalp.

He didn't understand what it was like for her. He was the King. He had people to check his social media. He had an army sworn to defend his honour. She'd been kicked out of the country the first time she'd done something wrong.

Even if she wasn't about to be deported again, would she be able to withstand the scrutiny and criticism that was sure to come her way if anyone got wind of the fact that she had slept with the King?

Did she even want to? Was it worth it?

You have to have a strong sense of yourself.

She did have a strong sense of herself. Much more so than when she was sixteen. She was Simone Auclair. She ran a second-hand bookshop in Paris. She loved books and reading and her mother. She loved her friends, Julia and André. She *knew* who she was.

And if she didn't have Paris and her bookshop then who was she? Her mother's daughter? Ed's friend?

She didn't want to be defined by being Ed's girlfriend. Once upon a time that might have been a dream come true, but if that was how she defined herself and then it was taken away from her...? Then who would she be?

Because if she didn't even know who she was, she certainly wouldn't be able to withstand the trolls.

CHAPTER THIRTEEN

AFTER A MEETING to decide on the final details of the coronation, and when he'd finished signing the box of papers for the day, his staff left him alone. Ed took out his phone and brought up the video of Simone singing. He watched it more regularly than he'd like to admit to anyone.

Remembering her words from last night, he didn't click on the link. To her, it was a betrayal for him to watch the video.

Simone in his arms was everything he'd never known he wanted—no, needed. All the dreams he'd been too afraid to picture.

She's your best friend, and for a precious morning was your lover.

His overwhelming thought after making love with Simone had been that she was the only person in the world he should be doing it with. That everything else in his life up to that point had been not quite right.

He'd put Simone into a mental box. Childhood best friend. And for years he'd kept her there, convinced that that was the only place for her.

Until Paris.

Until he'd finally seen her as the woman she was.

And now there was no going back.

Not that he wanted to. This Simone—this woman who'd lain with him the other morning—was magnificent. Soft and firm in all the right places. Warm and loving and everything he'd never even let himself imagine a lover could be.

Now when he clicked on the video he did feel he was betraying her by doing so. She had been genuinely traumatised by the fallout. She had been young. She'd had to deal with it alone. Worst of all, she genuinely believed that she had been banished from Florena because of it.

What a mess. If only she understood that she'd been sent away to boarding school because of the affair between his father and her mother and that it had nothing to do with the video. If only he could make her understand that... Clearly Alea had not divulged that secret.

For the first time Ed did more than glance at the comments below the video. There were thousands of them. Some complimentary, but most were vile. He'd dealt with online bullies in his time, but the vitriol reserved for women was on a different level entirely. And aimed at a sixteen-year-old girl?

Thank goodness he'd never have a daughter of his own. He didn't have the slightest idea how he'd prepare her for what she was likely to face from the trolls of the world as Princess of Florena.

Still, he didn't put his phone away and considered rewatching the video. Because Simone was gorgeous, and lovely, and her voice played on his heart strings like a maestro. Her singing was heartfelt...as if she was singing to someone.

Maybe he was a little obsessed.

But he was also curious.

Why had she been she singing? Why *that* song? Karaoke had been her idea. But something didn't feel right. It didn't feel like Simone. She wasn't a show-off. She wasn't shy, but usually she took a little persuading to put herself forward in a group where she didn't know many people. She must have had a well thought-out reason for singing.

You've been asking the wrong question. The right question is who was she singing to?

She hadn't known anyone at the party apart from her mother and the senior staff who had always been invited to those events. The rest of the guests had been either his friends or his parents' friends. Simone hadn't known most of those people. Ed hadn't even known many of those people.

Which meant…

His veins turned to ice and he froze.

He was such an idiot.

A special kind of stupid.

Seventeen-year-old boy stupid.

He couldn't believe he'd assumed that Simone's feelings for him had been running parallel with his. That they had only begun seriously in Paris, when his own feelings had.

But what if she had loved him…for ever?

When she'd declined his invitation to come back to Florena with him after the abdication he'd assumed it was because she didn't have feelings for him. Or that any feelings she did have were not strong enough.

But what if it wasn't that at all?

All this time he'd been thinking he'd just been reckless with his own feelings. Risking his own heart. That was one thing, but he realised shamefully that he'd been careless with hers too. He had assumed that he was the only one in danger of being hurt.

You don't know how she feels about you. You don't know anything for sure.

But it might explain why she'd been so upset about the fall-out from the video. It might explain why she'd been so reluctant to come back to Florena. He knew she'd been upset by the trolls and didn't want to risk further humiliation. And she thought she'd been banished once before. Those were all real fears and concerns.

But all this time he'd been assuming that her feelings for him were not strong enough to help her overcome those fears.

But what if he was wrong? What if it was the complete opposite and she didn't want to return precisely because she had feelings for him?

He took off his tie and jacket and threw on his casual sweater.

Even if he was a monarch, he could still be diabolically stupid.

Simone spent the afternoon in the kitchen, helping chop vegetables, cut pastry and wash dishes. Anything the kitchen staff would let her do to keep her mind off what had been happening between her and Ed.

Her mother had hired additional hands to handle the influx of guests over the coronation weekend and to cover for her. As the manager of the kitchen Alea was invited to the coronation and the ball, but she still had to co-ordinate the catering.

The kitchen work might not have kept her mind completely away from Ed. Or his hands. Or the things he could do with his tongue. But at least it had kept her from doing anything stupid. Like calling up André and asking him to run the bookshop on a permanent basis while she lived the rest of her life locked away in the palace as the King's secret mistress.

Of course she'd never do that.

Like everything else it was a silly fantasy. But now she was elbow-deep in grimy water, reminding herself that being with Ed in the long term and keeping her sanity were two diametrically opposed outcomes.

The large kitchen, which had been filled with laughter and chatter, suddenly fell silent behind her. She looked around to see what the problem was. Ed was walking towards her through a wave of bows and mutterings of 'Your Majesty'.

As he approached her he grinned, almost shyly.

But that couldn't be right.

He was never shy around anyone—least of all her.

When he reached her, she bowed too.

'Simone, would you like to have a walk with me?'

'I'm…' She was about to tell him she was busy and refuse his invitation, but then she saw all the eyes trained on her. 'Certainly, Your Majesty.'

He raised an eyebrow.

Simone dried her hands and followed him out of the kitchen. When they were out of earshot he said, 'What was all that about? The bowing…the "Your Majesty"?'

'In case you've forgotten, you're the King. If I don't bow people will want to know why. If I don't call you "Your Majesty" people will pretty much assume we're sleeping together.'

'They know we're friends.'

'The old staff do. But not the temporary staff here for the coronation.'

'They've all signed NDAs.'

'That's not the point, Ed.'

He stopped walking and grabbed her arm, so she stopped too.

'What *is* the point? Do you not want to see me?'

She sighed. 'We just need to be careful. And you know that more than anyone.'

He nodded. 'I don't know what I'd do without you,' he said.

She laughed wryly. 'You'll be just fine.'

Future tense. His life would go on perfectly smoothly and scandal-free once she'd left.

Hers, on the other hand…? She would be the one piecing her broken heart back together.

They reached the door to the garden and looked out. It had begun to snow. She looked down at her outfit. A long dress, tights and a long cardigan. He wasn't suitably attired either, with his dress shoes and only a thin sweater.

'It's too cold outside. Will you come to my room?'

This had now progressed from a casual walk and talk to a visit to his private rooms.

'Ed. I… I thought we'd talked about this. I'm not going to be the nearest warm body,' she whispered.

'What? You think I want to be with you just because you are close and warm?'

She glanced at the butler coming towards him and motioned for him to lower his voice.

'We're *definitely* going to my room for this conversation.'

He took her hand and pulled her in the direction of the royal apartments. She shook his hand away—but followed him anyway.

They walked quickly in silence to his room, greeting each person they passed with an overly friendly hello.

His apartment had a spacious sitting room, an office space, and an oversized bedroom. It was the same one he'd had for ever.

'Will you move into the King's apartments?' she asked.

He glared at her. 'Not the time, Simone. What did you mean, you don't want to be the nearest warm body?'

'Well… I didn't mean exactly that. But Paris…? The other morning…? And now you've brought me to your apartments.'

My heart may not be as important as a country, but I need it to live and breathe.

'I kissed you in Paris because I wanted to. I slept with you the other day because I've been dreaming about it since I left Paris. And because I wanted to—very much. Because after having you as my friend for so long…after so many years of taking you for granted as my friend… I finally see what an amazing and beautiful woman you are. I know I was slow on that account, but there you go.'

She could only stare. Amazing and beautiful woman?

'And, for the record, I don't just go around sleeping with women because they are close and warm. Do you actually believe what they print about me?'

She bit her lip. 'I don't…'

His look challenged her. She might as well get all her insecurities out into the open.

'But I know you've been with a lot of women, that's all.'

He let out a cynical guffaw.

'That's what you think of me? After everything you know about royal life, you still believe the headlines?'

'I don't need a number, Ed, but I see the photographs. I try my best not to see *all* the photographs, but I see them. And even if you only slept with a fraction of them, then...'

What? She'd run out of words. And she'd said too much.

He moved back to her. 'You try not to see the photographs? What do you mean by that?'

His voice was kind, and he raised a gentle eyebrow.

'Because...because I care about you, Ed.'

He encircled her in his arms and she pressed her face to his chest, so he wouldn't see the colour in her cheeks.

'Now we're getting somewhere. "Care..."?'

'Care is as much as you're getting now. We're friends. I like to know what you're up to.'

He pulled back to look at her with a broad smile. 'Again, for the record, it's not even a fraction of what the press would have you believe. And I do like it that you are close. And do I like that you are warm. But even if you weren't I'd still want to do this.'

He brushed his lips across hers.

She closed her eyes and breathed him in. There was no denying he was close...and very, very warm.

She let his speech run through her head a few more times, conscious that his hands were sliding up her back, sliding over the sensitive skin on her neck. Making her shiver.

'I've been dreaming about it since I left Paris... I finally see what a beautiful and amazing woman you are...'

She opened her eyes and sought out his lips.

CHAPTER FOURTEEN

THE KISS GREW deeper as they both fell into it. Fingers in each other's hair. Hands under one another's clothes. Tongues encircling one another's.

All the air left Simone's body and with it all her inhibitions.

She grabbed at the hem of Ed's sweater. Tugging. Pulling it out of the way. And he did the same with the buttons down the front of the dress she was wearing. He lifted her backside onto the nearest desk and she finally got his sweater over his head.

Ed pushed her lacy bra down, lifting and exposing one swollen, tender breast and taking it into his mouth. He kissed her painfully hard nipple and the room spun around her. He slid his hand up her thigh. Higher and higher.

Desperate need pooled inside her and came close to overflowing. She pushed him away. Very conscious of the fact they were in his apartment, not hers. And on his desk, no less.

'What if someone comes in?'

'They won't.'

'But...'

'Come.' He took her hand and led her to the other room. His bedroom. He shut the door behind him. 'I'm still just Ed. This is still my room.'

Simone swallowed hard. He was right. Ed was in front of

her. Pulling her towards his bed and everything she'd always wanted. She just had to find the courage to take it.

He stepped back to her, shirt awry. She reached out and undid the last of his buttons, ran her hand over his chest and slipped the shirt over his magnificent shoulders. She threw it to the ground and reached for his belt buckle.

'Don't rush. I want to savour every second of this.'

The subtext was that this might be the last time. It might not have been what he meant, but it was what she heard.

And he was right. If this was to be the last time she would commit every second to memory. Every caress, every stroke, every sensuous lick.

Ed kissed her all over as he slid her dress away, coaxed her bra off and eased her panties down. Waves and waves of pleasure washed through her.

She slowly divested him of the rest of his clothes. Committing each inch of his body to memory and each inch to her lips. She consumed his addictive scent, surrendered her body to him and was worshipped in return.

He trembled as he said her name.

'Yes. Yes…' she replied.

Protected and on the brink, they finally came together.

She closed her eyes and let go. Desire gathering, tightening, hardening…finally breaking apart. All her being seemed to concentrate on this one moment of perfect, terrifying clarity. She'd love him no matter who he was. She'd love him until the end of time.

She broke and so did he.

They lay in one another's arms, spent and satiated. For the first time since the other morning Ed felt normal and content. Like himself. And that was all because of Simone.

'I have a question for you,' he said after a while.

He felt her body tense in his arms. She knew him well enough to know that his question was going to be serious.

'Why were you singing? At my party?'

'Oh, that... I don't remember.'

'I don't believe that for a second.' He said it gently, but felt her body stay frozen nonetheless.

'We went over this before. You've got to get back to work and I'd better get back to Mum.'

'What are you not telling me? It wasn't like you to put yourself out there in front of a whole lot of people you didn't know. Why did you?'

He stroked her hair and felt her shift under him.

'I had a crush on you,' she mumbled into his chest.

He'd guessed as much, but to hear her say it still stirred up many emotions. Surprise, delight, worry...

'You *had* a crush on me? Past tense?'

She groaned, as if it was something to be ashamed of.

'Because *my* crush is very much in the present tense. Just so you know. And I'm not embarrassed in the slightest,' he said.

She giggled, and lifted herself up to look at him. Her blonde hair was tossed around her shoulders. Her lips still red and swollen from their kissing. She took his breath away. She was beautiful and she was Simone. *His* Simone.

'Yes, I had a teenage crush on you. Along with every other girl. Except it was mortifying because you were my best friend. You knew me and didn't share my feelings. Everyone knew how pathetic I was. That's why they sent me away.'

He couldn't believe that she believed everything she was saying.

He took her chin in his fingers. 'Simone, no. That's not why you were sent away at all. No one knows you had a crush on me!'

'They mocked me for singing to you.'

He rubbed his head. Was that really true? How could her recollections be so different from his?

'I think they were just laughing at the video. I don't think anyone thought you were singing to me.'

'Hashtag *palaceserenade*? That's pretty clear to me.'

'But…' It hadn't been clear to him. He sighed and bit his lip. He'd failed to notice a lot of things. 'Simone, I'm sorry I didn't notice.'

'You weren't meant to. I mean, you were only meant to re-alise if you shared my feelings. And I thought it worked, and you hadn't realised, and it all would have been fine except that then someone posted the video and made fun of it and everyone saw.'

The way she was talking in the past tense was starting to worry him. Was she over him? Had her feelings dissipated over the years, just as his were growing?

'Does any of it remain? Your teenage crush?'

She grinned. 'Ah, I don't know. My teenage crush was very… chaste.'

He laughed.

'This is something new.'

She trailed a finger down his chest and slid her hand under the covers. Just the thought of her fingers encircling him was enough to make his body react.

His fingers slid into her thick hair. He cradled her head and tilted her face towards him.

Something new.

But what?

It was powerful. And wonderful. But also dangerous.

This wasn't a chaste teenage crush or even an unchaste one. This was real life—both their lives—not to mention the future of his country.

He knew that. He knew that by continuing to be with Simone like this he could be putting all his carefully laid plans at risk.

Stay away from any hint of scandal. Be a monarch above all reproach. Beyond any criticism at all.

But this was Simone. She was next to him now and he needed her more than he needed air. No one needed to know. This would just be between them. She'd go back to Paris. He'd vowed to fulfil his royal duties alone. She didn't want to stay in Florena, and he accepted that, but that didn't mean they couldn't both make the most of this brief interlude in their lives.

Ed took a deep breath and knocked on the familiar apartment door. He heard movement inside and the door opened.

Alea smiled when she saw him. 'Eddie, sweetheart, come on in.'

He was instantly grateful that she had greeted him as usual, and hadn't curtsied or called him by his new title.

'It's lovely to see you,' she said.

'You too.'

'I'm afraid you've missed Simone. She's out having her dress fitted.'

'I confess I knew that. It's you I've come to see.'

Ed's throat was dry. Alea was one of the people in the world he felt most comfortable with, but what he'd come to ask was... delicate. He'd thought about coming weeks ago, before Simone had returned, and every day since then. But he wasn't sure what Simone had told her mother about the developments in their relationship. And he wasn't sure how she was going to react to his impertinent request.

'That sounds slightly ominous... Eddie, you know you're welcome here any time. Do you have time for a coffee?' she asked.

He nodded. They made small talk until the coffee was brewed, placed on the table with milk and sugar.

The coffee was sweet and robust, as always. Alea was a magnificent cook. But he was delaying. None of his etiquette lessons had ever taught him the art of raising one of his father's affairs with one of his old mistresses.

'I was wondering...that is... I don't think Simone knows about your affair with my father.'

There. No going back now.

Alea placed her cup down. 'I don't think she does either.'

'I was wondering if you had planned to tell her.'

'I hadn't really thought about it.' She crossed her arms.

'I wonder if you would like to think about it, now she's older.'

'Honestly, I'm not sure I planned to keep it a secret from her for ever, but it's in the past. You know that. Your father and I haven't been together for years. I don't think there's any need to dredge up the past. Particularly not now, with Celine and everything.'

'I know that. But I think maybe Simone deserves to know.'

'Eddie, I don't regret being with your father. You know it ended amicably between us. No harm done. You're an adult now. Old enough to know that people need company. People need touch. Companionship.'

Ed ran his hand over his head. This wasn't what he'd come to hear from Simone's mother.

'Alea, please, *please* don't think for a moment I'm judging you. I do understand. That's not it.'

'Then why raise it now?'

'Ordinarily I wouldn't, but Simone and I have…'

This was dangerous ground too.

Alea narrowed her eyes.

'Simone and I are close.'

'You always have been.'

'Yes, but recently I've realised we have this secret between us.'

'You've always kept this from her—what's changed now?'

No. Simone clearly hadn't discussed their relationship with her mother. Alea was smart, and she had probably guessed, but she was wanting confirmation. This was harder than he'd thought it would be.

'It's important to me that there aren't any secrets between Simone and I.'

That explanation would have to do. He wasn't about to tell Alea that he was sleeping with her daughter—especially as Simone hadn't.

Besides, she might ask him about his intentions, and he

wasn't sure that he could use the 'we're both consenting adults' speech back to her.

'It isn't your secret. It's mine and your father's.'

'I know. Which is why I'm coming to you and not Simone. The thing is, she believes she was sent away from the palace because of that video of her singing.'

'What video?' Alea asked.

'The one of her singing karaoke at my seventeenth birthday.'

'Where she sang *I Will Always Love You*?'

'Yes.'

'But that's absurd.'

'Yes, that's what I thought. But the clip went viral and she got a lot of horrible online abuse because of it.'

'But that wasn't why she was sent to school. The events were not connected.'

'I know that. But the timing was close and she never knew about the affair. It's what she believes, and I can see why she might. Rightly or wrongly, the abuse she received because of that video is one of the reasons she doesn't like coming back here.'

Alea paled. 'Really?'

'Yes—and it's why she plans on going back to Paris as soon as the coronation is over.'

Alea waved his suggestion away. 'She has a bookshop to manage. She always has to go back.'

'I want her to stay,' he said. 'Don't you?'

Alea held her face in her hands. 'Of course I do. And you're right. She should know the full story.'

Ed nodded, but then Alea shook her head and stood. She began to pace.

'But it isn't as simple as you suggest. We've all put it behind us. Your father, me, your mother… Even you. I know you and your mother accepted it as the way things were, but I don't know if Simone will.'

Ed hadn't been happy about the affair, but as his mother

had accepted the relationship he hadn't felt it was his place to rock the boat.

'I'm not sure we should dig up the past. It's over,' Alea continued.

But not for Simone. And not for him.

'Please talk to her. If you won't do it for me, maybe you should do it for you.'

Alea frowned.

'I thought you should know,' Ed said, before downing the last of his coffee and taking his leave.

CHAPTER FIFTEEN

SHE WAS GOING to go to the ball.

If only because if she didn't Ed, her mother, the dressmaker and the Queen's assistants wouldn't forgive her.

The Queen had only returned to Florena briefly since her divorce had been announced. However, Ed wanted his mother to continue to be called the Queen, and to maintain a presence in Florena to support him if necessary.

Queen Isabella was not returning for the coronation. She had told Ed she didn't want to overshadow him. Simone suspected the real reason was that the Queen didn't want to see the former King Edouard, who would have to be at the coronation.

With the Queen so often away, her staff were at a loose end—and the thread they had latched on to was Simone. Simone was getting her hair and make-up done twice on the day of the coronation, which felt absurdly excessive.

'They want something to do. They *need* something to do,' her mother had insisted. 'They're helping me as well—and any of the other staff who would like their services.'

Simone carried the cardboard box back with her from the dress fitting. Her mother's old dress hadn't needed much work. The waist had been taken in and the bust taken out a little.

Her mother wouldn't tell her when or why she'd bought the

326   BEAUTY AND THE PRINCE

dress in the first place, but the whispers she'd heard between the Queen's assistants had been curious.

'It's not ready-to-wear. It's bespoke. Looks like the aesthetic from a decade ago,' they'd murmured.

That would make it too recent for it to be a dress Alea might have worn when she was dating Simone's father. What had her mother been doing ten years ago, wearing a designer dress much less owning one?

When Simone opened the door to the apartment her mother was pacing the room, but she smiled when Simone entered.

'Do you have time for a drink?' she asked. 'I feel like I've hardly seen you at all since you got back.'

Simone took a seat. Alea was right to heap guilt on her. She had been seeing Ed every spare moment he had—which meant she hadn't seen as much of her mother as either of them expected.

'I'm sorry, Mum.'

'There's no need to be sorry. I know you've been busy. I just thought it might be nice to have bit of time together. Catch up with no one else around. Do you have plans?'

Simone shook her head. Her mother knew she had been spending time with Ed, but if she realised that their relationship had changed she hadn't let on. Maybe that was the point of this conversation? Would she approve or caution Simone against it? She had no idea.

You're too suspicious. She just wants to spend some time with you.

'Wine?'

'Yes, please.'

Alea poured them both a glass and joined Simone by the fire.

'You've been spending a lot of time with Eddie, I understand?'

Ah. So this wasn't just a casual chat.

'He's my friend, and it's a stressful time for him.'

'I know that—and I'm not judging.'

Judging? The word hung between them. Her mother saying she wasn't judging felt very much like…judgement.

Her mother played with the stem of her wine glass for a long time.

She knows about Ed and me. She wants me to tell her.

But Simone didn't know what to tell her mother. She didn't know what was going on herself.

'You and Eddie have been friends for a long time,' said her mother, 'but I wonder if lately you've become closer?'

Simone dropped her head. She wasn't going to lie to her mother. 'I'm not really sure what's going on between us,' she confessed. 'It's new, and difficult, but for the time being we're taking it day by day.'

That was what she was telling herself as well. Taking each day as it came. Enjoying it while it lasted. Definitely not analysing her feelings in any depth at all.

'I'm not asking you to tell me, but I want you to know that you can.' Alea's voice was warm.

'Of course I know that I can, Mum. I can tell you anything.'

Alea reached over, took Simone's hand and squeezed it. 'That isn't what I wanted to talk about. I'm sorry this has come out all wrong…'

'Oh?' Simone was as confused as Alea looked.

'There's something I need to tell *you*,' her mother began. 'Something I never told you before.'

Alea's expression was pained, and Simone's mind instantly jumped to a million conclusions. Her mother was sick. Ed was sick…

'It's about the King. That is…the former King.'

Simone sat upright. Was King Edouard sick?

'It's about Edouard and I…'

It was funny how you could know something the second before you were actually told it.

Suddenly Simone just *knew*.

Was she a good guesser or was she simply remembering something she had forgotten from years ago?

Suddenly some of the cryptic things Ed had said in Paris became clear.

'You had an affair,' Simone said.

'You knew?'

Simone shook her head. 'Not until this second. Is it true?'

Alea nodded. 'Yes. Yes, we had an affair. You were a teenager, and your father had been gone a long while. Edouard is charming. You know that.'

Simone nodded. Like father, like son.

'And I was lonely and flattered. The King and Queen had ended their intimate relationship years before, and sometimes two people...'

Simone held up her hand. She was in shock, and surprised, but she wasn't angry. She was just processing.

'It's okay, Mum. I get it.'

There were many things that were not okay. The fact that the King had been cheating on his wife. The fact that her mother had kept this secret from her all this time. But she did understand that sometimes these things happened. And if the former King had been as hard to resist as his son, then Simone really didn't blame her mother.

'Did you love him?'

'No, I don't think so. But I was terribly fond of him and we had a lovely time. He made me feel good about myself.'

Simone grimaced. Why had her mother not felt good about herself?

'I knew there was no future in it, and I didn't want there to be one. Heavens, I didn't want him to leave the Queen! We tried our hardest to be discreet. But there is one thing I feel bad about. One regret.'

'The Queen?' Simone guessed.

'Isabella knew. She told Edouard that at least I was age-appropriate and would be discreet.' Alea smiled, as if remembering something.

'The Queen knew?'

'Yes. It was all very adult.'

Simone wanted to be mature, but her stomach lurched at the thought of King Edouard—the philandering King—Alea and the Queen, all sharing this secret. The three of them might have been able to be calm about it, but Simone didn't think she would ever be able to treat such a situation in the same way the three of them seemed to have.

Perhaps she was just naive. Unsophisticated. Clueless.

'Why are you telling me now?' Simone asked, but she suspected she knew the answer. Ed had played a part in this.

'I regret agreeing to send you away to boarding school.'

'"Agreeing"? It wasn't your idea?'

'It was partly my idea. I did want you to get the best education you could. And I wanted you to have the opportunity to see life somewhere away from the palace. But it was Edouard who arranged it and paid for it. That is the part of the relationship I look back on with regret. It was only meant to be for a term or two. I thought you would come back. I always made it clear I wanted you to.'

It was as though her mother was telling her that the sky was green and always had been.

'I wasn't sent away because of the singing.' Her voice was soft.

'No. *No*. I can't believe you ever thought that.'

Simone had thought that the timing proved it. She'd made a fool of herself. She'd been asked if she wanted to go away and, feeling ashamed, she had agreed to go.

I was sixteen.

'It was to get me out of the way?'

'No, not as such… I thought it would be the best thing for your education. But I suppose that having you out of the palace may have been Edouard's intention.'

'I thought it was because of the singing… The video…' The contents of her stomach rose.

'I realise that now. And I'm sorry you thought you were being punished. That wasn't what it was about at all.'

'I wasn't in trouble?'

'Heavens, no, sweetheart. If I'd known how much that video had affected you I would never have sent you away to school to deal with it on your own. I'm so sorry.'

Simone took a sip of wine, but it tasted wrong in her mouth. 'Why didn't you tell me before?'

'I figured it was in the past.' Alea shrugged.

It was in the past.

The King had spectacularly moved on.

It was in the past for them—but Simone and Ed were still very much in the present.

And Ed knew. He had known all along.

The walls of the apartment closed in on her. Breathing became an effort.

They had all lied to her.

There was a lot to take in, and she couldn't do it here, in the warm apartment, with her mother looking on.

'I need a moment,' Simone said as she stood.

She had to get out.

She had to breathe.

'Simone, I had no idea the fallout from you singing that song had affected you so much. If I had I would have told you sooner.'

Simone nodded, but couldn't speak.

'Get some air. I'll be here when you get back if you want to talk some more.'

Alea looked stricken, but Simone couldn't worry about that now.

Everything she'd always believed had been turned on its head.

She grabbed her coat and left the apartment.

In summer the palace garden was the perfect place to sit

and think. With its thick green grass, shady trees and a riot of coloured blooms, it was a calm oasis from the bustle and formalities of the palace. In winter it was the only place to go without actually leaving the palace walls.

The snow had stopped, but the cloud cover remained so the air was not frigid. Simone had on proper boots and a thick coat. She walked around the frozen pond to the small playground. She'd expected to find it dilapidated—it had been years since any children had lived permanently in the palace—but she was delighted to find it well maintained.

She brushed the snow off one of the swings and sat. It was smaller than she remembered, but she could still fit on the seat and gently swing.

It's not smaller...you're bigger.

Yeah? Well, memory was a fickle thing.

With one conversation half the things she remembered about her childhood had been flipped on their heads. Her mother? Ed's father?

What did that make her and Ed?

The sensible voice in her head said, *Nothing. It changes nothing between you and Ed.*

But another voice, the confused, lonely voice screamed, *Everyone knew but me. They let me think I was sent away because of the drama with the song.*

They had all let her down. Even Ed. Though as the dark settled in and her emotions stilled she realised he'd thought she already knew.

And, as upset as Simone was with her mother, she realised she was right. Alea was always asking her to come back. The first term at boarding school had been Alea's idea. But every term after that, and then Paris, had all been Simone's idea.

Even now she knew she would go back to Paris. Florena was not her home.

The evening wore on and the cold seeped into her fingers,

but she wasn't going back inside. She didn't know these people any more. She didn't know her own mother.

Why had Alea had stayed working at the palace even after the affair was over? That didn't make much sense. Who would want to stay around to see their former lover every day once the affair was over?

'It was all very adult.'

Maybe she should just go back to Paris. It was her true home. Paris had never lied to her. She'd miss the coronation, but so what? Florena wasn't really her home. It hadn't been for years.

It was then that Ed found her, mentally booking her return flight to Charles de Gaulle.

'Hey,' he said gently, as if starting a conversation.

She had no time for niceties. 'You knew about the affair, didn't you?'

He took the swing next to her. 'Yes.'

'What I'm trying to understand is why she's told me now.'

'I asked her to,' he said simply.

Simone had guessed as much. 'Why?' she asked.

'Because I thought you needed to know. Not so much about the affair, but you needed to know why you were really sent to boarding school. It wasn't because of the singing or the video.'

'What on earth did you say to her?'

Oh, to have been a fly on the wall during that conversation…

He laughed. 'I was polite. So was she. I'm glad she understood where I was coming from.'

Simone rocked. The swinging was strangely calming.

'I felt bad that I knew and you didn't,' he said. 'But most of all I hate that you don't feel welcome here. I hate that you think you were banished.'

She could see his breath. He was wrapped up in a heavy coat and a thick grey scarf. His hair was slightly ruffled by the breeze. He looked as edible as ever.

Would there ever be a time when the sight of him didn't make her heart stop?

She might not have been banished because of the singing, but she'd still been sent away. They'd wanted to hide the affair from her.

'My mother and your father... Together.'

'My father and I have good taste in women. What can I say?'

'Stop! Ed, this changes everything. Between us.'

He got off his swing and stepped into her path, holding her swing still.

'No. It changes nothing between us. So what if our parents had an affair? It was ages ago. It's over.

She couldn't meet his eye. 'It changes the way I see my life. It changes things I thought about myself.'

It was also mildly uncomfortable to know that their parents had once shared a bed. But it was more than that.

Simone's mother was palace staff. She might live in the palace, but she lived in the servants' apartments. Simone and her mother were the type of woman Kings had affairs with. Nothing more.

Yet you don't expect anything more from Ed. You don't want anything more. You don't want to be the Queen.

Her chest ached. She didn't want to be the Queen, but that didn't stop her wanting to be with Ed. And not as his mistress, but for ever. She'd tried to push those feelings aside, but they were overwhelming her. They were too strong to overcome.

Now, even in the crisp open air, she felt the world closing in on her again.

'Ed, I'm not sure I want to talk now. This is a lot to think about.'

I want to be with you. For ever.

'I understand, but please don't mind if I stay here, to make sure you don't die of exposure. Your mother said you've been out here for at least an hour. Can you still feel your feet?'

'I can neither confirm nor deny.'

'At least come in somewhere warm. You can pace the Great Hall if you want.'

'No, I can't; it's set up for the ball.'

She kept swinging.

Swing back, breathe in...swing forward, breathe out, she told herself.

They both swung back and forth for a while, but thankfully he swung in silence and let her process her thoughts.

'Did it go on for long?' she asked after a while.

'I don't know. A year, maybe.'

'Do you think they loved one another?'

'You'd have to ask her that.'

She had, and her mother had denied it.

'Do you think he loved her?'

Ed scoffed. 'You know my father. I don't think he's ever loved anyone.'

Alea understood what Simone's heart couldn't. Loving a king was hopeless.

She looked across at Ed. Swinging as if he was a kid again. He'd spoken to her mother, asked her to divulge her greatest secret, and done it in such a way as to get her to agree.

Ed really was a world-class diplomat. And he'd done it for her.

So she wouldn't think she'd been banished. So she might stay in Florena.

But for what? So she could remain his secret mistress? Simone loved Ed, but she was never going to agree to that.

'I still have to go back,' she told him. 'You know that.'

Ed paused and took a few swings before he replied. 'I would like you stay, but I understand that it's not simple.'

'Ed, I'm not going to stay here as your secret mistress. My mother might have been happy with that kind of arrangement, but—'

'Oh, Simone! No! That was not my intent. I don't want you to be my secret mistress,' he blurted.

'But that's all I'd ever be.' She picked up his hand. 'This week has been lovely, but we both know that's all it can be.'

For a brief moment she let herself hope that he would contradict her. Tell her that not only did he love her, but that he wanted to marry her. Despite his vow. Despite his country. Despite everything, he loved her and would love her for ever.

But he didn't say any of that. He simply said, 'If we only have a few more days we'd better make the most of it.'

She nodded. A few days. They had only that interlude before life would go back to normal.

Ed stood up and came to her swing, lifted her from it. His green eyes sparkled in the moonlight and he pulled her to him. His lips were warm and she leant into the kiss, but even as she did so he pulled back.

'Sim, you're freezing. Let's go inside.'

'I can't go in. You can keep me warm.' She tugged him closer.

'And have us both get frostbite? Do you want them to find our frozen corpses out here?'

Despite herself, she laughed. 'Think of the memes on that!'

He laughed too.

CHAPTER SIXTEEN

'YOUR FATHER WOULD like to talk to you,' Ed's assistant said.

Ed stood before the full-length mirror in his dressing room. The suit was itchy. Its fabric stiff and weighed down with medals and embellishments. Coronation outfits were definitely not made for lounging in on the couch. And he was still expected to get a cloak over this. Not to mention a five-pound crown on his head.

'Great. Please send him in,' Ed said, desperate for some pointers about how to get through today.

His assistant looked at his shoes. 'No, sir. He's on a video call at your desk.'

Ed's heart sank. His father should be at the palace by now, in time for the coronation.

He sat at his desk and opened the call. His father had a white wall behind him. He could've been anywhere in the world.

'Father, what's going on?'

His father smiled sadly. 'You're dressed. You look wonderful. Very regal.'

Despite his status, Ed felt himself blush. 'Thank you. Where are you?'

'That's what I wanted to talk to you about. I've decided not to come.'

Not come? This was the most important day of Ed's life—how could he not be there? It was obviously unorthodox for a former king to be at his successor's coronation, but they had talked about it and Ed had decided he wanted his father to be there. No matter how unusual it might be.

'How can you not be here? We agreed.'

'I know we did, but I've thought long and hard about it. I know how important it is to you—which is why I can't be there.'

Ed had never seen his father look so uncomfortable. So not regal.

He isn't the King any more. You are.

'It isn't right for a former king to be at the new King's coronation. As much as I want to support you, I think I will serve you best by giving you space. If I'm there the focus will be on me, and that wouldn't be fair to you. They need to see you as the one and only King.'

'But you're still my father—not my former father.'

'A coronation isn't a family affair. It's about you and the country.'

His father had never intended to come. He'd just agreed so that they wouldn't have this conversation until it was too late.

Now he'd have to do it all. The diplomacy. The outmanoeuvring of Laurent. Everything.

It hit him, almost as if for the first time, that his country's future was on his shoulders and his alone. He'd have to please and placate Laurent and his cronies on his own.

'We'd be stronger and more united together, not apart.'

'I can't leave Celine.'

Having his father at the coronation would be a good thing—having Celine there would most definitely not be. She was a lovely person, but if she was at the ceremony the media would have a field day.

'Not even for a couple of days?' he asked his father.

'Not even for a couple of days.'

Was he serious? His father had changed dramatically since meeting this woman.

Another thought occurred to Ed. 'Is she well? Is the baby okay?'

'Yes, she's well, and so is the baby.' His father smiled.

'Then why can't you leave her for a few days?'

'Because I don't want to.'

'I don't understand…'

'Because I love her.'

Ed laughed. 'Oh, don't be ridiculous.'

His father didn't know the meaning of the word.

'I'm not being ridiculous. I love her with all my heart.'

'Like you loved Mother? Like you loved Alea? Like you loved every other one of them?'

'I like your mother—don't get me wrong. And I adored Alea. But I didn't love them.'

Ed shook his head. 'You didn't even love Mother when you got married?'

'No—and I don't think she loved me either. It was a fortuitous, diplomatic and financial match. I tried to love her. I wish I had loved her. But I didn't. If I had, our lives would've been very different.'

'You would have been faithful, you mean?' Ed knew he sounded like a kid, and yet he was about to be crowned.

'Yes, that's exactly what I mean. I'm not proud of the way I've lived my life, but from now on things will be different.'

Ed scoffed. 'Yeah, right. I don't think the Berringer men are capable of love.'

Countless generations of men before them had proven the Berringer bloodline to be fickle and disloyal.

'I thought that too once, but I just hadn't met the right woman.'

'And you have now?'

Ed knew his voice was laced with sarcasm, but he didn't care. His father had let him down. *Again*. First, by abdicating without even a discussion and now by leaving him to get through this day alone.

'Yes. I was a little slow to the game, and my meeting with Celine was a little unusual. But I love her deeply, truly and for ever.'

For ever? How could he even know that?

'For ever? Seriously? You're a Florenan King. Not one of our ancestors has managed to stay with one woman.'

His father laughed. 'You've read too many fairy tales. See them for what they are. Morality tales, at best. Propaganda from those in power, at worst. Laurent and his like use stories like that to their advantage.'

'Laurent didn't write the Florenan fairy tales. They've been around for years.'

'Yes. But he's using that story now, about the Cursed Kingdom, to try to persuade the people to get rid of us. It's a story. That's all. It has nothing to do with you.'

But Ed did know his family. His father. His uncle. His grandfather. And all who had come before them. He shook his head.

'Ed, son, you know as well as anyone that the stories the media tell about our family aren't true. Most of what they print about you is a lie. So why don't you see that story for what it is? A children's story. Marry the woman you love and you will not have any of the problems I had.'

His father ended the call shortly afterwards.

Ed stood and ran his hands through his hair, and squeezed his scalp for good measure. His father wasn't coming. His father was halfway across the world with his young girlfriend. He wasn't coming to the coronation—the most important day of Ed's life—because he wanted to be with her.

If he cared about you he wouldn't have got Celine pregnant in the first place.

If he truly cared for Ed he wouldn't have abdicated.

Objectively, from a public relations point of view, it did make sense for his father to stay away. But Ed had reasoned that having his father there would show the family was still united. And by seeming united they would appear stronger.

Although his father had a point as well. If he was there they would be sending a message to the world that his father was still around. It would look as if Ed was his father's puppet rather than his true successor.

If things had been different you wouldn't have expected your father to be at your coronation.

His death would have been the reason for his absence. But if things had been different Ed would probably have had many more years to prepare for this day. Not mere months.

No. He had to concede that his father had sound reasons for staying away. His absence was irritating, but it wasn't what was really bothering him. It wasn't the reason Ed wanted to run ten miles. Or scream until his lungs hurt. It wasn't the reason for this growing uncontrollable sensation in his chest.

He let out a cry and felt foolish. It was the other things his father had said. About Celine. About not wanting to leave her for a moment. About the fact that his father had never loved his mother.

'Marry someone you love and you won't have any of these problems.'

But how could he marry the woman he loved? It wouldn't work. There were too many things keeping them apart.

The fact that he hadn't told her he loved her was just the first...

Simone had chosen her coronation day outfit in Paris. White and red—the Florenan national colours—it was a knee-length white shift dress paired with a red jacket and red pumps. Her hair was down, styled into gentle waves and completed with a small white hat.

Simone wasn't used to dressing so formally—long cardigans and floral dresses were her usual look—so she felt self-conscious when she stepped out of her room to find her mother.

Alea had also chosen white and red—a white suit and a red hat.

'You'll steal the show,' her mother said.

'I'm hoping to blend into the background.'

'As if you ever could. Besides, we're up front.'

Simone was horrified. 'At the cathedral?'

'Who else would be?'

'The Prime Minister, for starters. Other heads of state. All the important people!'

'We *are* the important people. Eddie has seated us with his close friends and family.'

'How do you know this?'

'He discussed the seating plan with me weeks ago. We're seated in the first row. Not in the centre—that's reserved for his cousins and their families—but to one side.'

'How can we be at the front?'

On the screen. Photographed. Where her every move could be scrutinised. Her stomach rolled.

'What about the King?'

'If you mean the former King, I understand he hasn't returned.'

'What?

'It's hardly appropriate—'

'I need to speak to Ed.'

As soon as possible. He'd be devastated. When they'd spoken last night Ed had told her that the only good thing about the abdication would be his father being there to see his coronation.

Her mother gave her a quizzical look. 'Now?'

Simone didn't care what her mother thought. What any of them thought. This was between her and her best friend.

'Excuse me a moment.'

She went to her room and pressed Ed's number into her phone.

What was she thinking? He would be too busy preparing to get crowned to take her call.

But the phone clicked and he said in a whisper, 'Hello?'

'Ed, I just heard about your father.'

'Yeah, he called to tell me the good news.'

Simone heard muffled noises, a door closing, and then Ed said, 'Dropped it on me when it was too late to do anything about it.'

'I'm so sorry.'

'Don't be. I see why. He can't be seen to be supporting me. His presence will detract from me and it should be my day. Former kings don't usually go to their successor's coronations.'

'Except as ghosts,' she said.

'Except as ghosts.' He laughed. 'I guess I just thought he would be there…and Mother too.'

It hit her. He really was alone now. Left by both his parents. That was why Simone and Alea were in the front row. She'd have to sit there now. For Ed.

'If it helps, I'm sure he'll be watching—and your mother too. I know they're both proud, even if they can't show it. And I am too,' she said.

'I hope you won't chicken out.' His voice was tinged with uncertainty.

'I wouldn't miss it. I'll be there with bells on.'

'Bells? Really? Don't ring them. That'll only draw attention to yourself.'

She laughed. 'I'd better let you go. See you out there. Good luck—and remember to take the crown, not the baseball hat.'

He laughed.

It was so strange, sitting in the front pew at Florena's royal cathedral. She'd been in the cathedral before, but it looked remarkably different now, decorated with red and white flags and banners interspersed with evergreen branches from Florena's famous pine trees.

The place was packed—literally to the rafters—with guests. Special seating had been erected for the occasion, to allow even more people to attend. But the ceremony itself was to be traditional and austere.

Ed had donated the money that would have been spent on processions and lavish feasts for the select few to charities in the city itself. Tonight's ball would be the only official celebration. Though the coronation would still show the world that Florena was as strong and independent as ever. So much more than a crown rested on Ed's head and shoulders. It was the fate of the whole country.

Simone no longer marvelled that she'd had an invitation. It seemed as though half the country was there. Though she did have literally a front row seat. Just below the high altar, so that when Ed walked in and took his position he was directly in front of her. Despite her earlier reservations, she knew she wouldn't have missed it for the world. Laurent and Morgane were on the opposite pew, but once Ed arrived they blurred into the background and all she saw was him.

He's the King. Your Ed is the King.

For as long as she lived it would be hard to explain her emotions that day. But there was one in particular that stayed with her, and that was the way her heart had felt as the crown had been placed on Ed's head. He'd turned briefly to her, smiled and winked.

She'd resisted the urge to giggle, but her heart had never felt so full.

Because after everything he was still her Ed. And that realisation had been comforting and terrifying at the same time.

She'd hoped that maybe once the crown was on his head something would change. That *he* would change and become more distant and regal. She'd hoped that at the very least she would look at him differently. That it would make it easier for her to leave in two days' time.

But she still saw her Ed.

Only he wasn't her Ed any more.

He belonged to Florena now and would never belong to her.

* * *

After the ceremony was complete, and Ed had left the cathedral for photographs, Simone and Alea returned to their apartment to get ready for the ball.

'Stay.'

She sat on her bed with the silk of her dress spread out around her and put on her shoes.

What if she could do what Ed suggested and rise above her fears and stay? Learn to drown out the noise from the trolls? Trust that Ed and the palace would be able to shield her?

She had sat in the front row at his coronation and she had felt fine. More than that, she wouldn't have missed seeing that special moment for anything.

She'd miss out on so many experiences with Ed if she returned to Paris.

Wasn't he worth it?

Yes, but it wasn't that simple. She had a life in Paris, and she wasn't about to give that up to skulk around the palace with Ed until their affair ran its course.

Because it would. Ed wasn't going to marry—her or anyone else—so a secret affair was all it ever could be.

There was a knock at her bedroom door.

'Is everything all right?' asked her mother. 'We'll be late.'

Simone took a deep breath and emerged from her room. Alea brushed a tear from her eyes and sniffed another away.

'I knew that dress would look wonderful on you. You look spectacular.'

She carried her mother's compliment like a shield as they walked across the palace to the great hall. Did she imagine it or was everyone looking at her? It was probably because she was self-conscious, wearing such a magnificent dress. When she climbed the grand staircase up to the ballroom, she had to lift the voluminous skirt so she didn't trip.

Yeah, that would make a great photo. Her falling face-down on the palace stairs tangled in her dress.

But Simone made it to the top of the stairs without incident and more people turned. She walked through the doors. No, she wasn't imagining it. People *were* turning to look at her—but they weren't laughing. They were smiling.

Still, Simone's heart hammered behind the corset of the dress as she and Alea walked along the short receiving line.

She recognised Ed's closest relatives, his cousins the Dukes of Linden and Clichy, accompanied by their wives. And after them stood Ed. He was shaking someone's hand as Simone approached, but he stopped, paused for far too long.

Simone felt heat rise in her cheeks, but she focused on the two dukes. They greeted her warmly, though showed no sign of knowing who she was. There was no reason why they should, she reminded herself. They'd only met her as children. The last time she'd seen either of them had been Ed's seventeenth birthday, and they clearly wouldn't connect her to the teenager who had embarrassed herself in front of the world.

Maybe no one else would either.

Then she reached Ed. He kissed her mother on both cheeks first, and then swallowed hard. Simone was next. She held out her hand and curtsied, knees wobbling, unused to executing the movement in high heels. Once she'd risen he pulled her in for a kiss on the cheek, just like he had her mother. Only on the second kiss he held her shoulders and kept her close.

'Not only are you the most beautiful woman here tonight,' he whispered. 'But you're also the most beautiful woman I've seen in my entire life. If you dance with anyone else I think I'm going to have them sent to the dungeon.'

She laughed. 'Do you even have a dungeon?'

'I'm not sure. Just…' He pulled her close again. 'Please, save a dance for me.'

Simone floated into the ballroom.

CHAPTER SEVENTEEN

IF THEY HAD handed out dance cards Simone's would have been full. Particularly after Ed had singled her out for the second dance, after his obligatory one with the highest-ranking woman at the ball, the Duchess of Linden.

Simone had been worried she'd be standing next to her mother all night, like a spare part, as her mother spoke to her colleagues and friends, but Simone had met many people. Women she didn't know had come up to her and asked about her dress, and men had asked her to dance. They'd all been friendly and not at all intrusive. Conversation had come easily. Particularly when she'd divulged that she had grown up in the palace and now lived in Paris. People found her life story delightful and asked about her bookshop.

Not one of them thought she didn't deserve to be there.

Not one of them recognised her as the hashtag *palaceserenade* girl.

Later in the night, when her feet ached, she went to find her mother. She sat and reacquainted herself with some of the palace staff, past and present, whom she hadn't seen in years.

Then she and Ed snatched a brief moment together, as she

was on her way to the bathroom. They stood, respectably apart, and spoke briefly.

'Thank you for coming,' he said.

'Of course.'

'Not just for tonight. Thank you for being here this week. I don't know what I'd have done without you. I couldn't have got through today without you here.'

She smiled at him, unsure of what to say. She wanted to reach over and hug him, but knew that was out of the question with everyone looking on.

'If it were up to me I'd just dance with you all night,' he whispered.

'But you have to mingle.'

'I do have to mingle, and I fear that if I keep dancing with you then more than one person is bound to notice that I can't keep my eyes off you.'

Simone's body came alive at his words, and she wanted to slip her arms around him and press her body against his. But she knew he was right, so they parted. Ed brushed his hand against hers, sending sparks right up her arm. Two hands touching had never felt so exciting. She turned quickly, so no one would notice the blush in her cheeks.

She glimpsed Laurent and Morgane once or twice, but they didn't come close to where she was. She felt surrounded and protected by friendly people all night long.

When it was all over she and her mother returned, exhausted, to their apartment. Alea helped her undress and Simone went to the bathroom to wash off the make-up and brush out the styling.

She had survived the ball! Not only that—she had thrived. Her mind was dizzy with thoughts of the evening. She'd laughed and talked with so many interesting people. None of whom had thought she was out of place.

She heard soft voices and when she emerged in her pyjamas she saw Ed, standing in the living room. Like her, he'd changed out of his stiff uniform and formal clothes, and was wearing grey track pants and a soft blue sweater. Her fingers itched to stroke him.

'I'll bid you both good evening. Or is it good morning?' Alea said, leaving them alone.

He came straight to her and wrapped her in his arms.

'Should you be here?' she asked.

'It's my palace now.'

She swatted him. 'Here? Now?'

'Do you want me to leave?'

'Of course not.' They only had two more nights together. 'But my mother—'

'Knows you've been sneaking out to my apartment.'

Simone had suspected as much, and found she didn't mind her mother knowing about her and Ed. After all, if she ever needed to go to someone for advice about navigating a secret affair with a king she could think of no better person.

'I just want to hold you,' he said. 'I've never been so exhausted in my life and I just want to be with you.'

They fell into her bed and held one another. With her last ounce of energy she picked up his hand and entwined her fingers with his.

'Do you feel different?' she asked.

'I think maybe I do. But that isn't because of my new hat. I think it's because I now feel that my father really has left.'

Oh, Ed.

'But I realised something today. I'm actually lucky. I could've become King at any moment if he had passed away. But I'm lucky because I can still go to him for advice. He isn't dead. Just living somewhere else. Not many kings are that lucky.'

'I'd say hardly any at all,' Simone said.

'I just have a new job. And it's a job that I've been trained for. It's a job I think I can do.'

She squeezed him. 'I'm really glad to hear that.'

'But it's a job that would be much easier if I had someone else here with me.'

'Your mother?'

'No, Sim. You.'

'Oh, Ed. We've talked about this.'

'But have we really? We've skirted around it, but we've never really talked about it.'

They had, hadn't they? He wasn't going to marry anyone and she wasn't moving back here.

'What would happen?' she asked softly.

'You would move back here and be my girlfriend.'

Did kings even have girlfriends? And was that enough? Was a title and a ring important to her? Maybe not. They were Simone and Ed. Maybe it didn't matter what anyone called them or how their relationship was defined. Because they would always be Simone and Ed. Best friends. And nothing, no one in the world, could change that.

You'd have to move back to Florena.

For the first time she didn't panic at the thought. People had been so friendly and welcoming to her tonight. She'd had a marvellous time.

What was more, after Alea's revelation she understood that she hadn't been sent away to boarding school because she was an embarrassment, someone to be banished from Florena, but because of something that had nothing to do with her at all.

The people didn't think she was a disgrace.

Some of her own fears began to dissolve. Maybe she could start by returning to Florena more often and see how that went? And surely Ed would have to make some diplomatic trips to Paris?

'What would I do?' she asked. 'I couldn't work.'

'You could if you wanted to. You could do anything you want. I'd see to it. I am the King.'

Was he right? Or was he daydreaming?

'Do we have to decide now?'

Exhaustion was overwhelming her. Pushing her lids over her eyes. Maybe she could stay…? Maybe her fears were all unfounded…?

'No, we don't. I just want you to know that I want to be with you.'

Simone fell asleep in his arms and knew that.

Simone laughed, glowed, and looked as though she was having a wonderful time. He loved seeing her like this. Not just enjoying herself, but relaxed and thriving at the ball.

He tried to go her, but someone stopped him. He was stuck, listening to a boring conversation about the crown jewels.

He finally extricated himself as politely as he could, took two steps, but Laurent blocked his way.

Simone disappeared into the crowd. He pushed after her, but again his way was blocked—this time by two men who looked like Laurent.

He caught a glimpse of silver in the next room, but knew he could never reach her. She kept slipping further and further away…

Ed woke up drenched in sweat and shaking.

Simone had not slipped away. She lay next to him now, still fast asleep. Her golden hair was spread around her on the pillow. She looked so peaceful he had to stop himself leaning over and pressing his lips to her cheek in case he woke her.

It was still dark, but a glance at his watch told him it was after six and the palace would soon be waking. He should get back to his apartment as quickly as he could. He trusted his staff, but rumours had a way of leaking out, and the last thing he wanted was any undue attention being drawn to Simone. He could handle any bad press about himself—after yesterday he somehow felt more confident that he could beat Laurent at that game—but if Simone was spooked by internet trolls again she might never return.

As he walked back to his apartments he thought about which

rooms were empty and where Simone might be comfortable. Somewhere as close as possible to him. Maybe she could visit more often, or even divide her time between here and Paris. If she was going to do that she'd need her own space.

And then what?

The palace looked different this morning. The sun was slowly rising, and though he had already been King for three months, his being crowned officially had shifted something. Now his father really couldn't come back.

He'd meant what he'd said to Simone last night. He had made his peace with his new position and yesterday had been invigorating. He was going to be the best King Florena had ever had. He would make the Florenans proud of their country and its independence and make sure they put any idea of a union with France behind them as soon as possible.

'If you marry the woman you love then it will all be okay.'

His father was a lovesick fool, and probably rewriting history. He was sure his parents had loved one another once. Even if only for a short time.

What Ed and Simone had was stronger than anything his forebears had felt. Ed and Simone were old friends. Best friends. And amazing together in bed. Surely the odds of a long and happy relationship were stacked in their favour?

As he approached his apartments a staff member passed him and gave him a knowing wink. Why would the King be entering his apartments at six a.m. unless he hadn't slept there all night?

But what if Ed was just as weak as his father? What if he was the unreliable player everyone said he was?

The Playboy Prince? No. He had to block out those voices. They did not speak the truth. He wasn't a playboy. Or a womaniser, like the tabloids said. He was just Ed. A regular guy. Simone Auclair's best friend.

He couldn't imagine cheating on Simone. But if what one day, after those first heady days disappeared, that changed? What if he was as fickle as his father? And his grandfather? And every other King Edouard who had come before him?

What if he played right into Laurent's hands and showed him that the royal family was the disgrace he'd said they were?

He pushed open the door to his rooms.

No. He had to get Laurent out of his head. He would never cheat on Simone. She was his best friend. The person he felt closest to in the entire world.

In his suite, breakfast was laid out for him, and his valet stood by the table, holding the newspapers.

'Sir, there is something you need to see.'

Ed took one look at the front pages and knew that today was not going to go as planned. There was no way Simone would agree to stay now. She'd probably get on the first plane back to Paris.

CHAPTER EIGHTEEN

IT WAS LATE when Simone emerged from her room. Ed had left early. She hadn't expected him to stay. It was another work day for him. So she was surprised to see him in the kitchen, talking to her mother. He was wearing a suit and tie and she stopped. He looked handsome, but she decided she much preferred him wearing nothing at all.

They both turned to look at her when she entered.

'Don't you have a country to run? To save?'

She smiled as she said it, so he'd know she was joking. The truth was she was delighted to wake up and see her two most favourite people in the world.

Neither smiled back.

'Sim, darling, sit down. I'll get you a coffee.'

This wasn't good.

'What's the matter?' she asked as she pulled out a chair, her legs suddenly unsteady.

Ed sat next to her. 'There's been some media coverage.'

She pulled a face. Of course there was media coverage. It had been his coronation.

'Of you?'

They both shook their heads and it hit her.

'Oh... Me?'

But she hadn't done anything! She'd been one of hundreds of guests at the coronation. She and Ed had only danced once, as they had planned, and had only spoken to one another that brief time. They had been so careful not to do or say anything too intimate, in case they were filmed or overheard. Besides, everyone had liked her! No one had recognised her or known she was in that video.

'Can I see?'

Ed and his mother conferred with a look, and then Ed slid an open tablet across the table to her.

The King and the Crooner was the headline, and below it was a photo of the two of them dancing. But Simone's focus was immediately drawn to the next image. A still of the video taken at Ed's seventeenth birthday party.

Bile rose in her empty stomach and she scrolled down to the article itself.

Back to embarrass the Crown: the servant's daughter who managed to manipulate her way into the coronation and the celebratory ball. It seems Simone Auclair won't give up her ambitions with the King.

Simone even managed to trap the King into a dance. But we all know the newly crowned King is vulnerable to a pretty girl. It's no secret that he's known all over the world as the Playboy Prince.

Our sources tell us she is currently running a dusty bookshop in Paris, and it is still unclear how or why she managed to connive her way back into the palace after causing so much disgrace fourteen years ago.

A spokesperson from the Prime Minister's department has said they are looking into the matter and assessing any security risks.'

'Wow... This is...'

'Lies,' Ed said.

How did they know all this stuff? Only someone who knew her would be able to spin it this way.

'Yes, but not entirely. There's just enough truth in it, isn't there? That's what so awful. It isn't lies. Half-truths, maybe. But I *am* the daughter of a member of palace staff. I *do* run a dusty bookshop. I *have* been hiding in Paris.'

Simone opened up her own social media. She kept it very private, and her settings were as secure as they could be. She didn't even use her own name, for crying out loud, but went by *BookGirl*.

And yet there were many messages about the coronation and the ball. And they were all vile.

Her eyes went to a particular person.

MAL17. The thumbnail was an avatar, different from last time, but the words were similar.

Bad singer, bad dancer...why hasn't she died from embarrassment?

Her hand shook and Ed took the phone from her. He frowned.

'*MAL17*. That was one of the trolls from before,' she said.

The one who had told her to die.

'From when? The video?'

'Yes. I recognise the name. Or rather I recognise the comments. The words are the same. This is the same person.'

'I'll get Home Affairs to look into it.'

Home Affairs. The government.

If they couldn't trust Laurent, they couldn't trust his government. Ed was only a figurehead. He didn't control the government. Laurent did.

She felt even more exposed.

'No. Not them.'

'Why not?'

'Because...because Laurent is after you. Is there someone else you can ask?'

'Laurent wouldn't risk getting involved in something like this. It's too tawdry. Surely it's beneath him?'

'By attacking me he's attacking you. It sounds like his *modus operandi.*'

Ed and his mother shared a look. They thought she was over-reacting.

Maybe it wasn't Laurent. But she knew who else it might be. And once it occurred to her she wondered why she hadn't realised it before. It was so obvious.

'Morgane. His girlfriend. Morgane Lavigne.'

She saw their faces turn from incredulity to understanding.

'It's a long shot... Would she risk it?'

'*MAL.* Morgane Lavigne. I bet her middle name begins with an A.'

Ed and her mother were staring at her with open mouths.

'Oh, God. Am I paranoid? It sounds crazy when I say it aloud.'

'You're not crazy or paranoid. You've been viciously and unfairly attacked.'

'Do you want me to go back to Paris?' she said.

'No!' they shouted in unison.

She didn't want to be here, but even Paris might not be the sanctuary she thought it was. If this *MAL17* knew about her bookshop then she might be followed there.

She shivered. Where could she go? Canada? Australia? The middle of the Pacific Ocean wouldn't be far enough.

'Let's look at it before you go anywhere,' said Ed.

She opened a browser on her phone and typed 'Morgane Lavigne' into the search engine. The page opened with lots of glamorous shots of Morgane with Laurent, and also some from years ago, with Ed. Simone swallowed down bile and clicked on one of the links.

Morgane Adrianna Lavigne.

She passed it to Ed.

'I might be paranoid. I might be wrong. But I have this feeling...'

Ed nodded, and then pulled her into an embrace. He held her as if he was trying to protect her and give her strength all at once. She appreciated it, but knew that even he couldn't protect her completely.

No one could.

'I'll get someone to look into it.'

'But not anyone connected to Laurent. Promise?'

'I promise.'

He kissed her on the forehead and left.

'I hope you're right,' said Alea, passing her a coffee and a plate of warm pastries.

'Why?'

'If it's her they'll expose her. It'll all be over.'

Simone shook her head. 'I don't think it will ever be over. I know these things go on and on. She's just one of many.'

'But she's not a nobody. She knows the royal family and she's dating Laurent. She isn't a random person.'

Alea gripped Simone's hand. She started to speak again and then stopped.

Finally, just as Simone was losing sensation in her hand, her mother said, 'Simone, I'm so sorry again you had to deal with all this alone last time. I had no idea.'

Simone nodded. She had forgiven her mother. It was no one's fault except the internet trolls'. 'I know Mum. I know.'

'Can I cook you something?'

Simone couldn't drink the coffee, let alone eat anything. 'I think I want to go back to bed for a while. It was a late night.'

'Do you want to talk?'

Alea's eyes pleaded with her. But Simone didn't want to talk. She didn't want to be awake.

She shook her head. 'I just want to bury myself in my bed.'

And she did.

* * *

Simone woke a few hours later, not at all refreshed, and feeling just as beaten as she'd felt earlier that morning.

It was just like last time.

She'd been in this same room. The same bed. Looking at the same snowy view out of her window.

It was as though she'd been transported back fourteen years.

Nothing had changed. Including her sense of suffocation and the desire to get out of there.

Her flight wasn't until tomorrow, but that was less than twenty-four hours to go, and she had no intention of leaving the apartment. She still wasn't hungry, but her mouth was parched. She went to get a glass of water, but as she entered the kitchen Alea sat up, alert and concerned.

'Did you sleep?'

'A little.'

'Do you feel better?'

Simone frowned. 'I think I will when I get back to Paris.'

'Oh, Sim. No. Please at least stay and see how this all plays out.'

'There's no point. No matter what happens, I have to leave.'

'But why? If they find out who spoke to the paper... If they find out who wrote those things...'

'That won't change anything. Not really. Another troll will pop up in their place. You know that. And they will always dig up that video.'

Alea brewed new coffee and this time Simone accepted it, and curled up on the couch.

'The sooner I get back to Paris the sooner I'll be able to get away from all this embarrassment.'

'Why are you embarrassed?' Alea asked. 'You've done nothing wrong.'

But she knew she must have. Half the world was saying so.

'Mum, the comments are horrible. Some of them are telling me to die.'

Alea picked up her hand and squeezed. 'The comments *are* awful. Inexcusable. Criminal. But Eddie is getting someone to look into them.'

Simone nodded. She was out of words. She knew that no matter what Ed found these people would continue. Trolls always found a way. Being in the spotlight made you a target.

Alea scratched her head. 'How does Eddie do it, I wonder?'

'Ed? He was born into it.'

Ed didn't love the scrutiny, but he knew it was part and parcel of the job.

Simone sighed. 'He has a thick skin. He doesn't let things get to him.'

'Doesn't he?'

It wasn't a rhetorical question. Alea put her hands on her hips, as though waiting for Simone to think carefully about her answer.

'I don't know what I would have done without you.'

'I couldn't have got through today without you there.'

They weren't just the platitudes Simone had assumed them to be. Ed managed because he had supportive friends and colleagues around him. When the video of her singing had gone viral Simone had been alone. She'd had no one to help her deal with it. They had sent her away. Maybe things would have been easier if she hadn't had to go through it by herself.

'It does bother him, but he draws strength from the people he loves. Including you,' Alea said, echoing her daughter's thoughts.

Simone nodded. Then shook her head. 'I don't think I'm strong enough.'

'But you wouldn't be alone. You would have me. And Ed.'

'Oh, Mum, if I stay here it'll get worse. And if the government gets wind of the fact that Ed and I are more than friends then they'll use it as more ammunition. *The Playboy Prince strikes again*. I couldn't do that to him.'

'Then here's a crazy idea… Why don't you marry him?'

Simone nearly spat out the last of her coffee. 'He's not going to marry me.'

'Why not?'

'Because he's Ed. He doesn't believe in marriage. He's the Playboy Prince.'

Alea laughed. 'You know him. You know that's all nonsense, don't you? It's all made up by the press. Eddie hasn't slept with any more women than the average thirty-year-old.'

'How do you know?'

'Because I know Eddie. I live here. I see him. I know that pictures of him with pretty women sell papers. I know most of what's published in the press is lies.'

That was what Ed had said the other day, wasn't it? He hadn't slept with even a fraction of the women everyone thought he had.

But it was more than that. 'He's too worried about Florena. He thinks if he doesn't marry then there won't be any further scandal. He thinks not getting married is the way to save the royal family's reputation.'

Alea laughed. 'Really? That's nonsense. Being married—to the right woman—would do wonders for his reputation. And for the monarchy. Who doesn't love a royal wedding?'

'Everyone loves a royal wedding...until the inevitable royal divorce.'

Alea frowned. 'Oh, you two are impossible. What makes you think you and Eddie wouldn't last the distance? You do love him, don't you?'

Don't fall. Don't fall.

'He's my oldest friend.'

Alea raised an eyebrow. 'Sounds like a pretty good foundation for a marriage.'

'Ed hasn't asked me—and he won't.'

It was a ridiculous idea. Besides, she could never be with him. Being married to the King would draw even more trolls in her direction and make things worse than they already were.

* * *

Simone went back to bed. Just like last time, sleep was the only thing that stopped the thoughts in her head. Though she never stayed asleep for long.

The next time she woke it was nearly dark outside. She pulled on her dressing gown and went into the living room. Alea was sitting by the fire, still looking concerned.

'How are you doing?' she asked.

Simone shrugged.

'Eddie called while you were sleeping, but he asked me not to wake you. He has some meetings, and an official dinner, but said he will come by once he's finished.'

Simone longed to see him, but at the same time she knew it was the last thing either of them needed.

'He said to tell you he's working on it. He seems to think that your theory about Morgane may not be out of left field.'

Simone sighed. She should be happy to be right, but she wasn't. Knowing who it was didn't make it any easier to accept.

'I wouldn't be at all surprised if she was behind the video of Eddie's birthday party too.'

'Why on earth would she do such a thing? Why film me and then post it?'

'Because she was jealous.'

'Of me? Why? She was the one he was with at the birthday party.'

Simone could still remember how close Ed and Morgane had been. Their legs tangled in one another's on a sofa.

'Because Eddie loves you.'

Simone grimaced. 'He doesn't. And he certainly didn't then.'

'Oh, Simone. He always has. You're the love of his life. His best friend. He's always loved you. Just for a while he was too young to realise.'

Alea put an old movie on the TV and left Simone staring blankly at it while she prepared some food in the kitchen. A hearty chicken soup with fresh bread. Simone didn't feel like eating, but when the smell hit her she began to salivate.

They ate slowly in front of the television.

'Mum, where did you get that dress? The one I wore last night?'

'I was wondering when you would ask that. Edouard gave it to me.'

That made sense.

'When did you wear it?'

'I didn't.'

'Then why did he give it to you?'

'He wanted me to accompany him to a dinner. I thought about it, but refused. It wouldn't have been right.'

'So you broke up with him?'

'I suppose so. But these things are rarely one-sided. We couldn't give each other what the other needed.'

'Just like Ed and I.'

'No, Simone, not like that at all. You and Eddie are very different. You could find a way through if you wanted to.'

But her mother was wrong. There was no path forward for her and Ed, just as there had been none for Alea and Edouard.

Ed didn't love her. And even if he did he wasn't going to risk his country's future for her.

Besides, she'd never let him.

CHAPTER NINETEEN

AS SOON AS he'd cancelled his remaining appointments for the evening, Ed pulled off his tie and exited his office by the back door. He knew the quickest route to the apartment above the kitchens and took it, finding himself unable to stop smiling at every single person he passed.

He'd decided.

He laughed when he thought of how it had taken him so long when it was really the simplest and most natural thing in the world.

Alea let him in. Simone was reclining on the couch, tousled and gorgeous.

She sat up quickly when she saw him. 'I thought you had a dinner.'

Ed walked in slowly. He was suddenly more nervous now than he'd been entering the cathedral yesterday.

'I cancelled it. I had something more important to do.'

'What?'

'Talk to you.'

Alea cleared her throat. 'I have plans to meet a friend this evening. Have a good night.'

Simone looked at her mother, watching her leave. They both knew Alea had no such plans.

Ed glanced at the other armchairs, but chose the sofa, where Simone was ensconced in a pile of blankets. Guilt tightened around his heart. She wouldn't have to go through this again. He'd make sure of it. No matter how long it took, he would find out who was behind these attacks on her and make it stop.

Simone cleared away the blankets and he sat next to her. He moved to pick up one of her hands, but she put both in her lap before he could.

'I came as soon as I could,' he said.

'It's okay. You're busy. You didn't have to come.'

'Of course I did.'

'Mum said you might be able to trace the article to Morgane?'

'Possibly. We may not know for a few days. Would you…? Simone, why don't you stay until we know?'

She looked down and his heart crashed.

'I have to go back to Paris. My life is there.'

'What if your life was here? Your mother's here. And I'm here,' he said slowly, cautiously.

He had once thought that he would never marry, because marriage had only brought unhappiness and scandal to his family. But now he had figured out the way to stop that. The way to stop scandal wasn't to avoid marriage. It wasn't to avoid commitment. The way to avoid scandal was to make sure you married the right person and committed to them totally. Completely. And the right person—the only person—was sitting right next to him.

'I love you, Simone.'

She swallowed. 'I know you do. We're friends.'

'No. Not as a friend, but as my lover, my soulmate, my life partner. I love you in every sense of the word—body and soul. You are my match. And I want you to be my queen.'

She tilted her face back and closed her eyes. She drew in a deep breath and said, 'Love doesn't last. You said that.'

'That was before I knew what it was,' he said softly.

She shook her head. 'I know how you feel about marriage. I know that it's the last thing you want.'

'No. I've changed my mind. It was after I spoke to my father yesterday, actually. I've realised that the best way to avoid scandal is to marry the right woman. Marry the woman I love. Hiding from commitment won't help.'

Simone opened her eyes and faced him. 'I wish I could believe you.'

His heart thudded to the floor. He dragged both hands through his hair, gripping his skull. 'Why can't you?'

'You just said you want to marry me to avoid scandal. After everything you've told me, that doesn't make any sense.'

'Of course it makes sense! I love you. I'd never cheat on you. I'd never leave you.'

'It's been less than a week. Our relationship has barely begun.'

'It hasn't been a week. It's been a lifetime! I know you and you know me.'

Simone raised one perfect eyebrow and shook her head. 'I don't know that I do. Four months ago we sat by the Seine and you told me that you would never marry. That love didn't exist. And now you want me to upend my entire life? Ed, I care for you deeply. But this isn't the way to get me to stay here for longer.'

Why was she arguing?

Why didn't she believe him?

Because you've spent your entire life telling her you don't believe in marriage. You've spent your entire life actively avoiding marriage.

'Don't you…?'

At the last moment he thought better of asking the question.

Don't you love me too?

She'd loved him once. Loved him enough to stand up in front of everyone he knew and sing to him.

No. She had a crush on you when she was sixteen. Like every other girl her age in the country at the time. She's smart enough

*to know that the fantasy of dating a prince is far removed from
the reality of marrying a king.*

He wasn't Ed, telling Simone that he loved her. He was a
king, asking the woman he loved to turn her life upside down
for him. Simone was spooked by the press and not without
reason. She hated the spotlight. He'd been a fool to ever think
she'd say yes.

It felt as though his five-hundred-year-old palace was crum-
bling around him. Everything he'd ever told himself had been
wrong. Everything he believed his whole life had been wrong.
And now he was adrift. Alone.

'No. Never mind.'

He shook his head. It didn't matter. Even if a part of her did
love him, it wasn't fair of him to ask her what he was asking.

Duty would be his to fulfil alone.

'I love you.'

He'd said it. And Ed didn't lie to her.

He loved her as a friend...but big love? Everlasting love?

He'd told her that didn't exist.

'I'll go. I'm sorry.'

He stood and walked to the door.

Simone moved to get up from the sofa, but he waved her
back.

'Ed, I'm sorry...'

'Don't be.'

He shook his head, but wouldn't meet her eyes. Was he crying?

No. He couldn't be.

And he was out through the door before she could reach him.

'I love you.'

The floor felt unsteady. But that was probably just her entire
reality being tipped upside down. And shaken for good measure.

'I love you.'

She'd made the right decision.

The last thing Ed needed—the last thing the country needed—was someone like her in a relationship with the King. Rightly or wrongly, she brought controversy with her. Ed's main focus needed to be on improving the reputation of the monarchy, not defending her. She was a liability.

Ed's scheme to get married to avoid scandal was so bizarre that he'd wake up tomorrow and change his mind. He was panicked. Not thinking straight. That was all.

Because why would he want to marry her?

He loves you.

And you love him.

Simone buried her face in her hands. Of course she loved him! She'd never stopped. Not since that fourteen-year-old boy had arrived home from school that summer with broad shoulders and a whole new foot of height.

She'd loved him when she'd sung to him at his seventeenth birthday party. Promising that she'd always love him.

And she'd loved him when he'd arrived on her doorstep in Paris. And when they'd kissed by the Seine. She'd loved him then and she would always love him.

In fact, she loved him too much to tell him how much she loved him.

She loved him, she wanted him, she needed him to breathe.

I ache for you. I adore you. I yearn for you.

But it didn't matter what she felt. Love wasn't always enough, and she had to start protecting her heart.

Simone's phone pinged and she picked up her phone from where she had thrown it earlier. There was a message from Julia. She opened it, but her chest constricted when she saw that Julia had sent a photo from the ball. The one from the article Ed had showed her earlier.

OMG you two are adorable. This pic has made my heart melt! xo

Simone enlarged the photo on her screen and studied it properly.

The photo wasn't bad—that was part of the problem. They both looked lovely. They really did look adorable. She studied the way Ed was looking at her in a way that was impossible to do when he was actually looking at her. His eyes were soft. The skin around them creased. Any outsider who looked at this photo would know that the two of them were very much into one another.

They had both tried not to be obvious. Tried to be discreet all evening. But the photographer had managed to capture a moment between them when their gazes had been locked and slightly dreamy. It had just been one moment, she remembered, but it had been enough.

Was that how the world saw her?

Her hand shook as she opened her social media.

She was tagged in so many posts she couldn't count them. A quick glance showed her that while many were telling her how lovely she looked, most were less complimentary. They called her an upstart. A gold-digger. Ugly. Fat.

She threw her phone on to the couch and clutched a pillow.

If she stayed in Florena…if she stayed with Ed…it would always be like this.

She could ignore social media. She could stop reading the papers. But she couldn't divorce herself from reality entirely.

Even if Morgane turned out to be this particular troll and could be stopped, others would pop up in her place. The palace could protect her to some extent, but it was still up to her. Was she strong enough?

And then she did something she hadn't done in years. She clicked on the link to the video of her singing at Ed's seventeenth birthday party. Her hands trembled.

The opening bars of the song played and her muscles gave the familiar involuntary reaction they always did when she heard them. But this time the rest of the song was unfamiliar. Because *she* was singing.

She was so young…but also so beautiful and sweet. Why had no one told her how gorgeous she was?

She wanted to reach into the screen and shake that sixteen-year-old, tell her how beautiful she was. She was wobbly on her high heels, and she kept tugging at her dress, but her face was gorgeous. Young and bright and hopeful. Untouched by worry and strain.

There was also nothing particularly bad about her singing. She wasn't ever going to win a recording contract, but she held the tune.

She hadn't made a fool of herself. Not really.

No one should have posted that video. No one should even have been taking photos at that party. It had been in the palace, and the guests had all signed non-disclosure agreements.

She should have been safe.

None of this was her fault.

It was someone else's.

And the article published this morning had been lies.

She'd believed the trolls. She didn't blame herself for that. She'd been a teenager and all alone.

But not once had Simone done anything wrong or embarrassing.

And even if she had that was still no reason to attack someone on social media.

She wasn't being weak by leaving. She was being strong. She was leaving the man she loved because it was for the best. She was being strong for him, and she had to keep being strong.

She flicked through the posts until she finally fell asleep on the couch.

Ed would have been lying if he'd said that sitting across the desk watching Pierre Laurent sign his resignation letter wasn't deeply, deeply satisfying. A caretaker Prime Minister had been appointed, and would form a new government as soon as possible.

Ed understood that Laurent and Morgane planned to leave the country later that day. Their reputations were irretrievably ruined in Florena. But he hoped they wouldn't inflict themselves upon another unsuspecting nation.

Laurent looked at him and smirked as he pushed the paper across Ed's desk. Ed smiled back broadly and honestly.

Good riddance.

It turned out the French government had been keeping a close eye on Laurent for a while, given his declared ambitions. They had traced a lot of unusual social media activity to Morgane's PR firm. Simone was not their only victim. Morgane's firm had created a network of fake accounts to attack all kinds of people—especially Laurent's political opponents.

After that it hadn't taken long to also determine that Morgane was the source of the leaked video from Ed's seventeenth birthday party.

The fact that the PM and his girlfriend's private PR firm were leaking material to the press and running so many private social media accounts had caused the newspapers to publish many follow-up articles, and Laurent's resignation had come faster than anyone had guessed it would after his cabinet told him he had lost their confidence.

Laurent might be gone, but it was two days too late. If Ed had done something about Simone's trolls earlier he might have stopped this latest attack on her. Simone might have agreed to stay.

Now…? Now there was no way. How could he convince her to embark on a public life with him when he knew as well as she did that he'd failed to protect her? And there was no guarantee he'd be able to stop other attacks in the future.

The fact was he couldn't offer her his love and promise to protect her at the same time.

Ed had been right all along. It was best to remain single. To dedicate himself to his country and his duty and forget about love. Love was not his destiny.

He might have seen off Laurent and secured Florena's future for the time being. But it had come at the cost of his heart.

'Your Majesty?'

One of his aides had come in.

'Yes?'

'You have an unexpected visitor. It isn't in your calendar but…'

Ed sighed. He wanted to go to his room. Perhaps drown his sorrows in a few glasses of Scotch and take his frustration out on some video games. Not engage with lobbyists.

'No. Tomorrow. Or the next day. I've had enough.'

He stood.

'It's Mademoiselle Auclair.'

CHAPTER TWENTY

THE LAST PERSON Simone had expected to see as she waited outside the King's offices was the Prime Minister. She'd come to say goodbye. To see Ed one final time before she flew back to Paris.

A part of her—a very large part—wanted to leave without having to go through the hurt of a proper goodbye. But he was still her friend and she owed it to him.

And he loved her.

Or thought he did.

Because Ed didn't believe in love. Or marriage. Yet last night he'd claimed to have changed his mind.

Simone didn't have an appointment. She had no right to be rocking up unannounced at his office. Thankfully one of Ed's staff—a woman who had worked in the palace for years—had recognised her and hadn't sent her away at a glance.

'Mademoiselle Auclair, it's lovely to see you. What can I do for you?'

Temporarily shocked at this formal greeting from a woman who had known her since she was a child, Simone had told her that she would like to have a few minutes with the King, if at all possible.

'He is busy at the moment, but if you can wait I will let him know you are here.' She'd smiled and motioned for Simone to sit on the large sofa in the waiting room. 'Can I get you a coffee while you wait?'

Simone had shaken her head. Her nerves were jangling enough as it was, without adding another coffee into the jittery mix.

The door to Ed's private offices opened shortly afterwards and Simone stood, expecting Ed to walk out. Instead, she came nose to nose with Pierre Laurent.

The Prime Minister froze when he saw her, and Simone saw the exact moment he recognised her. His expression hardened.

But he couldn't hurt her. Nor could his girlfriend.

She met Laurent's gaze, held it, and straightened her back. She did not need to bow to this man. She certainly didn't need to smile. This man was trying to destroy her country—not to mention Ed's life.

And your life.

She held his eyes and dared him to look away first. He couldn't hurt her. She wouldn't let him.

Laurent lowered his eyes, nodded curtly, and left the room without acknowledging anyone else.

Wow.

Endorphins rushed through her. She'd looked him in the eye and nothing had happened.

Except…not nothing. There had been a rush. Exhilaration. Victory!

The double doors opened fully and there was Ed. Wearing a bespoke suit and filling it out like…like a king. He stood with a posture that was intended to say he was ready for anything, but the paleness of his face belied his confident pose.

She wanted to run to him and pull him to her. But she'd come to say goodbye.

Hadn't she?

'Simone. Would you like to come in? Have they offered you a drink?'

'Yes—and yes.'

She stepped into the offices and the large doors were closed behind them.

She looked around, took it all in. Ed's new offices. The King's offices.

'Welcome.' Ed waved his hand around the room. 'Have you been in here before?'

She shook her head. The King's offices were not open to children. Even a prince's playmate. In the centre of the room sat a large and imposing desk. The type that would have furniture movers balking. The walls were crammed with Old Masters and portraits of Ed's ancestors.

He led her to a circle of leather armchairs, in the most comfortable-looking part of the room, and motioned for her to sit.

'Unless you'd rather go somewhere less formal?'

She shook her head. Formal was good. Formal would remind her why she'd come to say goodbye.

'I thought about doing some redecorating. But this is an official reception room and when I'm in it I am the King. Having all this around me reminds me of that.'

'Duty first,' she said.

'Not always,' he replied.

Ed met her gaze and held it. The muscles in her chest tightened. Why was this so hard?

'I just saw Laurent.'

'Ah, yes.' Ed's face brightened. 'Good news…great news, actually. He's just resigned.'

'He's what?'

'Yes—just now. I suspect he's off to announce it.'

'Wow…' She saw her recent interaction with him through a new lens. 'Why?'

'Because his girlfriend was using her PR company and various fake social media accounts to harass people. Not only you. Also members of the media. Members of the opposition. And she was doing it at his behest. He's finished.'

Simone frowned. 'I'm glad. Really glad.'

'All talk of Florena being incorporated into France should end. For the time being. I don't expect it to stop for ever. And…' He leant forward. 'I can't promise that there won't be other trolls.'

She nodded.

No wonder Laurent had scurried away when he saw her. Laurent and Morgane had been exposed and it did make her feel slightly better. But there would always be another Laurent, waiting to find a weakness in the royal family. And there would always be another Morgane waiting to humiliate one or the other of them.

But you stared him down. You looked him in the eye and you didn't know he'd resigned. You stood in front of a powerful man, a man who had hurt you, and you didn't hide.

'Sim, why are you here?'

'I came to say…'

Goodbye.

Hadn't she?

Ed reached over and picked up her hand. He clutched it between his and her body flooded with warmth.

She never wanted to let him go.

'I meant everything I said last night. I love you, Simone,' he said. 'Not just as a friend. But as my lover, my partner, my other half. I want to spend my life with you.'

He made it sound so simple—but it wasn't.

'What if the country turns against you?

'Why would they?'

'What if they don't like me?'

'Sim, is that what you're worried about?'

'I'm worried about so many things.'

'There's only one thing you need to worry about. Only one thing we can't get through together. Do you love me?'

She opened her mouth to answer, but the words caught in her throat…behind the tears that had suddenly materialised.

She nodded. Swallowed her tears and said, 'I've always loved you. I never stopped. I tried and tried, but…'

And Ed was next to her, pulling him to her, crushing her against his chest, wiping her tears away.

'Oh, Simone… Oh, Simone… Thank goodness. We can do this. I promise. I love you so much. The people will love you when they get to know you. Besides…their King marrying his oldest friend? How can that be a bad thing?'

He was right. At least he should be. But their world would be filled with so many lies and half-truths. She'd spent fourteen years believing that she'd been sent away for embarrassing the palace, when in truth it had been for a different reason entirely. What if one of them stopped seeing the truth?

'But you're the Playboy Prince and I'm the palace crooner. What if…?'

'What if what? I don't believe any of those headlines and nor should you. You know as well as I do that they are all lies. All that matters is that you and I know what the truth is.'

He clasped her hands tighter.

'Ed, I love you,' she told him. 'With all my heart. More than anything in the world.'

It was such a relief to admit it.

He exhaled and smiled, pulling her to her feet and into his arms.

'So stay. And if the people don't like you we'll leave. I want you as my queen. But more than that I want you as my wife. I want you as my partner. Whether we're living in an attic in Paris, or in a boat on the Seine, or in a caravan in the Alps. I want you as my best friend…my soul mate.'

'Yes!' she sobbed into his chest.

'Yes to what? Living in Paris?'

'No. Yes to staying here with you.'

'Are you sure?'

'Yes. Neither of us have done anything wrong. And we will

be stronger together. I've loved you all my life, and I'm not going to let what other people do or say stop us being together.'

They *were* stronger together. Together they would keep one another safe and grounded. Together they would know each other's true selves. She wouldn't be complete without him.

'Then you and I will do this together. I don't want to be apart from you for a single day.'

And he wasn't.

EPILOGUE

THE LITTLE GIRL attempted her first steps in the lush palace garden. Her father held out his hands a metre away from her mother, who gently let her go. The girl took three steps before falling into her father's arms. Both parents hugged their daughter proudly.

'It's so lovely to see children in this garden again,' said the girl's father Edouard, Duke of Armiel.

Celine, the new Duchess, kissed his cheek and steadied their daughter, Alexandria, before letting her try walking again.

'I hope that there are more children soon.' The Duke winked.

'Hang on!' Simone said. 'We'll get there one day.'

Edouard and Celine laughed.

'We've only been married a few months. Give us a chance,' Ed added.

Children would come one day, but there was no rush. Simone was getting used to one new role already: Queen of Florena.

Ed was loving having her by his side every day, but was determined she would have her own projects as well. Things that had nothing to do with her walking three steps behind him.

Her choice had been to focus on charities concerned with teenage mental health, fighting against online abuse and bullying. She had also taken a place on the board for Florena's public libraries. Both positions into which she had thrown herself with passion and gusto.

She did still, on occasion, accompany Ed on his official duties as well. Which he loved. Because every moment she was by his side was easier and more pleasurable.

All the days.

And the nights.

Children would come in time. Children who would not be neglected or ignored. But for the time being he was enjoying having Simone to himself.

She was extremely popular everywhere they went. Any fears she'd had of being rejected by the Florenans had evaporated as soon as their relationship and then their engagement had been announced. The public had lapped up the story of two childhood friends falling in love. Furthermore, the new government had made it clear that personal and vicious abuse and threats to any member of the royal family—or indeed anyone in Florena—would not be tolerated.

Ed's father and Celine now lived in Paris, in a house much larger than Simone's attic.

Julia and André were now living in the attic, and André was running the bookshop full-time.

However, André's new landlord was a bit more relaxed than Mr Grant.

Ed had purchased the bookshop and the attic apartment for Simone as a wedding present.

She'd been horrified, but he had told her, 'I want you to always feel that you have somewhere to run away to. I don't want you to feel trapped here.'

Simone didn't feel trapped in Florina.

She felt at home.

Queen Isabella had been back for some visits as well. In fact both the former King and Queen had attended Ed and Simone's wedding, in a feat of diplomatic gymnastics that Simone still wasn't sure how they had managed to pull off.

But they had. Because together they were much stronger than they had been apart.

The wedding had been wonderful and the press commentary all positive, although neither of them had lingered too long in following it. Their trusted aides had told them what they needed to know. Besides, after the wedding they had enjoyed a very private honeymoon in a location no one had managed to discover—Tahiti—but they kept that to themselves.

'Your son will be King Edouard the Fifth,' said Ed's father.

'No. I am the last Edouard. The fourth King.'

The curse—if there really ever had been one—was lifted. By him marrying the right woman. By him making the woman he loved his queen. The kingdom would be cursed no more.

* * * * *

Subscribe and fall in love with a Mills & Boon series today!

You'll be among the first to read stories delivered to your door monthly and enjoy great savings.

WE SIMPLY LOVE ROMANCE

MILLS & BOON